'Is he a confirmed heavy

'Heavy' was a cor
nickname people used
the human immun
AIDS …

Smithson played with his pen. 'Just a suspect at the moment. Someone in the south London office brought in a carrier yesterday and he named Harris as one of his contacts.'

I looked at Harris's picture. 'So he's gay?'

Smithson nodded. 'According to the information south London got out of the heavy, yes.'

I could imagine how they got the information out of him; the tracers in the south London office were a mean, vicious lot.

'The trouble is, Gorman, that Harris's father is an important man,' Smithson continued, 'and the powers-that-be don't want any publicity. So we have to pick him and his contacts up in one quick swoop – without leaving any embarrassing loose ends.'

'But that's next to impossible!' I protested. 'I mean, there's no way we can be sure that he doesn't have contacts outside the circle of people we trace.'

Smithson sighed. 'Don't tell me things I already know,' he said. 'Our job is to get him and anybody else he's had contact with. Nobody at the Elephant and Castle is interested in the finer points.' He threw his pen onto the desk in disgust.

'His father must be important,' I said.

TRACER

STUART JACKSON

SPHERE BOOKS LIMITED

A Sphere Book

First published in Great Britain by Sphere Books Ltd, 1990

Photoset in North Wales by
Derek Doyle & Associates, Mold, Clwyd.
Printed and bound in Great Britain by
Cox & Wyman Ltd, Reading

ISBN 0 7474 0603 0

Sphere Books Ltd
A Division of
Macdonald & Co (Publishers) Ltd
Orbit House
1 New Fetter Lane
London EC4A 1AR

A member of Maxwell Macmillan Pergamon Publishing Corporation

I

FRIDAY,
18 FEBRUARY 1999

Friday, 18 February 1999

Time: 14.30 hours

I didn't like Terry Bannister. His bullet-shaped head with its cropped black hair, wide jowls and small bulging eyes gave him the look of a heavyweight wrestler. He appeared a hail fellow well met type, but he didn't fool me, or the people at the office; we knew that underneath his Cockney jocularity he was pure boar. In the course of our lunchtime drink I suffered his taunts about my lack of progress with Victoria and his unsolicited advice on where I was going wrong. Unfortunately, I had to admit to myself that he was uncomfortably accurate about three things: I had got it bad as far as Victoria was concerned; she was ten years younger than me; and my attempts to court her had so far been rebuffed with an indifference that bordered on the insulting. Terry had only been with the Department for five months and I stood at the bar with him wondering if he was married. If he was I felt sorry for his wife, Terry's idea of seducing a girl was to take his cigarette out of his mouth before committing rape – assuming her identity card said she was free of the HIV virus of course, not even Terry would take a chance like that.

I guessed he'd have probably played down the dark side of his nature at the interview with Sheila, the office's case manager. Not that he needed to have bothered, even if there were at least two jobs for every able-bodied person, we were so far below establishment Sheila generally took anybody who applied. Most people shunned us when they knew what we did. Despite the all pervasive health

7

education campaigns the myths persisted and the ignorant still believed that anyone who came into contact with the AIDS virus must be in danger of catching it themselves; while those who knew better gave us a wide berth in case any of their friends thought we were hunting them. Nowadays Sheila always rejected any applicant who wanted the job out of a sense of religious zeal or to get even for the loss of a loved one. She said they'd show poor judgement, and she was probably right; anyway, her system had ensured that so far none of the tracers in the Soho Square office had been convicted of causing grievous bodily harm to an AIDS carrier. I suppose the bounty money they paid us was mostly to blame for the violence – when you're paid for how many confirmed carriers you bring in to the holding compounds it tends to make you overreact when a confirmed carrier of the HIV virus is keeping back that last vital piece of information.

When we came out of the pub it was raining again. We walked down Tottenham Court Road and took the short cut through Sutton Street to our office in Soho Square and Terry had re-opened the subject of my lack of progress with Victoria when I glanced up the alley that runs behind the offices at the top of the square. For a moment I thought it was a bundle of rags which someone had left by the dustbins.

Standing over him it was easy to see the cause of his death and I watched while the patch of blood which was seeping from what had once been his head was chased away by the rain. Neither Terry nor I touched him; unlike the ambulance crews we weren't dressed in protective rubber suits and with all that blood about it was better to be careful in case he was a carrier.

'Come on,' said Terry, tugging at my arm, 'we're getting soaked. We can report it when we get to the office.'

'You go,' I said. 'I'll wait here.'

'Don't be bloody stupid.' He threw up his hands in frustration.

'What's the bloody point of staying here? There's nothing you can do for Christ's sake. He's dead. Anybody can see that. Come on, let's go.'

I didn't like the idea of leaving him but I could see Terry was right. After all it wasn't our business and the body would keep until we reported it.

As we walked across Soho Square I looked at the people who were going about their usual business, indifferent to the small tragedy we'd discovered in the alley. In the Square everything looked normal and it wasn't until you walked up to Oxford Street you noticed the difference. Only two years ago it had been one of the busiest thoroughfares in London, but that was before the United Nations Resolution had put a stop to the tourist industry – at least until we sorted things out. Now that international travel was restricted to government officials and those on legitimate business there was nobody to buy the junk in the souvenir shops, and they were boarded up and plastered with posters advertising the virtues of the British National Democratic Party. And with a sizeable segment of what the government called the sexually active population locked up in Special Care Centres there were less people around to sell it.

We're based in an anonymous-looking building in the south-east corner of the Soho Square, near to the offices of Twentieth Century Fox. We stood in front of the video camera over the entrance and Terry pushed the bell. The electric lock buzzed and we pushed open the steel-lined door. Inside the entrance foyer Bill Taylor, the young security guard, sat behind the reception desk, picking his teeth with the end of a matchstick.

'Phone the police will you, Bill,' said Terry. 'There's a stiff in the alley off Sutton Street, and let them in when they turn up, they'll probably want a word with Nick and me.'

He walked past the desk and went up the main staircase two steps at a time.

'You see it?' Bill called after him but Terry had disappeared from view.

I knew Bill was a supporter of the BNDP and an ex-football hooligan. He'd always struck me as a vicious

9

little sod and I knew the scar on his forehead beneath the shaved hair, so beloved by the BNDP's younger supporters, was the result of a fight with a group of young socialists when he and some of his pals had attacked one of their marches.

'No, we didn't. He's lying by the dustbins,' I explained.

'Right, Mister Gorman, leave it to me. After I've rung 'em I'll go over there. You never know, do you?'

No, I thought, you never do.

These days it was safer on the football terraces than on the streets; once the hooligan element in society had realised that fighting rival football supporters was far less exciting than the delights of opportunistic violence, which could be used against those the BNDP declared to be enemies of the State, they'd queued up in droves to take the Party's oath of loyalty. Violence on the streets was part of a way of life people had adjusted to; along with the midnight-to-six curfew, identity cards, compulsory blood tests, restrictions on travel and all the other new laws that had been introduced in an attempt to contain the AIDS epidemic.

I nodded to Bill before walking up to the tiny office on the first floor that I shared with Chris Brand. Chris and I were friends in an off-hand sort of way and we often went for a drink at lunchtimes if we were both in the office, which wasn't often. We didn't meet outside office hours or discuss our personal lives; we weren't that friendly and like everyone else at the office we never talked about what we did or where we went when we weren't out in the streets tracing down suspected AIDS carriers. But I liked Chris's sardonic humour and easy going manner and his wisecracks helped to lighten the sense of gloom which surrounded our work.

I went into our office, took off my wet trenchcoat and slumped into the chair behind my desk. The office's central heating radiator was far too powerful for the size of the room and it swamped the cold blast of air which came through the gap in the window we couldn't shut properly. After a few minutes the suffocating warmth began to pull at my eyelids. I'd been out half the night tracking down a suspect and I was on the point of slipping into a doze when Victoria opened the door and came in. Knocking on doors wasn't her style.

'I hear you've had an exciting lunchtime,' she said, looking past my shoulder at the grey sky on the other side of the partially closed window. 'All right for some.' She sniffed primly.

'Well, why don't you come? I've asked you often enough.'

'And be groped by Terry? No thanks.' She shuddered. 'Anyway, I don't want to stumble over corpses.'

I recalled Terry's advice on how to woo her and rejected it instantly. I knew it wouldn't work on a girl like Victoria Howard. She was around twenty-six, tall and willowy, with long thick blond hair and china blue eyes which were set in an oval face. Her high cheekbones and pouting mouth, slightly turned down at each corner, reminded me of a French movie actress of the 1960s. I couldn't understand why someone like her had transferred across from one of the Special Health Authority's Regional Offices into Tracing, unless she'd made a total foul-up of something her last boss thought important. She got results though; not as good as Chris or Terry's, or even mine, but enough not to draw our boss's attention to her performance indicators. I decided to persevere with my own approach to courtship. I'd been trying it with Victoria during the four months since she'd first come over to us.

'Why not come out this evening?' I gushed. 'I know a nice little Italian restaurant. The food's good and I promise to get you home by curfew.'

'No thanks,' she said. 'I'm going to church.' She looked at me squarely with her blue eyes. 'You should try it.'

I shook my head. We both knew she wasn't going to church, even though church-going had become popular again as the despairing sought solace in religion.

'Don't you believe?' she asked in mock seriousness.

'I don't feel guilty if I don't go, if that's what you mean.' We had this sort of guarded banter every time I asked her out. She wasn't a new convert any more than I was and I knew she took that particular line in order to avoid saying no outright. It was part of a game we played, or at least it had started out as a game and I don't remember when I first became serious about Victoria, but these days she crept into my thoughts like a thief. I looked up at her and she dropped her head to scan the piece of paper she was reading.

'There were some messages while you were out.' She dropped the paper on to my desk. 'I don't mind answering other peoples' calls, Nick, but next time don't divert your phone without asking me first. I'm a tracer like you, not one of the secretaries. Apart from anything else I shan't know if it's an important call, shall I?'

'Sorry,' I said.

I decided to try a different tack. I knew it was dangerous; not all the BNDP's members wore their Party's insignia.

'Tell me, Victoria, what's a nice girl like you doing, working in a place like this?'

'Oh come on, Nick.' She smiled. 'Even I've seen that movie. Can't you do better than that?'

'Seriously, Victoria, I'd like to know.'

'Why are you here?' she countered.

'I don't have much choice – not if I want to eat regularly. But you're different.'

'Am I?'

She turned to leave the office. I couldn't help myself.

'How about tomorrow then?' I coaxed. 'It's my birthday, you could help me celebrate.'

'Many happy returns, but no thanks, I'm going to see an old friend of my father's.'

'Sunday?' I almost pleaded.

She ignored my appeal and I watched her as her long slim legs carried her to the door; she'd probably chosen the calf-length black skirt and severe blouse to disguise the curves of her figure, but they didn't. I tried to remember the name of the French actress she reminded me of – Victoria had the same pouting look of anticipation. Our relationship – if that's what it could be called – had never got past the superficial level of a laugh and a joke and I sensed she was determined to keep it that way. I sensed too an inner fragility about her; I wasn't sure whether it was due to a busted love affair or something else, although with her looks I'd have expected her to break hearts rather than the other way round. Whoever had hurt her had done a first-class job of it because she kept her emotions tightly buttoned and I was one of the few people she seemed to talk to at the office, while she barely gave the time of day to Terry or Chris. Mind you, as far as Terry was concerned she wasn't unique in that – all of the women who worked at the office gave him a wide berth.

I was still looking through my messages when she put her head round the door.

'There's a detective here who wants to see you,' she said. 'Oh, and I forgot, the boss wants to see you in half an hour.'

'Which boss?' I wasn't being funny, in spite of the money we earned we were generally at the beck and call of anyone in a suit who didn't dirty their hands on the streets.

'Smithson,' she said.

I felt a momentary sense of alarm. I saw him so rarely I'd almost forgotten his existence in his lair on the fourth floor. Why should he want to see me?

'Did he say what about?' I asked her casually.

'No. He doesn't take me into his confidence.' There was hint of sarcasm in her voice.

'OK, thanks for telling me.' I smiled brightly at her. 'You won't change your mind about Sunday?'

'No,' she said with an air of absolute finality before closing my office door.

I swivelled round in my chair and looked out of the window. I wasn't insensitive to our age difference but I thought that at least she'd recognise I wasn't like Terry. Am I that unattractive? I thought. Outside it had stopped raining and low grey clouds were slipping across the sky. It would be dark soon. If Smithson wanted to see me it could mean trouble and if that wasn't enough I also had an interview with a copper. What a way to finish the week. There was a knock on my door and before I could answer a policeman opened it and walked in. He looked round the office and sniffed disdainfully before helping himself to a chair and sitting down in front of my desk.

'Would you like to sit down?' My sarcasm was more pointed than Victoria's had been.

The policeman gave me a long steady stare. 'Don't piss me about, sonny,' he said, evenly.

He looked about thirty which meant I could give him five clear years.

'All right, let's get on with it,' he said. He took his small tape recorder out of his pocket, checked it was working and put it on the desk in front of me. 'OK, talk to me,' he said, as he switched it on.

While he listened and the tape turned I explained how Terry and I had found the body in Falconberg Mews. After I'd finished he asked a few supplementary questions and before he left I asked a few of my own. He answered them indifferently while checking his tape recorder had recorded our interview; they'd found no identification on the body and because of that he guessed the man had been the victim of a mugging. It was likely his killer had either wanted money, or more probably the dead man's ID card. I'd had the same idea when I'd first seen him; it explained why his head had been beaten to a pulp. If you knew you were a carrier and couldn't afford the high price of a forged ID card, murder was the easiest way of getting one. It would only remain current until the date of your victim's next blood test; after that you either chanced it or killed again. As the policeman left he said he'd be in touch. We both knew he wouldn't.

Since the Health Emergency Act, police resources were fully stretched in regulating public movement aimed at stopping the spread of the AIDS virus and controlling outbreaks of politically inspired violence, and even murder took a back seat. I'd guessed they'd simply file it on their central computer. If the killer was a carrier we'd stand more chance of picking him up before they did – although I didn't bother to say that to him because I knew he wouldn't agree. There's no love lost between us and the police. They don't get a bounty for every successful arrest and because we don't carry guns or any other of the hi-tech equipment they do we have to call on their firepower if we think a suspect is armed, or likely to give us a hard time. It gets under their skins that while we get paid for the arrest all they get is the knowledge of a job well done. I've never understood why we don't get any real training nor why we aren't issued with personal phones or two-way radios, unless it's because the Conservatives can't break their habit of starving the National Health Service of cash – except when it comes to paying for the glossy advertising which says what a good job we're doing.

I was following the copper out of my office when my phone rang.

'Hello?' I said.

'I don't like to trouble you, Gorman, but I'm waiting,' said Smithson. 'Come up now, if you can spare the time of course, and don't bother my secretary, she's busy.' The line clicked as he put his phone down.

Smithson's particular style of management was a mixture of an overbearing uncle and a bad tempered sergeant major, in which the sergeant major usually had the upper hand. I was over five minutes late and it looked like our meeting had already got off to a bad start.

As I went up to his office I told myself there must be a better way to earn a living. I said it regularly. My trouble was that I'd gone into the National Health Service on leaving university and long years spent in hospital management had made me unemployable in the big wide world outside its narrow confines. I'd tried for different jobs years before, but I'd been a different person then and when I didn't even get invited to interviews I'd got the message. I knew that I was trapped in the Special Health Authority until I'd earned enough money to escape. I thought about the amount I'd built up in the deposit account at my bank as I knocked on Smithson's door and I had a warm feeling as I went in to see him – the way my cash was accruing it wouldn't be long before I could get out of my craphole of a job for ever.

Smithson was sitting behind his desk, surrounded in the glow of light cast by his brass desklamp. His bushy eyebrows, thin sandy hair and short thickset build reminded me of a dwarf in a storybook I'd read as a child. But whereas the dwarf in my storybook had been a jolly little man Smithson's small powerful body seemed to ooze malevolence. He had class, though; he'd furnished his office with some of his own antiques and people in Soho Square whispered that his house in an expensive part of Dulwich was full of them. I couldn't understand where he'd got the money from unless the rumours about him having a rich wife were true. As head of the London Region's four Tracing Departments he received an Assistant Secretary's salary plus ten per cent of his tracers' bounties, and it certainly wouldn't have been enough to keep him in the style to which he'd become accustomed after he'd got his job.

I stood in front of his desk waiting for him to acknowledge my presence. For some reason best known to himself he'd chosen the Soho Square office as his headquarters. Our division's general manager was based at the old Department of Health and Social Security building at the Elephant and Castle, in company with the other three general managers who ran the Special Health Authority and Antony Rayleigh, the Secretary of State for Health. It certainly made for easy communications between them; all they had to do was run up and down the stairs. And now that Rayleigh had forced the Social Security boys out of town there was plenty of room over there. I supposed Soho Square offered Smithson the advantage of close proximity to the Elephant and Castle while being far enough away to keep our general

16

manager's nose out of the day-to-day details of his business.

'Sit down, Gorman,' he said after I'd been standing, unacknowledged, in front of his desk for at least two minutes. Since he'd got his job he'd cultivated a tone of voice to disguise his east London accent. He nodded towards the antique chairs standing round his office, without looking up from the papers on his desk. 'Over there.' He nodded to a spot in front of his desk.

I chose the chair which I thought would most seriously disturb the carefully planned symmetry of his office and pulled it in front of his desk.

'Help yourself to some tea if you like,' he said, still studying his papers.

Not to offer tea when it steamed in a pot surrounded by cups and saucers would have been rude, even by Smithson's standards.

'No thanks,' I said, determined to keep our meeting as formal as possible.

I followed the simple rule I'd devised when I'd first joined the Tracing Department of keeping out of his office as much as possible; a cup of hot tea might prolong our meeting beyond its agenda – whatever that was. The chair creaked as I sat on it and Smithson looked over the top of his half-moon reading glasses at me for the first time since I'd entered the room. He put down his pen.

'Now, Gorman, I thought we should have a word or two together.' He saw my look of confusion. 'To see how you're getting along in the Department,' he explained.

I nodded sagely and tried to give him the impression that I wasn't bowled over by his uncharacteristic piece of behaviour. My arrest performance indicators were OK and I couldn't see any other good reason why he should want to have me in for a chat. Of course he could have been gripped by a sudden desire to play his overbearing uncle role, but the way he'd greeted me didn't suggest that was his purpose; when he was in that sort of mood he generally left his desk and greeted you at the door. He smiled at me. 'I think it's a good idea to have an occasional

17

talk with my best tracers. It's an opportunity for us to share ideas. Don't you think so?'

I smiled back at him and nodded with a sense of enthusiasm I didn't feel. 'Yes sir.'

I always called him 'sir', it seemed to humour him and it didn't do me any harm. I thought I'd got a fix on his technique now. About four years ago, when I'd still been in the NHS and a manager of a large hospital, I'd gone on a management development course, and as far as I could tell I was getting an action replay of a day I'd spent learning how to appraise and counsel my staff. I wondered whether Smithson had been on some sort of similar course recently and had decided to practise on me. It didn't seem very likely. I knew his friendly attitude was only skin deep. He wasn't the sort of boss who encouraged friendly relationships with any of his staff and whenever we'd talked in the past I'd always felt I was fending off a deadly snake; one wrong word and he'd strike. The only other thing which could explain his behaviour was some sort of religious conversion – had he been transfixed by a blinding light on his way to the office that morning and been turned into a human being? That seemed even less likely.

'Now, let's see,' he said, turning the pages in the file in front of him as I realised he'd been reading my personal details. 'You joined the department shortly after I set it up, and in that time you've traced ...' He found the appropriate extract from last month's computer printout showing our performance indicators and took in the number of arrests next to my name. 'That's a lot of bounties,' he said with approval as he closed my file. 'But I've always been pleased with your performance indicators. Well done.'

I sat there, mumbling something about how nice it was to receive recognition. With luck I'd be downstairs in my own office in a few minutes, laughing to myself at his counselling skills.

'Tell me, Gorman, why did you leave your career in the National Health Service? I mean, you were a good manager and you'd probably have been in charge of a district by now, wouldn't you?' He asked the question in a friendly enough way but the stare from his pale green eyes fixed me to my chair in a palpable demonstration of his trick of making you believe he knew when you were lying.

I stopped giggling inside at his counselling skills as I felt myself squirming under his cold, unblinking stare. This sounded like it was going to be a serious interview and I needed to keep my wits about me. I tried to recall the relevant part of the lecture on staff appraisal I'd heard on my management development course; in terms of interviewing technique I thought in Smithson's mind we were still at what they call the 'rapport stage'. Unfortunately for me he'd chosen the one topic which wouldn't break the ice between us. I hadn't given up my career in the NHS, I'd been forced out of it, and when I'd eventually appreciated the enormity of what I'd agreed to, it had been too late.

'I thought the Special Health Authority would be more interesting,' I replied.

If I'd had more notice of his question I'd have said something that sounded convincing, but without advance notice it was the best I could do.

'Come on, Gorman,' he said and smiled. 'Give me a bit of credit.'

His manner was still friendly but I could see he expected me to tell him the truth and I didn't want to cross him. He was ruthless with those surbordinates he decided to dislike and it only needed one word from him to our case manager and I'd be tumbling down the arrest performance indicator chart in a matter of weeks. He never told people outright that they were finished, he was a sniper, he picked you off from a distance and from behind cover when you least expected it. And after he'd made someone's life unbearable he had them in his office and told them to go.

I swallowed, my mouth had gone dry.

'Can I change my mind about tea?' I croaked.

He motioned to the tray with one of his dinner plate-sized hands. 'Of course.'

The cunning little pig knows I'm upset, I thought. I

helped myself to tea and sat down. My cup trembled in its saucer.

'Well?' he asked as I stirred my tea.

I took a deep breath. 'After my wife was killed things were very difficult. I was on sick leave for a long time and when I got back to work they were transferring staff across from the NHS. You know what it was like, the government established the Special Health Authority at lightning speed, and at the start they stripped the NHS of a lot of staff.'

It hadn't answered his question directly but I hoped I'd said enough to steer him away from the subject of my emotions at the time I'd joined the SHA.

'Why didn't you choose to join one of our other divisions?' Smithson wasn't going to be pushed off course.

'Well,' I said, 'research was going to co-ordinate information on all the scientific work that was being done to discover the cause of AIDS and they mostly needed scientific people; there wasn't much call for someone with my background in administration.'

He stared across his office at the tea tray. 'I see,' he said softly. 'Then why didn't you apply for the Care Centres? There'd be plenty of scope there for someone with your experience.'

'I didn't like the look of the prospects,' I said. 'I joined the NHS because I wanted a job that would let me help people. I was trained to be a hospital manager. I didn't want to end up as some kind of prison governor. And I was right, too, as things turned out. Most of the doctors and nursing staff left the Care Centres and went back to the NHS when they were offered the chance. And we both know why.'

His lips tightened as he noted my criticism of his Party. I'd never spoken out like that to him before and what I'd said had been an implicit criticism of the BNDP – my outburst was an indication of how rattled I'd become under his particular line of questioning.

'So? Why did you choose tracing?' His voice had lost its tone of sympathy.

'I'd only been back from sick leave a couple of days when I realised I couldn't just pick up things and start all over again … I wanted to do something different. They'd set up the SHA and Tracing got more publicity than anything else. I knew it wouldn't be like anything I'd done before and …'

I clenched my jaw to stop the words. There was no way I was going to share my grief with Smithson. When Ann's car catapulted off the M23 motorway and burst into flames on the way to see her sister I'd gone down so deep I thought I'd never climb out again.

'I wanted something that would completely occupy me,' I finished lamely.

'I see,' he said.

Except he didn't see. I regained control of my emotions. I was well past the period when I couldn't handle them. The embarrassments I'd caused friends when I'd cried in public were a memory, and so were the friends. After I'd resurfaced from my feeling of loss I'd cut off my past life completely. The new one didn't have the same quality, but I got by. In the last six months I'd begun to think positively again and to see my bounty money as the way of escaping to something. More recently, Victoria had begun to appear as part of my wide awake dreams. I told myself I was insane to link her to my plans and that the effort it would take to break through her tough outer coating might put the skids under me again, but even though I kept trying to extinguish it, her image kept re-appearing.

We sat in silence while Smithson's fingers played with his pen. 'And now?' he asked, dispelling the silence. We both knew what he meant; was I still a headcase?

'Now I'm OK.' I smiled.

I was. In the early months immediately after I'd been transferred over from the NHS I'd pursued my job with a mindless indifference and tracing HIV carriers had filled all my waking hours and crowded out the gap in my life. Its one reward was the steadily growing pile of money which would soon get me out of Smithson's clutches, but I was starting to despise myself for the way I earned it.

'I'm not surprised you're feeling all right with all the bounty money you've earned,' he said, smiling back at me.

He took every opportunity to impress upon you that he was the boss. I put it down to an inferiority complex – either about his height or his tough East End background – and I wondered whether he'd read my thoughts and was reminding me of his power to change my plans.

'Tell me, Gorman,' he said briskly, changing the tempo of the interview, 'what are we going to do about all this?' He extended his hands with their heavy gold rings in an attempt to capture the circumstances of our world which had been turned upside down by the AIDS crisis.

'I don't know,' I replied, looking at his hands. They were two or three sizes too big for his body and they'd always fascinated me.

It was a stupid question. My world had already been turned upside down when the size of the AIDS problem, which had been building up since the late 1980s, had buried every other item of news. In the months that followed the exposure of the real scale of its grip on us, when known homosexuals were attacked and burned to death by ordinary, law abiding citizens, I'd been walking around my flat locked up in grief over Ann's death. And by the time the TV news reports were showing pictures of the inner city riots, which had gripped virtually all of our big cities, as the white population turned in fury on the ethnic communities, I was a voluntary patient in a psychiatric unit. Gazing blankly at the montage of burning streets, running people and the hard-pressed squads of riot police I'd missed the significance of the spoken commentaries and we were already three months into the new parliament when I'd discharged myself.

The Conservatives had waited until the very last moment before they'd called for a general election, hoping for something to turn up which would put everything right. But when the votes were counted the pollsters' forecasts proved true; and in a matter of months the new British National Democratic Party had won enough of the vote to break the mould of our two-party system. And the Conservatives had been forced to offer them a share in a coalition government in which they'd become almost equal partners instead of the far Right lackeys which the Conservative Prime Minister had intended when he'd paid their price to let him hang on to power.

Even then I didn't understand how much our way of life had changed and it wasn't until the morning I'd driven from my flat in Finchley to the south London hospital, which I managed, for my first day back at work when I'd appreciated that the black population really had become prisoners in their ghettos. We were still some way from situations like the Warsaw ghetto in the Second World War but the heavy police presence and the large gangs of white men wearing BNDP armbands were as effective as any wall. Although I'd discharged myself I still wasn't well and despite his assurances to the contrary my boss hadn't relished the idea of relying on someone who'd had a mental breakdown. And while I'd been struggling unsuccessfully against his campaign to coerce me into joining the newly established SHA, Emmerson, the leader of the BNDP, and his supporters in cabinet, were forcing the Conservatives to accept more and more of their schemes to cope with the AIDS crisis. My mind came back into the room with a jolt – Smithson had asked me a question.

'Sorry sir,' I said. 'I'm afraid I wasn't listening.'

He nodded his head gravely. 'I understand,' he said sympathetically. 'It must have been a difficult time for you – losing her like that.' He paused. 'I was saying I had a special job for you.'

What special job? I was listening now, Smithson had my undivided attention.

'It requires a lot of discretion,' he continued. 'Do you understand?'

'Yes,' I said.

I knew the office sometimes got special jobs which Smithson dished out personally and I also knew he usually chose Chris or Terry, although they never talked about them. It wasn't favouritism on Smithson's part that made him chose them; Terry and Chris always topped the arrest performance indicators and he simply put his money on the people with the best form. And Smithson rewarded the pair of them by making sure they got the best jobs. Do this special job right, I thought, and you can bring your retirement plans forward.

Smithson took a buff-coloured file out of a drawer and pushed it across the desktop's maroon leather surface towards me. I picked up the file and opened it. The young man in the colour photograph clipped to the inside of the file smiled at me. He was a handsome-looking boy with an open face, even teeth and short brown hair. I guessed he was about Victoria's age.

'Who is he?' I asked Smithson.

'His name's Harris, Jonothan Harris,' replied Smithson. 'Or at least, that's the name on his ID papers. He may have changed them by now ... I want you to trace him.'

'Is he a confirmed heavy or just a suspect?'

'Heavy' was a corruption of HIV, and it was the nickname people used to refer to those who'd contracted the human immunodeficiency virus which caused AIDS. Tracers and other people in the office used the term too. I think a journalist on one of the down market tabloid newspapers had been the first to coin the term. It showed how little people cared for those less fortunate than themselves.

Smithson played with his pen. 'Just a suspect at the moment. Someone in the south London office brought in a carrier yesterday and he named Harris as one of his contacts.'

I looked at Harris's picture. 'So he's gay?'

Smithson nodded. 'According to the information south London got out of the heavy, yes.'

I could imagine how they got the information out of him; the tracers in the south London office were a mean, vicious lot.

'The trouble is, Gorman, that Harris's father is an important man,' Smithson continued, 'and the powers-that-be don't want any publicity. So we have to pick him and his contacts up in one quick swoop – without leaving any embarrassing loose ends.'

'But that's next to impossible!' I protested. 'I mean, there's no way we can be sure that he doesn't have contacts outside the circle of people we trace.'

Smithson sighed. 'Don't tell me things I already know,' he said. 'Our job is to get him and anybody else he's had contact with. Nobody at the Elephant and Castle is interested in the finer points.' He threw his pen onto his desk in disgust.

'His father must be important,' I said.

Smithson touched the small, gold celtic cross in the buttonhole of his black pinstripe suit jacket that told the world he was among the first thousand members of the BNDP.

'He is … Very important,' he said with a faraway look in his eyes.

I remembered again my management development lecture on interviewing techniques, and its emphasis on the importance of body language, and wondered whether Smithson's unconscious fingering of his BNDP emblem could mean that Harris's father was a big wheel in the Party. If he was and the powers-that-be were Smithson's political pals it was no wonder that he wanted the job to be handled with discretion. It certainly wouldn't look good for the BNDP if the media got hold of a story about how one of their top men had a gay son who'd caught the AIDS virus. And as Smithson was a member of the Party's National Executive Committee his colleagues would expect him to make sure the news didn't leak out. Office gossip said Smithson's sights were fixed on parliament; presumably, if he managed this job without any fuss, his cronies on the National Executive would put him up for a nice safe parliamentary constituency. Once he'd got himself elected he'd chart a course to take him off the back benches and into government, and with his considerable administrative talents and complete disregard for anyone else's feelings he stood an odds on chance of getting there.

I flipped through the file. It didn't take long. Apart from Harris's photograph it only contained a piece of paper with four addresses in London. It wasn't much to go on.

'There's not much to go on, Mister Smithson,' I said.

'You've found people with less information than that,' he said tartly. 'Anyway this takes priority, whatever else you're doing, drop it.'

It was true, I had found people with less information to go on, but they weren't special jobs and if my guess was right I had a feeling that Smithson was going to demand quick results. He smiled winningly. 'If I knew where he was I wouldn't ask you to look for him. Would I …? Find him and stay with him. You know the drill. We need a record of who his friends are. And when you do find him, don't lose him. Otherwise …' He didn't finish his sentence but his threat was plain enough. It was a warning that if I screwed the job up he'd see to it I got a list of carriers, whose trails had long since gone cold, added to my case load. We were required to spend a proportion of our time looking for these and even a ten per cent increase would bugger up my arrest figures.

'You're not to talk about this to anyone when you leave this room. Do you understand, Gorman?'

'Yes sir.'

No way would I do anything to upset him, yet. I didn't talk about my job to anyone outside the Department and there was nobody at the office I'd share a confidence with either, not even Victoria – I'd take my cue from Chris and Terry and keep my mouth shut when the subject of Smithson's special jobs came up in conversation. But when I was ready to walk out I'd tell Smithson a few home truths.

'You're not to approach Harris,' said Smithson, pointing his finger at me. 'I'll organise the pick up from here.'

I guessed that when the time came he'd probably parcel out the job of picking up Harris and his friends to make sure that nobody at the office could put the whole picture together. I cast round in my mind for anything that could upset the job and disrupt my short-term personal plans.

'What about Sheila? She'll know something's on when I don't fill in my weekly case reports.'

I was being generous to our case manager. She already

regarded me as a lone wolf and when I failed to complete my case reports she'd complain to everybody in sight; it would upset her office routines, not to mention the arrangements for reimbursing travel expenses, and if I disrupted her systems she'd make sure I suffered for it.

Smithson tapped the cover of my personal file with the index finger of his right hand. 'You haven't taken any time off in the current leave year,' he said. 'So we owe you four weeks. You'd better take some of it now. Fill out your request form and leave it in my pigeonhole.'

'Yes, sir.'

It meant I probably wouldn't see Victoria until I caught up with Harris – I'd miss her, but I wouldn't miss the rest of my colleagues. I tried to think of anything else that could lead them to guess I was doing a job for Smithson.

'One problem though,' I said. 'If Harris isn't at any of these addresses I may have to follow him into other peoples' territories and if it gets out that I'm working someone else's patch it's bound to cause trouble.'

He leaned back in his maroon leather armchair, folded his big strong hands over his barrel chest and looked up at the ceiling. I could see from the look on his face that he was struggling with the problem I'd presented him with.

A tracer's caseload of known or suspected HIV carriers was based on their last address and if the trail led outside our area we passed them on to the appropriate office. It was a simple and effective way of carving the work up. We got to know our own territory and it helped us build up a band of reliable informers. Unofficially, when a heavy skipped from one office's area to another inside the London region the tracers concerned would split the bounty. Of course if they escaped into one of our adjacent regions we'd try and snatch them back; our altruism only stretched as far as the London Region's boundary line – the lads in the sticks could look after themselves. It was an unofficial policy we'd devised to maintain some kind of harmony between all the tracers who worked in London. Other regional heads had stopped similar practices in their areas but although Smithson knew about our arrangement he chose to ignore it. That way Smithson could fool our division's general manager into believing it was his deft handling of his staff that contained any in-fighting. And of course it was in his own financial interests to turn a blind eye, because it meant his tracers didn't waste time arguing amongst themselves over the distribution of bounties.

He pursed his thick lips and studied one of his thumb nails. 'Don't worry about it, Gorman. I'll make sure your colleagues in the other offices won't cause you any difficulties and if there's any trouble I'll handle it. I'm glad you thought of it though. If anyone thinks you're poaching it could cause a lot of unpleasantness.'

I took some comfort from the fact he'd explicitly acknowledged the existence of our unofficial agreement, but I was nobody's fool and I knew he wouldn't be much help if my fellow tracers got nasty. On the other hand the financial payoff would be worth the risk.

'Send your travel expenses claims forms direct to me,' he continued. 'I'll make sure they're paid. And mark the envelope "Personal and Confidential". When you leave here tonight take everything you're likely to need.'

'Right,' I nodded. 'How long have I got to find Harris?'

'Until I tell you to stop,' he said. 'And as soon as you do turn him up I want you to phone me. After that I want you to provide me with regular reports of where he goes and who he sees. Don't put anything on paper. Is that clear? Use the phone, and don't come through the switchboard, use my private line.' He wrote the number of his private line on a slip of paper and handed it to me. 'When you find him I want to know, immediately. We need to get a result on this one.'

'Yes, sir,' I replied, putting the slip of paper he'd given me into the zip pocket of my blue corduroy windcheater.

'One more thing,' he said, pointing at Harris's file. 'I don't want that to leave this floor. No photocopying. You'll have to commit the photograph and addresses to memory. You can use the small committee room, I'll see to it you won't be disturbed. And bring it back to me when you've finished, I'll still be here.'

That was an understatement. Smithson had the worst case of workaholism I'd ever known. When he wasn't attending meetings at the Elephant and Castle or visiting the other London offices he was at Soho Square before any of his staff and stayed on late into the night, every night. And his weekends were either spent in BNDP executive meetings or at their rallies in pursuit of his political ambitions. Given the rumours about how rich his wife was I sometimes wondered why he didn't pay her more attention. But then, perhaps his domestic relations were as tortured as those I'd imagined for Terry.

I got up from his antique chair and put it back in its rightful place next to the window which overlooked the square.

'Can't I even make a note of these addresses, Mister Smithson?'

He looked at me as if I was a spoilt child. 'You did a degree in history and anthropology didn't you? You should be used to remembering facts.'

As usual, his attitude towards my university education caused me to bridle and I was determined to try to have the last word before I left his office. 'If I'm working directly to you will I still get the bounty?' I asked. 'If Harris is a confirmed carrier, that is?' Smithson gave me a hard stare but I ploughed on. 'And what about any bounties which might be due on his contacts when we bring them in?'

'Does it ever occur to you that there might be something more to life than just money, Gorman?' he said wearily, as if money meant nothing to him. 'Don't worry, you find Harris and I'll make sure you're looked after.'

I walked out of his office with the imaginary sound of cash registers ringing in my ears. Track down Harris, I thought, and you could be out of here in next to no time. There was no way I was going to blow this job, and if I did Smithson would have me touring the streets of London looking for heavies who were probably dead. Or he'd ease me out of my job, and my experience with my previous boss had taught me that employers don't look too kindly on people with a history of psychiatric treatment, even when they are desperate for staff. In either case the castles I'd been building in my mind when I'd gone into Smithson's office would fall through the clouds and smash into the dust. Where had the BNDP dug him up from? He was more like a gangster than a civil servant. Mind you, from what I could judge, a track record as a gangster seemed to be an essential point of entry into the inner circles of the BNDP. I couldn't begin to imagine his appointment interview. It would have been interesting to observe the civil service mandarins on the panel, trying to ask questions of a man who'd fought his way up from the back streets of London. Their in-jokes and allusions to great literature would have been lost on Smithson – he bought his antique books by the yard. But from what I'd heard he was a fairly typical example of the kind of political appointees which had been introduced into the civil service as part of a package of changes the BNDP had demanded from the Conservatives, before they'd accepted the offer of a coalition government.

II
WEDNESDAY,
23 FEBRUARY 1999

Wednesday, 23 February 1999

Time: 22.15 hours

I hadn't immediately started the search for Harris when
I'd left Soho Square on the previous Friday night. There
was a time when I'd have been out on the street minutes
after Smithson had given me the job of finding him and I
wouldn't have stopped looking until I'd turned him up.
But on Saturday I'd been to a match with Rob Foster, an
old friend from my university days, and afterwards we'd
gone for a meal to celebrate my birthday. We'd met up
again on Sunday to go to an exhibition at the Royal
Academy in Piccadilly and to see a movie. Going out at the
weekends was another sign I'd come to terms with Ann's
death and that I was getting myself together again.
Starting on Monday – two whole days after Smithson had
given me the special job – I'd begun the task of tracing
Harris.

It had taken me most of three days to trace him to a flat
in Earls Court. On Monday and Tuesday I'd chased down
a number of leads from the addresses on his file, but one
by one they petered out. And on Wednesday morning I'd
called on one of my police informers who'd agreed to
interrogate the police computer in return for the usual
kickback. But all she'd come up with were the same four
addresses Smithson had given me. So early on Wednesday
evening I'd gone to see Wally Jacobs. Wally ran a small
backstreet printing business in the East End,
photocopying for people who didn't have their own
personal copiers, local newsheets, that sort of thing. At

least that's what he did in the tiny room at the front of the shop; in the basement he practised the more lucrative trade of forging ID cards. I'd only found out his sideline by accident from a carrier I'd picked up. At first I'd thought about passing the information on to the police, then I thought more about it and decided it made more sense to strike a deal with Wally.

Before I went to his printing shop I'd taken the precaution of depositing a letter with a lawyer with instructions that it be sent, unopened, to the police if I should die in suspicious circumstances. Wally's face was a picture when I walked into his shop and showed him a copy of the letter and suggested we should talk. It took a little time to convince him that I wasn't interested in crude blackmail, but as soon as he grasped the shape of the deal I was proposing he told his two thugs to let me go and we talked business. Our arrangement had worked well; I kept my mouth shut about his criminal enterprise and he supplied me with information about the new identities of the special clients he didn't declare to the Inland Revenue. Since our agreement we'd both prospered and I'd picked up dozens of his ex-customers, none of whom could understand why their excellently forged ID cards hadn't protected them from arrest.

As soon as I'd drawn a blank with the police computer I'd guessed Harris had got himself a new identity. There must be other forgers in London besides Wally, unfortunately he was the only one I knew. But I was lucky, Harris had been to him. And armed with the information Wally had given me I had gone to a pub, off the Old Brompton Road, called the Golden Dolphin, just before closing time on Wednesday night.

I'd bought a drink and sat at a table in the corner of the bar by the side of an old juke box where I could keep an eye on one of the young barmen. If I'd gone over and asked for his forged ID it would have said his name was John Hartnell, but even though he'd grown his hair and dyed it blond I still recognised him as the young man in the photograph Smithson had shown me. I sat quietly, minding my own business and waiting on developments. It was about ten thirty when Harris went through the door behind the bar and I watched as he reappeared a few minutes later wearing his overcoat.

Once he got outside the pub he was as jumpy as a frightened cat and the job of following him back through the rapidly emptying streets had required me to use all the skills I'd learned since I'd joined the Department. Standing in the street in a seedier part of Earls Court and watching him turn on the lights in his flat I was certain he was home for the night. I was lucky again when I found a phone box in working order at the end of Harris's street and called Smithson on his private line. I'd expected he'd still be at the office and I wasn't disappointed. I told him I'd found Harris and he ordered me not to lose him. I'd already decided to stay outside Harris's flat all night and after Smithson had put his phone down I'd run back to the pub to collect my car and it was just after ten past eleven when I'd parked down the street from his flat in a spot which gave me a good view of the entrance.

I'd hardly turned off the motor when a taxi pulled up and Harris came out of the front door and ran down the steps and got into it. I was pretty sure he was taking care not to be followed when he'd switched cabs in the Bayswater Road and I'd nearly lost him, but when he'd paid off his second taxi before walking the last few streets to his destination I was positive he was on his way to an important date. I drew up on the opposite side of the street, about twenty metres from the house he'd gone into. He'd beaten the midnight curfew with a few minutes to spare. I'd thought about phoning Smithson but I was sure he'd have gone home and I didn't think Harris would have a curfew pass, unless the Home Office had gone gaga and started issuing them to barmen, and that meant I was stuck somewhere in a poorer part of Paddington for at least six hours.

It was fifteen minutes past midnight when the door of the house opened and Harris came outside and stood under the portico, looking up and down the street. Apart from the faint sounds of Beethoven's Seventh Symphony coming from a house close by it was dead quiet. He glanced back towards the house again, half turned towards it, changed his mind and ran down the steps and darted between the parked cars and crossed to my side of the street. I sat in my car watching him crouching down by the railings which ran between the entrances to the houses and I guessed he was deciding what to do. So was I; Smithson had told me not to give myself away – I couldn't follow Harris on foot through the deserted streets and I certainly couldn't go after him in my car because he'd have known in a minute I was chasing him. He made up his mind and sprinted to the end of the street and I watched as he looked up and down the main road before turning the corner. I decided to give him five minutes before going back to his flat, and I told myself that if he wasn't arrested by the police I'd pick him up again in the morning.

I sat, looking at the partly open front door and the shaft of light that seemed to be beckoning me to leave the security of the Ford and go inside. Why the hell hadn't Harris shut it behind him? Ignore it, I thought, in the morning you can phone Smithson and report what you've seen. But suppose Harris evaded the police patrols and decided not to go back to his flat? After all, I told myself, you've seen enough to know that he's frightened and in his state there's no telling what he'll do. And if I couldn't pick up his trail in the morning Smithson would be asking questions right, left and centre. He knew as well as I did that people didn't go out after curfew without a very good reason, and the first thing he'd want to know was why I hadn't followed standard procedure and checked the house out. But if I did, and I ran straight into one of Harris's friends there might be awkward questions. If that happened, and I couldn't get by with one of my perfected routines for avoiding awkward questions, like smelling for a gas leak, and Harris did get home safely, he'd probably do a runner seconds after his friend phoned to tell him about me snooping around outside the house. Either way I could lose him. And if I did that I was sure Smithson would carry out his unspoken threat to juggle my caseload. He might even decide to hold a formal disciplinary hearing just to make good and sure the people at the Elephant and Castle knew who was responsible for screwing up their instructions. Eventually I decided I'd have to chance being seen and give the house the once over – then at least I'd be able to argue I'd followed correct procedure. After that I'd go back to Earls Court and if Harris didn't show I'd get another of my police informers to check the curfew violation arrest lists in the morning.

I got out of the car, shut its door quietly and walked along the pavement in my rubber soled shoes, keeping close to the wrought iron railings. My heart was thumping as I walked up the two steps to the house and stood between the pillars which supported the portico. Suddenly someone opened the front door of a house further along the street and I instinctively shrank back into the safety of the shadow under the portico. There was a snatch of conversation before the person who'd opened the door shut it again. The cat, which had just been granted its nightly parole, padded past the steps to the house. It froze and considered me, then, satisfied I wasn't a threat, it continued on its journey.

Alone in the street, I peered through the partly open door into the hall. It was empty. The lion's sightless eyes on the tarnished brass door knocker stared at me impassively as I lifted the ring in its mouth and knocked. The door slowly swung open on well oiled hinges and I was embraced by the light in the hall. I listened for any sound from inside the house – nothing. It was too late for second thoughts. I stepped inside. 'Hello?' I called tentatively. 'Is anybody there?'

I waited for a reply. Nobody answered. I jumped as an old clock on the hall table chimed once to announce it was thirty minutes past midnight. I walked down the hall and called again, more loudly this time. The walls of the old house absorbed the sound of my voice like a damp sponge. Still no response. I stood in the hall, uncertain of what to do next. The first door on my right, opposite the staircase, was ajar. I moved towards it, hesitated, and knocked.

'Hello,' I called again. 'Sorry to disturb you.'

I poked my head round the door and saw a man sitting at the far end of the room at a writing desk. He was looking in my direction but his face was in darkness, outside the oasis of light cast by the desk lamp.

'Excuse me, sir,' I said, in the authoritative tone I always used when passing myself off as a cop. 'But your front door's open. Is everything all right?'

My imitation as a representative of the forces of law and order sounded OK to me but it didn't seem to do anything for him because he just sat there, his face in darkness, staring in my direction. I took two or three paces towards his desk.

'I said …' The words died on my lips.

His eyes were open but he wasn't seeing anything with them, he was never going to see anything with them again. I'm no doctor but my father had died from a heart attack and from the look of the man I guessed he'd met the same fate. The second shock hit me a lot harder than the first and even as I realised who he was, my mind was trying to deny it. I know I ultimately worked for him and I'd often seen him on TV but I'd never seen him in the flesh before, which was probably why I hadn't recognised him when I'd first looked round the door. There was no denying it; the dead man in the chair with a face like a basset hound and badly cut silvery hair was Antony Rayleigh, Secretary of State for Health, and Chairman of the Special Health Authority. I stood rooted to the spot while my thoughts and feelings rushed about inside me, bumping into each other. After what seemed like a very long time I decided to take the one piece of advice which my brain was transmitting at maximum power – I had better get out while the going was good. It was when my eyes swept across the top of the desk and over towards the door to make sure I was alone that I first noticed his papers. No one on my grade ever gets to look at a minister's papers until they've been boiled down and converted into a terse directive, and although my instinct for survival kept telling me to get out, my curiosity was telling me to have a look at what he'd been reading.

I compromised with myself and went back into the hall and through the front door and stood under the portico. Everything was quiet. I made my mind up and went back inside and closed the front door behind me, bolted it and slipped on its security chain before standing, with my back against it, wondering at my decision not to leave the house and drive away. Rayleigh must have used the place as a safe house, I thought, and perhaps others used it too. Others like him perhaps? Others who were gay? Did they meet Harris there, too? Christ! If that was the size of it, it was no wonder that Smithson had wanted to handle the messier details himself. But I was sure that Rayleigh must have found a foolproof method of slipping away from his State duties and I couldn't believe he'd been the type of man to risk a night away in a crummy house in Paddington unless he was very sure of his arrangements. There didn't seem to be much chance that his police minder would suddenly turn up, unless he was gay too, of course. No, I thought, it must be safe, otherwise Rayleigh wouldn't have risked it. Having satisfied myself I wasn't likely to be disturbed I went back into the front room. At one time the house had been a gentleman's home, but it had slipped one or two notches in the course of the twentieth century; it could still have been restored to its former Victorian glory but it would have needed money and a lot of loving care to do it.

The furniture in the front room was old and shoddy and I guessed Rayleigh had probably rented the place in a different name to his own. Shutting the door which led out on to the hall, I went over to the desk and had another look at the man who'd been my ultimate boss. I began to speculate whether Harris had been responsible for his heart attack; perhaps an argument or a struggle? I thought, but all the signs pointed to it having taken him completely unawares. I moved behind his desk and looked more closely at the papers with his jottings in the margins, which he'd brought with him in an official despatch box. I picked them up off the desk and took them over to an armchair someone had pulled up to the gas fire, which was standing in the old marble fireplace. An opened copy of *Private Eye* and a half-empty glass of scotch were on the floor by the side of a portable TV which looked fairly new and I assumed that Harris must have been sitting in the armchair when the Great Reaper had dropped in for Rayleigh. Settling myself into the armchair I started to peruse the dead man's papers in the light from an old standard lamp.

The Cabinet documents I'd read when I'd done research for my degree had discussed events which had long since become history; Rayleigh's papers were for a Cabinet meeting scheduled for the following Tuesday. I looked at the one with the reference to AIDS in its title first, the one which had excited my curiosity. Normally I'd have found a document from the Treasury boring, but its title – 'The Economic Implications of the AIDS Crisis' – touched on my business, and I quickly skipped through its first page. When I got to the bottom of the second page I went back to the beginning of the paper and started reading it again. When I'd digested the whole document I sat looking at the flames in the gas fire, trying to come to terms with the Treasury's analysis. It had only been specific about the economic implications of AIDS, it hadn't spelled out proposals to deal with them, at least not in detail, but its conclusions were inescapable.

The government was spending over £60,000 million a year on a National Health Service that the Conservatives had trimmed back as far as they dared over the preceeding fifteen years, and with the continuing increase in Britain's ageing population and the demands they placed on healthcare it was electorally impossible to cut NHS services any more. In addition, the Treasury's paper said we were now spending almost an equivalent amount on the Special Health Authority with most of the money going on its Care Centres which were looking after those who'd either caught the HIV virus or who'd progressed to full blown AIDS. To cope with that they'd trimmed spending on everything else to the bone, with the exception of the police and those parts of the Army who'd been diverted to assist them in controlling a volatile civilian population. To make matters worse a significant proportion of our population – those between the ages of twenty and fifty – who the country needed to do the work which would create the wealth to pay for the escalating costs of coping with the crisis, were the very people who were locked up in the Special Care Centres. It was an economic nightmare and it was one we shared with other Western countries, but in Britain's case, according to the Treasury, the effects of our shrunken labour force was made worse due to the decline in the numbers of school leavers which had been a problem since the early 1990s.

The second paper I came to had been tabled by Emmerson, the leader of the BNDP, who'd collared the job as Home Secretary when he'd done the deal with the Prime Minister to help the Conservatives stay in power. At the time he'd accepted his ministerial brief the newspaper editorials had argued it was a sign that the BNDP would be very junior partners in the coalition. However, as the extent of the AIDS crisis came to be more generally appreciated, Emmerson's relatively junior Cabinet role had grown in importance, until eventually the Home Office had become one of the top three departments, alongside Health and the Treasury, which were headed by Conservative Ministers, as it accumulated more and more powers to control the ordinary citizen's life. Reading the arguments and proposals it contained about my future I felt a growing sense of impotent anger. The Home Office wanted to take over three of the Special Health Authority's four Divisions – Environmental Health, Care Centres and Tracing – leaving Research to be absorbed into the Department of Science and Technology.

Swallowing more scotch from the bottle, I sat back in the armchair and tried to think more rationally about Emmerson's proposal. There was a certain logic to it. The three Divisions he was proposing to take over had more in common with the forces of law and order than health – Care Centres and Tracing particularly – and it made sense to bring the people who were working to contain the AIDS crisis into a single organisation; and it would create at least a semblance of unity between us and the police. I read the final part of Emmerson's paper and sat staring at the gasfire for at least five minutes, thinking about the connection between his plans and the Treasury's analysis of our economic position. I dismissed the idea that Rayleigh hadn't known about Emmerson's intentions and that he'd come to the house, read the Home Office paper and had a heart attack. It's ridiculous, I thought, after all, apart from being Secretary of State for Health, Rayleigh had been the SHA's chairman, and I couldn't see how Emmerson could have put his proposals together without reference to Rayleigh or his senior staff. I was sure that Rayleigh would have known what was going on inside his own domain and that the Home Office's paper would have been discussed in an inter-Departmental working party. Had Rayleigh been consulted about the Treasury's paper though? If he hadn't known about it and he'd sat at the desk, and like me, put two and two together, the resulting four would have come as a hell of a shock to the man who had been the leading liberal in the Conservative Party.

Could I have got it wrong? I thought. The Chancellor of the Exchequer and his officials at the Treasury didn't spell it out, but the conclusion was obvious – something would have to go before the whole economy came apart at the seams. And the final part of Emmerson's paper provided the solution; instead of maintaining the pretence that the Special Care Centres were hospitals, accept the reality that they were prisons and dispense with medical treatment entirely – that way we'd save on the thousands of millions we were spending on drugs and the skeleton force of medical and nursing staff. His paper had only alluded to the next stage of the programme and I hadn't understood what he intended until I'd set it alongside the Treasury's dire prediction that Britain was likely to be bankrupt within eighteen months and without hope of receiving help from the International Monetary Fund. It was blindingly obvious when you thought about it. In economic terms AIDS victims were a total liability.

However, those who'd caught the virus and who were still at the pre-AIDS stage had some utility to the nation's economy. Therefore, keep the HIV sufferers at work, inside the Special Care Centres and in a regime which rewarded those who achieved their work performance targets and punished those who didn't, and eliminate, quickly and painlessly, those people in whom the virus had progressed to AIDS.

I looked at my watch. It was well after half past one. I glanced at the title of the paper prepared by the Ministry of Defence. Don't push your luck, I thought, you're in way over your head as it is. I made sure all the pages were in the correct order before I got out of the armchair and went over to the desk and put them in front of Rayleigh. They'd ask a lot of questions when they found him and as things stood they'd decide he died from natural causes, but given the unusual circumstances they were bound to suspect someone had read his papers. The security services would be involved and from what I'd heard the whole lot of them were paranoid, and their suspicions would be confirmed if some sharp eyed civil servant discovered the papers were out of sequence. I couldn't understand how Rayleigh could have been so lax as to bring them with him. He must have been bloody sure he wasn't going to be caught, I thought. Still, he wouldn't have been the first to disregard the rules about the safekeeping of State documents.

I went over to the door and studied every part of the room. I hadn't disturbed anything and I was wearing leather gloves, so there would be nothing to show I'd been there. On a sudden impulse I went over and poured the scotch in the glass back into the bottle and stuffed the glass into the pocket of my leather coat together with the copy of *Private Eye*. I turned off the standard lamp but left the gas-fire glowing, before leaving Rayleigh, sitting at the desk in the glow of the desk light, and secured from the world's prying eyes by the thick brown velvet curtains which had been drawn across the windows.

I experienced a moment of indecision about whether to

turn off the hall light before opening the front door; I'd read my share of spy books and I knew it was inviting danger to stand in a doorway with a light behind you, because your silhouette made you a perfect target. Telling myself that nobody would be outside in the street at that time of the morning, and that Rayleigh must have known what he was doing when he'd chosen it as a safe house, I undid the bolts and removed the security chain. But I turned off the light before I opened the door. I shut it behind me firmly and crept to one of the pillars at the front of the portico and peered up and down the street. When I was sure it was all clear I ran down the steps and scampered across to my car. My hands were shaking so much I couldn't get the key in the ignition. Eventually I found the hole and rammed the key home, turned the engine over and narrowly missed hitting the car which was parked in front of me as I pulled out of my parking space. Christ! I thought, as I turned the corner at the bottom of the street, why the hell didn't you ignore standard procedure and follow Harris, anything, anything at all would have done, except going into that fucking house.

III
THURSDAY,
24 FEBRUARY 1999

Thursday, 24 February 1999

Time: 02.45 hours

I was stopped, driving along the Finchley Road, at a temporary checkpoint the police had set up beyond the roundabout at Swiss Cottage. There were three official cars in front of mine at the roadblock. The two police officers wearing flak jackets gave their occupants a cursory inspection and waved them through but they approached my Ford with suspicion and I saw the policewoman on my nearside remove the safety catch on her Heckler and Koch submachine-gun. I turned off my engine as required by the regulations and made sure my hands were visible. I always drove up to checkpoints at night with my window down and the door unlocked to ensure I didn't share the same fate as those people who had been shot by nervous coppers who'd sensed a threat in an innocent movement or gesture. I watched them relax as the tall policeman on my offside said something to his female colleague after he'd noticed my yellow windscreen sticker. He put his hand through my open window and I gave him my ID card stamped with the SHA's logo.

'Where've you been then?' he asked.

The last thing I needed was an inquisitive traffic cop, but I knew it wouldn't be smart to refuse to play his game.

'I've been after a heavy,' I said. It was the truth.

'Get him?'

'No. I had a tip-off, but she didn't show up. I'll get her though, sooner or later.'

'I'd kill every one of the bastards,' he said.

I'd no doubt he meant it; the reinforced plastic visor was pushed back on top of his steel helmet and I could see the hate in his eyes. Emmerson's plans to kill AIDS victims would certainly catch the policeman's vote.

'So would I,' I said with emphasis. It wasn't true but it was better to humour him.

'We'd soon see some changes if Emmerson kicked out the fucking Conservatives and became Prime Minister,' he said, returning my ID card.

So, I thought, he's a BNDP supporter. I wasn't surprised, most of the police were.

I nodded in agreement. The ID card he'd passed back to me said I traced carriers of the AIDS virus and he'd be surprised if anyone who had the job of catching heavies didn't share his regard for that grand old Party, the BNDP. His attitude was commonplace among the police and it gave credence to the complaints in what remained of the liberal press that they turned a blind eye to the violent activities of its supporters against gays and blacks.

'OK?' I asked permission to go like he'd already agreed to it. If Harris hadn't been picked up by the police patrols I knew after what I'd found out that my idea of picking up his trail again at his flat in Earls Court had been blown sky high and I had some serious thinking to do.

'All right,' he said as he straightened up and moved away from my window. He waved his hand and the drivers of the two armoured riot trucks, who were blocking the road ahead, reversed towards the kerb to give me enough space to pass between them. I started my car and raised my hand to the one on my right as I drove through the gap.

There were no other traffic checks on the way home. Apart from the occasional criminal or drunk the police rarely caught anybody at traffic checks and they'd come to place less reliance on them, preferring nightime raids on the homes of those they suspected were engaged in law-breaking activities. Decent people didn't go out after midnight; the one year statutory sentence saw to that. When the curfew was introduced it was challenged by gangs of working class kids, particularly in the inner cities, but that was before the BNDP sucked a lot of them into membership, or the white ones at least, as blind ignorance and bigotry became the basis of a political ideology. By then it was believed that over five million men and women in the United States had contracted the HIV virus and the last Conservative government had stopped publishing any figures after the reality of the crisis had been splashed across the front page of the popular newspapers. Up until then, knowledge of the scale of the problem had been owned by doctors, scientists and civil servants who'd believed massive publicity campaigns could contain the disease.

After the first wave of sensational news stories ordinary people didn't want to hear calm, reassuring views from experts and mainstream politicians who appeared nightly on their TV screens. It was easy to see why the BNDP's solutions for dealing with the problem touched a chord in the ordinary voter. They preached a message people wanted to hear and they supported Emmerson and the BNDP because of it. As far as I could see the only point where the Labour Party's comparison between Hitler and the Nazis and Emmerson and the BNDP broke down was over the latter's lightning rise to power; they'd done in months what it had taken Hitler and his pals years to achieve. Anyone who stopped to think about it could discern the historical parallel with Nazi Germany in the 1930s. In the last few months I had started to think about it a lot and I became scared when I thought about where we'd end up if the BNDP managed to elbow the Conservatives out of government. And if I needed it, Emmerson's paper on the future of AIDS victims had confirmed my worst fears about him and his bloody Party.

When I got back to my Finchley flat I made some coffee and poured myself a large scotch. I knew I'd stumbled into a bigger piece of trouble than I could ever have imagined. I needed a plan and I knew it had to be a bloody good one because sooner or later I might be linked with Rayleigh's death through my connection with Harris. I sat on my sofa, looking at the TV's blank screen, trying to think of a good story – something which would put me a ten miles away from the house in Paddington and something that Smithson might believe.

Time: 06.30 hours

I came awake with a start. In my dream Rayleigh had been laid out, dead, on my carpet and a car had just screeched to a halt in the street outside my flat; I knew they were coming to arrest me the moment I'd heard one of them push my door buzzer. It took a little time for me to gather my senses and struggle off the sofa before going into my bedroom to turn off the electronic buzz on the alarm clock which had intruded into my dream. I looked at the bed and decided to sacrifice my early morning run in favour of an extra hour's sleep. I reset the alarm clock for eight, kicked off my shoes, got into bed and pulled the duvet cover over my head and closed my eyes before my brain could realise I was awake. After all, I thought, there isn't any point in going out to look for Harris at this time in the morning.

Time: 08.00 hours

When the alarm woke me again I lay in bed for a few minutes trying and failing to convince myself that the previous night had never happened. Shaking off my feeling of tiredness I got off my bed and bathed, shaved and dressed while listening to the radio in case they reported the discovery of Rayleigh's body. The morning news programme had its customary slot on AIDS and I listened while a scientist discussed the prospects of success for the clinical trials of a new drug. Who's he kidding, I thought, as I took one of my suits off its hanger. Rayleigh didn't get a mention. Did that mean they hadn't found him or was it taking time to put a credible story together? I imagined the Prime Minister's Press Secretary would be working overtime to bury most of the details, but sooner or later they'd have to release something. I wondered how the Prime Minister would handle Emmerson and his pals; I thought Cabinet meetings were held on Thursdays and they'd be bound to ask questions when Rayleigh didn't put in an appearance.

During my breakfast of coffee and buttered toast I re-examined the appraisal of my situation which I'd made in the small hours. The cold light of day changed nothing. I was still in one hell of a jam. I started going over the usual recriminations – the ones which begin with 'if only' – until eventually I told myself that they were stopping me making progress. The only 'if only' that mattered was when I'd accepted the special job of tracing Harris that Smithson had offered me on the previous Friday afternoon. It was the one decision I'd had any real control over and if only I'd told him then to give it to someone else, this Thursday morning would be like any other morning and somebody else from the office would be sitting over their breakfast trying to decide what to do. I thought again about the plan I'd cooked up before I'd fallen asleep on my sofa.

It wasn't a good plan, but I'd covered my predicament from every angle and it still seemed to offer my best chance of steering clear of the whole business over Rayleigh. I'd thought about phoning Smithson and telling him Harris had skipped from his flat at Earls Court but I knew if I did that I'd have to go into Soho Square for the inevitable inquest over my failure to stick with him. And I might give something away under Smithson's cold stare, and if that happened the future I dreamed of would evaporate once I got myself a walk-on part in the biggest political sex scandal since Cecil Parkinson's secretary had announced to the world she was pregnant. If I'd been right in my guess that Harris's father was a big man in the BNDP, Smithson would crucify me. It wasn't only the drop in my earning power which worried me if I was implicated – there was also the prospect of a visit from a posse of the Party's well-wishers, and I didn't want to run the risk of spending the rest of my life in a wheelchair. So, however difficult, I'd have to try and pick up Harris's trail again.

I'd found him once before, I could find him again, or that's what I told myself, and as soon as I got him in my sights I'd ring Smithson and make some excuse to cover up my failure to ring him earlier. I knew that if I didn't ring in before the end of the day Smithson would give someone a special job of finding me, but I thought I'd got until at least the evening before I'd have to call Smithson, and at least his long office hours would be on my side. I glanced at the kitchen clock – it was nine thirty. I could probably delay phoning him until eleven in the evening. That meant I had over thirteen hours. I started to think about what I'd do if I didn't find Harris by then, but I pushed the thought to the back of my mind. There'd be enough time to worry about that later – then and there I needed to be out on the streets – and once I'd found Harris there was no reason why Smithson need ever know about Harris's midnight visit to Paddington. I couldn't believe Harris would volunteer the information; he'd keep quiet and so would I. The only evidence which could link Harris to Rayleigh's body was his copy of *Private Eye* and the whisky glass, and they were both nestling at the bottom of a litter bin along the Finchley Road.

I put on my leather overcoat and checked I had my wallet and keys. By the time I got into central London the pub off the Old Brompton Road would be open; I'd try to pick up Harris's trail from there. For the umpteenth time I thanked my lucky stars I hadn't known about his connection with Rayleigh at the time when I'd phoned Smithson; if I'd supplied my boss with the address of Rayleigh's safe house somebody really would have been ringing on my door in the early hours.

52

The landlord of the Golden Dolphin looked over my shoulder at the near empty bar. It was early yet and there were only a couple of customers, sitting at a table over by the window.

'You just can't get the staff,' he said, turning his eyes towards me. 'Not anyone that's reliable. You set 'em on and before you can turn round they've upped and left. Well you can understand it, can't you? Look at the sort of wages people can earn; everybody's falling over themselves to offer more money to get people to work for them.'

'It must be difficult,' I sympathised. I drained my glass and slid it across the counter for a refill. 'Would you like one?' I asked him. I wanted to keep him talking.

'It's a bit early for me ... but yes, I'll have one with you, thanks.' He filled two glasses and brought them back to the bar. 'Haven't I seen you before?' he asked, after he swallowed some of his beer.

'Mmm.' I took a mouthful of tomato juice. 'I was in yesterday. I'm working around here this week.'

'What are you up to, then?'

'I'm in the insurance business,' I replied. 'Don't worry,' I added as I saw the look in his eyes which said he wasn't interested in buying any. 'I'm not going to try to sell you any. I was here last night about half past ten. I was over there.' I pointed towards the far end of the bar. 'Waiting to be served when your barman walked out.'

'Him!' He snorted. 'Don't talk to me about him! Do you know?' He took a mouthful of beer. I didn't know, but if I kept him talking I soon would. 'Just put on his coat and left! And after I told him he couldn't! He just walked out and left me to serve all by myself. Little bastard!'

'It must have been important,' I said.

'Important! Jesus!' he swore. 'He gets a phone call about half past nine and tells me – tells me, mind you – he's got to leave early. I told him. I said to him, you're on 'till we close, you can bloody well go then and not before. He just looks at me and goes back behind the bar. And then, at half past ten, he just walks out. I said to him, you're not getting paid, you know … little bleeder.'

He broke off our one-sided conversation and went to serve a customer. I looked at my watch. I'd find out what I could about Harris from the landlord and then I'd go round to his flat. The landlord gave the woman customer her change and came back to my end of the bar.

'Why did he go off like that?' I asked.

'Search me,' he said. 'He'd only worked here for a few days, casual staff, you know.' I knew. It meant the landlord didn't have to fill out any forms about who Harris was; most of the pubs worked on the same basis and the police ignored their breach of the employment law aimed at keeping track of people's movements because they preferred to keep the dregs of society in places they knew where to find them. 'He wasn't one of my regular staff,' the landlord continued. 'I'd have finished him anyway on Sunday when the wife gets back from her mother's.'

'He's not coming back then?' I said. I was stating the obvious but I wanted to be sure.

'You're joking!' he said. 'I wouldn't have him back even if he walked through that door and got down on his knees and begged. I'd rather manage without him. Mind you, I blame myself, I should never have taken him on. I knew he was gay. Well, you can tell, can't you? But,' he ran his hand over the top of his head, 'I thought I'd take a chance. It's the last time though. You know how it is?'

'Yes,' I said. 'You can't get the staff.'

A man came into the bar and he left me again.

'I tell you what though,' he said as he re-joined me. 'It'll be a bloody good job if the BNDP do get their way. It's about time we made it illegal.'

I shrugged my shoulders. 'Won't it just drive them underground?'

'Underground?' He laughed. 'That's where they ought to be.'

I forced myself to grin at his red puffy face and small

eyes shining with bigotry. 'So? What was so important he had to leave?'

'Who?' The landlord looked puzzled and I could see his mind was focused on the current debate about the Homosexual Offences Bill which had been introduced into parliament the previous week.

'Your barman,' I said.

'I don't know,' he said. 'Probably one of his boyfriends. I didn't know anything about him and I didn't want to. As long as he could serve my customers, that's all I wanted to know.'

I looked at my watch. I was losing precious time as well as my temper and I could see the landlord was on the verge of spewing out the BNDP's line on gays and blacks and I didn't want to get into an argument.

'Well, duty calls,' I said, and left. Talking to the landlord had cost twenty minutes and I'd learned nothing which could help me find Harris.

I stood outside the pub and surveyed the sky; the previous day's dull clouds had been replaced by a pale sun, but dark grey clouds were massing to the south – I guessed it would rain later. I still felt fragile from my lack of sleep and I decided to walk the relatively short distance to Harris's flat. I couldn't believe he'd gone back there after running out of the house in Paddington, but I still needed to check it out, and without any lead on him I needed the same sort of luck I'd had the day before.

I'd only just turned the corner into the street where Harris lived when I got the feeling I wasn't alone. It was nothing you could put your finger on, just a sense of being watched. Without slackening my step I took out my packet of cheroots and fumbled with my lighter. As I intended, it slipped through my fingers and fell to the pavement. I took a half step past it, stopped and bent down to pick it up. There were two or three people in the immediate vicinity and they treated my mishap with total indifference, and more particularly no one stopped in mid stride, or found a sudden interest in their shoelaces. I picked up my lighter and put it back in my pocket. In real life it's difficult to bring off the subterfuges used by characters in detective novels, but I thought my simple ruse had looked natural. Of course, anyone who knew the business would have guessed what I'd been trying to do and they'd have known I was on to them. I knew there was nothing I could do about that and I took a cheroot out of its packet and lit one whilst telling myself I was tired and that my sixth sense was nothing more than an overworked imagination. Convinced by my explanation I continued walking along the street towards Harris's flat.

Harris lived on the top floor of a house conversion. The builder who'd done the work had probably been looking for ways to save money on the job because the house's front door wasn't protected by a remotely controlled electric lock. I walked into the front hall and up the stairs to Harris's flat and knocked on his door. There was no reply. I knocked again. After waiting for two or three minutes I decided there was no one at home and I took a piece of plastic from my wallet, slipped the lock and eased the door open. There was no security chain attached on the other side. OK, I thought, you can't hang around here all day, and taking a deep breath I slipped round the door and closed it behind me. My guess had been right: the flat was empty.

I started to poke around the two rooms and the small kitchen and bathroom until, after about ten minutes' worth of searching, I asked myself what I was looking for. I'd sat down to think of a good answer when my thoughts were interrupted by the sound of a key turning in the lock on the door to the flat. My brain presented me with a couple of ways to get me out of the fix I was in but my body stubbornly refused to execute a single one of them, which was just as well since I was on the top floor and all my ways of escape had centred on jumping out of the window into the street below. So, his first sight on entering the flat was of me, sitting on a chair, staring at him. If there is a God, at that moment he was on my side, because I instantly recognised that the young man staring at me was even more scared than I was. Can I bring it off?

I thought. I was wearing my military-style leather overcoat – the type favoured by detectives in the new national police force – and I told myself that as long as I kept my nerve I could deceive him into believing I was one.

'Well, well,' I said evenly in my best tough policeman's voice, 'and what have we here?' I slid my right hand inside my leather overcoat and held it under my armpit. 'Who are you?'

He started to speak and then hesitated. I could see he believed I was armed. I got off the chair and walked across to him.

'I asked you a question,' I said, pushing the door closed behind him. 'Now. Do I get an answer or will you need a bit of help?'

It was enough pressure; the threat of official violence unlocked his tongue. 'I live here,' he stammered. 'My name's David Johnson, this is my flat.'

'Come on, you little bugger,' I said. 'I know better. You share it, don't you? Isn't that right?'

He looked down at his feet. 'Yes,' he said softly.

'And where's your partner? That's what you call one another, isn't it? Partners?' I sneered.

Now he really was scared and I was certain if I kept harrying him he'd spill everything he knew about Harris. He was tall, about my height, and very slim and although his hair was cut in a very masculine style it couldn't disguise his delicate, almost girl-like features. I felt sorry for him. And for me – when I'd finally emerged from my cocoon of grief over Ann I'd promised myself I'd cut out the violence. Up until now I'd kept to it. I swallowed down the taste of self disgust and thought myself into the role of a gay-hating copper and prepared to act in the way Harris's flatmate would expect.

'Look!' I said, pushing him hard in his chest with my left hand. 'I know you're queer – it sticks out a mile. I'm after your friend, we're looking for him.' He stared at me, momentarily numbed by my second round of shock tactics. 'As things stand I've no evidence against you,' I continued pressing home my advantage. 'We can get it though, can't we?' I pushed him hard in his chest again. 'Two minutes with the police surgeon and we'll know.'

He closed his eyes and for a moment I thought he was going to faint. Christ! I thought, you're in a fucking dirty business, Gorman. But he was my only chance of finding Harris and I'd no choice but to continue.

'Are you going to tell me what you know or ...' I curled my fingers round his shirt collar and pulled him towards me.

'Can I sit down?' he whispered. 'Please. I don't feel very well.'

'If it's going to help you talk. Sit down,' I said, taking hold of his shoulders and propelling him towards the chair I'd been sitting in.

'I don't know where Jonothan is,' he mumbled after he'd sat down in the chair.

'You'll have to do better than that,' I growled.

'I haven't seen him since yesterday.' He looked up at me. 'Honestly. He came home from working in the pub last night and then he went out again and he never came back.'

He began slowly to rock backwards and forwards on the chair, with his arms huddled around himself, like a confused and frightened child. Oh Jesus, I thought, why didn't you tell Smithson to stick his special bloody job.

'You didn't report it?' I pushed his shoulder.

Failure to report a curfew infringement was an offence which also attracted a statutory one year prison term. I doubted he would have done in case it led to questions which he dared not answer; even though homosexuality still wasn't a criminal offence it wasn't smart to alert the police to your sexual orientation, unless you were heterosexual. Once they knew he was a homosexual they'd pin some crime on him, sooner or later. Nevertheless, I needed to be sure he hadn't reported Harris missing because it was crucial to the story I intended telling Smithson.

'Did you report it?' I hissed.

He shook his head in despair. 'Is it likely?'

I pushed his shoulder again. 'Any idea where Harris is?'

'No.' His denial was barely audible.

'I'll ask you again,' I said, feigning anger.

'Look, I don't know where he is,' he said. 'I don't understand what's going on.' He started to cry softly.

Self pity I didn't need, it might lessen his fear of me and make him defiant. I slapped him hard across his face.

'Don't start snivelling!' I shouted, taking Terry Bannister's method of dealing with suspected carriers as my role model. 'That kind of shit won't work with me. Your sort turn my stomach. Make no mistake, sonny, if you don't come up with something better than that I'll spoil your sweet little life for ever. Now! Where could he have gone?'

'There's an old friend,' he said quietly. 'He might have gone to stay with him … We had a fight you see.' His shoulders shook as he wept. 'I said some very cruel things to him.'

'Where does his friend live?'

'I don't know.' He looked up at me and I raised my fist. He cringed. 'He runs an art gallery called Pastels. I don't know the address, honestly,' he pleaded.

'Is that the best you can do?' I said, trying to sound bored.

'I've told you all I know,' he cried. 'It's the only place I can think of. What do you want him for? What's he done?'

'That's my business,' I said. 'Now understand me, if you've told the truth I'll forget about you. If not, I'll find you and by Christ, you'll suffer before you go down.'

He took his head out of his hands and looked up at me again, his face creased with tears. It was open season on gays and with each day that passed I was becoming more and more sickened with my damn job. Another six months and I'd be able to chuck it. First of all, though, I had to find Harris. I'd walked to the door of the flat and opened it and I only asked the question out of curiosity, or maybe it was because I wanted him to believe I wasn't all bad.

'What was the fight about?' I asked.

'Money,' he said as he wiped his face on the sleeve of his overcoat.

I smiled. 'Everyone fights about that.'

'This wasn't like that.' He sniffed. 'I wanted to know where he was getting it from. He only works occasional jobs as a barman. I thought he was going with somebody else.'

'How long have you known him?' I said in a conversational tone.

He wiped his damp sleeve. 'Only a couple of months, but we're a couple. I'm clean. I was scared he'd pick something up.' We both knew what that 'something' was.

'Was he seeing someone else?' I asked, standing with my back to the open door.

'He said he wasn't. I didn't believe him.' I could have given him a few clues about who Harris was seeing and presumably Rayleigh would have paid well for his pleasures.

I left him sitting on the chair, crying softly and hugging himself. When he stopped he'd get his possessions together and clear out, and he'd be deep underground before I reappeared to harass him. That's OK, I thought. Smithson need never know that Harris shared a flat with someone and if he told the tracer at his shakedown interview I'd just play dumb. Johnson was a loose end and I'd stitched it up nice and neatly. Now I needed a London telephone directory and a stiff drink to get the taste of Terry Bannister's interviewing technique out of my mouth.

Time: 14.00 hours

Pastels was one of those bijou art galleries you only find in Mayfair and I guessed it was patronised by types who believed the function of art was to oil conversations at cocktail parties. The catalogue for its current exhibition said the Spanish artist who'd chosen to emigrate to England believed that only children could perceive the true form of the human body. Although his drawing hadn't progressed much beyond matchstick people the price list showed he'd got straight 'As' for arithmetic. I felt out of place and I must have looked it because as I stood inside the door, casually looking at the paintings and flicking through the catalogue I was firmly accosted by a young woman.

'Can I help you?' She had the voice of what used to be called a debutante and pretensions to match. But she was pretty, with dark brown hair and grey eyes, set in a round face with a pert nose and red moist lips.

I'd prepared for such an eventuality. I took a clipboard from under my arm and went into my routine as the pompous gasboard official. It was one of the many roles I'd perfected in order not to alert people I was hot on the path of one of their friends.

'There's been a report about a gas leak,' I said slowly and stentoriously in the way that self-important men from the gas board are wont to do. 'Nothing to worry about, but we can't be too careful, can we?'

She looked at me with distaste. I wasn't sure whether she didn't like me, or merely men from the gas board.

'Are you sure?' It was a challenge rather than a question. 'I haven't smelled anything.' She sniffed the air in the gallery. 'I hope you're not going to cause any mess.'

I examined the papers on my clipboard. 'Not according to this,' I said. 'I'm only checking really. It's the men who come after me who'll do the job.'

If she'd looked more closely at my papers she would have seen the forms were printed with the SHA's logo. But she didn't. A clipboard complete with printed forms is the universal mark of officialdom and to dispel any lingering doubts she might be harbouring I flashed the gas board ID card I'd had forged for moments such as these.

She showed me round the gallery and the storerooms at the rear while I sniffed officiously, examined the meter and asked the kind of questions that were the stock in trade of a gas board official. She answered all of them in a bored voice; there were no gas appliances in the gallery apart from the central heating boiler; and yes, the Victorian style wrought iron spiral staircase which wound upwards to the first floor led to an upstairs apartment; but no, she didn't have the key to the apartment and unfortunately the owner of the gallery was out and she wasn't sure what time he would return. I would have liked a look at the upstairs apartment but I didn't press her – I didn't want to appear too pushy.

We'd completed the tour and were standing by her desk when two potential customers came. I could see she wanted to get rid of me so that she could concentrate on extolling the finer points of the indecipherable scratchings of the Spanish artist which were hung on the gallery walls. I recognised that now was the time to find out what I really wanted to know.

'Can I just check my records, miss,' I said, examining the papers on my clipboard.

'Really!' she exclaimed quietly. 'Don't you have better things to do?'

'Let's see,' I said slowly, ignoring her show of pique. 'According to this the gallery belongs to …' I shuffled the papers pretending to look for the right one.

'Mister Motte,' she said, supplying me with the name I wanted while she looked greedily at the two punters who were examining the paintings.

'That's Mister D. Motte?' I replied, oblivious of her increasing agitation. 'D as in David?'

'No. C … as in Charles. Look! Have you finished? Because I'd like to talk to our clients.' She started to move towards the gallery's door, expecting me to follow. I stayed by her desk.

'I do need to have a look at the apartment upstairs,' I said. 'Haven't you any idea when Mister Motte will be back?'

'He should be back later this afternoon,' she said as she crossed her arms across her breasts, defying me to ask her another question. I looked at the swell of her breasts underneath her pale lemon and grey cashmere sweater and wondered whether she had any upstairs duties. If she did I envied Motte. Does she know he's bisexual? I thought.

'I'll try and come back later then, miss,' I said. 'If not I'll have to come round this evening. Will he be in?' I wrote Motte's name on the top page on my clipboard.

'I'm sorry,' she said tightly as she cast another look at the clients. 'I really don't know.'

'Well, I'll try anyway. I'm sorry I've taken up your time.' I put the clipboard under my arm. 'Thanks for your help, miss,' I said as I went past the two customers on my way out of the gallery.

I walked across the road to my car, unlocked it and got inside. From its position in the side street where I'd parked I had a clear view of the gallery. I sat and waited until the two clients had left and then I went back and put my head round the door. She was sitting behind her desk, filing her red lacquered fingernails. I picked up my pen off the carpet where I'd purposely dropped it on my way out and apologised for disturbing her before making what I hoped looked like an embarrassed exit. Re-crossing the road to my car I felt quite pleased with my little performance. From what I'd seen I didn't think I'd raised her suspicions; if Motte was up to something either he hadn't taken her into his confidence or he was somewhere she couldn't phone him to report an unexpected visit from the gas board. Congratulating myself once more I got back into my car and prepared to wait for Motte.

Time: 16.50 hours

A dark blue Jaguar stopped outside the gallery just before five o'clock and I watched as a tall man got out and went and kissed the female assistant. I thought it was usual pleasantry people like them exchanged until she put her arms round his neck and thrust her body against him. So, I thought, she does have upstairs duties, I wonder whether she was lying about not having a key to his apartment. Was Harris hiding up there? Somehow I didn't think so.

Shortly after, she collected her coat from the back of the gallery and came out on to the street. Motte locked the door behind her. There was enough light inside the gallery for me to watch him go to its far wall and climb the spiral staircase to his apartment. After a few minutes a light went on in a window on the second floor and I could see Motte's silhouette as he closed the curtains. The spy stories are right: he did make a perfect target. What should I do now? I thought. It was entirely illogical but I'd expected Harris to be with him when he came back to the gallery, and I had to admit to myself that I hadn't thought beyond that. I sat in the car looking at the glow from Motte's window, wondering whether I'd wasted most of the afternoon on the word of a frightened boy. I looked at the digital clock on the Ford's fascia panel – there was less than six hours before the midnight curfew and if I didn't report to Smithson by then my only way out was suicide.

I'd been sitting in the car and fretting for nearly half an hour when the light in the window of Motte's apartment went out. After a few minutes he came out of the gallery's front door and climbed into his car. I only had one choice; and as the Jaguar glided away from the kerb I swung out of my side street and took up a position three cars behind it. Motte came out on Piccadilly and at Hyde Park Corner he took the Park Lane exit. It wasn't until we were driving north along the Edgware Road that I guessed he was probably heading out of London.

As we approached the roundabout at the bottom of the MI motorway I got close behind Motte's Jaguar to make sure I wouldn't lose him in the crush of jostling cars. In spite of my aggression towards the homeward bound motorists I got boxed in as the heavy traffic crawled its way round the junction and I only just managed to catch a glimpse of his Jaguar as he took the access road on to the motorway. I knew that if he put his foot down I'd never catch up with him in my Ford and the second I got on to the motorway slipway I pushed the accelerator pedal to the floor. I needn't have worried; Motte was a sedate driver and I'd gone less than three miles when I saw his Jaguar in the orange glare from the overhead lights. I slowed down and tucked in behind him. I didn't think there was much chance he'd notice me in the streams of cars taking their owners home from a day's work in the city.

After ten minutes steady cruising I turned on the car

radio to hear the news, in case the story of Rayleigh's death had broken since I'd driven off from Motte's gallery. I wasn't expecting the BBC to reveal all the lurid details; there'd be a short announcement of his death, followed by an obituary prepared at the time he'd become Secretary of State for Health, then their chief political correspondent would come on to say what a loss it was to the country, how he was a great family man and a pillar of the Church – the usual garbage. The other facts, like how he was secretly a homosexual and that he'd died in down-at-heel property in Paddington would be omitted in the interests of good taste; at least they would if the Prime Minister's Press Secretary had anything to do with the story. The news broadcast didn't mention Rayleigh. Did that mean they still hadn't found him? It probably wouldn't be easy because there was no doubt in my mind that he'd have taken meticulous care to hide his secret. What would the Prime Minister do? I wondered. I hadn't paid too much attention to politics until the last few months when I'd find finally shaken off the effects of Ann's death, but even a political illiterate could see that Rayleigh's death could shift the balance of power in Cabinet, and with things as they were Emmerson would be the one who was most likely to benefit from it.

Motte's nearside rear indicator started flashing as we approached the junction for Hemel Hempstead. I was relieved; we weren't all that far from the outer London limit and once we went past the Luton exit we'd come on to the London Zone traffic control point. I hadn't got a pass to let me into the South Midlands Zone and if Motte had I'd lost him. I let a couple of cars get in front of mine as we drove along the exit road to the traffic checkpoint to make sure he wouldn't notice my Ford as we sat in the queue, waiting for the police to check our ID. As I drove up to the barrier I followed my usual procedure to ensure against being shot by accident. It was unlikely the police would be jumpy at that time of night but it was prudent not to take chances.

The policeman looked at my ID card under the bright arc lights.

'Do you know your period is almost up?' he asked. 'Your

blood tests are due next Tuesday.'

'It's OK,' I said. 'I haven't forgotten.'

'Well, make sure you don't.' His manner was firm but polite.

'Even if you are a tracer you'll still be locked up.'

'I won't,' I said as I took back my ID.

I drove away from the checkpoint and followed Motte along the dual carriageway into Hemel Hempstead. The copper had given me good advice, whatever happened I'd have to go for my test. All those between sixteen and fifty who weren't confined to the Care Centres, had to take their compulsory three monthly blood tests. There were no exceptions to the rule and failure to have it meant that the person concerned was flagged on the SHA and police computers as a suspected carrier. Whether you turned up later to apologise or you were caught by a tracer made no difference, once Environmental Health got the daily returns from the Test Stations and placed you on its 'Expired Test' list you were taken to a Care Centre's holding compound, where you were tested and held for three months. After the incubation period was over and if your test was antibody negative you were released. If the test was positive you were questioned by a tracer who would record all your sexual contacts and while you went under armed guard to a Care Centre the tracer went out to hunt down those who might have contracted the HIV virus from you. It was an inconvenience we'd learned to live with and most people accepted the BNDP's argument that it was one of the few effective ways the State could monitor and contain the spread of the disease.

Motte skirted Hemel Hempstead's town centre and took the road to Leighton Buzzard and a couple of miles outside the town he turned left down a minor road. Although I knew it was going to be difficult keeping in touch with him if he kept to country lanes I had no alternative but to drop further back and rely on picking out his red tail lights and the glow from his headlights. After following him for a couple of miles I drove through a series of S bends before coming to a long stretch of straight road. Apart from my car there was nothing else in sight. I'd lost him. I drove as fast as I dared for about two miles, but it was no use – there was no sign of Motte's Jaguar.

I stopped my car and sat in it, with the engine idling, while I considered my next move. I was sure Motte hadn't known he was being followed, and even if he had, he didn't strike me as an ace driver and he'd have had to be up to rallying standards to get so far away from me. I hadn't even seen a faint glow from his tail lights when I'd driven round the last S bend, and the road beyond it was virtually straight for over half a mile. I decided there was only one explanation; he must have turned off, either going through the bends, or immediately after. I turned the car round and drove slowly back towards Hemel Hempstead, looking for a side road.

I discovered the driveway to a house just before the start of the S bends. It was on my nearside and so well concealed that I very nearly missed it, and it was easy to see how I hadn't noticed it when I'd been coming from the opposite direction. I drove past without slowing down and stopped beyond the bends in an entrance to a field – that way I could circle round on foot and approach the house from the rear. I closed my door quietly, locked it, climbed over the gate and dropped into the field. I struck off on a diagonal route which would take me to its far corner. It was years since I'd been out in the countryside at night. The rain which had threatened earlier in the day had failed to materialise, the moon was up and without any cloud cover the temperature was dropping.

Silence is definitely a human concept and in the middle of the field, as owls hooted and small creatures I couldn't see went about their nightly habits, it seemed noisier than Piccadilly Circus. The first three weeks of February had been very wet and the ground was sodden. I hadn't gone very far before my shoes and trouser bottoms were soaked. As I squelched across the field I offered thanks to the farmer for not ploughing it up. It wasn't until I'd nearly reached the far corner of the field when I realised that although the moonlight had helped me to see where I was going it would also have made me visible to anyone who might be watching. I cursed my stupidity, but it was too late to change my route and I wasn't going back to the gate to start again. I'd had a hunch when Motte left his gallery and I was going to play it out; I was sure Harris was at the house, whose rooftop I could see above the trees, and all I had to do was confirm it. The luminous dial on my watch said it was nine seventeen; my time was running out.

I found a gap in the hedge that bordered the house which was sufficiently large enough for me to squeeze through. At least that was my plan. However, I'd nearly pushed myself through it when the bloody thing seemed to come alive. It was like being sucked into a man-eating plant; the thorns on its branches snagged at my leather coat and scratched at my face as I struggled to extricate myself from its clutches and force my way through. I'd nearly escaped its prickly embrace when I made another discovery; there was a shallow water-filled ditch on the other side. I dragged myself over the lip of the ditch and flopped on to the wet grass like a beached whale and lay there, breathing heavily and listening for the sound of approaching feet. I couldn't have made much more noise if I'd driven through the hedge in a tank and I knew that if there was anyone on guard outside the house they couldn't have missed the sound of my approach. After a few minutes my breathing returned to normal and as I lay on the grass, straining to hear the sounds of someone coming in my direction, I comforted myself with the thought that I'd gained some benefit from my early morning running.

When I was sure I was alone I got to my feet and ran, half crouched, to a small clump of trees. The rear of the house was in darkness and I decided to make my way round to the front. From what I could see in the moonlight my best way lay on the field side, where the trees came to within ten metres of the house. I crept through the undergrowth beneath the trees, praying I wouldn't step on a rotten stick which might crack in the still night like the sound of a gunshot. After I'd covered a short distance I could make out a dim luminosity at the front of the house.

I covered another ten or so metres until I could see part of a gravel driveway – it was bathed in an arc of light and the shape of Motte's Jaguar and a BMW parked alongside it were clearly visible. Another couple of metres and I could see the light came from a downstairs window on my side of the building. Alright, I thought, you've come this far, all you have to do now is get up to that window. The ground between me and my final destination consisted of a large flowerbed. I'd already accepted the fact that my shoes and trousers would defy any attempt at salvage. I could have walked across the gravel and knocked on the house's front door and spun a story about my car breaking down, but I dismissed that idea because I guessed the people inside would take one look at me and begin to wonder why I'd decided to swim for help rather than walk up their driveway from the road like any other normal person. There was nothing for it, I decided, I'd have to take the risk of them discovering my footprints in the flower bed when the sun came up.

I started towards the corner of the house, feeling naked and vulnerable outside the cover of the trees, even though I knew I was in the shadow of the building. I reached the corner of the house and edged towards the window, aiming for the gap between the closed curtains which was sufficiently wide for me to see into the lighted room. I reached the side of the window, squatted down and inched myself along the wall until I was directly below the gap in the curtains. Easing myself up slowly, I looked into the room. I guessed the house was Edwardian – not too large – it was the sort of place you could easily imagine yourself living in.

The room I was spying into had probably been used as the principal one for the family who owned it. Motte was sitting in a leather armchair, facing me, and talking to another person, in a matching armchair, on my side of the fireplace. Both chairs had high backs and I couldn't see who was sitting on my side of the fireplace. Now I've got so far I'm not leaving this bloody place until I've seen Motte's friend, I thought. A log fire was burning in the grate and the room looked warm and cosy. I shivered. My body temperature had taken a dive since I'd fallen in the ditch; I was beginning to feel the cold and the muscles in my legs felt like they were seizing up. I shifted my position to combat the first signs of cramp, hoping that Motte and Harris – if it was Harris sitting with his back to me – were the kind of people who believed in early nights. Ten minutes passed. At any moment I expected Motte to glance up at the window and see me staring at him, but he kept his eyes on the other person in the armchair. I tried to hear what they were saying but an old record deck was playing one of Bach's Brandenberg Concertos and I could only make out the murmer of their voices.

Motte finished his scotch, raised his glass and nodded to the other person. I ducked below the window ledge as he got out of his armchair. When I peered over the ledge again he was standing by an ugly Victorian sideboard with his back to me. Perhaps my mystery man in the other armchair will get up and stretch his legs, I thought. He didn't. Motte lifted the lid of the ice bucket standing on top of the sideboard, looked inside and shook his head. There was no ice. You should have my problem, I thought. I watched as he walked to the door of the room, opened it and called to someone and as he turned back from the door I dropped down below his line of sight. My mystery man was a woman, and she'd left her armchair and was standing with her back to the log fire.

Generally I only watch movies on the TV, but I'd seen enough of the stations' scheduled viewing to know I was looking at Alice Townsend, who hosted a twice weekly political chat show, laced with veiled criticisms of the BNDP; she was even better looking in the flesh than on the tube. Both she and Motte were talking and looking at the door, anticipating a delivery of fresh ice. The moment they'd been waiting for arrived as the door opened and I saw the man who'd brought it – it was Harris. Thank you God, I breathed, I've found him, now I can report to Smithson. I slipped away from the window and slushed through the thick wet earth in the flowerbed. My experience since I'd left the car had convinced me I was a city boy and I vowed that from that time on I'd keep it that way and that the next time I got close to Mother Nature would be when I was in my grave.

Time: 21.50 hours

I walked down the drive under cover of the overhanging trees and back along the road rather than face a return bout with the hedge and it took me about ten minutes to get to my car. Before driving back to Hemel Hempstead to find a phone I changed out of my wet clothes into the black tracksuit and training shoes I carried in the Ford's boot for emergencies. Even in the dim light offered by the moon I could see my suit trousers and Italian shoes were ruined beyond repair. I'd always regarded myself as a good dresser and the suit had been one of my favourites. I wondered whether my tailor had enough material to make another pair of trousers, if not, the jacket, too, was bound for the dustbin. I got into the car and drove out of the gateway, trying to solve the puzzle of what Harris was doing in the company of Motte and an illustrious celebrity like Alice Townsend. By the time I'd driven back through Hemel Hempstead and parked outside a hotel I'd spotted on the dual carriageway when I'd driven off the motorway I still hadn't solved it. I'd decided on my way past it, going into Hemel Hempstead, that if I found Harris it would be easier to phone Smithson from there rather than hunting round the town centre for a call box in working order. I locked up my car and looked at my watch – it was ten twenty. With luck, Smithson would still be at Soho Square.

I managed to get a drink in the hotel bar although the woman who was serving wasn't too happy with my appearance, and I carried my double brandy with me to the phone booth in the hotel's small lobby.

When I rang Smithson's private line at the office he answered immediately.

'It's Gorman,' I said.

'Where the hell have you been?' he asked, dispensing with the Oxbridge vowels he so carefully cultivated. 'I told you to keep in touch. It's bloody nearly twenty-four hours since you last called. What's been happening? Why haven't you called in?'

'I've been following Harris, Mister Smithson,' I said, trying to sound like an innocent schoolboy who's been brought up before his headmaster. 'I've been at it all day.'

'Who's he seen?'

I could visualise Smithson's pen poised over his jotting pad. I knew this was the tricky bit. I had no idea where Harris had gone after he'd left the house in Paddington. He'd been on foot and he'd have had to dodge police patrols and I guessed he must have made his way to Motte's gallery either sometime during the early hours of the morning or when curfew was lifted.

'I traced him to a man called Motte,' I said truthfully.

There was a long silence at Smithson's end of our conversation and I thought for a moment we'd been disconnected.

'Hello?' I said.

'I'm still here,' said Smithson's voice down the line. He hadn't reverted to his mock Oxbridge accent. 'Are they together now?'

'Yes, sir.' I was about to say where they were when Smithson's voice cut across me.

'Where?' he asked urgently.

I gave him a description of the house's location and when I had to repeat it several times I guessed he was writing it down. I kept quiet about Alice Townsend; I didn't believe a woman like her would go to bed with someone like Harris and on those grounds I decided I could reasonably leave her off his list of contacts. Anyway, you couldn't see her BMW from the road and if I hadn't trekked across the field and spied on them through the window I wouldn't have known she was there at all. I recognised the faults in my logic but Alice was political and after last night's discovery I wanted to keep well away from that particular area of social activity.

'This Motte?' Smithson enquired casually. 'What's his first name?'

'Charles,' I replied. 'He owns an art gallery in Mayfair,' I added.

There was another long silence from his end and I was on the verge of asking him for further instructions when he spoke again.

'Alright, Gorman, go home.' He'd spoken to me as if I was a disobedient dog. 'Forget about Harris. I shan't need you anymore.'

I thought about the bounty money I might lose and I knew if I didn't stay with Harris I'd have no idea who his contacts were and Smithson could tell me anything he wanted.

'Don't you want me to stay with him?' I asked Smithson anxiously. 'I mean, I've only turned up one other person.'

'Gorman!' He yelled my name down the phone at the top of his voice. 'Just do as you're bloody well told.'

'Alright, sir. Sorry,' I said, trying to placate him. 'I'll be in tomorrow. Shall I come up and see you?'

'Gorman,' I could almost feel his ice cold anger. 'I've told you once, now I shan't tell you again. For the last time, go home and stay there until you hear from me. Now fuck off.'

The line went dead.

I jumped as someone rapped sharply on the side glass of the phone booth and as I turned round the hotel's porter pulled open the door.

'Excuse me sir,' he said. 'Are you a resident?'

'No.' I smiled. 'I was just using the phone.'

'Well in that case you'll have to leave,' he said, dispensing with civility. 'We shut the doors at ten thirty.' He looked at my torn leather overcoat. 'There's plenty of pubs in town. You can go there. I'll take that, if you don't mind.' He snatched the empty brandy glass from my hand.

I looked at him properly for the first time. He was a short bald man, about fifty, and he had the air of one of life's lance corporals. In his case the armed service was the

BNDP, but unlike Smithson the celtic cross in his buttonhole was the bronze variety – the one worn by ordinary Party members.

'Have you got anywhere to go to?' His eyes were full of suspicion and the tone of his voice told me that I'd better have or he'd be on to the police as soon as I left the hotel.

'Yes,' I said quietly. The phone call had made me angry and I was on the verge of losing my temper.

He sighed deeply. 'I see,' he said. I could see he thought I was lying. 'You'd better get off home then, hadn't you?'

He took hold of my arm and walked, or rather escorted me, to the hotel's front entrance. When we reached the door I swung round to face him. 'If you lock the doors how do the residents get in?'

'They ring the bell of course. If it's before midnight I let 'em in. After that I call the police, unless they've got a curfew pass.'

Of course you would, I thought. It was silly of me to ask – in his book they were law breakers and they'd deserve their one year's prison sentence.

I walked across the hotel's carpark to my car, got in and drove down the dual carriageway towards Hemel Hempstead so I could turn back on myself at the first roundabout and head back for the motorway. At least, that was my intention, but I was seething with rage over my phone call to Smithson and the humiliating way I'd been shown the door by the hotel porter and before I realised it I was back on the Leighton Buzzard road again. I pulled off the road into a small side street which ran parallel with it and slammed on my brakes in anger as I relived my humiliation at the hands of Smithson and the bloody little BNDP shit at the hotel. After about ten minutes, when I'd calmed down, I started to talk to myself about me.

All your life you've taken the soft option, I told myself. You made a conscious decision to go into the National Health Service from university because it offered the certain prospect of security and when you got into it it took you years before you were confident enough to handle the medical consultants. Look at how you fooled yourself that you were in charge when all the time you were running around the edges, bowing and scraping and carrying out their wishes. But I learned, I argued with myself, I learned how to handle them, not at first, but after a time I was assertive and confident with them. In fact, I was good at handling people, and I was good at my job and Smithson was right when he said I'd have been a top manager if I'd stayed in the NHS.

I didn't bother to ask myself where everything had gone wrong – I already knew that. The car accident which had killed Ann and the baby which was growing inside her had killed all my ambitions too. After that I'd just drifted through my life, not caring about anything or anybody, particularly myself. I'd discharged myself from the psychiatric unit as soon as I thought I could cope. With hindsight I knew I should have taken my psychiatrist's advice but I wanted to get back to work. Once there I'd been unable to stand up to the perpetual harrassment from my boss, aimed at getting me to accept a minor administrative role, and rather than taking his offer of a grindingly monotonous job in hospital supplies I'd allowed myself to be pushed out of the NHS and into the Special Health Authority.

At first I'd fooled myself into believing the SHA offered a means of escape, instead I'd found myself trapped, and I'd been trying to escape from it ever since. But I knew I was telling myself a lie; I'd been running around, tracing AIDS carriers, who generally collapsed and wept when I arrested them, without thinking positively of a way to get out. Even my aim to buy my way out was wishful thinking; I'd made no plans, nor had I any realistic ideas about what I'd do when I left. In the early days, after I joined the SHA, it wasn't so bad – then, I'd been so wrapped up in my own anguish that I'd barely noticed that of the people I arrested, but now their faces were beginning to haunt me. More than that, I was beginning to doubt whether my job was really necessary, whether it did contain the spread of AIDS, or whether its real purpose was to help the BNDP maintain a climate of national terror.

If mother and father could see you now, I thought. What would they think? What would they think of their only son, the little lad who they worked so hard for? All those long hours my father had worked in a Sheffield steel mill in order to make sure my life would be better than his. And my mother, working in a small factory and putting her money away to pay for private lessons so that her boy could go to university and not feel less favoured than his new middle-class friends. Christ! I thought, all that for nothing. They'd been so proud when I'd got my degree, my mother had cried through my graduation ceremony, like it was my wedding. She'd cried through that too, not because she knew I was in love with another woman, but from happiness that I'd chosen a sweet girl like Ann. And look at you now, I thought. Look at you! You don't help people anymore, do you? You hurt them. Look at you, running around at Smithson's beck and call – 'Yes, Mister Smithson,' 'No Mister Smithson,' 'Just say the word, Mister Smithson, and I'll fall to my knees and lick your arse, Mister Smithson.'

I thought again about the way Smithson had dismissed me on the phone and I began to wonder whether he'd known all along about Harris's connection with Rayleigh. If he had known I'd be the perfect stooge to uncover it for the BNDP. After all, what was I? An insignificant cog in the machine who worked the streets while Smithson sat behind his desk and worked the levers. And if he had set me up to expose Harris and Rayleigh I'd be trapped between one or another group of political interests. Sitting in the car, oblivious to the cars heading home in time for curfew, I was honest with myself for the first time since Ann's death. I'd behaved like a performing seal when Smithson had offered me a special job. I might have told myself it was the prospect of the bounties that made me take the job without asking any questions, but deep down I'd taken the soft option. And I'd sat in front of his desk and let him manipulate my feelings in a way that had let him run our meeting, from start to finish. Thinking about it, I was sure he'd only raised the subject of why I'd joined the SHA as a way of getting me to remember Ann's death and how I'd been after the accident, and in playing our meeting that way he'd ensured I was too upset to ask him any difficult questions.

I dragged myself out of the swamp of self pity, turned on the car's radio and fiddled with the tuning button until I found a local radio station. There was still no news about Rayleigh on the half hourly news summary. I made up my mind; if Smithson was putting me into the frame surrounding Harris and Rayleigh I wanted to know the whys and wherefores before I went down. Motte, Harris and Alice Townsend were the strangest ménage à trois I'd ever seen and I wanted to get to the bottom of why they'd been together in that house. After that, if there was an 'after that', I'd go back to playing it safe until I'd decided what to do with the rest of my life. In a way Smithson had done me a favour, thanks to him I still had three weeks leave – plenty of time to find out why he wanted Harris. To hell with it, I thought, I've finished with soft options. And if everything falls apart I'd saved up enough money to quit London and make some sort of living. If I didn't do something now I'd stay with the SHA for safety's sake until my whole life turned to ashes. Smithson was a shit. He might be clever, but without the insidious spread of AIDS he would never have got a senior job in the civil service. Fuck him! I was as smart as he was, and I was going back to Motte's house – if it was his – and Smithson could stick his orders up his arse.

Time: 23.30 hours

I was nearly out of Hemel Hempstead when I was waved down at a temporary roadblock. Permanent traffic checks are only feasible at key points in or near large cities and on motorways or main roads; elsewhere, control of the travelling public is achieved by more transient arrangements. In this case two police cars were parked across each side of the road, leaving a space between them which was just wide enough for a single vehicle to squeeze through. A driver sat behind the wheel of each car, ready to close the gap if anyone tried to drive through without stopping. As I pulled up I noticed the steel 'hedgehog' they'd stretched across the road to cover the gap between the two police cars. On one occasion I'd been chasing a heavy who'd driven over a hedgehog at speed and its forest of steel spikes had stripped the tyres off all four of his car's wheels. It was a sign that this bunch of coppers weren't taking any chances.

A single policeman came up to my car. He pointed his Hessler and Koch submachine-gun at me through my open window and asked for my ID. I passed it over and he studied it in the light from his torch, clipped on to the front of his flak jacket.

'Expecting trouble?' I asked, nodding towards the hedgehog.

'You're a bit out of your way, aren't you,' he said, ignoring my question, as he examined my ID. 'According to this you're based in London.'

This was the first test for the born again Nick Gorman. 'You want me to let the guy get away?' I asked truculently.

'What guy?' He took his submachine-gun out of my face and bent down and looked at me.

'What does it say on that?' I nodded at my ID card in his hand.

'I'm a tracer and I'm after a heavy. He skipped out of London and I want him.'

He straightened up and looked at my ID again. 'When was this?'

'This morning,' I said. 'He must have known I was after him. I think he might be at his sister's.'

He glanced back towards the two police cars. 'Aren't you supposed to hand him over to the local lads?' he asked, turning back to look at me.

He was right. Leighton Buzzard was inside the area covered by our South Midlands Region and technically I was poaching a heavy from their Tracing Department.

'Look pal,' I said, allowing a note of anger to creep into

my voice. 'You get on with your job and let me get on with mine. OK? You're holding me up.' I leaned out of my window and snatched my ID card from his hand. 'What's the matter? You feel sorry for them? Fancy a bit of arse do you?'

The dark on the other side of his torch's beam hid his face and I couldn't see his reaction.

'Get the fuck out of here!' he snarled as he waved to a colleague behind the nearest police car.

He was blazing with rage but I could hear the note of fear in his voice. The steel hedgehog scraped against the road's surface as a policeman dragged it clear of the gap between the two cars.

'Don't worry, mate,' I said grimly. 'I won't come looking for you so long as you don't come looking for me.'

I slipped my Ford into first gear and negotiated the space between the two police cars. This time I didn't bother to wave my thanks.

I watched the traffic cop in my rearview mirror as he walked back to the police cars. We'd both appreciated the threat behind my insult and I was sure he'd keep his mouth shut about the incident – there'd be no embarrassing report to the South Midlands Tracing Department about a London tracer called Gorman straying over into their territory. The copper knew I had carte blanche to call up anybody's profile on the SHA's computer – well, almost anybody – and it only needed the slightest hint that a tracer was nosing around for a person to suffer complete social ostracism. The suicide rate of suspected heavies was depressingly high because, even when their blood test was antibody negative and they were declared to be free of the virus, their friends and neighbours preferred to stay clear in case we started to investigate their past and present sexual habits. The policeman's response to my veiled accusation about his sexual preference was typical of man in general. Paradoxically though, homosexuals were a minor category in my caseload, for, in spite of their public abomination, most of them had changed their lifestyles and taken the necessary precautions against the virus at the time of the second Thatcher government's publicity campaigns in the late 1980s. It was the young men and women who'd casually screwed each other, either ignoring the warnings or believing that AIDS couldn't possibly happen to them, who formed the vast majority of our diseased population. And I was sure if Emmerson had his way they were destined to pay the highest price of all for their past indiscretions.

IV
FRIDAY,
25 FEBRUARY 1999

Friday, 25 February 1999

Time: 00.05 hours

I was still thinking about the Home Office's paper when I pulled off the road and parked in the gateway of the field near the house where I'd spied on Motte and Alice Townsend. After opening the gate I drove my Ford into the field and parked it alongside the hedge, out of sight of the road. The moon was shining and it was freezing. I stooped and scooped up a handful of cold wet mud and smeared it over my cheeks and forehead before closing the gate behind me and setting off, down the road towards the entrance to the house's driveway; I wasn't going to repeat my recent experience of effecting an entry via the field and I knew it wasn't likely that there'd be a guard prowling around in the house's grounds. I walked down the driveway, taking care not to walk on the gravel, until I arrived at the edge of the turning area in front of the house. It was in darkness and Motte's Jaguar and the BMW, which I was sure belonged to Alice Townsend, had gone. I crouched down, under the cover of the trees, and pondered on this unexpected turn of events for some minutes; when I'd left I'd assumed that Motte and Townsend were intending to stay the night – of course it was possible they were still there and that they'd put their cars under cover at the rear of the house. I knew there was only one way to find out.

Skirting along the side of the house and retracing the route I'd taken earlier, I made my way to the garden at the rear. Still under the cover of the trees I crouched down again and studied the whole area carefully in the moonlight. I could see what looked like a walled garden beyond the long, wide lawn and on the far side of the house, across the lawn, I could make out the shapes of a greenhouse – its glass panes reflecting the moon's rays – and a large outbuilding. The moonlight ruled out the possibility of walking across the grass, but on my side the lawn was flanked by mature rhododendron bushes and my safest route to the outbuilding seemed to be to work my way through the bushes to the walled garden. That way I could keep close to the wall and get across to the far side of the garden without being seen from the house. Taking a deep breath, I left my cover under the trees and ran, at the double, towards the line of rhododendrons.

I reached the walled garden and with my back pressed firmly against its bricks I stood for a few moments, getting my breath back and straining to see if there was anyone watching from one of the windows at the rear of the house – nothing, I thought. Making my way along the wall, I kept close to stay in its shadow, and I didn't stop until I'd reached its far corner. Standing there, my leather overcoat rubbing against the wall's bricks, I estimated the large outbuilding was something like fifty metres away. From what I could see I thought it looked like it could be used as a garage because a gravel driveway ran up to it from the front of the house. To get to it I had to cross open ground, but my biggest concern at that moment was what lay around the corner of the wall. I told myself there was no point in guessing – I'd have to look.

I inched up to the corner and peered round it. The area I could see looked like a grass tennis court but beyond that there were thick bushes. If there's someone on guard out here, I thought, and if he's hiding in those fucking bushes with a gun he'll cut me to pieces before I'm halfway to that outbuilding. I forced myself to take a good, long look before I ducked back behind the corner. All my instincts told me I was alone out there. Come on, I thought, you can't stand here all night. I sprinted across the lawn to the side of the outbuilding, but it wasn't until I'd crept round to the front that I realised someone was inside.

To be precise, a person had been inside the outbuilding, but they were in the process of leaving when I appeared round the corner and caught them in the act of closing the doors. The man – I was sure it was a man – was about two metres from me and dressed in an anorak with the hood up, which probably explained why he'd been unaware of my approach. He turned towards me and dropped his torch with surprise. A karate master once told me you never lost the basic technique, although your instinctive reactions slowed down with the passage of time. But at that moment my adrenalin was pumping at full bore and I knew I had surprise as an ally. I moved forwards in the fighting stance and kicked him immediately below the knee and as he fell forwards, towards me, I hit him full in the mouth with my gloved fist, with my forearm stiff and rigid. He didn't cry out or stagger, he simply fell with a thump on the gravel and lay as still as a stone. I rolled him over on his back, pulled the anorak's hood off his head and felt for the pulse in his throat. It was regular and slow. Harris would be alright but I knew he wouldn't present any problem for some time.

I rolled him over on his side and left him lying on the gravel while I went inside the outbuilding. The faint smell of oil and petrol said I'd been right in my guess that the building was used as a garage. But it was empty and that meant that Motte and Alice Townsend had gone and it looked like Harris and I were alone. I dragged him into the garage and made sure he was lying on his side and wouldn't choke to death before I retrieved his torch. After that I shut the garage's doors and sat on a workbench while putting some order to the questions I was going to ask him when he came round.

Time: 00.50 hours

Harris was compos mentis in about fifteen minutes. While he'd been unconscious on the garage floor I'd had a look at him in the light from the torch. Apart from his new hairstyle and broken tooth the photograph in his file had been a good likeness. In spite of the scanty information Smithson had given me I'd built up a mental picture of him, and the tone of his voice when he first spoke caught me unawares. I'd expected him to have the sharp London vowels of his flatmate, but Harris was a product of the upper classes. His friend's concern about his sudden wealth didn't ring true – in my experience money was usually a precondition of an accent like his – unless his folks had fallen on hard times, but then, Smithson had said his father was an important man.

'Who are you?' He asked the question he'd asked me a few minutes earlier, when I hadn't replied.

It was an understandable question in the circumstances. I swung myself off the workbench and pulled him into a sitting position on the cold concrete floor with his back resting against the wall. He flinched as I bent down to haul him upright. I took his torch out of my overcoat pocket and shone it into his face. He blinked and turned his head away from the light. He couldn't shield his eyes with his hands; while he'd been lying on the floor unconscious I'd found a spool of nylon gardening cord on the workbench and tied his hands behind his back. And, as it had seemed a shame to waste it, I'd tied his feet together too.

I decided I'd kept him waiting long enough for my answer.

'I've been following you,' I said. 'I've been after you since last night when you left the pub where you work.'

'Oh Christ,' he said in despair. Please don't let him cry, I thought, I don't think I could handle that.

He didn't cry. He was an ex-public school boy and an experience like that prepared you for being knocked unconscious and trussed up like a chicken in a cold, dark garage in the middle of the night. I shone the torch on his face so I could watch his reactions.

'All right, Jonothan Harris,' I said. 'Is that your real name by the way?'

He nodded.

'OK then, Jonothan,' I said. 'I'm going to ask you a few

questions and you're going to give me the right answers. Don't forget, I know a lot about you, so it wouldn't be smart to upset me.' I sounded like an irritated nanny. It was a style I thought he'd respond to.

'Have you been to the flat?' he asked.

'Yes.'

'Was David there? Did you hurt him?'

I liked him for that. If the boot had been on the other foot I hoped I'd ask about someone I cared for rather than worrying about myself.

'He was all right when I left him,' I replied. 'He's probably moved out by now though.'

'Why?' he asked sharply. 'What did you threaten him with?'

The interview wasn't going the way I'd planned at all; Harris was tied up and on the floor and I was supposed to be asking the questions. Was it because my upbringing had programmed me to be polite to my social betters? I stood away from the bench, shrugged off my sense of class inferiority and prepared to break my promise about using violence in cold blood.

'Shut up!' I said, without emotion, and kicked his injured leg. He yelped with pain. 'Now. Is there anybody else in the house,' I continued smoothly.

'No,' he said, speaking through his teeth as he fought against his pain.

I bent down and held the torch close to his face. 'Where did Motte and Alice Townsend go?'

He tried to hide his surprise but he had the sort of open face which betrayed inner feelings.

'I told you, I know a lot about you,' I said, exploiting the advantage I'd just won. 'Now tell me. Where are they?'

He moistened his lips and tasted his blood. 'They went back to London.'

'Impossible!' I said. 'There's no way Motte could have got back to his gallery before curfew. Unless he has a pass. Does he?'

I wondered whether I was going to have to repeat the

performance I'd given his flatmate. I hoped not. I knew that these days I didn't have the mental attitude it takes to start hurting someone who was tied up and helpless. When I'd first joined the Department I had, and I did, but that was in the past. I stood up and walked towards the door trying to psych myself up – it was no good, I couldn't break that promise to myself and I didn't share the same attitude as my fellow citizens towards homosexuals, and no matter how hard I tried I couldn't bring myself to see a dangerous pervert lying on the floor, all I could see was a frightened, defenceless young man with a damaged leg.

'They only had to get to Stanmore Hill, it's only an hour from here,' he said quickly and I realised he'd misinterpreted my silence as the calm before my storm.

I thought about what he'd said. If they came off the motorway at junction 4 it wouldn't take long to get to Stanmore Hill, not at this time of night.

'When did they go?'

'About half past ten.'

It occurred to me that they'd driven past, going in the opposite direction, when I'd been sitting in my car at Hemel Hempstead reflecting on the way I'd fucked up my life.

'Why did they go to Stanmore Hill?'

'Alice Townsend lives there, I think,' he said. 'I don't know her address. I'd never met her before this evening.' It sounded like the truth.

He started to shiver. It was freezing in the garage and I was feeling the cold too, but he'd also had a bad shock and I decided it would be better for both of us if we continued our discussion in more civilised surroundings.

'Tell me, Harris, why did you come out to the garage?'

'A fuse blew and the lights in the house went out. I came out to see if I could find some wire to mend it.'

'Did you find any?'

'It's in my pocket.'

I went over to him, bent down and searched in the pockets of his anorak. He winced and bit his split bottom lip as my hand brushed against his right leg. I knew I'd kicked him a lot harder than I'd meant to and I hoped it wasn't broken.

'OK,' I said when I'd found the fuse wire. 'We're going over to the house. You'll feel better once you're in the warm.'

I unzipped the pocket of my leather overcoat and took out my Swiss Army penknife and pulled out one of its blades. 'I'm going to cut the cord from your ankles,' I said. 'Don't worry, I'll take it easy. I don't want to hurt you.'

After I'd removed the cord I helped him to his feet. His leg wasn't broken, but he couldn't walk on it and he hopped all the way to the house's back door with me supporting him – I didn't want him sprawling face first on the gravel drive, one way and another I'd caused him enough pain. I helped him through the back door into the kitchen and once inside I shone the torch round the room until its beam picked out a large pine table and matching chairs. I hoisted him across to one of the chairs and he sat down and let me lash him to it with the spool of nylon cord I'd brought with me from the garage. He didn't seem to have much fight in him, but I wasn't taking a risk; big, sharp knives are a standard kitchen fitment and I didn't want to come back from fixing the fuse to find him sporting a carving knife, even if he would be hopping about on one leg like Long John Silver.

I fixed the fuse, and then, with the lights on, I checked the front room where Motte and Alice Townsend had been, making sure the curtains were closed in case the house was the victim of a second visit from a peeping tom. The fire was low but its embers were still glowing so I opened up the draft, ripped some pages out of an old magazine and added some slender logs and watched until they caught and started to burn. Finally I made a quick tour of the house's other rooms, noting the dustsheets which covered the furniture, before returning to Harris in the kitchen.

He was slumped in the chair and his face was drawn and grey with pain. I sponged the blood off his mouth, made two mugs of sugary tea and took it through to the front room before going back for him. After I'd cut the bonds from his wrist and from around the ladder backed pine chair and retied his hands in front of him I helped him into the front room and sat him in the armchair where Motte had sat, and gave him his tea.

'Let it cool down before you try and drink it,' I cautioned. 'Otherwise it'll hurt that broken tooth.'

Motte's scotch decanter on the sideboard looked inviting but I decided against a drink. I'd had a long day and it looked like I was going to have an even longer night and I knew the alcohol would dull my senses. So far the new man inside me had done OK but I knew if I relaxed my guard the old one would creep back.

Time: 01.20 hours

Sitting in the armchair opposite Harris I started in on the questions. I opted for the gentle touch for starters.

'How's the leg?' I asked him.

He moved it and winced. 'It hurts like hell,' he said. 'Who are you?'

'Haven't I told you?' I asked innocently. 'I'm a tracer.'

Even as I told him I realised it was stupid to reveal my identity, apart from anything else he'd probably go to pieces once the significance of what I'd said dawned on him. As I'd predicted his face turned a shade paler.

'Have I got it?' he asked anxiously.

I smiled. 'Got what?'

'You know what I mean. Don't play games. Have I got AIDS?'

'You can't get AIDS unless you previously contracted the HIV virus,' I said soothingly, repeating a passage in the SHA's information booklet which had been distributed to every household.

'Tell me!' he shouted.

'Do you know any gays who live in south London?'

'Certainly not!' he said, as if he wouldn't be found dead

with anyone from south London.

'In that case you probably haven't,' I said. 'Anyway, I'd have thought you'd have more important things to worry about.'

He looked down at his shoes to prevent me seeing the expression on his face. 'I thought your lot didn't receive any special training,' he said.

'We don't,' I said, assuming he was referring to my karate skills, but knowing he'd only said it to divert me from the subject I most wanted to discuss. 'It's a natural talent.'

'Thank you for bringing me in here,' he said. 'I was beginning to feel quite poorly in that garage.'

I smiled to myself at what I imagined was a typical example of British upper class understatement. He'd struggled from the garage without a murmur, when, given his circumstances, he could easily have fallen apart. In another world I'd have been glad to have been his friend.

'So,' I said, slowly, 'you don't know anyone in south London?'

He looked up and shook his head. 'No. Should I?'

Yes, you bloody well should, I thought, because Smithson told me you'd been named by a confirmed heavy who'd been picked up by the south London office.

I got out of my armchair and put some larger logs on the fire. According to the determinants of our case work, if the south London office had nabbed the heavy he'd have lived in their area. I believed Harris when he said he didn't know anyone from south London and somehow he didn't strike me as a promiscuous type and with Rayleigh in the background it wouldn't have been very clever of him to have a string of lovers. That left me with another possibility – Smithson had been lying about him from the start. He might have lied to protect Harris's father, but there again, he might not. I sat back down in my armchair and saw that Harris had been studying me carefully.

'Aren't you afraid of catching it?' he asked, pointing to his face.

'Look,' I said, 'I don't think you've got the AIDS virus

and anyway I know how you catch it. Remember, I work for the SHA, we understand these things. Provided I don't go to bed with you or shoot up drugs with the same syringes I'm not likely to catch it by just wiping the blood off your face.'

The fire was well alight and I pushed myself out of the armchair again and fed it with the biggest logs from a deep wicker basket which was on my side of the hearth. Standing in front of the fire and watching the flames licking around the base of the logs I couldn't picture myself working him over if he wouldn't talk. You'd never have made it with the Spanish Inquisition, I thought. That thought triggered another and I picked up the short poker from the hearth and looked at Harris, before plunging it deep into the heart of the fire. I guessed he'd caught the drift of my thoughts when I saw him shudder.

'Does the SHA teach you to torture people?' he asked quietly. 'Or is it just another natural talent of yours.'

'Understand me, Harris,' I said. 'I'll do whatever's necessary to find out what I want to know.'

I'd sounded like I meant it although I knew it was a bluff. Never mind, I thought, there's plenty of tracers who would and Harris is bound to have heard about some of the grislier parts of my business.

'There'll be questions,' he protested.

I grinned at him. 'Do you think anybody gives a damn about a gay with a few scorch marks. If it comes to it I'll say I stopped some people who were trying to burn you to death when I caught up with you.'

I let him think about it while I settled back in the armchair and when I looked at him again it wasn't difficult to see he was afraid.

'OK. Let's start at the beginning,' I said. 'How long have you known Rayleigh?'

He looked at me and at the poker which was beginning to glow in the fire before he spoke. 'All my life really,' he said. 'He was a friend of my father's.'

'Was?' I tried to ask my question matter of factly.

'My father was killed in a flying accident about three

years ago. They were in business together, in the City, before Rayleigh went into politics.'

'I see,' I said.

'No you don't!' he snapped and the sound of anguish in his voice reminded me of the way I'd felt in Smithson's office when he'd been questioning me about Ann.

'Tell me then,' I offered.

'I hadn't seen Tony for a couple of years until we met again at a party about two months ago. It was at my mother's, it was her fiftieth birthday ... I don't see much of her these days, but I felt I ought to go.'

'Go on,' I prompted.

'Tony was there and he asked me what I was doing. I tried to lie but he'd known me since I was a boy and when I admitted I was working in bars he was very upset.'

'Why are you doing that sort of work?' It had interested me from the time I'd heard him speak. 'I'd have thought your father must have been well off.'

'He didn't approve of me.' He paused. 'I wasn't the son he wanted.' He looked at the fire.

'You mean he knew you were gay?'

'We had an understanding,' he said, ignoring my direct question. 'He paid me an allowance and I kept out of his way and avoided any embarrassment ... After he was killed I found he'd left his money so I couldn't get at it.'

I thought of my own father, a hard unforgiving man who found it difficult to express his feelings, but despite that I'd always known that he loved me. How could a father simply reject his son and refuse to have anything to do with him? You're wasting time, I thought, never mind Harris's unhappy childhood, get on to the subject of him and Rayleigh.

'So? Rayleigh was upset, and then what?'

'He asked me to go and see him. He said he wanted to help me.'

'Did he know you were gay?'

'It never occurred to me at the time,' he said. 'But I suppose he must have. Anyway it all came out when I went to see him.'

I was virtually on the edge of my seat. 'How?'

'I went to see him in his London flat about six weeks ago. He used it when Parliament was sitting.'

'Not the place in Paddington then?' I interjected.

He shook his head. 'I got dressed up in my best suit,' he continued. 'I wanted to make a good impression, you see. It was a good job I did otherwise I wouldn't have got past the policeman outside his front door ... Tony was charming, he gave me a drink and we sat down and talked. It was the first decent conversation I'd had for a long time. David's OK, but ... well ... we come from different backgrounds.'

That's putting it mildly, I thought, as I struggled to think what he and his flatmate could have in common outside their sexual orientation.

'How long have you and David been together?'

He thought for a moment. 'About three months.'

'So? You were with Rayleigh at his flat. What happened then?'

He started to speak and then changed his mind. I looked at him and then I stood up and moved the poker to a hotter part of the fire. His eyes narrowed as he watched my every movement.

'After we'd been talking for about half an hour Tony suddenly looked me straight in the face and said "I know Johnny." I just sat there, staring at him.' Harris slowly shook his head from side to side as he recalled the scene. 'I ... I couldn't think of a bloody thing to say.'

I could understand he'd be lost for words when a Minister of the Crown, no less, was accusing him of being a homosexual.

Harris smiled to himself. 'It was then the penny dropped. I'll never know why I hadn't recognised it before, I suppose it was because he'd been a friend of my father's. And he was married with children. I mean, it never ever occurred to me. Christ knows how he'd kept it from everyone.'

'Did you ...' I searched and failed to find an appropriate word, 'do it in his flat?'

'Don't be a bloody fool.' He laughed. 'Tony said he'd always cared about me and he was terribly sorry to see what had happened ... My father was an absolute pig,' he said venomously. 'Not just to me, he made my mother's life a misery as well. I can't remember a single time when he showed me any affection, not even when I was a child. But Tony was always kind ... he used to remember my birthdays and bring me presents at Christmas.' Harris looked into the fire and I guessed he was seeing moments from his childhood in his mind's eye. 'Tony might have been getting on but ...' He fell silent.

Unfortunately I didn't have time to indulge him in silent reminiscences. 'When did you start seeing him? Don't forget, Harris, I know about the house in Paddington,' I said.

Harris sighed. 'I can't remember when exactly. We tried to meet as often as possible. It wasn't easy. Tony had a lot of commitments and he was always busy, he couldn't slip away to see me very often; if anything happened and he was missing ...' He didn't bother to state the obvious. 'I suppose we only met about half a dozen times.'

'Always in the house in Paddington?'

Harris nodded. 'He gave me the money and I rented it using a different name.'

'Did he pay you, apart from the rent, that is?'

He looked at me with loathing. 'People like you never understand. It wasn't like that. I ...' He stopped and choked back his tears. I'd learned enough about grief at first hand to recognise it when I saw it – Harris had cared for Rayleigh. 'He gave me money because he cared about me and he wanted to help me,' he said. 'My mother couldn't, because she only received a small allowance from my father's estate.'

I took his empty mug of tea and put it on the mantelpiece. 'What happened last night?'

'I arrived just before midnight,' he said. He was looking into the fire again.

'You can skip the details,' I said coldly. 'How did he die?'

'You know that?' He was shocked. '... Tony was finishing his papers and I was reading when he suddenly clutched his chest. He was in terrible pain. He died before I could do anything.' He was on the verge of crying but I cut into his grief.

'What was Rayleigh reading?'

Harris was re-living the events of the previous night and he didn't hear me. I asked my question again.

'I don't know,' he sniffed. 'They were secret. He never talked about his work at all usually, but ...'

'But? But he did last night?' I asked.

Harris swallowed. 'Yes. He started to talk about Emmerson – you know – the leader of the BNDP ... Tony was very angry. I'd never seen him like that, he kept talking about a conspiracy.'

'What did he say, precisely?'

'I can't really remember. I'm not interested in business or politics or things like that. All I know is that it had something to do with Nazis – whoever they are.' He shrugged his shoulders. 'Something like that.'

'Do you know anything about history?'

'Fraid not,' he said dismissively. 'I was a duffer at school. I suppose that was another reason why my father was the way he was.'

I couldn't believe it; here was someone who'd probably had the best education that money could buy and he had no knowledge of the second worst catastrophe of the twentieth century.

'You must have been good at something,' I said.

'I liked tennis.'

I wondered whether to revise my earlier assessment of him. I'd assumed the stoicism he'd shown since I'd disabled him outside the garage sprang from a sense of effortless superiority the upper classes breed into their children – a gift usually denied to someone of my humble origins. But in his case its source seemed to be inherent dullness. I'd been wrong earlier when I'd thought we could have been friends in another world; in another world he'd be helping himself to money in the City while I'd have been an overworked and underpaid functionary.

'Tell me, Harris, what did you do after Rayleigh died?'

'I rather lost my nerve, I'm afraid. I just picked up my coat and left. I didn't want to leave him there like that. But what else could I do?'

'Where did you go after you left the house?'

'I hid in Hyde Park and waited for the end of curfew. After that I walked round for hours and hours until I eventually decided to go to Charles's place.'

I stopped leaning against the mantelpiece and sat in my armchair and rubbed my shoulders against its cool leather. I was tired, but knew I had to keep going until I'd squeezed everything out of him.

'Why did you go to Motte? Is he gay?'

Harris rubbed his eyes with the back of his hand. He was tired too.

'No. I was his fag at school. The others were horrible to me, but he was nice. He owed me a favour and there was nowhere else I could go. Most of my friends are gay and I knew they wouldn't be able to help, but Charles knows lots of important people.'

I supposed Alice Townsend came into the category of 'important people'. But I didn't believe him.

'How did you get out here, Harris?' I said, deciding to let him think he'd convinced me about why he'd gone to Motte.

'Charles drove me out this afternoon.'

'What time did he leave?'

'About three, or three thirty.'

I gave his answer some thought. Motte had turned up at his gallery around five – the times seemed to coincide.

'Did you tell Motte about Rayleigh?'

'No.' He shook his head. 'Not at first. Charles knew I was gay of course, but I thought it best not to, but then … well … I just had to tell someone.'

'How did he react?'

'He was angry at first, angry I'd come to him, I mean. Then he went quiet and he said he'd help me.'

His answer confirmed my suspicion as far as I was

concerned – he was lying. The public school code wouldn't extend to harbouring a gay who was in tow with a dead Secretary of State. Motte had another reason and Alice Townsend was part of it. And if Harris wasn't lying and he really did believe that Motte would risk his life to help him because he'd been his school fag he was the stupidest man I'd ever met. No, I thought, Motte extended the hand of friendship because of what Harris had told him.

'Did Motte say how he was going to help you?'

'He was going to get me a new ID card, you know, things like that,' he said. 'I told you, Charles has lots of important friends.'

'He must have,' I agreed. 'Why did he come back with Alice Townsend? Was talking to her the price of Motte's help?'

He nodded, but I still didn't believe him, or at least, if he believed it, I didn't.

I had a good idea of the answer but I asked my question anyway.

'Anything specific she wanted to know?'

'She was very interested in the papers Tony had been reading. I had to go over everything he said before he died.'

Surprise, surprise, I thought, as he gave me the answer I was expecting.

'And what did you tell her?'

'The same as I've told you,' he said dully. 'Look, I wasn't paying attention to what Tony was saying, not really. I just wanted him to finish reading his bloody papers so we could talk and be together. I already told you, we didn't see one another very often.'

'What else did she want to know? The address in Paddington?'

He nodded. 'Yes.'

'Did you tell her?'

'No,' he said firmly. 'No way.'

'Why not, Jonothan?' I said sarcastically. 'After all you'd told her everything else she wanted to know. Why stop at that?'

He sighed. 'You still don't understand, do you?' he said

wearily. 'I knew I had to tell her if I wanted Motte to help me. But I wasn't going to let her destroy Tony. She just saw it as a story for her fucking television show.' He looked at me defiantly. 'She didn't fool me. I'm not stupid whatever you might think. I could see right through her and all her shit about wanting to help. Bloody cow! She just wanted to know for herself, so it would make her look big.'

Had she? I thought. The snippets of her shows that I'd seen definitely suggested she wasn't on the side of the BNDP. And even if her bosses let her serve up the story of Rayleigh on prime time TV, would she do it just to further her career, even though she'd know it would help the BNDP sink the Conservatives?

'And you didn't tell either her or Motte the address in Paddington?'

'No,' he said emphatically. 'And I wouldn't have told you either.' He looked at the poker. 'Whatever you'd done to me I wouldn't have betrayed Tony.'

The tone of his voice persuaded me that he meant it. But part of my mind was struggling with the significance of what he'd said; if he hadn't told Townsend or Motte where Rayleigh was, he and I were the only two people who did know. I was sure Motte and Alice wouldn't simply give up and walk away without getting a secret like that out of him.

'Why did they both go off and leave you here? Wouldn't it have been better if they'd taken you with them?'

'Charles thought it was safer. After all, nobody but he and Alice knew where I was.' He paused. 'You haven't told anybody, have you?' he asked anxiously.

'No,' I lied. 'Wasn't Motte worried you'd run away? If you were caught you might talk and then he'd be in trouble.'

'Where would I run to? I'm trapped wherever I go until he can organise a new ID for me. It's better I stay here. Nobody knows where I am, the phone's been disconnected. I'm safe here,' he half smiled. 'Or at least I was until you turned up.' He slumped back into his armchair and closed his eyes.

I don't like this, I thought, I don't like this one bit. I tried to, but I couldn't understand why Motte had taken the chance of helping him. And I wasn't sure whether, if I'd been Motte, I'd have left him, on his own and miles from anywhere, although I could see it could be safer than taking him back to Alice Townsend's place in Stanmore.

'Harris, why did ...?' I stopped speaking; despite the pain in his leg he'd gone to sleep.

Time: 01.55 hours

I sat forward in my armchair, looking at the dying fire and wishing I was safe in my flat. I was fairly certain Harris had told me most of the story, or most of the story as he saw it, but I was still no nearer to finding out why Smithson had sent me to find him. My boss was hardcore BNDP; he wouldn't have set me to catch Harris if he'd already known about the Rayleigh connection. He'd have gone straight to Emmerson, wouldn't he? And Emmerson would have handled the whole business and Smithson would have collected his reward. Or had Smithson decided to do all the legwork and hand the whole thing over to Emmerson on a plate? But then why send me to look for Harris? Why not someone from the BNDP? Someone Smithson would know he could trust. Even worse, I thought, had Emmerson and Smithson known all the time and decided to use me so they could keep out of it until I'd discovered Harris and Rayleigh together? The more I thought about it, the more confused I became, because unfortunately, the way Smithson had briefed me about the special job fitted all three scenarios. I threw the last three logs on the fire and went over to the sideboard, poured myself a scotch and tossed it down my throat in one gulp. Admit it, I thought, you haven't got a fucking clue what's going on.

My watch said it was nearly two o'clock. I went into the kitchen and held my head under the tap until the ice cold water revived my flagging senses, and on my way back to the front room I turned off the lights. Harris was still dozing in his armchair and he'd got some of his colour back. I stood, looking at him; there were two missing links and he had the answers, or some of them. I knew I was fishing in dangerous waters and I had to find out how deep it was and if there is such a thing as a sixth sense it was telling me to get a bloody move on. Could I lay the poker across his face if he wouldn't tell me what I wanted to know? Still, I told myself as I seized both his shoulders and shook him awake, you only need to convince him you will do it.

'OK, Harris,' I said, pulling the poker out of the fire and threatening him with it.

He jerked away, hitting his head against the high back of the armchair.

'Look at me,' I yelled.

His eyes were wide with fear and I could see I'd convinced him I'd use the poker on him if it came to it.

I held his eyes with mine. 'Now,' I said through clenched teeth. 'Let's go over a few details. And this time I want the truth.'

I moved the poker as close to his face as I dared. He screamed and I moved it away quickly. His scream had unnerved me and I was almost as frightened as he was. At that moment I didn't like the new, born again Nick Gorman.

'Come on,' I said grimly. 'Tell me about Motte. The truth, not that crap about you and him being at the same school together.'

He swivelled his eyes towards the poker. 'I used to help him.' His words came out in a rush. 'I used to give him bits of information when I was …' He hesitated.

'Come on! Come on! Spit it out!' I shouted, moving the poker towards his face again. 'When you were what?'

'You have to understand. I was absolutely broke, I didn't have a penny. I'd never have done it otherwise. I …' He hesitated.

'Done what!' I shook him by his shoulder and moved the poker towards him until it was almost touching his cheek.

'I was a prostitute,' he cried, sobbing in terror.

I took the poker away from his face. 'And you passed

101

information about your clients to Motte? Is that right?' I shook him again. 'Who were they?'

'I don't know. I used to describe them to him. They must have been important. Mostly they didn't say anything but some of my regulars did.'

'Who did Motte tell? Come on! Who did he pass your information to?'

'I don't know.' The poker brushed lightly on his face. 'I don't know. Please,' he screeched, 'if I did I'd tell you, but I don't. Please, please believe me.'

I turned away from him and put the cooling end of the poker back into the fire's red embers – I wanted him to believe I was sadistic enough to apply it to his face again when it was good and hot. I thought about the old promise I'd made to myself to cut out the violence. I'd breached it when I'd questioned Harris's flatmate and now I'd broken it entirely. I felt sick. Should I just clear out and leave the poor little devil in peace, I thought. But I knew it was too late for that. If I'd wanted to get out I should have followed Smithson's instructions and gone home to bed like a good little boy.

'I told you before, Harris,' I said, standing over him, 'I'll do whatever's necessary to find out what I want to know. Well? The choice is yours, we can wait until the poker hots up, or you can talk now. Which is it?'

He dropped his head on his chest in submission. I bent down and put my hand under his chin and lifted his head so I could look into his eyes. His cheek was blistered but as far as I could tell I hadn't inflicted any permanent injury on him, and inwardly I breathed a sigh of relief.

'OK,' I said. 'So you don't know who Motte passed your information to. So, let's talk about something you do know. How long have you been on the game?'

He averted his eyes. 'I'm not doing it anymore.'

'Why not? Because you'd met Rayleigh?'

'No. I'd stopped before then. It was before I started to live with David.'

'Why did you stop?'

He tried to move his head away but I held his chin firmly.

'Look,' I said, 'we can do it with the poker if you prefer.'

'I ran into someone in Knightsbridge. He was getting out of a car. His wife was with him. At least, I think it was his wife.'

'Who was he?'

'I don't know. Honestly, I don't, except I think he was in the BNDP, but we recognised each other straight off and I guessed it would mean trouble, so I chucked it and moved away from my old flat in case they sent someone after me.'

That's it! I thought, and suddenly, all my questions about why I'd been given the special job, were answered and everything fell into place.

'When you were on the game did you ever have a client with sandy hair and pale green eyes? Short, but he'd have had a strong and powerful body. Looked a bit like a dwarf, with big hands and lots of gold rings on them?'

He thought about my description of Smithson for less than a second. 'No,' he said.

'Are you sure?' I almost shouted.

'I'd hardly forget someone who looked like that.'

'OK. Ever heard of the name "Smithson"?' I was so anxious he'd prove my theory I was pressing his head back against the armchair.

'No,' he answered immediately. 'I don't know anyone with that name.'

I relaxed my grip on his chin while I thought about what he'd told me. If Smithson hadn't been one of his clients, had he sent me after Harris on the instructions of the man he'd met in Knightsbridge? If the man was BNDP there might be a connection there.

'You said "they" before, "they would come after you". Who's "they"? Did you have a minder?'

'I never saw anyone,' he said. 'Someone used to phone me and give me the name and address of a hotel.'

'So how did you get into it in the first place? The days of gay pubs are over.'

'A man phoned, late one night and said he knew I was

gay and if I didn't want any trouble I'd do what he told me.'

His answer wouldn't have been plausible a couple of years ago but I was prepared to believe that what he'd said was true – terror reigned everywhere.

'And you never saw this ...?'

It wasn't a loud noise, but I heard it. When I'd been spying on Motte and Alice Townsend they'd had Bach playing in the background. Now, apart from Harris's rapid breathing, the house was as silent as a tomb. I heard it again; someone was walking across the gravel. I moved quickly to the door to turn off the room's centre light and my hand was almost touching the switch when there was a crash of breaking glass as something punched through the window and its flimsy curtains and hit the wall a few inches away from my head. I stood by the door, paralysed by the sight of a tear gas cannister, spinning away from me across the floor and spewing out its evil looking white vapour.

It was the sound of them smashing out the rest of the glass in the window a micro-second later which snapped me back to my senses. I yanked open the door as the first bullets, fired from a softly drumming silenced submachine-gun, came through the window. As I ran along the hall to the kitchen Harris screamed, a scream which at first was sharp and clear but which finished in a gurgle as the blood in his lungs rushed up his windpipe and choked him.

He was dead, I knew that, and my one thought was to get out of the house and across the garden to safety. As I entered the dark kitchen I saw his shape, in the moonlight, through the back door's opaque glass panels and I realised they must have planned a simultaneous attack from the front and rear of the house, and the man outside had been slow off the mark. My old karate master had been wrong, when you're fighting for your life your instinctive reactions return. I knew two things. He would be wearing a gas mask and he'd be coming from out of the bright moonlight into the dark kitchen – both would seriously restrict his vision.

He kicked open the door and rushed inside and I threw myself bodily at his ankles, causing him to fall over the top of me. He crashed full length on the kitchen floor on top of the silenced submachine-gun he was carrying. It stuttered softly and he gave a hoarse cry as the bullets meant for me ripped into his body – I guessed that there'd be two bodies to cart away. Rejecting the idea of losing precious seconds by hauling his body off the gun, I grabbed hold of each side of the door frame, checked my forward momentum, looked outside the door, left and right, and launched myself through it like a sprinter springing away from his blocks. I raced across the lawn, into the rhododendrons, tore my way through the gap in the hedge and flung myself into the field beyond it. They might have found the car, a voice inside me said – I'd have to manage without it. Not daring to expose myself to the moonlight outside the shadow of the hedge, I ran along the field's perimeter until I came to a fence on the far side. I climbed over it and set out across country.

After a mile of running and falling and getting to my feet and running again I came across a disused barn in the corner of a field. I stopped and listened for the sounds of pursuit and when I was sure they weren't coming after me I went inside and huddled in a corner. I guessed that as soon as it was light they'd make a sweep of the country round the house and I thought I could safely rest inside the barn until I'd sorted myself out. I checked the time – it wouldn't be light for at least three hours. That meant I could stay there for half an hour while I decided what to do. From now on Smithson would be after me and I had to discover what he was up to – it might give me something to bargain with – and I couldn't see I had any other options. I'd no doubt that he'd organised the attack on the house; while we occasionally used violence to obtain information from confirmed heavies, tracers didn't get into the really rough stuff, we left that to the police. The face of the man who'd come in through the kitchen door might have been hidden by his gas mask but I'd have recognised him anywhere and I had to discover why Chris Brand, the tracer who'd shared my office and whose sardonic humour had made me smile, was back at the house, lying on the kitchen floor, with his guts torn out.

While I sat in the barn getting my breath back I tried to create some sort of order out of the chaos which had ensued after the tear gas cannister had crashed through the window. I knew it wouldn't take Smithson's people long to put two and two together and decide I'd been in the house with Harris and that I'd escaped. Apart from the fact Harris had been tied up they'd find my leather overcoat; my wallet was in the hip pocket of my tracksuit trousers but there were some papers in my coat's inside pocket. And there was Chris Brand's dead body. And if they were still uncertain my abandoned Ford would leave them in no doubt who'd been at the house when they'd called. It explained why Smithson had been so insistent that I go home when I'd phoned home from the hotel; that way he'd know where to send his people to kill me. OK, I told myself, your decision to be your own man for a change saved your neck, now all you have to do is to try and keep it in one piece.

I thought the odds were against any police involvement because the subtlety of using silenced submachine-guns wouldn't have occurred to them, but if Smithson was working directly for Emmerson they might be drawn into the hunt. As Home Secretary, Emmerson was supremo of the new national police force and it would only take one phone call to mobilise the entire network, and once that happened my chances of survival were pretty thin.

On the other hand, since I'd been with the Department I'd learned a good deal about hiding and with Smithson after me I'd have to put those lessons into practice. Getting back to London would be dangerous, but I had to try. It was still the best place to hide and once there I could contact Motte; if I could discover where he fitted into the picture I might be nearer to finding out what I was doing in it, and more importantly, how I could get out of it.

Leaving the barn, I took a route across the frozen fields which would lead me south and west of Hemel Hempstead and towards Watford. I could catch the Underground into central London from there.

I reached the outskirts of Watford at seven forty-five and made my way to its Underground station.

Time: 08.15

Standing at a bus stop and pretending to read a newspaper I watched the people going into Watford's Underground station. As far as I could tell there was no sign of the police and everything looked normal. I waited at the bus stop for a further ten minutes before walking along the street and stopping opposite the entrance to the station, even then I hesitated before crossing the road. According to my theory Smithson had masterminded the previous night's happening – but what if I was wrong and the police were involved? There was only one way to find out. I crossed the road, joined the throng of people in the station and bought a ticket and went down to the platform in the jostle of commuters. When the next train left for London I was on it.

I sat in the carriage counting off the stations and looking at my fellow passengers. A year ago most of them would have been wearing surgical masks in the panic which had followed newspaper reports that the AIDS virus had transmuted itself into an airborne agent. The news came out immediately before the General Election and the BNDP had seized on the reports and used them to attack the Conservative's overall handling of the crisis. The economy had taken a terrific pounding; I'd been receiving treatment in hospital at the time, and I missed all the social upheaval, such as the waves of absenteeism from work when people had stayed in the safety of their homes. At the height of the hysteria it hadn't even been safe to appear in public with a common cold. Learned men had appeared on TV to pour scorn on the sensationalised reports but the BNDP had produced its own experts, who argued that as the virus was unique it might not be bound by the known laws of virology. The BNDP had kept the issue on the boil until the last couple of weeks before polling day, but afterwards, when they'd taken a share in government, they'd accepted the arguments of the scientific community. Nevertheless it wasn't until after Emmerson had armed the police and relaxed the rules for their use of firearms that the lawlessness had abated.

Although none of my fellow passengers appeared to show the slightest interest in me I got off and crossed over to the Jubilee Line at Wembley Park to make sure I wasn't being followed. While I was waiting for a train to continue my journey into London a gang of skinheads wearing BNDP sweatshirts came on to the platform and began distributing copies of their party's daily newspaper. I watched as they stopped and exchanged a few words of greeting with people who were wearing BNDP badges and like the rest of those standing around me I took one of their papers when it was thrust into my hand. A man further down the platform refused, but quickly changed his mind when they threatened to throw him on to the rails. Over the last six months I'd noticed that more and more people were wearing BNDP badges. I wasn't sure whether they were joining the Party to protect themselves against its roaming bands of young supporters or whether they believed in its policies, although I hoped their new found conviction stopped before the ballot box.

The paper's front page had a picture of Emmerson and a piece claiming success for the health measures which he'd forced on the Conservatives. I knew enough about AIDS to recognise the distortions of fact in the article. When I'd been a manager in the NHS it was impossible not to hear whispers of growing alarm as both the reported numbers of HIV carriers and the probability of them progressing to full blown AIDS kept increasing. Perhaps, if steps had been taken at that time to require doctors to notify local health offices of anybody who'd caught the virus things might have turned out differently. But unfortunately, the policy of protecting the confidentiality of individual victims meant that we had no clear idea about how far it was spreading out into the general population, until, shortly after Ann's death, one of the gutter tabloids had examined the official and not so official statistics and printed the probable numbers of people with the virus. After it had revealed the true scale of our problem everyone got in on the act as newspapers published everything about AIDS they could get their hands on, including a secret government report, leaked by a civil servant in the Department of Health, on the dangerous side effects and dubious success rate of the new all-purpose vaccine. A vaccine which, according to Rayleigh's predecessor as Minister of Health, was not only completely safe but would also eradicate the disease in its entirety. After his lie had been found out nobody believed the Conservative's confident, don't-worry-folks-everything-will-be-all-right-on-the-night misinformation statements, and all their attempts to placate the electorate were overshadowed by rabble rousing editorials and Emmerson's speeches about the cause of the disease.

I flicked through the pages of the BNDP's newspaper. The message it preached was always the same; AIDS had been the result of a lack of decent, Christian and national moral values, and those responsible – gays, black, socialists and anyone who opposed the BNDP's views – should be made to pay for it. I threw the paper away in disgust as the train arrived and the platform's loudspeaker switched on automatically to play its loop tape, warning passengers whose surname began with the first three letters of the alphabet that this was the last day designated for their three monthly blood test.

I got off at Baker Street, handed in my ticket and hung round in the vicinity of the barrier, examining the faces of people coming up from the platform. There was no one I recognised from the office and although I knew Smithson wouldn't necessarily have chosen people from among my work mates, it seemed a safe bet. When I was sure I wasn't being followed I went to the machines and bought a ticket before going down to the Circle Line's westbound platform where I caught the second train. At Notting Hill

Gate I jumped off the train and ran to the eastbound platform. I got into the first train and stood by the open doors, and as they closed I leapt out. I was the only person left on the platform as it pulled away to Bayswater. I caught the next train and changed at Edgware Road to the Metropolitan Line for Shepherds Bush.

I knew I needed help. I'd thought about making contact with Victoria but I'd decided I couldn't chance it. Now that I'd discovered Chris Brand had been working for Smithson on some sort of secret basis I couldn't be sure that Victoria wasn't involved as well, and although Chris and I had never exchanged intimate details about our lives I thought I knew more about him than I'd ever found out about her. Coming in from Watford I'd decided that Rob Foster was the only person I could trust, and the rules of friendship demanded that I made sure I didn't arrive there with Smithson's band of murderers on my tail.

Time: 10.30 hours

I came out of Shepherds Bush Underground station into bright sunlight and walked quickly to Rob's garage. When we'd left university we'd gone our separate ways and we hadn't met each other again, until, six months previously, we'd literally bumped into each other one Saturday morning outside the Haymarket Theatre. Rob had had an armful of packages and after we'd retrieved them from the pavement we'd simultaneously recognised each other. Initially it had been a meeting between strangers but after half an hour we were talking as if we'd been in regular contact over the intervening years. I'd studied history and anthropology at university and Rob had been doing a degree in engineering and we'd met through our mutual interest in karate. While I'd gone on to work in the NHS, Rob had sacrificed a good degree for a black belt, but the combination of a small legacy, good business sense and an intuitive feel for machinery had been enough for her to establish a niche in the motor trade.

I walked into the garage and spoke to the feet pointing

out from under a car who told me to go to the office. As I pushed open the door of Rob's small sanctum, smelling of oil and crammed with paper and car maintenance manuals, she got up from her chair and kissed me. It was a platonic kiss. There'd been a time when I thought things might develop between us but that was before I'd met Ann and seen the way Rob acted when she was in the company of her brother, Martin. After I'd seen the closeness of their sibling relationship I'd backed off, confused and suspicious about whether a brother and sister should touch each other in the way they did.

'How are you, lover?' she said, motioning me towards a chair by the side of her desk.

I sat down and looked at her. Rob was tall, over five feet nine, and slim, with a walk that reminded me of a cat. I wouldn't have described her as pretty, her pale face was slightly too squared for that, but her large mouth and straight nose set between wide apart almond-shaped large green eyes were striking, and I'd noticed the way men eyed her when we walked down the street together. Few women look good in flying suits, but the black one she was wearing suited her.

'You tell me,' I said, as I sank back into the hard wooden chair. I felt exhausted.

She stared at my bedraggled appearance, looking at me properly for the first time since I'd walked through her office door.

'You look awful,' she said. 'What's happened to you?'

I didn't reply immediately. A feeling of safety was creeping over me and reducing the high energy level which is common in animals when they're hunted. Rob knelt down in front of me and held my hands in hers while her green eyes studied me. She'd had her Titian-coloured hair cut in a pageboy style since the weekend and it suited her. She squeezed my hands gently and I felt the strength in her wrists and the hardness of her fingertips – she was in really good shape, certainly better than me.

'Come on, Nick,' she said, 'tell me what's happened to you?'

I didn't know what to tell her. Our chance meeting outside the Haymarket had marked the start of my re-emergence into the world and since then we'd seen a lot of each other. Rob had reached third Dan and she was the master at a karate club in Shepherds Bush. She'd got me to take up the sport again and I'd worked hard at it and on the previous Saturday I'd represented the club in a match with a team from west London. I knew I'd never become a master but I was getting back to the level of skill I'd reached at university before I'd decided to settle for my brown belt and concentrate on my degree. The trouble was that since we'd met up again I hadn't told her about my job as a tracer. I always meant to but somehow the time had never been right and it had been easier to let her think I was still working in the NHS and, if I'm being honest, she was my only real friend and I wasn't sure how she'd react to the news that her chum was a modern day bounty hunter.

'You may not like it,' I said.

She looked at me quizically. 'Will you stop pissing about and tell me what's happened to you.' She'd always been direct, even at university.

'I'm on the run,' I said.

She let go of my hands and shrank back against the desk. It was a natural reaction.

'Don't worry,' I said. 'It's not that. I'm not a carrier ... I ... I'm on the other side.'

She didn't move. 'What other side?'

'I work for the Special Health Authority.' There's no going back now, I thought. 'I'm a tracer.'

She moved away from her desk and went over to her office door and shut it. As she walked behind my chair it occurred to me that she could easily overpower me if she chose. After all, she was a master, and from past conversations I gathered she'd mixed with some pretty rough company when she was getting her business off the ground. She left the door and came back to her chair and sat opposite me – I noticed she'd judged the distance between us to a millimetre and in my present state I knew she'd hit me to pieces before I could muster any sort of defence. 'So tell me,' she said without emotion.

I gave her the bare outline of my life since my interview with Smithson on the previous Friday afternoon when he'd given me the special job. I omitted any mention of Rayleigh or Motte and Alice Townsend. I'd decided it wasn't in Rob's interest to know the whole story because it might put her in danger. She was tough and she'd be able to handle Smithson's thugs, but Special Branch and MI5 played in the top league and if she didn't know anything she couldn't give herself away under questioning. I finished my tale and we sat in silence, looking at one another. Will she believe me, I thought? Even to me my story had seemed scarcely credible. She stood up and without saying a word she went over to a small table in the corner of the room, on the opposite side to the door, picked up the glass jug of a Cona coffee maker, poured coffee from it into a mug and passed it to me.

'You're a shit,' she said, as she sat down in her chair. 'A complete shit. Do you know that?'

I took a sip of coffee and tried to avoid her green eyes.

'We've been seeing one another for … what is it? … six months? And you never said a word. Not a bloody word. Tell me? Why in God's name should I help you?'

'I've nowhere else to go,' I said. It seemed a poor excuse for involving her in my problem. 'I can't go back to my flat, that's the first place they'll stake out.'

'You lied to me, Nick!' she said, hitting the arm of her soft, executive-style swivel chair. 'I thought you worked for the National Health Service.'

I took another sip of hot coffee. 'Well,' I said. 'I do. In a way.'

'No you bloody don't! You hunt people for money. Jesus Christ! I think we should lock them all up, but your lot are worse than the bloody filth.'

Her vehemence shocked me. I suppose I'd still pictured her as the easygoing girl I'd known at university and I should have realised that, in her business, visits from unfriendly coppers were an occupational hazard. I could see her point of view, you knew where you stood with the police; money or information could easily be exchanged for a blind eye. By comparison, although tracers purveyed a sense of security they might suddenly turn up and point an accusing finger at you and our bounty tended to offset the possibility of a bribe.

'I'm sorry, Rob,' I said quietly.

'So you bloody well should be,' she replied. 'I think what hurts most is you couldn't give me credit in the first place. Why didn't you tell me?'

'I couldn't ... I tried to, but I knew you'd ...' It had been a mistake coming to Rob for help, I realised that now. I stood up and walked over to the coffee maker and put my mug down beside it. 'I'm sorry Rob, I shouldn't have involved you in this.'

'Sit down, you pathetic slob,' she said as she stood up and steered me back towards my chair. She pushed me down on to it. 'I didn't say I wouldn't help. It's just the shock, that's all ... Now, are you sure you weren't followed here?'

'No,' I said, shaking my head. 'There's nobody behind me.'

'Are you sure?'

'Positive.'

'Who is after you, Nick,' she said, sitting down in her chair.

I sighed. 'My boss, I think.'

'That's bloody marvellous,' she said sarcastically. 'Don't you bloody know?'

'Not for sure.'

'Why is he after you?'

I debated with myself about how much of the detail to tell her.

'I'm not sure,' I said. 'He gave me a special job. I had to find a young gay.'

'Don't you know why he gave you the job?'

'If I could work that out I'd know what Smithson was up to and I wouldn't be here, bothering you. I'd be trying to bargain my way out.'

114

'You must have some idea?'

'It's either something to do with the BNDP – Smithson's on their National Executive. He could have chosen me to expose someone important.'

'Who?'

'Look Rob,' I said, leaning over and putting my hand on hers. 'It's better you don't know, honestly. For your own sake it will be safer if you don't know any names.'

She sighed and patted the back of my hand. 'OK. I can see that. But why should your boss choose you, you're not in the BNDP.'

'I don't know … He could be up to something he'd prefer the BNDP not to know about of course.'

'Such as?'

'I'm not sure, but it would explain things if he was trying to cover up something.'

'So? What do you think he's up to?'

I shook my head. I didn't want to share the explanation that had occurred to me – no matter how unlikely it was – but since I'd escaped from the house at Hemel Hempstead I'd been thinking a lot about what Harris had told me and I was beginning to wonder whether Smithson had been the brains behind the voice which had blackmailed Harris into becoming a prostitute.

'I can't be sure,' I said.

She raised her hands in exasperation. 'Christ, Nick,' she sighed softly. 'Does your boss know about us? That we're friends?'

'No,' I said. 'I've never talked about you to anyone at the office. As far as they know you don't exist.'

'Well,' she said. 'I suppose that's something in your favour.'

She stood up and pulled her chair towards me and lifted my feet on to its seat.

'I want you to stay here,' she said. 'I need to think about this.' She walked over to the office door and paused with her hand on its handle. 'Try to get some sleep, you look like you could do with it. Don't worry, Nick. I'm not going to shop you.'

As she went out of the office and closed the door behind her I told myself I had to trust her – I had no choice – and I knew if I tried to leave against her will I'd never make it. Apart from Rob there was her mechanic, whose feet I'd met on the way in, and the feet I'd spoken to belonged to a body which was very big. I'd made my decision to come to her when I'd hidden in the old disused barn and now I had to let Rob make hers. Until she did I was safe and I guessed the worst she'd do was to throw me out. I lay back in my chair and with the warmth of her small office adding to my sense of temporary security I fell into my first sleep for over twenty-four hours.

Time: 12.55 hours

Rob woke me a few minutes before one o' clock. I'd been asleep for around two hours and I felt a little better.

'Sorry it's only junk food,' she said, putting a small red and white waxed paper box containing chicken and french fries on to my lap. 'It's the best I could do around here.'

I gobbled the food while she sat on her desk, slowly swinging her long legs to and fro, and looking at the floor. After I'd finished eating she got off her desk and sat in her chair facing me while I waited in silence to find out whether a late breakfast was the only help I was going to get.

'OK, Nick,' she said, in a brisk no-nonsense voice, 'this is what I'm going to do.' She raised her head and looked at me. 'I'm going to take you round to my place so you can clean yourself up. And I'll give you some of Martin's clothes.' She pointed with distaste at my filthy tracksuit. 'You can't go about looking like that … I've fixed you up with a car. Nothing flash, but it's got plenty of go in it.' She saw my sudden look of concern. 'Don't worry, it's not hot, I keep out of that end of the business, but it can't be traced back to me either. When you've finished with it just park it and throw the keys away. All right?'

I nodded in grateful agreement; hot food, a bath and

116

some of her brother's clothes were more than I had a right to expect, given my previous dishonesty about my job.

'Thanks, Rob,' I said. 'I don't deserve it. I shan't forget it.'

'Well,' she said. 'I thought about it and I thought I ought to give you the benefit of the doubt. You must have had a terrible time when Ann died. I'm doing it for her as much as for you. I know we lost touch after we left university, but I always had a soft spot for her. She was a smashing girl.' She sighed. 'What would she say if she could see you now …? I'll take you round to my house, but I want you out of it and gone in an hour … Deal?'

I nodded again while I pushed down feelings of self disgust which had overtaken me when she talked about helping me because of Ann. Christ, I thought, even after all this time it won't go away, it's always coming back to haunt me.

Rob took a small bunch of keys out of the top pocket of her flying suit and turned in her swivel chair towards her desk.

'Have you got any money, Nick?'

'It's OK,' I said. 'I've got enough, but thanks anyway.'

'Well, if you're sure,' she said, getting out of her chair and picking up my empty mug and the paper box containing chicken bones.

She looked round her office to make sure there was nothing else to show that I'd been there, before holding out her hand to me. 'Come on, Nick, let's get you out of here.'

She helped me off my chair and pushed me gently towards the door and out of her office.

Her big Rover was parked inside the garage immediately outside the small office.

'Here,' she said, passing the paper box and mug to the big Jamaican mechanic who was standing by her car, wiping his hands with an oily rag. 'Wash up the mug and burn the box. OK?'

They exchanged a look which said more than volumes of books ever could.

'Right. In you get,' she said, opening the Rover's back door for me to get inside.

She closed the door and got into the driver's seat.

'Lie across the back seat,' she said as she started the engine. We drove out of the garage and turned right with me lying across the Rover's back seat to ensure I wouldn't be seen on the way over to her home on the fashionable side of Notting Hill.

Her's and Martin's house had a garage and as she squeezed the Rover through the narrow gateway its electrically operated doors swung open. Once we were inside she got out of the car and shut them before holding open my door while I inched myself out and into the tight space between her Rover and the garage wall. We entered the house through the connecting door which led into the kitchen and while I sat down on one of the bright red stools by the breakfast bar she turned off the squealing delay tone on the burglar alarm.

'Come on,' she said, hustling me out of the kitchen.

She took me into the bathroom that led off her bedroom. 'Take your clothes off.' She bent down and turned on the bath taps. 'There's a robe behind the door. You can wear that. I'll go and find you a razor.' She went out of the bathroom, closing the door behind her.

I was in the bath when she knocked. 'You can come in,' I called.

'I'm leaving a razor on the floor outside the door,' she called back. 'I couldn't find any shaving foam so you'll have to use ordinary soap. And don't go to sleep, you've only got forty-five minutes left.'

I climbed wearily out of the bath and retrieved the razor. After I'd rubbed myself down and shaved I put on her dark blue bathrobe and went into her bedroom. Rob had laid out a collection of men's clothes on her bed; underwear, two suits and a selection of shirts and ties.

'You can choose from these,' she said, pointing at the clothes.

'You and Martin are about the same size and I don't think he'll mind. He hasn't worn them for ages.' She

118

opened one of her wardrobe doors and produced a black nylon overnight bag. 'Take both suits and a change of clothes in case you have to check into a hotel. You know how careful they are, if you don't have any luggage they're likely to phone the police.'

She left the room while I got dressed. I was glad she was thinking for me. The sleep in her office had helped but I still wasn't too sharp. Hotel guests had to show their ID cards to get a room and the police checked all the hotels' registers every twenty-four hours. It would have been an impossible task when London had bustled with tourists but since the restrictions on international travel many of the hotels built in the 1970s had been closed, or turned into Special Care Centres, accommodation for suspected heavies. Rob had been right; if I tried to check in without any luggage the receptionist would have been reporting me to the local police station about the time I'd be opening the door to my hotel room.

Martin's grey suit was a reasonable fit, although anyone who looked closely might wonder why I hadn't insisted the tailor take more accurate measurements – over all, though, I looked fine. His black leather shoes were a half size too big. Still, I told myself, better than a half size too small.

'When is Martin coming back from New York?' I called to Rob as I sat on her bed tying up my shoelaces.

'Next week,' her voice replied from Martin's room.

I'd never understood how a brother and sister could be as different as they were; while Rob had used her share of her father's money to launch herself into the rough and tumble of London's car trade, Martin had gone into banking when he'd left university and he'd risen to a senior job on the international investments side. He was a couple of years younger than her and I'd wondered about the nature of their relationship from the first time I'd seen them together, and when Rob and I had bumped into one another after nearly fifteen years I wasn't surprised to find neither of them had married.

'Is he OK?' I asked her as she came into her bedroom.

Martin had been away in New York during the whole of

119

the six months Rob and I had been friends and in all that time we'd hardly mentioned him; on my part, I'd guarded against being inquisitive in case my questions had accidently wandered into territory which I was sure was taboo, and she seemed not to want to share anything about him.

'He's fine. I wish he wouldn't work so hard though, it's not as if we need the money.'

There it is again, I thought, the assumption that she and Martin will always be together.

'What's it like? Travelling, I mean.'

'Well, Martin goes first class and he never has any trouble with the health immigration people because he's got a green card.'

Lucky Martin, I thought. A green card was only issued to high level travellers on legitimate business and it generally covered politicians, diplomats, the military and businessmen or anyone else of importance who could convince the Foreign and Commonwealth office they had a legitimate reason to travel. It was rumoured that now the AIDS virus had largely been contained, at least among the industrialised countries, green cards might be extended to a wider group, like sportsmen and movie stars.

Rob opened an old plastic washbag and showed me its contents. 'I'm giving you a razor and a flannel and some soap,' she said, putting it into the overnight bag along with Martin's blue suit and a white shirt and a change of socks and underwear. I looked at her and at the bed. It was an innocent look, but Rob wasn't taking any chances.

'Forget it, Nick, I'm not interested.' Her tone had an unmistakable note of finality.

'Don't worry,' I said. 'I'm not up to it. Anyway, the thought never crossed my mind.'

I let her propel me through her bedroom door and down the stairs to the hall and while I looked at my appearance in the mirror at the bottom of the stairs she went to the walk-in cupboard and emerged with a half-length, dark brown sheepskin coat.

'What will Martin say about you giving his clothes away?'

I asked, as I slipped my arm into the coat.

'It never suited him anyway,' she said. 'And I'll find a way to make it up to him.' There was the tiniest hint of a double meaning.

The coat, like the rest of Martin's clothes was of very good quality and fairly new. In fact, on re-checking my appearance I decided I was better turned out than I had been when I'd left my flat on the previous morning. That was good. I had to look right. It fitted with my plan.

We left the house the same way we'd gone in and I lay across the back seat and out of sight as she backed her Rover down the short driveway and into the road.

After driving for about twenty minutes she stopped the car. 'You can sit up now,' she said.

I sat up and looked out of the Rover's windows. 'Where are we?'

'In a road on the south side of Holland Park.'

She pointed to a silver coloured Ford, parked about twenty metres further along the road. I guessed it was about two years old, two models up the range from mine, with multi-point fuel injection – the sort driven by fast-rising young executives.

Rob leaned between the Rover's front seats and gave me the keys to the Ford. 'It's got a full tank and there's maps and a London A to Z in the glovebox,' she said.

'I don't know how to thank you, Rob,' I said. I leaned forward to kiss her but she turned her head away.

'I haven't got much time,' she said. 'I'm due back at the garage to see a customer.' She turned round again and looked at me. 'It's for old time's sake, Nick. If you're caught I expect you to keep me out of it. Understand?'

'Don't worry about that.'

'I'm not. Now go on, get out of here.'

I started to open my door. 'What about Martin's clothes? Look, I'll send you some money when this is all over.'

'Don't bother.' She twisted round and pushed open my door. 'I don't want to see or hear from you this side of my fortieth birthday. Now get the fuck out of here before I change my mind.'

As I got out of the car she opened her electric window. 'Take care, Nick, and try to remember what I've taught you these last six months. If you get in a jam wait for an opportunity – you always were better on the counter attack.'

I turned to face her and bowed stiffly from my waist as befits a pupil taking leave of his master.

'Good luck,' she said. She gunned the Rover's twin-cam engine and drove away. Its tyres screeched as she took the corner at the end of the street.

I went over to the Ford, unlocked it, got in and started its engine and turned on the radio. There'd be a news bulletin on the half hour and I thought there might be some kind of an announcement about Rayleigh. As I drove towards Motte's gallery I thought about Rob's instruction to keep well away from her – five years was a long time. Perhaps by then I'd have gathered up sufficient courage to get round to the subject of her relationship with Martin. To do that though I'd still have to be in one piece, and as things were I wasn't too confident about that.

Time: 15.05 hours

Motte's gallery was closed when I got there. I rang the bell and waited, then I kept ringing it, but nobody came to the door. I went and found a phone. The directory listed two numbers, one for the gallery and one for Motte's apartment. I rang them both. Nobody answered and after two or three minutes I admitted to myself that either he wasn't at home or he was dead; I knew something must have happened to make him shut up the gallery on a Friday afternoon. I went back to the big Ford and sat in the driver's seat, staring into space for some time. Eventually I decided to drive out to my flat in Finchley. It was too early in the afternoon to follow the only other lead I'd got and I thought if I stayed in the road outside my place and kept out of sight I might learn something to my advantage.

I cruised slowly along the road where I lived until I spotted a parking space in a good position; too far away from the flat for Smithson's men to take any interest and near enough for me to watch for any telltale comings and goings. I drove into the space and reversed until I was almost touching the car behind. The Ford was much longer than the model I was used to and if I had to get away in a hurry I didn't want to be shunting backwards and forwards between parked cars. I turned the engine off but I kept the radio on with the volume turned down so that I could just hear it. There'd been no news about Rayleigh on the last bulletin and I'd guessed that could only mean they still hadn't found him and, with Harris dead, I was the only person alive who could tell them where to look.

It's an axiom of a tracer's job that people generally return to their territory when they know you're after them. I'd heard it said about animals too, and I suppose there's not much difference between them and us when we're being hunted. Anyway, I was sure Smithson would leave someone in my flat in case I turned up there. The weather had changed with the previous night's full moon; the skies were a cloudless bright blue and the air outside the car was clear and cold and I reckoned there was still a good forty-five minutes of daylight left. By now my hunters will be getting restless, I thought, and with any luck they might do something to give themselves away. If I could catch a glimpse of one or more of them it might give me an advantage, at the very least I wouldn't be unknowingly killed by someone I knew at the office. I looked at my watch – they'd be recording Alice Townsend's current affairs chat show in a few hours.

I'd been sitting in the Ford, watching my flat, for about thirty minutes, when I saw the curtains in the window of my living room move – they didn't move by much, but enough to tell me that someone was waiting inside and that they were getting bored and careless. I guessed they probably didn't have too high an opinion of me either, and I couldn't say I blamed them, for by then even I'd come to the unflattering conclusion that Smithson must have regarded me as a hapless yesman. I hoped he'd continue to underestimate me.

I saw the small Ford, the model leased by the office, approaching me from behind in my car's door mirror and I slid down in my seat as it passed and parked in a space further along the road, almost opposite my flat. I knew from its number plate that it was one of ours and, as I watched, Terry Bannister got out of it, walked across the road and stood outside the front door of the house, pushing the bell to my flat and blowing in his bare hands and rubbing them against the cold – somehow I'd always known that he'd be in charge of operations on the ground. The people inside my flat pressed the button on my intercom phone and Terry pushed open the door and went into the house and after ten minutes he reappeared with another man who I'd never seen before, and they walked across the road to the office's Ford. At the moment when Terry started his car I decided I'd do more good following him than sitting outside. As he reached the end of my road and turned left I started my engine and swung out from between the parked cars and went after him. Terry's appearance at my flat was confirmation of part of the theory I'd put together while I'd huddled in a corner of the disused barn in the early hours of the morning and I hoped he might lead me to the final proof I needed.

I caught up with them before they turned right into Finchley High Road. Terry was an aggressive driver and I nearly lost him when he jumped the lights going over the North Circular, but I kept on his tail as we continued down Archway until, just past Seven Sisters, he turned down Camden Road. The rush hour traffic was starting to build and I knew it would be difficult to stay with him if he started using the back doubles. We turned left into Royal College Street then right into the maze of little streets at the back of St Pancras railway station where he suddenly slowed down and pulled into the kerb. I continued past him and took a left into the next side street, drove down to the bottom, turned round on myself at the T junction and cruised slowly back up the street and found somewhere to park. Terry's car was around the corner – less than ten metres from where I was waiting – and I guessed he was receiving new orders.

Ten minutes later Smithson's car drove past the end of my street with Terry's following behind. I counted to ten, quickly, and followed them. At the bottom of Pancras Road they both went left along Euston Road, but at the junction outside Kings Cross railway station Smithson turned right into Grays Inn Road, while Terry turned north up the Caledonian Road. I gambled on Terry going back to my flat and I followed Smithson. I gambled wrong; Smithson drove back to the office – it was a dead end. Turning north into the Tottenham Court Road I decided against confirming my gamble about Terry's probable destination; I had the final proof of my theory and it would be better for me if I disappeared for a few hours.

I knew the names on the registers of the cheap hotels were always the first to be fed into the police computer and that I would be safer hiding in a place where my expensive clothes would blend with the ambience. I headed towards Bloomsbury; there was a good hotel in Russell Square with a car park and an Underground station close by, and if I had to leave the hotel in a hurry I'd have some alternatives. I left the Ford in the nearly adjacent multi-storey carpark, walked to the hotel under the street lights in Russell Square and registered for one night. Once I was in my room I stripped and got into bed. Before I went to sleep I phoned through to reception and asked them to call me at eight and for room service to bring me a light meal fifteen minutes later.

Time: 20.00 hours

The bedside phone's insistent ringing dragged me protesting out of a troubled half sleep at eight o'clock precisely and I pushed the bedclothes away and went into the ensuite bathroom and let the shower's icy cold water lash me into full consciousness. I'd dried myself down and dressed before room service knocked on my door. After the waiter had left I turned on the TV and sat down to eat my cold beef salad. I could have eaten more but I knew a large meal would make me drowsy and I needed to keep wide awake.

Alice Townsend's programme started at eight thirty. After the titles had finished rolling across the screen her good looking face appeared in close-up to tell me what I was going to see in the next half hour. In the first part of the programme she interviewed the same research scientist I'd heard on the early morning news the day before. After his simple explanation and supporting diagrams, she thanked him and the interview finished on a note of optimism; it was the customary don't-worry-there's-a-cure-just-round-the-corner note of optimism which the media usually used to conclude such interviews.

I'm no scientist and my Department never saw a doctor, let alone a medical researcher, but I understood enough to know from the information that filtered down to us that so far the constant changes in the virus's composition had defied all attempts to make a safe vaccine. It was a virus which seemed to have been designed to resist all attacks and that was probably what had caused the speculation that it was an experiment which had escaped from some germ warfare research establishment. Its method of attack was to colonise the complex system inside us which enables us to survive in a world full of bacteria and the people who caught it were like walking time bombs, with the virus inside them, ticking away and subverting their body's immune system. Worse still, a carrier was permanently infectious and could pass it on to other people through sexual contact. AIDS itself developed later – twenty years later in some cases – either after a minor illness or something more significant; even now I didn't think the scientists were absolutely sure what triggered it. After that the infected person went into a progressive decline with periods of relative good health until their

126

immune system declined to the point when their body was wide open to any form of ailment that came along.

I smoked a cheroot and watched as the programme continued with various items and comments on our current domestic political scene and a quick round-up of foreign news. Aside from Europe and the United States, events beyond Britain's shores received relatively little coverage and there'd been nothing at all on Africa since the series of shock programmes on the effects of AIDS throughout the continent south of the Sahara. I supposed it was because the industrialised countries were too hard pushed to cope with their own problems over the disease and that someone had probably decided it would be better not to distress the viewing public when there was so little we could do to help. Perhaps, too, they thought it might provoke another round of attacks against our own black population who the BNDP had accused of being the source of the disease. It was all very depressing.

Alice wished all her viewers goodnight, and wound up a programme whose only reference to Rayleigh had been a series of shots showing his attendance at a conference two weeks previously. I turned off the TV and considered my own predicament. In the immediate future the prospect of being fished out of the Thames was a damn sight more depressing than the national problem with AIDS. I got off the bed and put the tray with the remains of my dinner outside, in the corridor, and stuck the 'Don't Disturb' sign on my door. As I left the room I took Rob's overnight bag with me in case I didn't return. I went down the hotel's main staircase, stopping to scan the people in the foyer before I walked down the final flight of stairs. Pushing my way past the people who were standing by the reception desk I made my way to the hotel's small side bar and came out on to Bernard Street, where I turned right and sauntered round the block so I could approach the multi-storey car park from the south-eastern corner of Russell Square.

The car Rob had given me was standing in its parking bay waiting for me. I dropped on to my haunches and looked under it and, to be doubly sure, I opened its bonnet and surveyed the engine compartment before turning the ignition key. I didn't think Terry knew anything about explosives, but there again, before he'd burst into the kitchen in the house at Hemel Hempstead, I'd always regarded Chris Brand as a OK sort of guy. As I drove between the bays of parked cars I thought again about contacting Victoria. I'd called her number before I'd left the hotel but the second she'd answered I'd decided that contact with her was too dangerous, and I'd put the phone down on her 'Hello'. I might care about her but she'd done nothing to make me think she felt anything for me and a one-sided relationship like ours wasn't a good basis to ask for her help. Perhaps, if she'd been one of our secretaries, I might have taken the gamble, but she was a tracer, and she might be part of whatever game Smithson was into.

I came out of the car park and drove round Russell Square and took the north exit. At Euston Road I turned left and kept going until I met the Edgware Road. There I went north towards Stanmore Hill and Alice Townsend's house. I'd found her address in the phone book in the hotel's public callbox before I'd gone up to my room. When I'd rung it and got the number unobtainable tone I guessed she'd probably gone ex-directory since her rapid rise to fame. One thing intrigued me, though – she'd only made the big time in the last year and the British Telecom's directory in the hotel's phone booth had been over two years old and I couldn't understand how she could have afforded a house on Stanmore Hill when she was still an ordinary working girl.

Time: 22.15 hours

Alice Townsend lived in a road very near to the top of Stanmore Hill in a small close of individually designed and exceptionally desirable residences, each of which was surrounded by a piece of land that was large enough to let you have a blinding row with your nearest and dearest without fear of disturbing the neighbours. I stood in the narrow road looking at her house, which was built in the style of a large, single storey Scandinavian log ranch house, and decided the fixtures and fittings in her not-so-little nest would account for most of the bounties I'd saved – I couldn't even contemplate the possibility of buying the place. Although the doors on the house's double garage were closed and there were no cars in the drive, the light over the front door was on and I hoped it meant that she was at home. The gossip pages in the newspapers said she was unmarried, but she might have visitors and I thought that since Motte hadn't been at his gallery there was a chance he might be with her. With that in mind I'd taken the precaution of leaving the car in a car park behind a small row of shops halfway down the hill; I didn't relish the idea of confronting the pair of them but if he was with the delectable Miss Townsend and things turned out badly, and I had to run for it, I preferred to race downhill. The prospect of curfew – that continual spur to conclude one's night time activities – was beginning to exercise my mind, and in spite of the immunity provided by my tracer's ID card I wanted to be tucked up in bed in Russell Square or in another hotel by midnight. While I stood in the road looking at Alice Townsend's house I was losing time.

I walked up the driveway and went up the steps, hearing for the first time the faint sounds of Mahler's Fifth Symphony that were escaping from inside the house – she must be at home, I thought. The exterior wall of the house, which ran away to my right, was made of dark, smoked plate glass and as far as I could see it appeared to form the outer wall of a corridor which ran the whole length of the ranch house. I rang the bell and the music stopped. A door opened towards the end of the corridor on my right and I watched as a figure appeared, framed by the light from the room they'd been in when I'd rung the doorbell. The figure walked along the corridor towards the front door and opened it to the limit allowed by its security chain.

'Yes?' said a woman's voice. I recognised it as belonging to Alice Townsend.

'Miss Townsend?' I asked tentatively.

'Yes?'

I figured I had about ten seconds before she closed the door in my face.

'I'd like to talk to you about a man called Jonothan Harris,' I said, using my senior official's voice.

'I'm sorry,' she said quickly, 'I don't know anyone by that name.' She started to close the door.

I spoke quickly. 'When a minister of the Crown disappears all sorts of nosey people start to ask questions and when he's found in mysterious circumstances they get tougher and so do the questions. If you close that door, Miss Townsend, I'll go and find the nearest phone and ring somebody I know. And I'll only say one sentence.'

She looked at me properly for the first time through the gap in the door. 'And what will you say?'

'Anthony Rayleigh is dead and Alice Townsend knows all about it.' I heard her sharp intake of breath. 'Now,' I continued, 'you can talk to me or you can spend the rest of the evening talking to some gentlemen from Special Branch.'

'Wait a minute,' she said before she closed the door and removed its security chain. 'You'd better come in,' she said, opening the door wide.

As I entered she looked past me and outside, into the close. 'Don't worry,' I said. 'I'm not an amateur. I paid off the taxi and walked here.'

It's a good job she doesn't know the way I've unthinkingly obliged Smithson in his whims, I thought, otherwise she would have shut the door in my face. His part would have to come later, at that moment I had to convince her I was a streetwise operator. She closed the door and put on its security chain before leading me down the corridor and through the door where she'd first appeared, while I listened to my sixth sense telling me that it thought we were alone in the house.

The house's main living area was on two levels, with

130

wood panelled walls and a huge window which appeared to make up one side of the room which overlooked the garden. The floor-to-ceiling curtains were drawn across it and despite the room's size it conveyed a feeling of warm intimacy. Alice Townsend walked over the deep oatmeal-coloured carpet and down the steps to the room's lower level, which contained three two-seater settees, covered in soft leather, drawn up on three sides of a Scandinavian style fireplace. Small blue flames licked at the coals in the fire which were imprisoned behind its heat resistant glass. Personally, I prefer old houses although I like modern architecture when it's of high quality. I followed her down the steps, looking around the room – I'd been wrong when I'd looked at the house from the road, my bounties wouldn't begin to cover the cost of the fixtures and fittings.

'It's a nice place.' I said it as if I was used to living in nice places.

'I'm glad you like it,' she said with a brief smile as she invited me to sit down on one of the two seater settees.

I took my eyes off the room and turned them on Alice. Howard Hawks, an old Hollywood film director, once said that the camera either liked you or it didn't. It certainly liked Alice, but it still didn't do her full justice. She was a living example of the sort of beautiful women you sometimes see in classy fashion magazines, like *Vogue* or *Harper's Bazaar* – utterly desirable but totally out of reach. On the TV programme she'd had her jet black hair scraped away from her face in a severe style, whereas now it was down, and touching the tops of her shoulders. The shape of her face, the texture of her skin and her bow-shaped lips reminded me of a doll, but her high cheekbones and slightly hollowed out cheeks below them guarded against any hint of the pudginess of a doll's face. The way her slim body had moved under her dark blue silk kimono reminded me of Rob, although the curves of Alice's body were much softer. I'm glad Rob's brother has expensive tastes in gentlemen's suitings, I thought, because if I'd have turned up here in my tracksuit and training shoes, the delicious Ms Townsend would have undoubtedly shown me the door.

Alice Townsend looked me full in the face. 'I'd like to see some identification please. Are you with the police?'

'My name's Gorman, Miss Townsend, Nick Gorman,' I said. 'No, I'm not with the police, nor with MI5 or any other department you will have heard of. For the moment let's just say I'm a special sort of civil servant.' I said it in an understated you-know-what-I'm-talking-about-so-don't-let's-play-games tone of voice. My introduction rolled smoothly off my tongue, like it had been finely honed by years of practice; I'd rehearsed it in the car on the way out to her house until I'd been word perfect and I could see she was taken in by my performance.

She sat down on the settee facing mine and I caught a glimpse of her outer thigh through the split in the side of her kimono. She didn't have Victoria's bloom of youth – I guessed she was around my age, in her mid thirties – but she was still the best looking woman I'd ever seen close up. Pull yourself together, I told myself; short of rape you don't stand a hope, get on with what you came for.

'You said outside that you wanted to talk to me, Mister Gorman,' she said coolly. 'I'm afraid you've caught me in the midst of some work. I hope this won't take too long. Now, won't you tell me what's brought you here?'

'Of course. I'd prefer to come straight to the point,' I replied. 'Last evening, Miss Townsend, you met a young homosexual in a house near Hemel Hempstead. Agreed?'

She caught her top lip with her bottom teeth and held it for a few seconds while I congratulated myself for deciding to start with a bodyblow of a question.

'I meet lots of people,' she said, quickly recovering her composure. 'Do you want to arrest all of them? Because if you do, let me warn you that some of them are very influential.'

'The homosexual's name was Jonothan Harris,' I said, ignoring her hint, which I thought might have been designed to winkle out my position in the pecking order. 'He's a friend of Charles Motte. Motte drove Harris out of

132

London to that house. It was supposed to be safe. Later on, you drove out to the same house in a BMW. Shall I tell you the registration number?'

I fished out my wallet and took out a small white card; it had 'Chinese Garden Takeaway Restaurant' printed on the side I was looking at, but she didn't know that. I wanted to look and sound official.

'I don't have to tell you anything,' she said, in a voice which had lost a lot of its self-assuredness.

'I think that would be unwise, Miss Townsend. I hoped we could keep our little talk confidential – you know, just something between the two of us. I can assure you that those who come after me won't be quite so understanding. Life could become very difficult indeed.'

We sat in silence while I put the card back in my wallet and while she assimilated my unspoken threat to bring in the State's heavy mob.

She pursed her lips. 'Would you like a drink, Mister Gorman,' she said, interrupting the brooding silence.

'Scotch on the rocks would be very nice.'

She walked over to the drinks cabinet which stood on her side of the fireplace and put ice and scotch into two chunky, cut glass tumblers. She gave me one of the tumblers and sat down again, opposite me, looking at her glass as she twirled it in her long slender fingers, making the ice tinkle softly. Her nails were painted in a subdued red which matched her lipstick.

'I'm a journalist,' she said, looking up at me. 'You never know.' She shrugged her shoulders. 'A good story can come from all sorts of unlikely sources.'

I had to admire her; my reference to Rayleigh must have come like a thunderbolt, and I'd mentioned the possibility of involving Special Branch and MI5 on two separate occasions, yet so far she'd ignored my opening shot.

'Will you confirm the details of my story, Miss Townsend,' I said. 'It would be a great help if we could make progress. Otherwise,' I turned in my chair and looked round the room, 'I shall have to borrow your telephone to make a call.'

She drank some of her whisky. 'All right,' she sighed, 'I did go to the house as you said.'

'Was this after Mister Motte contacted you?'

She nodded.

Junior barristers are taught to avoid asking questions of a hostile witness unless they already know or think they have a good idea of the likely answer, and it seemed the likeliest way she'd have got to know about Harris being at Hemel Hempstead, but I knew that from now on I couldn't take the risk of second guessing her answers. I wanted to give the impression that I already knew most of the details and one wrong assumption on my part might lead her to think of questions about me I couldn't answer and if that happened *she'd* start talking about needing to phone someone, except in her case she wouldn't be bluffing.

'How did Motte contact you? By phone?'

She nodded again.

'Now that must have been about ...' I said slowly, hoping she'd supply the last words of my sentence.

'Around five o'clock. I was at the studios ...' She paused. 'Discussing tonight's programme,' she added.

Her answer fitted with my version of events; Motte's car didn't have a phone aerial and I thought it likely that he'd called her after he'd closed the gallery and gone upstairs to his apartment. I drank some of my scotch before I asked my next question.

'Tell me, Miss Townsend, after you left the house at Hemel Hempstead, where did you go?'

'Back here.'

'Were you alone?'

'Yes.'

'That's not what I meant,' I said. She threw me a sharp look. 'I know that Mister Motte left with you and he couldn't have got back to his gallery in Mayfair by curfew, unless he has a curfew pass. Did he stay here?'

'Yes,' she sighed. 'But before you ask, we're not lovers.'

I was pretty sure she wouldn't have said that if the idea of her and Motte being lovers had never occurred to her.

134

'But you were.' It was a question, but I tried to make it sound like a statement.

She nodded. 'God!' she said softly. 'You've got a bloody nerve.'

'I'm sorry,' I said. 'I'll try not to pry into your personal life.'

It was a lie of course, I wanted to know as much as I could about her personal life, and I particularly wanted to know how Charles Motte figured in it.

'Why did you go out to the house at Hemel Hempstead, Miss Townsend?'

She held out her hand, palm downwards and studied the back of it before answering. Come on, I thought, stop playing for time.

'Charles said I might learn something of interest,' she said, putting her hand into her lap.

'Does he often give you leads on possible stories?'

'Sometimes.'

'Is that why you went?'

'I was intrigued when Charles rang me. He was very excited and that's unusual for him.'

I wished I knew something about Motte. Could he be tied in with Smithson? I wondered, as I remembered the way Smithson had asked questions about him when I'd phoned in from Hemel Hempstead. I looked at Alice and tried to decide whether she might be tied in with Smithson too – it seemed very unlikely. I hadn't found anything to connect them in the questions I'd asked so far. Unless …

'Did Motte mention Harris's name over the phone when he called you at the television studios?' She shook her head in answer.

It had been a long shot. I knew from my work that the police were tapping phones all over the place and I thought it was likely that they'd have listened in to the BBC's lines.

'Then did you tell anyone about the call?'

'No,' she said.

'How do you come to know Charles Motte?' I asked, breaking my earlier promise not to pry into her personal life.

She smiled to herself, but whether her smile was in recognition of my broken promise or because she was remembering scenes from her past life I wasn't sure.

'We met at a party at Cambridge. We were both at the university, not at the same time of course, Charles is a lot older than me. It was about two or three years ago. We've been friends ever since.'

I guessed that in Alice's world you could be friends as well as lovers, it was an exclusive world and a lad from my background seldom got an invitation to join, unless it was to play the role of buffoon.

'Would you regard Motte as political?' I asked.

'Charles!' She was drinking the remains of her scotch and she almost choked on it in surprise at my question. She laughed. 'Political? You must be joking.'

I wasn't. And what was more, I knew she was lying; Motte rang her because he was political, if he'd only been interested in art and arty women, like his assistant, I was certain he'd have either bundled Harris off into quiet obscurity, or more likely he'd have contacted the police. A man doesn't offer sanctuary to a homosexual, particularly when he knows he's been having a love affair with a freshly dead Secretary of State and then ring up a journalist and offer exclusive rights to the story, not if he wants to stay healthy.

I knew enough about journalists to know that gossip was their lifeblood and letting Alice in on Harris's secret might set off a host of rumours; sooner or later it would leak out and when it did Special Branch would start to nose around and eventually Motte would be implicated. Of course, I thought, that would only apply if Motte had called her as a journalist, but supposing he did it for another reason? Harris had said that Motte knew a lot of influential people and that he'd supplied him with snippets of his clients' pillow talk. The more I thought about it the surer I became that Motte had involved her because they were working on something together and Harris's information was crucial to the people they were working for. Although I'd never met Motte I'd long since classified him as a Tory 'wet' and Alice was probably one as well. She could be a Labour supporter of course, except I didn't think she'd be the kind of girl who backed losers. Was Motte connected with Smithson in some way? I turned the question over again in my mind and then dismissed it. If he was involved with Smithson why bother to involve her in the secret, why not go straight to Smithson? I thought again about the way Smithson had reacted when I'd told him about Motte – was Smithson's attack on the house intended to take Motte out as well?

'We live in interesting times,' I said, quoting an old Chinese proverb to re-start our conversation. 'How well do you really know Mister Motte?'

'I know Charles better than most I suppose,' she said off-handedly.

I found myself wishing she'd known me in the way she'd once known Motte. However much I'd tried I couldn't stop my eyes slyly darting towards the split in her kimono and the narrow strip of her exposed thigh. Never mind her leg, I lectured myself, just keep your eyes on hers, that way you might have a better chance of keeping in touch with her answers to your questions.

'Have you seen Motte today?' I asked, in the hope she could explain his absence from his gallery.

'Not since he left here this morning.'

'When he left here this morning, did he go back to Hemel Hempstead?'

She drank the last drops of scotch from her cut glass tumbler. 'No,' she said. 'He had to go to the gallery first thing but I think he was going back to the house later on this morning.'

Christ! I thought, if he went back to Hemel Hempstead and if Terry had left a small rearguard at the house it's no wonder he's not at his gallery. I tried to fit Alice's seeming lack of concern about Motte's whereabouts into another picture which was forming in my mind.

'Aren't you a little worried about him, Miss Townsend?'

'Charles? No. He's OK.'

I noticed she hadn't asked me why she should be

worried. She knows I know about Harris's secret, I thought, she must do, otherwise she would have asked what Motte had to fear. And the way she'd answered my question suggested she was absolutely confident she knew where Motte was.

I drained the last of my scotch from the cut glass tumbler.

'Would you like another drink?' she asked as she got off the settee.

I held out my glass. 'Did you get anything interesting out of Harris,' I asked her as she took it.

'Not really,' she replied as she went to her drinks cabinet. 'He seemed to be a very stupid sort of person. It was a complete waste of my time.'

Well, I thought, that's the second lie she's told me since I walked through her front door.

Alice gave me the refilled glass and sat down again. She took a sip of her scotch and I guessed she was on the verge of saying something I would want to hear.

'Look.' She leaned forwards. 'I realise you people have your own little ways, but when you came to my door you mentioned somebody else's name.'

'Anthony Rayleigh you mean?' I asked her innocently.

'Yes. But I thought you said …' She didn't finish her sentence.

'That he was dead?' I finished it for her. 'Yes. But we both know that, don't we, Alice? We've known it for sometime, haven't we?'

I said it quietly, trying to create a sense of intimacy between us – a shared secret – because I hoped that if I could inject a sense of intimacy into our relationship it might stop her throwing me out into the street if my own identity became a topic of conversation. Calling her Alice somehow seemed natural and I promised myself I'd do it again.

'Who else knows?' She'd asked her question in a matter of fact way but I could tell she was extremely interested in my answer.

'You tell me, Alice?' I fenced off her question. 'You work in the news media, after all.'

'Rayleigh's ill,' she said. 'He's at his home in Chichester,

138

confined to bed with a bad attack of 'flu, or at least, that's the official story.'

'Why haven't they put it out?'

She smiled. 'Cabinet Minister catches bad cold. It's hardly red hot news, is it?'

'What about your friend Charles Motte? Will he keep his mouth shut? I mean, you said he wasn't political, will he introduce the subject of Rayleigh's death into a conversation over cocktails?'

'He's not stupid,' she snapped. 'Don't worry, Charles knows his way around.'

I noted her retreat from the first impression she'd tried to convey of Motte as an empty-headed fool. They were engaged in some sort of political activity together; I was certain of that now. OK, I thought, now's the time to hit her with your other piece of bad news.

'Harris is dead too,' I said and took a mouthful of scotch.

'When?' She gasped, genuinely shocked.

'After you and Motte left him.'

'How did it happen?'

'Somebody attacked the house,' I replied casually. I drank another mouthful of scotch. 'He was shot.'

'How do you know?'

This is your moment of truth, I thought, so far you've found out enough to tell you that she and Motte are working together, but you've found nothing to link her and Motte with Smithson. It was why I'd come to her house in the first place and I'd already come to the conclusion that as far as that particular topic was concerned I'd come to a dead end. But I knew what had happened when she and Motte were tucked up safely in bed – and despite what she'd said about them no longer being lovers I wasn't sure whether they'd been in separate beds – and more importantly I knew the contents of Rayleigh's Cabinet papers and the address of the house in Paddington. I'd have preferred to have bidden her good night, but I knew I was in too deep for that and I was beginning to think I might have found an ally in my fight against Smithson. Come on, I thought, tell her, you got yourself into this game of poker and the most dangerous thing you could possibly do now is to get up and walk away from the table.

'Because I was there when it happened,' I said. 'I only just managed to escape.'

'There's nothing about it on the news services. I'd have heard.'

'I suppose it's all been hushed up.' I said. 'Or perhaps they haven't found Harris yet. After all, the house is a bit off the beaten track.'

Alice sank back into her settee. This time I saw more than a glimpse of her thigh.

'Jesus Christ,' she sighed. 'What a fucking mess.'

'Not if we keep our heads, Alice,' I said reassuringly.

She raised her glass to her lips and sipped some of her scotch. 'Where do you fit into all this, Nick?' she asked looking at me over the top of her glass.

I'd anticipated her question before I'd left the hotel in Russell Square and I'd worked out a plausible answer. The trouble was that at that time I hadn't anticipated that it would be asked while a pair of big brown eyes were boring into mine.

'I've been following Harris for some time,' I said. 'We suspected he and Rayleigh were involved together.'

'So when did you know Rayleigh was dead?'

'Shortly after it happened.'

She sat upright so quickly that she spilt some of her drink into her lap.

'Don't worry,' I said, watching her brush drops of scotch off her kimono and showing more of her legs in the process. 'I'm not exposed like you … Tell me, Alice, did you find out what you wanted from Harris?'

'You tell me,' she said, readjusting her kimono. 'You're in the secrets business.'

The way she'd regained control of herself after the shock I'd just served up was impressive and I realised I'd have to find another way to prise out of her how much she knew about the circumstances of Rayleigh's death. Still, I

140

thought, at least we've arrived at a point when she's tacitly admitting that she'd lied about wasting her time with Harris.

I smiled and bowed my head. 'Deuce,' I said. 'All right, let's put our cards on the table, shall we?'

She smiled back at me. 'You first, Nick.'

'I had a long talk with Harris before he was killed,' I said.

'And?' she prompted.

'I know you were especially interested in the papers Rayleigh had been reading when he died. Not surprising really, I suppose, they were very interesting papers.'

'How do you know that?' she said sharply. 'Harris couldn't tell me anything about them.'

'Perhaps I was more persuasive.'

'What does that mean? What did you do to him, or do you enjoy hurting ...' she sought for a description of homosexuals, 'his sort?'

It was an intriguing euphemism. Media people were supposed to be liberal – even libertine by the standards of our time – but then, Alice seemed to have more than her fair share of female hormones and I wondered whether homosexuality affronted her femininity.

'I don't get a kick out of hurting people,' I said. 'Either homosexuals or anyone else.'

'So?' She leaned forwards in her settee, her eyes glowing with interest. 'What did you find out?'

No way, I thought, you can't trap me like that lady.

'It's your turn to show a card,' I countered. 'Why do you want to know so badly?'

'I'm a journalist.'

It was a neat, simple explanation, but unfortunately for her I'd already thought about it when she'd said that Motte had invited her out to Hemel Hempstead to give her career a boost. A journalist's sources had long since ceased to be privileged and I could think of a couple of examples where they'd succumbed to pressure and fingered their moles in government departments. These days it didn't need the threat of the courts; and it only needed a small

141

amendment on a computer to brand you as an AIDS victim. If Motte knew his way around so did Alice, and I was sure she'd have heard of the dark little practices which occurred in the crevices of government.

'Even if you could use it,' I said quietly so that it didn't sound like a challenge. 'We both know your editor would kick it into touch the moment you suggested putting it on the air.'

Before she could reply the phone rang.

'Excuse me,' she said as she went out into the glass sided hall to answer it.

I got quickly out of my settee and went up the steps and listened. I breathed a long sigh when I knew she was only speaking to one of her girl friends about having lunch the following Wednesday. As she put her phone down I moved away from the door and when she re-entered the living room I was back on my settee.

'Tell me, Nick?' she asked when she'd sat down again. 'Do you believe in God?'

It seemed an odd question in the light of where we'd left off our conversation when her phone rang.

'I don't know,' I said. 'Perhaps when I was a child, but a lot's happened since then. Why do you ask?'

But I thought now I knew why she'd asked. If I had have been a practising Christian, especially one of the fundamentalist variety I wouldn't have denied my belief, I'd have declared it out loud like the Christian fundamentalists at the office, and Alice would have a clear view of where I stood politically.

'I just wondered,' she replied.

'Is this answering my earlier question about your editor?'

'It depends.'

'On what?'

'On whether you give me a straight answer to my question.'

I sighed. 'As I understand Christ's message it's about love and charity,' I said. 'From what I've seen lately, Christianity is being used to support political ideas – it should be the other way round.'

'Are we to conclude from that you're not a BNDP supporter?'

I hesitated while I tried to decide whether my earlier guess about her politics had been accurate. I was certain she wasn't BNDP – her programmes showed that – and as long as she wasn't one of them I didn't think it mattered too much who she supported.

'No,' I said, 'but lots of people are, their membership seems to be going up in leaps and bounds.'

'I know,' she said grimly.

'And you don't approve?'

'Do you?'

'No,' I said, and sighed again. 'It scares the hell out of me.'

I could have said a lot more, but I thought I'd done enough to confirm that whatever else we couldn't agree on we were on the same side as far as the BNDP was concerned. Anyway, I knew that if I really got talking about the BNDP and what I thought about them I'd be there all night, and I was beginning to worry about the curfew and the idea of being stopped by a police patrol who had the name of 'Gorman' in the forefront of their minds as a result of their pre-duty briefing.

'Well,' she said. 'That's why I wanted to find out what was in Rayleigh's papers. Charles told me the story when I arrived at Hemel Hempstead and he seemed to think there was a connection between what Rayleigh had been reading and his heart attack. I wanted to see if it was true.'

She paused for a drink and I thought about her explanation. 'If what Rayleigh was reading was so terrible why don't his supporters leak it to the press? I mean it would have the same effect. After all, there's plenty of other Conservatives in the Cabinet,' I added.

Alice put her glass on the small coffee table which separated us and pushed back her hair from her face and I suddenly realised it was one of her unconscious mannerisms when she came across a difficult interviewee on one of her shows.

'British governments have always lived by secrecy,' she

said. 'Surely you of all people realise that.'

'But they also leak information if it suits them,' I argued. 'There's nothing secret in Whitehall.'

'You're wrong,' she said shortly. 'These days there's as much secrecy inside the Government as outside it. The BNDP isn't part of the Conservative Party, it's in coalition with it. And the BNDP's very well disciplined. What's more, they have a lot of support inside the Civil Service and among some sections of the Conservative Party. A lot of people think we should have done some of the things they've pushed on to the Prime Minister a long time ago. Cutting back on social security payments and unemployment benefit, and hounding those who claim it are things that many of the Conservatives would have done years ago if they'd have had the chance. And it's quite conceivable the BNDP have some sort of secret alliance with the top Civil Service mandarins, there're even rumours of talks between the BNDP and the Conservative's own lunatic fringe. Remember, that's where Emmerson came from and if he hadn't walked out on the Conservatives to become leader of the BNDP it would never have got off the ground – his political skills and charisma are the driving force behind his party.'

'You seem to like the man,' I said. 'A few minutes ago I got the opposite impression.'

She shook her head. 'I despise everything he stands for,' she said, hotly. 'But I recognise his political talents and his genius for getting his message across. In spite of his upper class background he still has the uncanny knack of knowing what ordinary people think and how to communicate with them, just like Margaret Thatcher did. You only have to look at his party's rallies on TV to see that.'

'Speaking as an ordinary person, I can't stand the sight of him,' I said. 'Even if he does look good on television.'

'Even though he never held government office,' she continued, ignoring my interruption, 'he still had a lot of influence in the Conservative Party. Look at his pedigree – old school tie, links with the aristocracy – if the old

144

Chancellor of the Exchequer hadn't been virtually nominated as prime minister by Margaret Thatcher when she stood down, Emmerson would have had a good chance in an election for the Conservative leadership. After all he was one of the reasons why the new prime minister offered the BNDP a coalition in the first place – he and the rest of the Conservative's old guard made the mistake of thinking that Emmerson was really one of them.'

'What about the new Chancellor of the Exchequer?' I asked, thinking about the connection I made between the Treasury and Home office papers I'd left on Rayleigh's desk. 'Does he get on with Emmerson?'

'They're supposed to get on well together. Why?'

'Oh, no reason,' I said. But I was sure now that my earlier suspicions, that Emmerson's Home Office and the Treasury had colluded over their two papers, had been correct. 'The Conservative Party Chairman doesn't like Emmerson, though, does he?' I added.

'That's not surprising,' she said. 'In spite of all his tough talk, Harper's a Tory "wet" and he knows Emmerson could tempt a lot of the Conservative's ultra-right wingers over to the BNDP by offering them government jobs if they supported him. If that happens ...' She stopped and looked down at her hands. '... Rayleigh was an old fashioned "wet" too and the sort of Conservatives he represented have a lot in common with the Labour Party, and if Emmerson succeeds in splitting the Conservatives Rayleigh might have tried to form an alliance with some of the Labour people.'

It was Alice's job to know about political in-fighting and I gave her credit for knowing a lot more than I did. She spoke with the sort of conviction that came from knowledge. I thought she was probably right about the shifting alliances that were taking place in response to the BNDP's undoubted success in putting the Prime Minister through the wringer; they might be the junior partners in coalition but so far Emmerson had played every card with consummate skill. And her analysis had expressed what had been in my mind for a long time, as I'd watched and heard stories about how the BNDP's tentacles were gradually spreading into all the centres of power.

'You only have to look at the way things have gone in the United States,' she said, interrupting my thoughts. 'Look at the way the Moral Majority Movement have subverted the Republican Party; if their candidate wins the presidential election next year we're going to have a Christian fundamentalist from the deep South in the White House. Think about it – a man who doesn't accept the principles of man's evolution from the apes and who still thinks Russia represents the devil is going to have his finger on the nuclear button ... Oh Christ,' she swore despairingly. 'We all seem to be going down the same road.'

Hearing a call of despair spoken by a member of the same bloody news media which had awakened and whipped up the dormant bigotry of the populace in the first place I couldn't suppress my smile of irony. But she was looking into the blue flames of the fire and she didn't see it. The lights dimmed and came back to their original level of brightness. It happened twice more as the privatised electricity generating board covering the London area played with the voltage to indicate the start of curfew was ten minutes away and that I'd lost track of time. I'll never make it to a hotel before curfew, I thought.

'Won't your wife be worried about you, Nick? Or is she used to late hours?'

'She's dead,' I said.

'I'm sorry.'

I guessed what might be in her mind. 'She was killed in a car accident a couple of years ago,' I said. 'In a way I suppose she was lucky, at least she escaped all this.'

Alice gave me a long look. 'Would you like to stay here? I wouldn't want you to get shot by accident. I'm afraid I haven't changed the sheets on the spare bed since last night when Charles stayed, but if you'd like to stay you're welcome.'

I bet I am, I thought, the last thing you want is for me to get shot, at least, you don't want it to happen until you've had a chance to find out more about the Cabinet papers, not to mention the little matter of whether I know where Rayleigh's body is presently resting. But if I did accept her offer it meant I wouldn't have to hazard police patrols, and her house was a safer hiding place than the hotel in Russell Square; I couldn't believe Smithson would be on her weekend guestlist and there was no way he could know that I was staying with her.

'I'd like to stay if it's not going to put you to any trouble,' I said. 'Thank you.'

'No trouble,' she replied, shaking her head. 'Would you like something to eat? I usually have a snack about this time on the nights I've done my programme. I can never get to sleep until late, I suppose it's the tension.'

She found me a towel and showed me to her guest room and while she was preparing some food I used its ensuite bathroom to freshen myself up. Looking into the mirror of the bathroom cabinet I conjured up a picture in my mind of her smooth white thigh peeping through the split in her kimono; I liked her, and it wasn't simply straightforward male lust. I told myself to stop being stupid, but on the off chance I put the packet of condoms, which were sitting on the bottom shelf of the cabinet, into my pocket before I turned off the light over the mirror.

V

SATURDAY,
26 FEBRUARY 1999

Saturday, 26 February 1999

Time: 00.15 hours

When I went back into the main living area, five minutes later, she'd already prepared our food.

'I thought we'd have it in here,' she said. 'Would you open the wine? There's a bottle of Chianti in the wine rack in the kitchen and the corkscrew's in the top draw of the dresser.'

I followed her through to her kitchen, which looked as if it had been designed by Smallbones, and opened the wine before carrying the bottle back into the dining area, on the upper level in the main room. She'd dimmed the lights and lit the candles which stood in the middle of the dark teak table laid out for supper. I was still speculating whether the dim lighting and candles were significant when she came in carrying two steaming plates, a wooden bowl of salad and a stick of french bread on a tray. 'It's only lasagne I'm afraid,' she said. 'I don't have much time for cooking, I usually buy stuff from Marks and Spencer's.'

I tried to think of a compliment, but I couldn't, you can hardly compliment someone for a culinary skill which consists of buying pre-prepared food from a department store. I kept my mouth shut and poured the wine.

We indulged in small talk as we ate. I asked her questions about her job and her private life; nothing intrusive – the sort of surface details that people exchange at the start of their first meal together. She liked talking about herself, which was just as well, because if she'd

151

started asking questions about my job and personal background our conversation would have come to an abrupt halt. It may have been an unconscious act on her part not to ask me personal questions, or perhaps she was convinced by my cover story and had decided not to ask questions to which I couldn't supply any answers.

It came as a surprise when she told me something of her family background and I discovered she wasn't the little rich girl I'd supposed, when I'd stood outside in the road surveying her house. What she had she'd made for herself through the application of her own talents and business acumen and I felt more at ease when I knew that, like me, she'd grown up in small town in an ordinary family and that her father had been a manual worker like mine. But her parents, unlike mine, were still alive and she'd bought them a house in the same small town of her birth and visited them regularly.

'Cambridge University must have come as a shock,' I suggested. 'Given your background, I mean.'

'Shock?' She shook her head and smiled. 'I don't think I'd been in its hallowed precincts for more than ten minutes when I decided I wanted to go back home. I felt so out of place, all those people speaking posh and looking at me as if I was something the cat dragged in, it was awful.'

'But you didn't?'

'No.' She smiled to herself. 'I kept my mouth shut for a couple of days and listened to the way people talked, then I locked myself in the loo for an hour and practised speaking the way they did and when I came out of the loo I had this new voice and suddenly everything was lovely; people wanted to know me, I got invitations to parties, men wanted to take me out and my opinion seemed to matter.'

'Do you slip back into your hometown accent when you go to see your parents?'

'Of course not,' she said. 'They'd think I was patronising them. I am what I've become but I'm not ashamed of my parents, if they hadn't pushed me to better myself I wouldn't be where I am now, would I?'

The echoes of my recent recollections of my own parents

152

and what I'd become sounded in my mind.

After we'd talked about her parents our conversation became more relaxed, or at least I felt more relaxed. We discovered our mutual interest in movies and we started swapping ideas of our favourite films. We'd got on to the horror genre, and the plot of a especially nasty movie brought our discourse back to the subject of the reason for my visit.

'I'm still not sure why you came to see me?' she asked sweetly.

I hadn't intended telling her about Smithson when I'd rung her doorbell but I was positive by now that she wasn't connected with him and I was seriously considering whether she might be an ally.

'I needed to check you out,' I said, deciding I wouldn't mention Smithson's name. 'I don't like being on the business end of a submachine-gun.'

'Is that what happened when the house was attacked?'

I nodded.

'Who was it? Do you know?'

'I didn't stop to find out.'

'Well? Have you checked me out?' She smiled. 'Am I innocent?'

I laughed. 'I don't know about that,' I said. 'But I don't think you were involved in the raid at Hemel Hempstead ... Tell me, why did you and Motte go off and leave Harris out there?'

'Charles thought he would be safer there than anywhere else. He took a big enough risk taking him there in the first place. We couldn't take him back to London in case we were stopped by a police patrol, and as we had to go through a checkpoint when we got on to the motorway, it seemed safer. The house belonged to Charles's parents, they're dead, and he seldom goes there now, but he keeps some food in the freezer. And a woman goes in once a fortnight to clean and keep an eye on the place. We didn't think there was much chance anyone would find Harris.'

Her story coincided with the version Harris had offered me, and it seemed plausible, except ...

153

'Why didn't Charles stay out there with Harris? Just to make sure he didn't run away.'

'Where would Harris have run to? He couldn't phone anyone from the house because it isn't working. And even if he did, who would have helped him? Charles was his only hope. Anyway Charles couldn't stay, he's in the process of organising an exhibition for Ramone Gonzales.' I remembered that Ramone Gonzales was the Spanish artist whose pictures were hanging on the walls of Motte's gallery. 'This morning he had an early meeting at his gallery. He couldn't stay at Hemel Hempstead.'

Harris had told me much the same thing. But do you believe her? I thought. Would you have driven off into the night and left Harris alone in your parents' old home? It was difficult to supply an answer, because I wasn't sure whether I'd have helped Harris in the first instance.

'How long was Charles going to leave Harris out there?'

'I really can't say,' she said, getting up from the dining table. 'Shall we go and sit by the fire? I find these chairs become uncomfortable after half an hour or so.'

We picked up our cups and the coffee pot off the table and took them down to the sitting area.

'Why did you offer to let me stay?' I asked her, as we were putting them on the small coffee table, standing in the square of space in the middle of her three small settees.

'Because you're a small town boy, like me, and I knew you were safe.'

'Safe?'

'You don't have the look of a rapist,' she said.

I sat on the settee that was facing the fireplace. She sat next to me, drew up her legs underneath her and turned towards me with her left arm resting on top of its cushions. We were very close and the smell of the discreet perfume she wore gently invaded my senses.

'What did Harris tell you, Nick?'

I could recognise the Mata Hari approach, particularly when Mata Hari's knees were almost touching me.

'He told me about Rayleigh,' I said. 'His father and Rayleigh had once been business partners.' She knew that anyway, probably.

'What did he say about Charles and me?'

Her question sounded innocent enough, like the casual enquiry you'd make to someone when you know that a shared acquaintance has been talking to them about you.

'Nothing I didn't know already,' I replied, equally casually.

'I knew you'd visited the house and I guessed Charles owned it. Harris simply confirmed it.'

'What else did Harris say about me?'

'He said you kept asking him about Rayleigh's death.'

'What did he say?' She asked the question with all the nonchalance she could muster.

'He said you kept asking him questions he couldn't answer. Perhaps you didn't ask him in the right way,' I suggested.

'Perhaps I didn't … But you did …'

She didn't ask her next question. It was there though, hanging, unspoken, in the space between us.

'Yes I did,' I said. I was going to make Alice work for the information she was so desperate to get out of me. According to my cover story I was some type of government agent and people in that line of work aren't supposed to reveal secrets at the drop of a hat, or a kimono come to that

'Well?' She said the word in a soft husky voice, as if she'd previously asked me her unspoken question.

'Do you really want to know?' I fenced. 'It may not be in your best interests to know any of the details, that way you'll have less to fear if things turn nasty.'

Alice moved her hand away from the top of the settee's cushions and squeezed the top of my right arm.

'It's very sweet of you to worry about me.' She gave me a smile. 'But I can take care of myself.'

I looked at her and smiled while I wondered whether she really could look after herself if things did get nasty. I wasn't sure whether, if it came to it, and Special Branch, or MI5, or whatever department was given charge of the investigation into Rayleigh's demise, I could stand the bad treatment they'd undoubtedly dish out to anyone who was a suspect. And I wasn't sure that her public position would be a deterrent against the sort of thugs who'd be looking for answers to their questions. She could die at the hands of a death squad and be discovered in the Thames just as easily as I could.

'Have you told anyone else, Nick?'

'I operate on long lines of delegation,' I replied.

'That's not an answer,' she purred.

'It's the best I can do.'

She squeezed my arm again. My heart was pumping at the same rate it usually reached after the first mile of my early morning runs through the park. I knew I had to say something – if nothing else I wanted to find out what Alice would do next to prise my information out of me.

'I know why the papers came as a shock to Rayleigh,' I said as evenly as I could.

'Tell me. Please.'

She moved closer. A casual observer might have seen her movement towards me as an interesting illustration of body language; as a sign of increased attentiveness. He should have been at my end of the settee, he'd have known better.

I resisted the feeling of needing to swallow. 'Rayleigh found out there are proposals to remove some parts of the Special Health Authority and put them under the control of the Home Office,' I said. 'As he was the Secretary of State for Health and the Chairman of the SHA I suppose it would have been a bit of a shock – if he didn't know what was planned.'

Alice moved a fraction closer. Her knees weren't quite touching the side of my right leg, but her kimono was.

'Which parts?'

I swallowed. 'The Care Centres, Environmental Health and the Tracing Divisions.' I said. There was a note of huskiness in my voice now.

'Their job is to control the spread of infection, isn't it?' she asked, looking at me from under her long eyelashes.

'It's a polite way of putting it,' I said. 'Environmental

Health record all the cases where people either fail their blood tests or fail to turn up at the Care Centre's Test Stations and then they notify Tracing who have to round up the people who didn't register for a test, or the contacts of those who've been confirmed as antibody positive.'

I'd taken care not to use the word 'heavies' when I was describing the SHA's primary functions for catching people who'd contracted AIDS, because I guessed that in the social circles Alice moved in they'd be called 'carriers' or 'victims', and I thought she might wonder why someone of my supposed character was using street terms.

'You seem to know a lot about it,' she said.

'I had a thorough briefing when I was given the case.' My reply sounded reasonable; my mythical secret government department wouldn't send me out to spy on Rayleigh without giving me the deep background.

'I've only ever met one person from the Tracing Division,' she said and my pulse rate leapt up to 150 beats per minute. Had I found a connection between her and Smithson? 'I interviewed him for one of my programmes.'

My heart slowed down. I remembered that show, when I'd come in from a bad day and turned on the TV to see her, interviewing a tracer from our west London office, who'd acted like a shifty-eyed crocodile when she started to ask him whether the rumours about the violent questioning of confirmed carriers were true. When he hadn't answered, and her questions had got hotter and hotter, he'd sat back in his chair and quoted the Official Secrets Act at her before acting as if he was deaf and dumb. On the morning after his interview I'd dropped into the office to pick up my expenses and found my colleagues calling Alice every obscene word they could lay their tongues to. After I'd collected my expenses I'd gone to a pub and sat down with a drink and had a good think and that same evening I'd promised myself that I'd stop using violence when I was questioning confirmed heavies about their contacts.

'I'm afraid I missed that programme,' I said.

'The tracer I met was nothing more than a thug, he

could have been recruited straight from an underworld gang.'

You don't know how true that is, Alice, I said to myself, thinking about Smithson and Terry Bannister and some others from among my esteemed colleagues; apart from the Christian fundamentalists most of them gave the impression they'd been pretty gangsters in one dirty trade or another before they'd joined the Department. And their murky backgrounds was the principal reason why I couldn't understand how Victoria had chosen to go into the work.

'Well,' I said, 'they're not doctors or nurses. They track people down who either don't know they've got the virus or do know and want to stay outside the Care Centres. I suppose you'd expect them to be a bit rough at the edges, the work can't be very pleasant. It must be like being on a treadmill, they deliver suspected carriers to the holding accommodation and if their tests are positive they find out their contacts and go after them, and when they find those contacts they start in on the questioning again.'

'But we've had compulsory tests for over a year ...' she said. 'I'd have thought they'd have arrested everyone by now.'

'There's still a lot of people who went missing when they were introduced and it's a fair bet they ran rather than take the blood tests because they knew it was possible they'd got the virus. As far as I know Tracing hasn't even begun to make inroads into that group.'

'But is it all necessary? I mean, they're sick, they're not criminals.'

'That's fine coming from someone who works in the media,' I said. 'It's a pity your lot didn't take that attitude at the start, instead of treating them like lepers.'

'I wasn't one of those who demanded their persecution,' she said, defensively.

I had to get off this topic; it was too close to home for comfort and besides, I didn't like to think about the part I'd played in the whole gruesome business. And in the last twelve hours I'd made a decision that whatever happened between me and Smithson I wasn't going back to being a tracer, no matter what, I'd sweep the bloody streets before I'd go back to a job I hated.

'I know. I'm sorry,' I said. 'I wasn't suggesting you were. But there were precious few who spoke out against the witch hunt.'

'You're sorry for them, aren't you, Nick?'

It was the first time I'd considered the direct question of the way I felt about the people I'd hunted down. I'd got near to it, particularly during the last few months, but I suppose I'd always avoided asking myself that question.

'Yes, I suppose I am,' I said, voicing the thoughts which had begun to haunt my dreams. 'They are sick. And to blame it all on them is ridiculous. We're all to blame. It's not the fault of the gays or the blacks, we're just using them as scapegoats.'

'You surprise me.' She smiled. 'I'd have thought that someone like you, who worked for the government, would be playing the line that they're a threat to society.'

'Just because I work for the government doesn't mean I can't think for myself. It's easy to blame the gays and the blacks for starting the disease, it appeals to the voters, they want simple answers to complex problems. Tell them that it's the fault of a small group who planned to destroy a decent white Christian society and a lot of people will believe it. They want to believe it. It's a nice simple solution, those who've caught the virus are responsible for everything – gays, blacks, men, women and children – hunt them down and lock them up. Don't think to stop how lucky you are and what might have been if you'd gone to bed with someone who'd got it. That's too difficult. And it might start questions; about the bloody hypocrites who protested against explicit advertising in the early days. They're sitting pretty now – cheering on the bloody BNDP. And when they've finished with their favourite scapegoats of the moment it'll be someone else's turn – Jews probably ... When you believe God's on your side and that He abhors anyone who thinks differently from you, you don't need to bother about facts, blind faith provides the answers ...' I stopped and paused for breath, surprised by the force of my feelings. Shut up, I told myself, in this sort of mood you could give something away about yourself.

Alice looked at me and I could see a new light of interest in her eyes.

'But why don't people do anything to stop it?'

'Because they don't care, or they don't want to care,' I said, answering her question in spite of myself. 'We've had twenty years of the Conservatives and their ideas about the freedom of the individual and fuck those who can't look after themselves, so it's hardly surprising that those who're free of the virus couldn't give a damn about those who aren't. Perhaps if a few national figures had been prepared to shout down the initial hysteria things might have been different, but they were too concerned to protect their public image or to make some mileage out of it. Perhaps if they had, we'd have taken a more sympathetic view of those who'd caught it, at the very least they might have been spared the Special Health Authority's Care Centres.'

I suddenly realised it wasn't the closeness of her body that was loosening my tongue and it wasn't the sudden torrent of emotions and ideas I'd bottled up about my job either; I was succumbing to the technique of a polished TV interviewer.

'They're supposed to be terrible places,' she said. 'Have you ever been to one?'

'Christ! What a question to ask,' I replied. 'Of course I haven't.'

It was the truth; the last I ever saw of a carrier was when I delivered them to the Care Centre's holding accommodation and people were let out of holding accommodation if their tests were OK, so they couldn't be too Spartan.

'They're supposed to be terrible places,' she repeated. 'More like prisons than hospitals, even if they have soaked up the long-term unemployed.'

That's it, I thought, you're not going to draw any more out of me on this particular subject.

'It's another example of Emmerson's political skills, I suppose,' she said.

I agreed with her; when Emmerson had suggested the Conservatives should withdraw unemployment benefit from people who hadn't had a job for over two years unless they 'volunteered' to work in the Care Centres most of the electorate had cheered him to the rooftops, but I was determined not to reply.

'So Rayleigh was going to lose virtually everything,' she said reflectively, when she realised I'd finished saying all I was going to say on the topic of AIDS victims.

I was prepared to talk about Rayleigh, though, because I wanted to know her views on the subject which had been exercising my mind since I'd read his Cabinet papers.

'He'd still be responsible for the Research Division,' I lied. 'And he'd keep the NHS, of course.'

'But he'd lose a lot of clout in Cabinet,' she said, speaking her thoughts out loud.

'I guess he wouldn't have gone down without a fight,' I offered.

'Come on,' she said. 'Rayleigh had already lost. My guess is that the first time he knew about Emmerson's proposals was when he read them in his Cabinet papers.'

'What about the prime minister? He's big pals with Rayleigh, surely he'd have told him what was going on?'

'Prime ministers rely on the Cabinet Office to tell them what's going on in their ministers' departments. He wouldn't know about it if his civil servants didn't tell him. I told you, there are all sorts of stories circulating about deals between the BNDP and the Civil Service heavyweights.'

'What about the other Conservatives in the Cabinet?'

'I don't know,' she said thoughtfully. 'Margaret Thatcher weeded out most of the independently-minded people years ago and now she's gone there's not much backbone among those at the top of the party.' She smiled. 'Anyway, this shouldn't be news to you. Who are you working for, Nick?'

'I'm on the side of the angels,' I said.

She gave me a look that said she didn't believe me and I dropped my eyes and played with the cuff of Martin's suit jacket while I tried to think of a way to divert her away from the supplementary questions I knew she was bound to ask in an attempt to find out which department I worked for.

'Did Harris know anything more about Rayleigh's papers?' Her question caught me momentarily off guard.

'Not that he told me,' I said, deciding to keep up our pretence that she'd gone to the house at Hemel Hempstead in the role of an eager journalist. 'I'm afraid what I've told you isn't much good, even if you do decide to use it.' I shrugged my shoulders. 'Nothing more than an inter-departmental re-shuffle really.'

She looked at me archly. 'It depends what lies behind it, doesn't it, Nick?'

She was right about that and if she knew what I'd read in the Treasury's paper she'd have the full picture. It had taken me a little time to put the whole scenario together and now that she'd told me Emmerson and the new Chancellor of the Exchequer were chums I was absolutely convinced that my scenario was correct – the Treasury and the Home Office were in cahoots – and it would take her less than ten seconds to work it out.

Alice moved her position slightly and her arm slid quite naturally on to mine. She looked at the embers of the glowing coals behind the heat resistant glass in the fireplace while she absent mindedly stroked the back of my hand. I tried to pretend her action wasn't having an effect on me while I prepared myself for her next question – the one which went, 'Tell me, Nick? Do you know where Rayleigh is?'

'Tell me, Nick?' she said, still looking at glowing embers in the fire. Here it comes, I thought. 'Are you armed?'

'I don't normally carry a weapon,' I replied, wondering why she'd chosen such a oblique line of attack to get to the question she most wanted to ask.

She turned her head slowly and looked straight into my

eyes. 'Really?' There was no mistaking her double entendre.

I looked at her squarely in the face for the first time during our game of hide the truth. I might be inexperienced in the finer points of the new game she seemed to want to play but I knew enough to recognise the offer in her expression. Nevertheless, I kept my eyes open as I moved forwards to kiss her; I wanted early warning if I'd misinterpreted her signal. Alice wasn't alarmed. She unwound her legs and wrapped herself around me. We kissed with our lips slightly open. Contracting HIV by exchanging saliva is relatively rare, but unless you're really sure of your partner it's better not to take risks. She got off the settee and led me into her bedroom and my night ended in sweet hot blindness.

I had a good idea why she'd decided to take me into her bed but I wasn't sure what she expected when we got there. Perhaps she thought she'd get a quick orgasm from me and a long goodnight kiss. If that's what she'd planned she must have had a surprise because I hadn't had any form of sexual experience since Ann had died. I let Alice take the lead at the start and I knew she was faking the first time. The second time, when she was clawing the back of my neck with her fingernails and her heels were pressing down, hard, on my shoulder blades, I thought she was beginning to let herself go. But the third time, when she sat astride me and seized hold of my ankles and pulled herself backwards and moaned as I penetrated deep inside her, I felt her cum, even through the protective skin of the condom. Afterwards, she sank down on top of me and lay with her head on my shoulder. We stayed like that for a long time.

Time: 08.35 hours

I slept through my body's alarm clock and woke a few minutes after eight thirty. Alice was still asleep. My neck and chest were sore from where she'd scratched me with

163

her fingernails. I might have breached her mental defences during our lovemaking but she was a practised lover and she'd handled my locked up libido without any trouble. And I knew she hadn't invited me to stay and then beckoned me to her bed because of my blue eyes; she wanted to know what I knew about Rayleigh and Harris. She thought she'd found out what Harris knew about the Cabinet papers and she'd soon be turning to the question of whether I happened to know where Rayleigh's body could be found. If I left her house without answering that particular question she'd never forgive herself and I knew she'd decided that our making love was the best way possible to keep me there. I was sure that sleeping with me wasn't part of her ususal repertoire of journalistic skills for obtaining information, but on the other hand, I was in possession of information that only fell into the lap of a journalist once in a blue moon. And there was Motte of course; he fitted in somewhere and it was possible that the reason she'd gone to bed with a stranger had nothing to do with her job as a journalist. Still, I thought, she hasn't scaled the heights of her profession without making a few compromises.

She might have been a practised lover but she wasn't a whore, nor a nymphomaniac, she was a girl from a small town who'd seized the opportunities when they'd presented themselves and in the process of carving out a career for herself she'd acquired that element of ruthless determination which characterises those who know what they want. And I gave her full credit for being a bloody good interviewer. While I'd only got hunches about what she and Motte were up to, she'd found out about Emmerson's paper and its implications for Rayleigh. She knew her politics too and I wasn't ashamed to admit to myself that without her knowledge about what was going on inside the Government I'd still have been fumbling about in the dark about the significance of the Cabinet papers. But I knew it was a poor exchange, because, apart from the pleasure of her delicious body, everything I'd got in return was on display for anyone who was interested enough to look at what was happening around them. Emmerson had a lot of support from the ultra-right wingers in the Conservative party and they'd desert the prime minister and join the BNDP once Emmerson got the upper hand in the coalition. And once he'd split the Conservatives the small rump which supported the prime minister might form an alliance with the Labour Party's right wingers, or with one or more of the minority parties. And more immediately, I was walking around with a piece of information which would give Emmerson the final lever he was looking for to ease the Conservatives out of power and on to the Opposition benches.

I slipped my chunky diver's watch on to my wrist and turned over and studied Alice's sleeping face, wondering how many men she'd brought to her bed. Suddenly I found myself wishing it was Victoria who was lying beside me – I'd imagined a scene like it often enough. Why had she become a tracer? I wondered whether I'd have had more success with her if I had taken Terry Bannister's advice, or watered down version of it, and dispensed with the usual ritual that's expected of men and told her outright that I wanted to look after her and that she could trust me. I'd thought about doing it but I'd always stopped myself at the last minute in case she'd responded with a scornful laugh. Well, I thought, you'll never get the chance now, and I felt something which approached the same pang of loss I'd experienced when the police had broken the news to me about Ann's fatal accident.

I pushed my memories out of my mind, rolled on to my back and returned to my problem with Smithson. I was no nearer to discovering his purpose than when I'd rung Alice's door bell; every idea I'd explored had finished in a blank. On one level I'd begun not to care. I'd never been hunted before and I didn't like it. The memory of my blind panic in Motte's house had dulled since I'd been in Alice's company but I was tired, physically and mentally, and when I really thought about the trouble I was in, my brain went numb. My reaction to being chased had given me a new perspective on the behaviour of heavies I'd pursued in the past, like the young girl, she couldn't have been more than seventeen, who eluded me for weeks. When I'd eventually cornered her in a disused warehouse down by the river in Southwark she'd just sat down and buried her face in her hands. At first I'd thought she was crying, but when I'd put the handcuffs on her I'd realised it was emotional fatigue, mixed, in a curious way, with relief that I'd caught her at last and that she didn't have to run anymore. I'd helped her to her feet and she'd gone with me to the holding accommodation like an obedient little girl and while I'd checked out her ID on the computer in the holding accommodation's reception area she'd stood by the desk, staring into space, almost as if she was no longer part of the world. It was the first time I'd felt sorry for an AIDS victim. In fact it was the first time since Ann's death that I'd felt anything about anyone, even myself. The experience had jolted some life into me and I'd begun to ask questions about what I was doing.

In the cold light of day, lying in Alice's bed, and thinking about the girl, I knew for the first time how she'd really felt. I felt the same way – shut out of society and hunted to the edge of exhaustion. I had no plan and I was fooling myself if I thought I could come up with one. All the smart money was betting that Smithson would catch up with me, sooner or later. Whichever way I looked at it I was trapped inside Smithson's territory; he only had to reprogramme my computer entry to show I'd contacted HIV and he could loose the whole London Department after me. Once they'd caught me it wouldn't do any good to protest I was clean; tracers and Care Centre staff were immune to heavies' claims about mistaken identity. They'd fix it so my blood test showed I was antibody positive and my only hope then was to convince a friendly doctor – if I could find one – that I was the victim of a conspiracy. And I didn't set too much store by that because the sympathetic ones didn't have much regard for men like me, who chased people for money. No, I thought, I'll be incarcerated in a Care Centre where no one will pay any attention to my ravings of political intrigue.

Conversely, Smithson could sit back and wait for me to register for my three monthly blood test. He only needed to patch in to the Environmental Division's main computer and he'd know which London Test Station I'd gone to as soon as a clerk typed in my ID number, and the chances were that Terry and his merry men would be waiting to pick me up the moment I stepped outside the station's doors. I was trapped. I'd no warrant to travel outside the Greater London Zone and even if I evaded the traffic checkpoints and headed out into the country I couldn't check into a hotel, or buy petrol without one. And without a new ID I couldn't get a job. I could get forged papers but that was an option I'd only take as the very last resort. Once my money ran out and I could no longer afford to pay for the forged test results I'd be back to square one and into the mugging business.

I swallowed down my feelings of despair and slid out of Alice's bed, without waking her, and went into the kitchen to make us some breakfast. Perhaps, I thought, if I'm right about her, and she and Motte are working against the BNDP, I might be able to strike a bargain with her in exchange for the address of the house in Paddington. When I took her coffee and toast back into the bedroom she was already awake. She gave me a good morning kiss and while she started to drink her coffee I got into bed next to her with the morning papers, which I'd picked up off her door mat, and scanned through them quickly – there was nothing in them about Harris or Rayleigh.

Alice put her cup on the bedside table and turned to look at me. 'You're on the run, aren't you?' she said softly. 'They want to kill you as well, don't they? Don't deny it, Nick … it's written all over your face.'

There was no point in denying it. She took the *Guardian* out of my hands and laid it out on the bed.

'Why do they want to kill you?'

'Is that why you let me make love to you?' I countered. 'Granting the condemned man a last night of happiness?'

'Why do they want to kill you?' she repeated ignoring my facile remark.

'I'm a loose end.'

'Who are they, Nick?'

'I don't know,' I lied. I still didn't know enough about her to talk about Smithson openly. 'Look, I'm sorry, I shouldn't have got you into this. I'll get out of here and leave you in peace.'

I left her and went into the guest-room and showered and shaved, using a razor I found in the bathroom cabinet. To tell the truth, in saying I'd leave, I wasn't sure whether I'd acted out of a sense of honour, or whether I wanted to see if my imminent departure would push her into offering me a bargain. I was getting dressed when she tapped on the door of the guest-room and came in wearing a black, thigh-length silk dressing gown.

'Where will you go?' she asked in a voice which sounded like she was really concerned about me.

'Don't worry,' I said as I put my wallet and car keys into the pockets of my trousers. 'They won't find me.'

'But I am worried.' She left the door and came over to me and took my hand and kissed it. 'I don't want you to be killed.'

'What is this, Alice? Be kind to dumb animals week?'

She let go of my hand. 'I thought you had more style than that, Nick.'

'I'm sorry,' I said, shaking my head. She was right, whatever game we were playing I shouldn't have said that to her. It was cheap. 'Please, I'm sorry. It's just that ...'

'OK, no offence taken,' she said, patting my arm. '... look, why don't you stay here for a few days, it'll be safer than dodging around London. There's nothing to connect us together, is there?'

I shook my head. 'No.'

'Well then, you'll have time to decide what to do next. What do you think?'

I thought that if circumstances were different the idea of being locked up with her for a couple of days was too good to miss.

'Why should you risk your neck for me?'

'I like you, Nick. You haven't talked about yourself but

168

I'm pretty sure we have a lot in common. And you're against the BNDP and I think you're on the run from them, and,' she punched me lightly on my chest, 'you're nowhere near as tough as you make yourself out to be. In my book that's a good enough reason to offer to help someone. Do you want me to get on my knees and beg you to stay?'

I put my hands on her shoulders and touched her forehead with my lips. 'You're a great lady, Alice. I'm sorry about my cheap remark earlier … I don't want to involve you in this business, it could be very dangerous.'

'Think about it,' she said.

I knew myself well enough to know that I'd spent the last couple of years in an emotional desert; making love to Alice had turned my feelings about her into a hopeless tangle and something told me that if I stayed, she'd probably wheedle the whole story out of me while we lay in bed together. But if I stayed with her I'd be well out of Smithson's way. The only clue to my whereabouts was the Ford Rob had given me, parked a quarter of a mile away down Stanmore Hill. I trusted Rob and she'd told me it was clean, I didn't think there was the slightest chance Smithson could trace it to me. Finally I told myself that if I stayed with Alice I'd get to know her better and I could start talking about a bargain for my information – before she got it out of me through her sexual endeavours.

I walked into Alice's kitchen with my mind made up to accept her offer.

'I'd like to take you up on your offer, if that's OK,' I said, standing by her fridge with my thumbs hooked in my trouser's belt loops, like I was Gary Cooper in *High Noon*.

She smiled. 'Good. Help yourself to some more coffee and go and read the papers. After I get dressed I'll start the lunch. After all,' she said, giving me a sly smile, 'we have to keep your strength up.'

She was a perceptive girl, but then, it didn't take much to see through my disguise in that area of our newly formed relationship.

The sun of the previous day had disappeared behind gunmetal cloud and light snow was falling as we sat down to lunch and the door bell rang.

'I'll get it,' she said. 'I'm expecting a packet from the studios.'

She was on her way out before my mental faculties had begun to work at full speed. I ran out of the kitchen and along the glass walled corridor and I was within a metre of her when she unwittingly opened her front door to a gun, with a man's hand on the end of it. The door shielded me from his view but his partner had seen me coming down the corridor and he shouted a warning. I kicked the door and he bellowed with pain as it banged against his wrist, knocking the gun out of his hand. I threw my weight against the door and fumbled with the security chain, ignoring his renewed scream. The gun lay on the carpet just out of my reach. I started for it, but I checked and drew back as I saw the end of the other man's gun barrel poking through the gap. He fired and the bullet from his silenced revolver buried itself in the corridor wall, missing Alice and me by centimetres. I grabbed her arm and raced back down the corridor, pushing her in front of me. Our only way out was through the back door, unless there were three in the team. I opened the back door and I was pushing Alice through it when I heard the front door crash open. The chain had bought us less than ten seconds. I hoped it would be enough.

We were half way across her lawn when Alice slipped on the thin layer of snow and fell. I turned to help her but the uninjured man was within ten metres of her and moving fast. I saw him raise his gun and I stopped in my tracks.

'No!' she screamed, struggling to her feet.

He'd intended jumping over her half prone body but his feet slipped on the wet snow at the moment he took off and he fell on top of Alice. They both tumbled into a heap on the grass. He had the reactions of a professional and I stood there, paralysed, as he rolled away from her, aiming his gun at me.

'No!' Alice screamed again as she threw herself at his rolling body. He was lying stomach down on the grass and his attempt to push her away lacked power. She only jolted his gun hand momentarily. It was enough, and for the second time in less than a minute a bullet whistled past me. He tried to roll away from her to give himself the space for a clear shot.

I went through it afterwards, over and over again in vivid detail and while I was doing it I kept telling myself I couldn't have got to him before he'd squeezed off a third shot. I had to leave her. I know what heroes are supposed to do in situations like that, but looking into the black hole of his gun I knew I wanted to live. I didn't care for how long, just to live was enough. As I leapt over the low boundary fence and sprinted across Alice's neighbours' gardens the sound of her scream echoed and re-echoed in my head. She tried to save you! I kept thinking. And what will she get for it? I reached the main road which runs down Stanmore Hill, knowing that Smithson's people would take her away and get what information from her they could. And then what? The same treatment they'd given Harris? If that happened I might not be the one pulling the trigger but that was mere detail, I'd led them to her house and I was the one who'd really killed her. I knew one thing as I ran full pelt down Stanmore Hill to my car – I was going to see my business through with Smithson to the very end, no matter what it cost.

The car was standing in the small car park half way down Stanmore Hill where I'd left it. There was no time to check it for a bomb. I ripped a parking ticket off its windscreen and threw it away before getting in and driving south, heading back down the hill towards central London. I drove as fast as I dared, keeping an eye on the rearview mirror, until, when I reached Cricklewood I found myself in a stream of slow moving traffic. The light snow flurries were insufficient to keep the Saturday afternoon shoppers indoors and I made poor progress in the line of stopping and starting cars moving at a snail's pace along Cricklewood Broadway. Five cars behind mine was a red Volvo that had been with me for the last couple of miles. I turned right across the path of an on-coming truck and accelerated down a side street, took the first left and kept on going. I checked the mirror; the red Volvo was nowhere in sight. Keeping to the side roads I skirted Willesden and came out on the Harrow Road, near Kensal Green, and turned east into central London. It was a long way round but I knew I'd have a better chance of spotting if I was being followed.

Time: 15.05 hours

I parked the car in a side road off Baker Street just after three o'clock – almost three hours since I fled from Alice's house. I needed to disappear and I needed time to think about what the hell I was going to do next. I got out of the car and retrieved Rob's overnight bag from its boot before locking the doors. I shivered as the gentle blow of warm air from the car's efficient heater was replaced by a blast of icy cold wind that cut through my thin shirt; if I didn't get into the warm soon I'd freeze to death. Keeping a firm hold on my bag, I jogged back along the side road towards Baker Street, where I went into the first cinema I could find. As I paid for my ticket I thanked the gods for making me put my wallet and car keys into the pockets of my trousers when I'd been dressing in Alice's guest bedroom.

Downstairs in the waiting area outside the cinema's auditorium I went to the men's toilet, found an empty cubicle and proceeded to change into Martin's blue suit. I stuffed the grey trousers I'd been wearing into the bag and went and checked my appearance in the mirror before going out of the toilet and through to the nearly empty auditorium and settling myself into a large soft seat, immediately adjacent to an emergency exit. OK, I thought as the warmth begin to return to my body, what the fuck do I do now?

I looked at the images on the screen. The new morality insisted that film makers concentrate on showing the wholesome side of human life – movies about happy families with loving parents and cute kids and even cuter family pets. It was a million miles away from the reality of my world which existed outside on the streets. The fear of AIDS, or the casual, bruising encounter with a gang of BNDP toughs were no part of the fantasy existence of the smug, white, middle-class family in the movie, whose only concern seemed to be that their peaches and cream daughter would marry a nice boy with an even nicer job. Even when judged on its own terms the family portrayed on the screen seemed to lack a vital ingredient. Perhaps it was because they never showed any outward sign of love, like a kiss, but since actors' unions everywhere had banned their members kissing in any performance, out of fear of AIDS, film directors had had to fall back on gestures or close ups of their character's eyes to indicate their feelings.

It wasn't a movie I'd have seen out of choice. When Ann and our unborn child had been killed I'd realised a loving family had been denied to me for ever and thereafter I'd been careful not to expose myself to any situations which would prompt me to reflect on my life as it might have been. My mind blanked out the argument on the screen about who were to be the eldest daughter's bridesmaids and I returned to the problem of how Smithson had traced me to Alice's house. During the drive back from Stanmore Hill I'd thought of nothing else and I'd decided there was only one possible explanation.

When I'd been watching my flat on the previous afternoon I hadn't given a thought to whether one of Smithson's team might be sitting in a car parked further along my road. Terry knew his job and he was good at it, and it was just the sort of precaution he would take to ensure the people he'd left in my flat wouldn't be caught off guard if I suddenly turned up. But I'd been so busy waiting to see if anyone was inside my flat I'd never given the matter a moment's thought. The more I thought about it the more sense it made. As soon as I'd driven off after Terry, the guy in the car would have given me a couple of minutes and then set off after me, to become a third member of our little convoy and I'd been so concerned to keep up with Terry it hadn't occurred to me to check to see if I was being followed. The only difficulty with my explanation was that I couldn't understand why Smithson hadn't picked me up earlier; he'd had plenty of opportunity, both at the hotel and on the way out to Stanmore Hill. But perhaps by then, I thought, he was more interested in finding what you were up to.

The house lights came up and I looked at my watch – it was just after four fifteen. It would still be light outside the cinema. I went out to the thinly peopled foyer, bought some chocolate and returned to my seat. I was back in my seat in the darkness, unwrapping the silver foil from the chocolate bar when the feeling of remorse, which I'd held at arm's length since I'd driven away from Stanmore Hill, finally overtook me. How could you have run off and left Alice? I askd myself, over and over again. How could you? At first I told myself I'd had no choice, but I knew I wasn't telling the truth. The truth was that I was fit and I'd had a better than a fifty fifty chance to disable the man with the gun. If I'd tackled him when he'd tripped over Alice and gone sprawling on to the lawn I could have kicked the gun out of his hand and knocked him senseless in a few seconds.

You know the moves you should have made, I lectured myself. Christ, you're almost as good as you were when you were at university, you'd have taken him easily, but you didn't, did you? While Alice was fighting to save your life you just turned and ran. And now Smithson's got her. You spineless bastard, Gorman. What happened to all those brave thoughts you had when you were in the car at Hemel Hempstead, eh? All those things you promised yourself, like not being pushed around anymore and standing up for something. What happened to them? Your tough guy act didn't last long, did it? You let Alice do the fighting. And what's happening to her now? Have you thought about that?

I tried to shut out the images, not the honey sweet cloying images on the screen as the BNDP's advertisement pleaded for all good and decent English men and women to join them to create a cleaner, brighter, make believe world, but the images of the real world. The world being created by the BNDP, in which a dangerous psychopath like Terry Bannister could get a job in the civil service in a department headed up by someone like Smithson. I knew what Terry did with good looking girls he caught before he took them to the Care Centre's holding compounds. He was careful not to draw blood for fear the girls would be confirmed as antibody positive, but you couldn't catch AIDS from bruises caused by a thick leather belt. And that's what Terry used on them; he'd take them to a deserted house, strip them and thrash their naked flesh while they screamed and begged for mercy.

The wardens at the holding compounds couldn't care less about the state of the people we brought in and if they did, or if the girls Terry had beaten complained, it was a waste of time. 'Resisting capture' was the standard get-out if a heavy complained and even if they were found to be antibody negative and released they were unlikely to get redress, unless they had money or influence, and Terry and those like him took care not to indulge their pleasure on people like that. When I'd found out what he did I'd gone to see our case manager, but Sheila had told me to mind my own business unless I wanted trouble. I began to think of what he might do to Alice: she wasn't infected by the virus and he'd know that ... my stomach went tight and I threw the chocolate on the floor as I imagined her terrified screams.

Time: 17.00 hours

I came out of the cinema on to Baker Street filled with a cold resolve. As I saw it I had to continue with my original plan to discover why Smithson had had Harris killed; if I could find out something to blackmail him with I might be able to bargain for Alice's life and mine. If all else failed I'd have to kill him, because as far as I could see it was the only way to stop him hunting me, and if he'd killed Alice I'd kill him anyway.

I'd almost reached the side road off Baker Street where I'd parked the car when I met a small gang of BNDP skinheads. There were three of them and they were taunting a couple of young Pakistani kids – a boy and his girlfriend.

'Here!' The tall, brawny skinhead with the letters BNDP tattoed across his forehead grabbed hold of my arm. He looked about eighteen. 'What do you think of this mate?' he asked hoarsely. I could smell the beer on his breath. 'I mean, look at these two.' He pointed at the two Pakistanis. The girl was clutching her boyfriend's arm, her brown eyes wide with fright and reddened with tears. 'Fucking cheek,' the skinhead swore, 'out on the streets of London like this. This is our fucking country. You fucking niggers,' he shouted at them. He turned towards me. 'What do you say, mate?'

'Go home,' I said to the Pakistani boy, whose eyes were darting at each of the skinheads in turn. 'Get a taxi and go straight home. It's not safe to be out on a Saturday night.' The young Pakistani tightened his grip round his girlfriend's shoulders but before he could start walking the skinhead who'd accosted me pushed him in the chest.

'You stay where you are, you black bastard,' he shouted. 'We'll sort you and your piece of black cunt out in a minute. Now, you nigger lover –' he said taking a half pace towards me.

I don't know what the skinhead expected, but what he got was the heel of my palm hitting him upwards on the point of his chin. My forearm was stiff and rigid and I wasn't in the mood to worry about things like not killing him. I felt and heard his jawbone crack, and as he fell backwards on to the pavement I knew that for the next month or two he wouldn't be in any condition to shout foul-mouthed taunts at young Pakistani couples.

'You f ...' the oath from the fat skinhead stopped as I

hit him below the heart and as he doubled over and his head dropped level with my waist I took a half step past him, drove the point of my right elbow into his right kidney, pivoted on the balls of my feet into the crouched fighting stance and kicked his legs from under him.

'You want some too?' I hissed at the third skinhead as his fat friend face's slapped hard against the pavement, but I could see by the look in his eyes that he didn't. He turned and ran off down Baker Street.

I looked around, but passers-by were walking quickly and finding all sorts of interesting things to look at on the blank windows and walls of the empty office buildings on the other side of the road.

'Where do you live?' I asked the Pakistani boy, ignoring his offer of thanks.

'Willesden,' he said.

'Have you got enough money for a taxi?'

'Yes,' he said, 'But they won't stop for us.'

'Then why in Christ's sake didn't you get home in daylight? Don't you know how dangerous ...' I stopped. Why shouldn't he be out after dark? What sort of a world were we in when he and his girlfriend couldn't go out and enjoy themselves like everyone else. 'Look, I'm sorry. Let's see if I can help you. Come on,' I said, stepping into the road and flagging down a taxi.

The cab pulled up and the driver leaned over and pulled down his nearside front window. He was in his early forties with deeply set eyes.

'I'm not taking them,' he said, looking past my shoulder at the two young Pakistanis. 'You're OK. But not them.'

I took out my tracer's ID and shoved it under his nose.

'Recognise this?'

He looked at my ID, then looked up at me and gulped.

'Yes.' I nodded conspiratorially at him. 'You recognise it all right.' I gave him my most intimidating smile. 'These kids live in Willesden. What's the address?' I asked the Pakistani boy who was standing next to me, holding on to his girlfriend. He said it loud enough for the cab driver to hear.

'You hear that?' I asked the driver.

He nodded his head.

'You take 'em there.' I opened the door for the couple to get in the back, before looking into the front nearside window at the cable. 'I've got the number of your cab, so you make sure you take them to where they want to go. If I hear otherwise I'll look you up on the computer and next time you see my ID I'll be on official business. Got me?'

He swallowed hard. 'I'll take 'em guv. Don't worry.'

'I'm not worried,' I replied. 'I won't be the one in a Special Care Centre,' I added to make my threat explicit.

'Thank you so much,' called the girl in the second before the cab drove off.

'Forget it,' I said. 'You wouldn't understand but in a way you've helped me too.'

I stepped back on to the pavement as the taxi drove off.

'Did you do this?' asked a short, thickset man, pointing at the two prostrate skinheads. I noticed the bronze celtic cross in the lapel of his cheap leather coat.

I looked down at the two street level representatives of the BNDP. The one with the broken jaw who'd thought I was his mate was moaning softly while the other one was still out cold. It was a cardinal rule among those who did karate as a sport that you didn't use your lethal skills in the street unless there was no alternative. I knew my first reaction had been to hurt them, and hurt them badly, and I'd never even considered reasoning with them. I knew I should have felt guilty, but I didn't.

'Come on, Eric,' said the man's wife, tugging his arm. 'It's none of our business.'

He swung round on her. 'What do you mean none of our business?' he almost shouted. 'These two lads,' he pointed to the two skinheads stretched out on the pavement, 'are Party members.'

'Do you want to join them?' I asked fiercely, sticking my face in his. ' 'Cos if not you better fuck off. Now!'

'Come on, Eric,' repeated his wife, still pulling him by the arm.

Come on, Eric, I thought as I recalled the sight of Alice

struggling with Smithson's gunman, just open your fucking mouth once more and I'll close it for you. Eric gave me one last look before allowing his wife to drag him away, but I knew he'd be giving my description to the first policeman he met. I picked up my bag, turned away and ran down the poorly lit side street to where I'd parked the car. Don't fool yourself, I told myself as I unlocked the car and settled myself in the driving seat, those two skinheads weren't in your division and they don't even begin to put you in credit for running out on Alice. You can feel proud of yourself when you start hurting Smithson. But you moved well, I thought, you know now that you've still got that old instant reaction and you going to need it when you're up against guys like Terry.

I drove to the bottom of the side street, turned right and headed towards Mayfair and Charles Motte's gallery. The previous night I'd been sure that Alice and Motte were involved in something together and it was something which had outlasted their love affair. If Motte was still alive he might be able to answer some of my questions about Harris and Rayleigh. He might be a useful ally too, and God knows I needed one. It wasn't much, but it was a start, and if he refused to help me I'd take the fight to Smithson.

Time: 17.40 hours

I walked past Motte's gallery on the other side of the street. I deliberately didn't look across at it because I wanted to scout round before I did anything and I'd parked the car a couple of streets away, just in case some of Smithson's representatives were already at the gallery. Mayfair isn't the sort of area you find people loitering around in shop doorways and there was nobody watching his place that I could detect. Nevertheless I walked back up the street to make sure. When I was certain I turned round again and stopped opposite the gallery.

It was full of people with wine glasses in their hands. I

hadn't anticipated walking in on a viewing. Still, I thought it was a good sign because it meant Motte must still be alive and there was a reasonable chance we'd both stay that way if I could talk to him in a crowd. Smithson might be involved in a secret BNDP project but even they wouldn't want the risk of a wild shooting in a crowded Mayfair gallery; they might kill some of their rich supporters for one thing and even their publicity machine would be hard pressed to put a gloss on an act of terrorism of that magnitude. I shivered. Without the sheepskin coat I was cold. I counted to five before walking across the road and in through the gallery's grey smoked glass doors.

'Do you have an invitation?'

I'd opened the gallery's door and found myself face to face with Motte's female assistant.

'Do you have an invitation?' she insisted haughtily, looking me up and down, taking in my appearance.

The blue suit was only slightly crumpled and I hoped it gave me the air of careless wealth. I could see by the look in her eyes that Motte's assistant approved of Martin's tastes. I searched my inside jacket pocket and then patted its other pockets absentmindedly while I scanned the crowded gallery for a sight of Motte.

'I'm sorry, I must have left it in the car,' I said, giving her my best smile. 'Surely you're not going to make me go out in the cold and get it?'

I'd always tended to go by my first impressions of people and so far she'd done nothing to shake my opinion that she was an upper class bitch who regarded anyone outside her own immediate circle as a lower life form.

'Well …' she hesitated, half convinced I was someone who it might not be politic to be rude to. She looked carefully at me. 'Haven't we met before?'

'Rather,' I replied, trying to sound like an officer in the Life Guards. 'I'm always at jaunts like this.'

She eyed me narrowly, perhaps she didn't know any Guards officers.

'Wait a minute,' she said, putting one of her perfectly manicured hands against my chest to prevent me moving

180

away from the gallery door. 'You're the man from the gas board.' Her attitude changed in a moment. 'I'm sorry,' she said curtly pushing me in the chest, 'but you can't interrupt Mister Motte now. He's far too busy to see someone like you. You'll have to come back on Monday.'

She started to move towards me. With most people it would have been a signal to edge backwards rather than invade her personal space. I stood my ground and scanned the crowd for Motte, ignoring her request for me to leave. I glimpsed a sight of him in the middle of a small huddle of attentive viewers; he was talking animatedly and pointing at the pictures on the walls.

'I'm sorry,' I said, taking her hand away from my chest and forcing my way past her. 'I have to speak to Charles.'

Before she could stop me I was inside and politely but firmly pushing my way through the crowd. I heard her surprised cry of 'Wait!' behind me, but I kept going. I snatched a glass of champagne from a passing waiter's tray and insinuated myself into the group of people around Motte and reached over and touched his arm.

'Alice sent me,' I said as he turned to look at me. 'It's very urgent.'

His eyes narrowed as he gave me the once over. At that moment his assistant joined the little throng of people.

'I'm sorry, Charles,' she said breathlessly. 'He simply forced his way in. I couldn't stop him.'

'That's all right, Gwen,' Motte replied. 'This gentlemen has a message for me.'

But his voice said he and I knew that in his opinion I was no gentlemen and the expression in Gwen's eyes confirmed it. He took hold of my arm and steered me into a quiet corner, away from the viewers, by the spiral staircase that went up to his apartment. He was very tall – nearly half a head taller than me – and he had the body of an athlete. A rich diet had stretched his girth and puffed out his cheeks but he was still pretty fit and I began to decide the best way to take him if things got rough. Good lad, I thought after I'd noted my reaction, you're getting sharper.

'Now,' he snapped, once we were out of earshot of the crowd. 'What the hell's all this about? Who are you?'

'That doesn't matter right now,' I said. 'Look, I've come here to warn you.'

'Warn me about what?'

'Alice Townsend's been kidnapped. She might even be dead.' I said it without emotion.

Motte's handsome, dark, almost Latin good looks crumbled and his brown eyes went misty. He looked like the skinhead I'd hit under the heart. As he rocked backwards I grabbed both his arms to steady him and helped him sit on the bottom step of the spiral staircase. Gwen, who'd been watching us, came over and knelt beside him and put her arms round his shoulder. With his face and physique and easygoing charm it was easy to see how he held women in thrall.

'Darling, what's the matter?' she whispered softly, her voice full of concern.

It wasn't the sort of concern an employee might show to an employer, even if he was good looking and benevolent. I guessed she was in love with him.

She turned on me. 'What have you done?' Her eyes shone with anger. 'Who are you? What do you want here?'

This time I instinctively moved backwards as her anger invaded my personal space.

'You bastard!' she hissed. 'Get out of here or I'll have you thrown out.'

She looked past me, trying to catch the eye of one of the waiters.

'It's all right, Gwen,' Motte reassured her. He rose, none too steadily, from the step. 'Let's not make a scene,' he said, glancing at the viewers.

Most of them were in the main area of the gallery with their backs towards us and no one seemed to have noticed the emotional eruption which was boiling beneath the smooth surface of the laughter and smart talk about art.

Gwen took hold of Motte's arm and looked up at him. 'What has this man said to you, darling?' she asked him earnestly, while giving me a look of unconcealed hatred.

'It's OK, darling,' he replied and patted her arm with his free hand. 'It's about Alice. It came as a bit of a shock, that's all.'

Motte had regained his composure; apart from his slightly flushed face he showed no sign that anything untoward had happened. I wondered whether it was something they taught you at Cambridge.

'Please tell me, Charles,' she pleaded. 'It must be awful to have upset you so terribly.'

'I'm fine now, honestly.' He bent down and kissed her lightly on the cheek. 'Now, we're ignoring our guests.' He scanned the crowd. 'Look, poor old Gonzales has been trapped by that terrible woman. We don't want one of his famous tantrums, it'll be bad for business. Go and rescue him, there's a love. I'll tell you about it later. I promise.' He patted her bottom and pointed towards a short, dark, swarthy man dressed in a pale green suit.

Gwen gave me another savage look and made her way over to the Spaniard whose work was the cause of all the admiration while Motte took hold of my arm again and steered me towards the spiral staircase.

'We can talk upstairs. Gwen can handle things down here,' he said as he bowed stiffly from the waist, indicating I should go up to his apartment.

Time: 18.00 hours

Motte showed me into his sitting room, turned on the table lamp, closed the curtains and asked me to sit down.

'I need a drink first,' he said. 'I expect you could do with one too.'

I did need a drink. His reaction to my news about Alice had rekindled all my feelings of self-recrimination and I wasn't sure I could talk about her without some alcohol inside me.

'Scotch or brandy?' he asked, peering into the genuine art deco drinks cabinet.

'Scotch,' I replied. 'Please.'

'Damn,' he said softly. 'I told her to get some more in.'

'Brandy will be fine,' I said. I didn't care what it was as long as it was alcohol.

'No, it's OK. I've another bottle in the kitchen.'

Motte excused himself and slipped into the kitchen. I looked round his sitting room with its muted gold and blue Sanderson wallhangings and contrasting covers on the sofa and armchairs and his expensive prints and knick-knacks. There was no doubt about it – Motte was doing very nicely flogging off Senor Gonzales's pictures. He came back with a bottle of scotch and two glasses he'd already filled with the golden brown spirit. He put both glasses and the bottle down on the small glass topped table in front of me.

'Would you like anything in it?' he said pointing to the glass nearest to me.

'No, I'll take it straight,' I said.

'Me too,' he said.

For some reason I can't explain I suddenly remembered an article I'd read in a Sunday colour supplement years earlier which had criticised the practice of giving your guests a drink which you'd poured out in another room. According to the socialite who'd written the article it was a habit to be frowned on by those who mixed in the right circles. On an impulse I got out of my armchair and went over to the window and peeped through the curtains. Someone had parked a Mercedes on the other side of the road immediately opposite the gallery.

'Do you know anyone who owns a silver Mercedes?' I asked Motte.

'Christ! You weren't followed here were you?' he replied, as he started to come over to the window. 'What's its number?'

I left the window before he joined me there and went back as quickly as I dared to my armchair.

'Recognise it?' I asked as he drew back a corner of the curtains and looked into the street.

'No,' he said. 'But, I think ...' I made sure his attention was absorbed with what was happening outside in the street and then swapped our glasses.

'It's OK,' he said. 'They've driven off.' He breathed out a sigh of relief.

'Don't worry,' I said. 'I took care not to be followed.' I raised the glass he'd intended to drink from to my lips.

'Cheers,' I said and swallowed some of his scotch.

He came over and sat opposite me, picked up the glass he'd originally offered to me and took a large gulp from it.

'Now, Mister ...?'

'Gorman,' I supplied him with my name. I couldn't see the point of being devious. He might be a useful ally and a lie wouldn't be a propitious way to start an accord.

'Look,' I said. 'I know you want to hear about Alice but it will be simpler if you let me tell the story from the beginning. Believe me, it will make more sense that way.'

Motte stared at me. 'Is Alice dead?'

'I don't know.' I drank some more of the scotch. 'She may be.'

Motte held up his hand to his forehead. 'Oh my God! How?'

This is it, I told myself, there's no going back now, your hunch that Motte and Alice are on opposite sides from Smithson had better be right.

'By a man called Smithson,' I said. 'Well, not actually by him, but some people who work for him.'

Motte stared at me again. I wasn't sure whether he believed me, but I'd noted he hadn't reacted when I mentioned Smithson's name.

'Who are these people, Mister Gorman?'

'Smithson is in the SHA. He's in charge of the London Tracing Departments.'

'I see,' said Motte quietly. 'No I don't see. What's all this got to do with Alice?'

'Well ...' I said, but Motte broke into my explanation before I could continue.

'How are you mixed up in this,' he asked.

'She was putting me up?'

'Putting you up?' he spluttered incredulously, as if the thought that she'd even let me over her front door mat was preposterous.

'Yes,' I continued. 'Putting me up. I was with her when they came to her house.'

'But you escaped?' His question sounded like an accusation.

I couldn't tell him the truth; I felt too ashamed about running out on her, and I wasn't going to expose myself to his superior attitudes about what a decent fellow would have done. When I'd worked in hospital management most of the medical consultants I'd regularly crossed swords with had been 'decent fellows'. My experiences with them had taught me that 'decent fellows' were rude, sexist and tyrannical with their staff and anyone else whom they perceived to be subordinate to themselves.

'I managed to get us out of the house,' I said, 'and we were running across the garden when ...' I couldn't finish. I sat, looking at the carpet through a wet mist.

'How did you get away, after ...' He couldn't bring himself to say the words either.

I told him about leaving the Ford in the car park at Stanmore Hill.

'And you're sure you weren't followed?' He got up and went over to the window and peered through the curtains again.

I swivelled round in my chair and watched him looking up and down the street. 'I was careful. I've told you, don't worry, there's no one on my tail.'

I was sure now he and Alice were working together. That left me the problem of finding out who they were working for – the Conservative Party was still my best guess. He and Alice both seemed like types who would be ardent supporters of the Conservatives.

Motte left the window and sat down in the armchair opposite me. 'Why did you come here, Gorman?'

I made a mental note that he'd stopped calling me Mister Gorman. Was that because he'd pigeonholed me as a working-class lout, or was it because he'd decided to think of me as a friend? It's always difficult to be sure of these things with the British upper-middle classes. But his question was a reasonable one and on the drive over from

Baker Street I'd thought of a couple of answers. I considered them and decided that the truth would be best.

'I know you and Alice were involved with Harris,' I said.

'I see,' he said evenly.

He drained the rest of his scotch in one swallow and refilled both our glasses.

'There's plenty of time, Mister Gorman. Gwen can manage things downstairs. Drink your scotch and tell me your story. I'm sorry, I interrupted you before. I think you're right.' He sat back in his armchair. 'It probably would be better if you started from the beginning.'

Back to Mister Gorman, I thought – was that significant? But there was no retreat now. I'd have to tell Motte the whole story, or parts of it, anyway. I felt an irresistible urge to tell him, or anyone, about how I'd spent my time over the last forty-eight hours. I remembered an article I'd read somewhere on the psychology of interrogation and how people felt the need to confess, even to things they hadn't done. It was working on me. I suppose it was also a reaction to the shock of what had happened at Alice's house. I was going to keep back two pieces of information though, because once Motte knew the whereabouts of Rayleigh I wouldn't be any use to him and I thought it safer to keep quiet about the plot I'd discovered to solve the long term problem of the AIDS crisis.

Motte sat quietly while I drained the last of the scotch in my glass and cleared my throat. I hadn't got farther than telling him where I worked when I noticed he was having difficulty keeping his eyes open.

'Are you OK, Motte?' I asked.

'I'm fine, Gorman, just keep talking,' he slurred.

He wasn't fine – anybody could see that. Motte tried to lever himself out of his chair but his legs buckled under him and he collapsed on to his knees on the Indian carpet. I stood up.

'You …' He looked dozily at me, then at the empty glass in my hands and at his half empty glass on the small glass topped table.

I nodded. 'Just a simple precaution, Mister Motte,' I said

as he fell face forwards onto the carpet at my feet.

I whistled once, softly, through my teeth. My instinct about him filling the glasses in the kitchen had been right – he had put some sort of knockout drug in my glass – and if I hadn't acted on impulse and switched our glasses I'd have been the one stretched out on his beautiful Indian carpet. I bent down and rolled Motte over on to his back. His breathing was strong and regular. I felt his pulse – it was OK too. I took his wallet out of his jacket pocket and emptied its contents on to the carpet; money, credit cards, a book of stamps and half a dozen of his business cards – that was it. I checked the rest of his pockets and found some small change and a black and white spotted silk handkerchief.

I was sure if Gwen had known of Motte's intention to drug me it wouldn't be long before she came up the spiral staircase to the apartment. I rolled Motte over on to his side to make sure he wouldn't choke to death on his tongue before searching quickly through the drawers in his small writing desk. There was nothing. Or to be more precise there were lots of things in his drawers; my problem was I didn't have too much of an idea about what I was looking for, except perhaps an address book, and I couldn't find one of those. The only thing I found which had any utility was an automatic pistol with a box containing twenty-five bullets. I don't know much about guns, but I can read, and the inscription inside the top of its black leathercloth presentation case said it was a Walther PPK and I'd seen enough spy movies to know it was supposed to be a reliable automatic with a lot of stopping power. Well, I thought, as I stuffed the Walther in the waistband of my trousers and the small box of eight millimetre bullets in my pocket, courtesy of Charles Motte, you've now got the means to kill Smithson, all you've got to do is to find him.

I let myself out of the sitting-room and walked slowly down the spiral staircase. Gwen must have seen my descent because as I reached the bottom step she was coming through the crowd to meet me.

'Is Charles all right?' she asked anxiously.

188

'He's fine. He said he wanted to be left on his own. He'll be down in about ten minutes.'

'What did you tell him about Alice?' she asked viperously.

I wondered why Gwen disliked me so much, or was she jealous of Alice because she knew Alice and Motte had been lovers. Apart from deceiving her in my role as a gas board official I couldn't see that I'd given her any reason to be so hostile.

'How much do you know about Charles's business?' I asked casually.

'Just because you've come from the General, don't think you can intimidate me.' She said it fiercely enough, but her eyes told a different story, and I realised, in the instant, that her dislike of me had nothing to do with our respective social positions – she was scared of me, very scared. And I was sure it was because she thought I'd come as a messenger for someone known as 'the General'.

Motte must work for him. And Alice too? Was that why they'd been together with Harris at Hemel Hempstead, because they both worked for the General? But who the hell was he? And how was I going to find out? A scene from an old 1960s American movie I'd seen recently on TV came into my mind. Its main character had been an anti-hero criminal, played by an actor called Lee Marvin, who'd pursued a single-minded vendetta against a crime syndicate. It occurred to me that I had a lot in common with the movie character; each move he'd made had led to him getting more entangled with the people he was trying to outwit. I moved very close to Gwen and she backed away until her shoulders made contact with the wall by the side of the spiral staircase. I put my arms round the small of her back and pulled her body close up to mine, so that she'd feel the hard steel of the Walther pressing against her flat belly.

'What has Charles told you about the General?' I whispered menacingly, my mouth next to her ear.

She caught her breath. 'Nothing,' she gasped. 'Nothing. He hasn't told me anything. I only know he works for him.'

'And Alice too?' I said, as if I already knew the answer to

189

my question.

She didn't answer.

'Come on, Gwen, tell me what you know about Alice,' I said, doing what Lee Marvin had done in an almost identical situation. The frightened woman he'd been intimidating hadn't stopped him brushing her neck and cheek with his lips and Gwen didn't try to stop me either. I could feel her body trembling through her thin dress.

'I think she and Charles both work for the General, but that's all I know. Please, let me go.'

'Tell me what Charles has told you about the General.' I whispered, my lips touching her ear. Her perfume smelt heavy and hypnotic.

'Oh please,' she whimpered. 'Don't hurt me. Charles hasn't told me anything. I just know he works for someone called the General, that's all. I don't know anything more, please, I don't know any more, honestly.'

I moved my hands up her back and held her away from me by her shoulders and studied her face. The sheen on her skin and her professionally-applied make-up reminded me of Alice; both of them could have found work as fashion models for *Vogue* or *Harper's Bazaar*, but her cool air of self possession had vanished and she now had the same look that I'd seen in the eyes of the young Pakistani girl.

'Please,' she whispered, her breath coming in short gasps. 'Don't hurt me, please.'

'So you don't know anything about the General?' I said, wondering whether she was telling me the truth.

In the movie, Lee Marvin had dragged the woman into a room, and once out of sight of a crowd of party goers he'd pushed the barrel of his gun into her mouth and threatened to blow her head off if she refused to tell him what he wanted to know. I thought about taking Gwen into the storeroom at the back of the gallery and doing the same thing, but I hadn't the stomach for it and I reckoned I'd learned everything I could from her.

'Take a tip from me, Gwen.' I growled, stroking the side of her cheek with the back of my hand. 'Keep it that way, it'll be safer.' I let her go, turned on my heel and made my way through the crowd.

'My, my,' said a woman who was standing near the edge of the crowd, as she put her hand on my arm. 'Don't tell me you're Gwen's, too? She is a dark horse. Where's she been hiding you?' she purred.

Like the character Marvin had played I knew anyone who'd been watching my close encounter with Gwen would have jumped to the conclusion that we'd been sharing a swift embrace while Motte was upstairs in his apartment.

I looked through the crowd towards Gwen, who was standing by the stairs hugging herself. I knew it was a reaction prompted by fear but I could see how the woman who'd accosted me could perceive it as a manifestation of sexual hunger.

I smiled at the woman. 'Gwen and I are just good friends, er …?'

'I'm Amanda,' she said. 'Well, my dear, she seems to be very upset about you leaving. You must have something to make Gwen feel like that.'

Amanda tightened her grip on my arm. She was a good deal older than Gwen, I guessed in her mid forties, but I could see she came from the same stable. Tall, sleek and glossy, she had a young woman's body that belied the lines on her face that she'd skilfully concealed with cosmetics. She turned her head and her well-cut silver blonde hair brushed the shoulders of her mink shawl.

'He's mine,' she said, pointing to an Italian-looking boy who looked about twenty-five years old who was talking to Gonzales. 'A bit wild, but such a dear.' She turned back and looked at me with the same frank, lustful arrogance which some men bestow on women that they crave for; I felt like a stallion being inspected by a prospective owner. 'If you and Gwen fall out, why not give me a call?' She smiled apologetically. 'I shall want to see your ID though of course. Just to be sure.'

I patted her arm. 'Do I get to see yours?'

'Well, naturally,' she said softly. 'One can't be too careful these days. Can one?'

'No,' I agreed. 'One can't.'

'We're going on to dine. Would you care to join us?'

'I'm sorry,' I said. 'I have a previous engagement.'

'Anyone I know?'

'I don't think so. It's a bit of a chore really,' I said. 'I'd much rather be having dinner with you.'

'Anytime,' she said. 'What's your name by the way.'

'Gorman, Nick Gorman,' I said. 'Charles can tell you all about me.'

I decided to play out the role she'd cast me in to the end. 'Bye,' I said, leaning over to kiss her cheek.

She slipped her hand round my neck and kissed me hard on my mouth.

'Bye, darling,' she breathed as she released me. 'Keep in touch.'

I came out of the gallery, wiped Amanda's lipstick off my mouth and smiled as I thought about a scene in which we inspected each other's blood test dates to be sure neither of us had the virus before we got into bed. I'd never had the inclination for casual sex, even before the crisis, but for those who still felt the need to be promiscuous an inspection of each other's blood test dates was an obligatory part of the courtship ritual.

As I walked back to my car I tried to picture the scene after Gwen found Motte fast asleep on his sitting room carpet. It would probably be at least a couple of hours before he emerged from the effects of the drug he'd intended for me and when he did he'd probably call the General – whoever he was – and by that time I'd be the other side of London.

Time: 20.30 hours

I pulled up and reversed into a spot between two cars, turned off my lights and looked round. The part of Dulwich where Smithson lived was quietly fashionable and aside from the cars parked on both sides of the road and the lights on in the windows of the houses there was no sign of life. I counted off the numbers on the large properties on the opposite side of the street; Smithson lived in the tenth one along from where I was parked. There were lights on in a downstairs room and I could make out his big Rover in the drive. I took out a match, split it in half and started to prise out the remains of one of MacDonald's double hamburgers from between two of my molars. I estimated I'd lost thirty or forty minutes through stopping to eat, but I hadn't had a meal since I'd breakfasted with Alice and I'd decided that I'd be better equipped to handle Smithson with some food in my stomach.

Digging out the trapped piece of ground beef from the gap in my teeth, I tried to decide whether Gwen had told me the truth. She didn't seem the sort of woman who was strong on physical courage. Christ, I thought, as I recalled the fear in her eyes, how did I get into this? With every twist and turn I was getting myself deeper and deeper into the mire. Now I had someone else to worry about; the General. Gwen's reaction when she thought I was working for him said he was a man to be feared. Was he someone who masterminded the BNDP's strongarm tactics, or did he operate on the other side? With politics the way they were it was impossible to be sure whether he worked for them or the Conservatives. I didn't think there'd be too many Generals who'd throw their weight in with the Labour Party and anyway, Labour were only spectators in the current struggle between the Right and the far Right. If he was a senior army officer I was sure he'd favour a party on the Right. But how far to the Right? He must be working for the Conservatives, I told myself. I was positive now that Alice and Motte both worked for him in some sort of clandestine role and I couldn't imagine them as BNDP supporters.

I gave up the struggle of trying to decide whose side the General was on; until I knew more I'd stick with my theory that he was with the Conservatives and he'd have to remain a mystery, and Gwen's reaction suggested it might be safer for me if I kept it that way. I thought again about the way she'd squirmed in terror as I'd pressed her body close to mine and she'd felt the Walther in the waistband of my trousers. What had happened to that nice guy in the white hat who'd ridden to the rescue of the Pakistani couple? Where had he gone? Was he the same man who'd experienced a thrill of sadistic pleasure while he'd held Gwen captive and touched her flesh with his lips. What was happening to me?

I tried to remember the way I'd felt when I'd first gone into hospital management; the feeling I'd had of wanting to help people. I'd carried that feeling like a torch. Had it burnt out when Ann had died, or while I'd been in the psychiatric hospital, or had it been extinguished in the slime and shit which surrounded everyone who worked as a tracer? That's the last time you hurt someone who doesn't deserve it, I promised myself, the very last time, from now on you're going to be the good guy wearing the white hat.

So what are you going to do now? I asked myself, you can't just walk up to Smithson's door and ask him what he's done with Alice. I'll wait here, I thought, and see if anything develops. I pushed the lever fixed into the side of my seat and reclined it a couple of notches. I'd taken a cheroot out of its packet and was on the point of lighting it when I had second thoughts; someone sitting in a car and smoking was a dead giveaway. I put it back in the packet and looked at the highly priced house that Smithson could never have afforded on the salary the Special Health Authority paid him. If the office rumours were right and his wife had the money she must have plenty of it.

Unlike some of the lower priced areas of London, Smithson's part of Dulwich had largely escaped the disastrous property slump which had followed on from the AIDS crisis. The houses in his road were owned by professional people who'd either stuck to one sexual partner or who'd taken precautions when they were having sex with people they didn't know well. It was the working-class girls and boys who'd ignored the warnings about the disease who constituted the majority of the

Special Care Centres' populations. They weren't kids any longer of course, most of them were in their late twenties and early thirties, but their lives were over, and the home-owning democracy that had been a vision of Margaret Thatcher had turned to ashes, as the houses which property developers had built for young and socially mobile working-class couples in the affluent South stood damp and empty, while the people who were supposed to buy them were housed in the Care Centres.

A car's headlights blazed momentarily in my driver's door mirror and I slid down in my seat. It drove past and stopped in the middle of the road, about two cars' lengths away from my Ford. I reached for Motte's Walther, took off the safety lever and cocked it. I'd stopped in a side street after I'd eaten my MacDonald's hamburger and spent a good ten minutes discovering how to load and cock it. I'd seen people doing it plenty of times in movies, but doing it for real was different and I'd taken my time to ensure I wouldn't fire the damn thing accidentally. Apart from the attention I'd draw if it went off, I was anxious not to blow a hole in myself. I cocked the Walther and pointed its evil-looking snout at the car. If they get out and come over I'm going to have to start shooting, I thought.

There was only one person in the car and he didn't get out. Instead, he flashed his headlights. I wound down my window a few inches and heard a car engine start up farther down the road. Christ! I hadn't been alone after all. A Nissan drove out from the rank of parked cars and the car which had just arrived followed it down the road, stopped and reversed into the newly vacated space. Now what's all that about? I thought. Did Smithson take the precaution of having someone on guard outside his house? And were they changing shifts? I'd seen enough of his street work to know it was the sort of thing he would do. But where would he get them from? The BNDP? Nobody in the office had ever mentioned it and besides he would need to employ at least three or four people to keep watch on his house on a twenty-four hour, seven days a week basis. Or was there two of us secretly watching him? And who was my fellow watcher working for – the General, perhaps?

I shifted my position to get a better look at the newcomer. The car was one of those small fast Renaults. I remembered I knew someone with a car like that and it was the same colour too. Its driver took off his hat and his long hair tumbled down to his shoulders. I was wrong, it wasn't a man, it was a woman. Surely it couldn't be her? She lit a cigarette and I caught a glimpse of her profile in the brief flare of her cigarette lighter. Holy Christ! I swore softly. It was her! What should I do? I sat quietly and thought about the answer for more than five minutes, until I decided my best idea was to seize the initiative. I eased myself over on to the passenger seat, checked the Walther again and put it into my jacket pocket before distributing the remaining eighteen loose bullets among my pockets. How could I get out of the car without the courtesy light going on when I opened a door?

After taking out a match from its box and sticking it between my front teeth I pulled back the handle on the passenger door and opened it wide enough for me to slide my hand into the gap between the front inner edge of the door and the door pillar, while my fingers hunted for the push switch that operated the courtesy light. It was nearly at the limit of its travel; another couple of millimetres and it would make the contact and the courtesy light would come on. I pushed it back inside the pillar with my thumb nail, opened the door wide with my other hand and edged myself out of the car and squatted on the pavement. Still holding the push switch inside its sheath with my thumb, I took the match out of my mouth and inserted it into the gap between slightly protruding switch and the barrel of its sheath. I pushed hard and the match slipped inside the sheath jamming the switch against the side of the barrel. With luck it would stay jammed when I removed my thumb. I took my thumb off the push switch; it stayed inside its sheath. I closed the door quickly, taking care not to shut it completely; it could stay like that until I came back to the car.

Crouching down, so that my head and body were below

the level of the windows of the vehicles which were parked on my side of the road, I worked my way along the pavement until I was about two cars behind the small Renault. The most difficult part of the manoeuvre would come when I crossed the road; the street lights weren't very bright, but if she glanced across at the mirror on her passenger door she'd see me for sure. My ears caught the sound of a car driving up to the junction further up the road, if the driver turned left and came down past Smithson's house he'd give me the cover I needed. The car stopped and drove off – it was coming my way. Taking the gun out of my pocket, I scurried into the space between two parked cars as it drew level with me and the second it passed I ran at the double across the road, on to the opposite pavement and past the car parked behind the Renault. As I put my hand on the driver's door handle on the Renault I prayed she'd worked in the office long enough to assimilate tracer's habits – because if she'd locked her door I was fucked.

The door was unlocked.

'Freeze!' I hissed urgently, leaning inside the Renault and jabbing the Walther's barrel against her right side. 'You make a sound and I'll kill you!'

Her mouth was open with shock.

'I mean it, Victoria, you make a noise and I'll kill you,' I repeated.

She closed her mouth and looked at me. It seemed to be my night for meeting women whose eyes were wide with fear.

I jabbed her again with the gun. 'Move over,' I ordered. She pushed herself on to the passenger seat and swung her legs over the Renault's gear lever.

I suddenly remembered I hadn't pushed the Walther's safety lever down. Still, she didn't know that, but it would be better to take precautions in case she tried to resist. I was glad now that I'd spent nearly all of my leisure time since I'd joined the SHA watching old movies.

'Sit on your hands,' I said.

'What?' she whispered.

'Sit on your hands,' I hissed back at her. 'Now!'

She shrugged her shoulders and put her hands under her backside. I got into the driver's seat, closed the door and locked it and sat looking at her in silence.

'What are you doing here?' she asked incredulously, breaking the tension.

I waved Motte's Walther at her. 'Shut up! I'm asking the questions.'

'Please,' she moaned softly. Her eyes seemed to be hypnotised by the gun. So much for the guy in the white hat, I thought, realising the promise I made to myself hadn't lasted more than twenty minutes. I clamped my back teeth together. For all I knew she was one of the members of Smithson's team, she could have spent the last few days hunting me. What choice did I have?

'Let's understand one another right from the start,' I said. 'If you shout out or do anything, anything at all except answer my questions I will shoot you. I mean it Victoria. Now, what are *you* doing here?'

She looked away from the gun and I saw her lips tighten. Victoria was a lot tougher than Gwen and I guessed she'd mistaken my initial silence when I'd got into her car as a sign I wasn't sure what to do. So what are you going to do, Gorman? I thought, this is the girl you were falling in love with, you can't hurt her, not unless she gives you good cause, you know you can't. I touched the safety lever on the Walther to check its safety was locked on.

'Victoria,' I said.

She turned her head and looked at me and I made sure she saw me pull the gun's hammer back. It clicked as it reached the limit of its travel. She tried to swallow but there was no saliva in her mouth.

Taking hold of her coat lapels I dragged her towards me and put the gun up to her mouth like Lee Marvin had done in the movie. Her body went rigid and she moved her head back instinctively as the end of its barrel pressed against her lips. I kept it against them; if she'd thought it was a toy gun its cold steel would have told her otherwise.

'I want you to think what will happen if I squeeze the

trigger …' I whispered. 'Just think hard about what you'll look like when the back of your head is running down the rear window …' I counted up to fifteen in my mind, hoping that this time the silence would be working for me. '…Now, for the last time, what are you doing here?'

Her body relaxed and I sensed her feeling of resignation. It was an attitude I'd seen before when I'd had to call for police help to pick up heavies who I suspected were armed. When the moment of decision came and they had to shoot or surrender and they realised that death, in the form of a stream of bullets from a police submachine-gun, was a guaranteed outcome, they'd resigned themselves to my custody. I suppose that life was so precious they preferred to opt for a grisly existence in a Special Care Centre rather than forgo life itself. The dull look in Victoria's eyes told me that she'd chosen the same option – life at all costs – and that I was in control. I took the gun away from her lips and she breathed out.

'I'm watching Smithson,' she said.

'Why?'

She hesitated and I brought the Walther up to her face.

'I've been watching him ever since I joined the Department. That's why I joined the Department – to watch Smithson.' The words came tumbling out of her mouth.

'Why?'

'To find out what he was up to. We couldn't understand where he was getting all his money from.'

'Who's "we"?'

'The people who sent me to work in the Department.'

'I know that, you stupid bitch.' I switched quickly to another line of attack. 'I thought his wife was supposed to be rich?'

Victoria shook her head. 'She's got some money, but nothing like the amount he's spending.'

'So where is his money coming from?'

'You work for him. Don't you know?'

'Me? Work for Smithson?' I smiled to myself. 'Don't fuck me around Victoria, I'm not in the mood for our office games. Now, where's does his money come from?'

'You don't work for Smithson?'

'I told you. No. Now stop fucking about.' I stuck the end of the Walther against her right cheek and pushed it gently. 'You're out of time, Victoria,' I said, tightening my grip on its butt as if I was bracing myself against the recoil as I fired it.

'He's using the SHA's computer to blackmail people,' she said quickly.

'Gays, you mean, don't you?' I said as I realised the implication of what she'd told me. I took the gun out of her face.

It was a scheme which had occurred to me during periods when I'd been at a spiritual low ebb and trying to find a quick way to make a lot of money. When the Test Stations had first been set up everyone between sixteen and fifty had been required to complete an official questionnaire which had included a question – the infamous Question 10 – which asked males to indicate their sexual orientation. At that time the concept of individual freedom was still alive and the National Council for Civil Liberties and Gay Rights groups had mounted campaigns to protest against Question 10 and the State's intrusion into the sexual preferences of its citizens. Rayleigh, who'd just been appointed as Minister of Health had placated the nation's male population by assuring us we wouldn't obliged to answer that particular question, and when the questionnaire was published Question 10 commenced with a preamble in bold type which said that while it wasn't obligatory to answer it, the information was necessary to help combat the AIDS crisis.

In common with the vast majority, when I'd answered Question 10 I'd put a cross in the box labelled 'heterosexual' and my name had been coded 'NS' (meaning 'not suspect') when it had been fed into the SHA's computer. Those who'd been fooled by the Government's publicity and had put a cross in the box labelled 'homosexual' were coded with a double H, while those who exercised their freedom not to answer the question were coded with a single H, on the assumption that since it would be abnormal for a man not to admit he was heterosexual if he didn't answer the question he was probably gay.

The coding system was never revealed to the public of course, and I only found out after I'd joined the SHA. The other thing I found out was that after the answers to Question 10 were put on computer the SHA had run a cross check with Central Criminal Records to pick up any males who'd had been convicted of an offence associated with homosexuality; if they lied about their sexual preference, or if they hadn't answered the question they'd been re-coded by the SHA. A couple of months later, when the issue of Question 10 had been overtaken by successive tides of public hysteria over the AIDS crisis, the SHA had run another cross check. This time there was no official announcement and only the SHA and family doctors were privy to the secret sweep of every citizen's medical records.

At that time I'd only recently joined the SHA and I'd only heard rumours about why we were suddenly told that all leave was cancelled and that we'd been put on emergency standby to provide administrative support to a major police operation. Months later, when I'd got to know my way around, I'd discovered that many family doctors had objected to an SHA directive requiring them to provide a report on every patient who'd consulted them over a sexually transmitted disease during the previous twenty years. The doctors had seen the directive as a grave threat to their clinical freedom and had called on the British Medical Association for support. It had rallied to their cause and threatened the SHA with a press conference at which it would reveal the existence of the directive and call on public support to resist this newest development towards a police State.

In the event, the press conference never took place and the secret stayed buried in the British Medical Association's headquarters in Tavistock Square. And because nobody outside their headquarters knew what was going on, nobody saw anything sinister in the car accident which resulted in the death of the Association's President on the day before he'd threatened to call his press conference. Nor were any questions asked about the sudden short illnesses which suddenly afflicted family doctors up and down the country. After all, only a small proportion of people go to their doctor at any one time and doctors can get sick like anybody else, so nobody was likely to suspect anything. People who attended their local surgeries for treatment were seen by those members of doctors' practices who'd seen the sense in co-operating, or by doctors who been conscripted in from the armed services (although the people they'd treated didn't know that).

It was obvious to me that Rayleigh and his top managers in the SHA had planned the whole operation with the police weeks before they'd issued the directive. I didn't know, but I suppose there were only a handful of doctors, probably bachelors, who'd stuck out for their clinical freedom during their three or four days of incarceration. I also didn't know who'd been the instruments of State terror; BDNP thugs drafted in for the purpose by Emmerson, perhaps; or maybe coppers who'd joined the police because they saw it as an opportunity to exercise personal power and inflict pain, while they were safe, inside the immunity offered by their uniform. I do know that if I'd answered my front door bell in the early hours of the morning and been whisked off my doorstep and locked up and told my wife and children would be hurt if I didn't co-operate I'd probably have come to the conclusion that my responsibilities as a husband and parent meant more to me than my hypocratic oath. And I guessed that had been the decision of ninety-nine per cent of family doctors, because within eight weeks the information demanded by the SHA had been fed into its computer and cross-tabulated with its existing data.

Anyone with a criminal frame of mind, who also possessed basic computer keyboard skills and the high security pass code necessary to access the SHA's national list of sexually-deviant males had the means to blackmail on a grand scale. I'd realised the possibilities months ago, but I hadn't got the necessary clearance to call up the national list. Smithson, on the other hand, had a terminal for the SHA's computer plugged into his office and, as Head of the London Tracing Department, the right to access any programme he wished. Once he'd decided to exploit the information all he needed to set up in business was a stock of cheap envelopes, writing paper and a typewriter.

'So,' I said to Victoria, 'Smithson's getting the names of the rich and famous from our computer's list of male sexual deviants, is he? And then what? Dropping them an anonymous letter threatening to send their names to the Sunday newspapers or the BNDP's muckraking rag if they don't pay up.'

She nodded. 'Yes.'

Smithson was doing precisely what I'd once fantasised about doing.

'How does he collect the money?' Out of curiosity I wanted to see how far my fantasies coincided with Smithson's practice of blackmail.

'The letters tell people to send the money to an address in Whitechapel,' she said. 'Then Terry goes along and picks it up.'

I wasn't surprised to discover Terry was in on the racket, but I was surprised with Smithson's lack of subtlety.

'It's not very sophisticated,' I said. In fact it was downright crude. In my imaginary scheme, collection of the blackmail money had involved two messenger services, who would have been unaware of what they'd been transporting across London, and three separate places for them to deliver.

'It doesn't have to be sophisticated does it? From what we …' She stopped and corrected herself. 'From what I've discovered Smithson doesn't bleed them dry. They make one single big payment.'

'How big?'

'Depends how rich they are.'

'He must have made …' I paused and tried to make a

realistic assessment of Smithson's haul. I couldn't see him doing it for small change. 'Millions,' I suggested. '... But where the hell is he hiding it?'

'Don't be stupid,' she said. 'He's not keeping it, it's going to the BNDP.'

Of course, I thought, why didn't I think of that. I knew why; if I was going to share my money, ill gotten or otherwise, I'd have thought of people to share it with. The last thing I'd have done was to hand it over to a political party – I'd have rather made a bonfire of the bloody lot. But Smithson was a different kind of animal from me. He'd give the money to the BNDP knowing that in return he'd gain more influence in its inner circle and a cash bonus in recognition of his efforts on the Party's behalf. By now he must have become one of the principal fundraisers for the BDNP. I sometimes wondered where they'd got the sort of money they needed to pay for the succession of national advertising campaigns, their daily newspaper – the *Bulldog* – their shops selling Party books, pamphlets and other paraphernalia and their mass rallies. Now I knew the answer; how Emmerson must be laughing over the irony whereby his Party were being financed by the very people they defamed.

'And it's not just money,' Victoria continued. 'Smithson's not just going after rich men who're gay, he's blackmailing anyone who's listed as homosexual who might be in a position to do something to help the BNDP. Politicians from the other parties, officers in the armed forces, senior civil servants, the police; you name anyone who might be a closet homosexual and Smithson's either made an approach, or intends to approach them for some kind of favour in return for his silence.'

'Jesus Christ,' I swore, realising the scale of his blackmail network. In my fantasy I'd envisaged touching about a few dozen people for enough money for me to live on after I'd walked out on the Tracing Department.

'Who else is involved in the Department?' I asked, knowing from what she'd told me that Chris, the lately lamented tracer who'd shared my office, must have been working on Smithson's secret project. How many other of my colleagues had been involved in a conspiracy which had operated below the ordinary everyday routines at the office?

'I don't know about the other London offices, but at Soho Square it's Terry and Chris. And you of course.'

How could someone be so right and yet so wrong?

'I've told you, Victoria. I'm not working for Smithson.'

She snorted. 'Don't give me shit like that. Of course you are. He gives you special jobs doesn't he?'

'What do you know about the special jobs?' I said, wondering how she'd found out that Smithson had asked me to find Harris.

'I know Smithson sends Chris to frighten people who refuse to pay up, and Terry too sometimes. You've been away from the office for over a week. You don't think I believed all that crap in the memo Smithson circulated saying you'd taken leave because of domestic difficulties. You were sent to do a special job. Your being here now proves it.'

So that's how Smithson had covered my absence.

'That's true,' I said. 'He did give me a special job, but it was the first one he'd ever given me. And it was the last,' I added grimly.

An idea occurred to me.

'Tell me, Victoria? Does the name Harris mean anything to you?'

She tried not to show any sign of surprise, but I was close to her and looking straight into her baby blue eyes, and I saw her blink with shock.

'No,' she said.

It was a lie, she knew about Harris, I was sure of that. I was also sure that she wasn't working for Smithson. Did she know about Rayleigh?

'Who's "we" Victoria?' I asked. 'A couple of times now you've said "we" – who are you working for?'

She pressed her lips together and shook her head. I put the barrel of the gun against her face.

'You better shoot me, Nick,' she said, 'because I'm not going to tell you.'

There was a note of finality in her voice.

Transferring the Walther to my left hand I held it against her stomach while I reached down to the floor by her feet and picked up her handbag, opened it, and shook out its contents on to her lap. There was the usual collection of things women carried in their handbags like tissues, a small powder compact, lipstick, a couple of nailfiles, her purse, a bunch of keys, a small pencil torch and her ID card. I picked up the torch and inspected the assortment of odds and ends lying in her lap before throwing them one by one on to the car's back seat.

'And what have we got here then?' I said, shining the thin beam of light from her pencil torch at the All Areas Pass.

I'd seen them before, although the weren't issued to us. I turned it over and shone the torch on the back of the plastic coated Pass to see who'd issued it. The official stamp said it had been authorised for use by the headquarters of the South Eastern Army Tactical Group (SEATAG for short), one of the four Army Groups in England with responsibility for providing military support to the police in maintaining civil order. Each Group was under the command of a general. Was the general in charge of SEATAG *the* General, the one Motte worked for, and did Victoria work for him too? It sounded plausible enough; SEATAG'S HQ was in a Ministry of Defence building in Horseguards Parade and I couldn't imagine they'd issue All Area Passes to just anybody.

'So,' I said, 'you work for the General too, do you?'

Victoria looked away from me. I prodded her in the stomach with the gun.

'I asked you a question, Victoria. Do you work for the General too?'

She sighed deeply.

'Whose side is he on? The Conservatives?'

'Yes,' she said, nodding her head in resignation. 'Yes, he works for the Conservatives.'

Thinking about her admission I could see it answered all the questions I had asked myself about her since she'd started working at the office. I'd always tagged her as a Conservative supporter. Girls who had been to a good boarding school simply weren't the type who'd slither around in society's shit out of choice. If I'd thought she was out of place it seemed likely that Smithson would have been equally surprised by her choice to work in his Department.

'How did you manage to get a job at the office?'

'What do you mean?' she asked.

'Oh, for God's sake, Victoria. You stand out like a sore thumb. Surely Smithson must have been suspicious.'

'The story was that I'd been transferred because I'd had an affair with Alan Murray. Don't you remember all the fuss when he killed himself?'

I remembered. Alan Murray had been the Assistant General Manager of the SHA's Oxford Region and he was supposed to have committed suicide after his mistress left him. I remembered something else too – the area covered by the Oxford Region came within the operational orbit of SEATAG.

'Were you his mistress?'

'No. His suicide was just an excuse. He killed himself when he found he'd got cancer.'

I thought about her answer. People who'd known Murray had been shocked by his suicide. We lived in ruthless times and I wondered if it was conceivable he could have been murdered to provide a cover story for Victoria's transfer to Smithson's department. I recalled again the way Gwen had trembled with fear when I'd started to question her about the General – was he ruthless enough to have Murray killed as part of a plan to get Victoria close to Smithson?

'He's coming out of the house,' Victoria whispered.

I forgot about the General and turned my head in time to see Smithson climb into his Rover. The illuminated digital clock on the Renault's dashboard was showing ten minutes past ten. Where was he off to? And what the hell was I going to do about it? He started his car and backed it out into the road. The Rover's reversing lights went out as

Smithson put the car into first gear and drove off in the direction of the main road, fifty or so metres away. Whatever I was going to do I had to do it quickly, because once he reached the main road I'd lose him. Come on, Gorman, I thought, make your mind up.

I snatched hold of the All Areas Pass, took her car keys out of the ignition and got out of the car.

'Get back into the driver's seat,' I said urgently. 'Go on. Move!'

She swung her legs over the gear lever, her dress slipping up her over her thighs, and before she settled herself into the driver's seat I'd skipped round to the passenger door, opened it and got back inside the Renault. I gave her the keys. 'Follow him!' I said, as Smithson turned right at the junction at the bottom of his road.

He's going into central London, I thought, in the moment before the Renault's turbocharged engine burst into life. I put on the seatbelt quickly in case Victoria decided to accelerate fast away from the kerb, hit the brakes and pitch me head first into the windscreen.

'Go on!' I almost shouted, flourishing the Walther at her as Smithson's rear lights disappeared from view.

Victoria pushed hard down on the accelerator and I felt the pressure against my back from an invisible hand as the needle on the turbocharger dial swung over and the little Renault raced down the road. She reached the main road, glanced right and left and drove after Smithson, with the car's cold engine howling in protest as she took it up to maximum revs through each gear. We'd travelled less than a quarter of a mile when I picked out Smithson's car.

'Get closer and then stick with him,' I ordered.

'And what are you going to do with me when we get to wherever he's going?' she asked, as she swung out to overtake a taxi. 'Kill me?'

It was a much better question than her pal Motte had asked me earlier. I'd gone to him, convinced he was on opposite sides to Smithson, looking for an ally. Now, fate had led me to Victoria and I was almost certain that she and Motte worked for the same general, and that their general was the officer in charge of SEATAG. The very last thing I wanted was to get myself mixed up in a cloak and dagger war between the Conservatives and the BNDP, even when I'd gone to Motte I'd hoped to strike some sort of deal which would allow me to fade into the background, but I was in it now – in it up to my neck. And by now Motte would have contacted someone close to the General, if not the man himself, to report that a tracer called Gorman was the last person to see Alice Townsend before she was grabbed by Smithson's men.

I glanced across at Victoria. My fantasies about her had long since supplanted my silly schemes about how I might be able to get out of the Department by blackmailing rich gays. In my imagination I'd seen our first out-of-office hours contact being accompanied by soft lights, a meal and a bottle of good red wine. Well, I sighed to myself, it's not the best way to start a partnership, but in the circumstances you're rather short on viable alternatives. Sooner or later the General would catch up with me and I could imagine he wouldn't be best pleased if I'd hurt Victoria. On the other hand if she and I worked together he might be the man to help me get out of the bloody mess I landed myself in, because if I had to tell someone about Rayleigh and Harris I'd choose to tell the Conservatives rather than the fucking BNDP.

'I asked you a question,' said Victoria.

'What?'

'Are you going to kill me when we get to where your boss is going?'

'For Christ's sake, Victoria,' I said, looking at her and smiling. 'I thought the Conservatives would have been able to afford people with brains. How many times do I have to tell you I'm not working for Smithson? It must be obvious by now that I'm telling the truth, even to you.'

'So? Who do you work for?'

'I don't work for anybody, except myself. It might seem strange to someone like you, but your party, the Conservatives, they used to emphasise things like the freedom of the individual,' I said. 'Now ... since we're

209

both working against Smithson and the fates seemed to have brought us together I propose we become partners.'

'What does that mean?'

'I'll help you and you help me. Partners. OK?'

She was silent for a moment or two and as we came to a roundabout she turned her head and looked at me. 'Does that mean I get to have your gun?' she asked, following Smithson down the exit which led into central London.

'Let's see how well we get on, shall we?' I replied.

In the last few days my life seemed to have consisted of a succession of compromises, but I wasn't even prepared to think about making a compromise of that magnitude.

Time: 23.15 hours

We hadn't talked much on the drive into central London until I'd put the Walther away in my jacket pocket. After that Victoria had been more prepared to answer my questions, or at least she'd answered questions about herself. From her answers I'd gained a much clearer picture of the girl who was skilfully following Smithson through the traffic. I'd been right in thinking her family had plenty of money which had bought her a good education and all the other things which the fees from her doting father's legal practice could bestow on an only child. Then, like the lives of millions of others, her life had been shattered by the AIDS crisis; and an imminent marriage to a young and successful barrister, her job as a journalist and the prospect of producing grandchildren for her proud father had vanished overnight.

Both her father and her fiancé had been outspoken opponents of Emmerson and the BNDP and they'd tried to galvanise opinion within an association of Conservative lawyers in the hope that, if sufficient of their colleagues came together, they could form a pressure group against the ultra-Right members of their profession. One Friday night, shortly before the last general election, the two men she loved had spoken at a meeting at the Dorchester

Hotel. I'd been in hospital at the time, unaware of the new vogue in politics, where people who opposed the BDNP were beaten up on the street by persons unknown. Nowadays of course they'd have been murdered by a death squad made up of either off-duty police or army personnel, but before the general election political violence still retained an amateur status.

Since her fiancé was intending to spend the weekend with her, at her parents' house in Virginia Water, it seemed sensible, once the meeting was over, for him and her father to drive there in the same car. Like most people who'd grown up in the old England, the two men still believed in the liberal ideal that people had the right to think and say what they liked. They discussed their affairs openly and anyone who knew them would have known that they were going to share the same car. So, at the end of the meeting, they shook hands with one or two people, walked out of the Dorchester's swing doors, got into her father's car, he turned on the ignition and the bomb in its engine compartment blew them to pieces.

Victoria had used her contacts as a journalist to try to discover who'd planted the bomb, until her efforts came to the attention of her editor. On the morning he'd sacked her she'd had a call from her dead father's partner to say that a senior member of the BNDP wanted to buy her family home. She'd refused outright, but when she'd got home that evening she found her mother had received a visit from her father's partner, in company with the thug from the BNDP who wanted the house. The pair of them had been and badgered her mother into signing the contract. It hadn't taken Victoria long to find out her dead father's partner had quietly joined the BNDP a week after the meeting at the Dorchester Hotel. The last shock had come when they'd found out that the amount on the contract her mother had signed was only a fraction of the house's true value. Six weeks later they were ejected from their home and the money they got for it was just enough to buy a small flat in Pimlico.

Victoria's mother had died a month later; she'd been fit

211

and healthy when her husband had been killed, but the shock of his loss and everything that followed had been so great she just seemed to give up on life. After her mother's funeral Victoria found that there were complications with her father's partnership agreement. The 'accidents' began after she'd phoned her father's partner and accused him of trying to cheat her out of what was rightfully hers; her car mysteriously caught fire, her mother's faithful pet dog was poisoned, her flat was burgled and ransacked, and then, one night on her way home from her temporary job as a typist she was stopped by three men. These weren't BNDP skinheads, they were in their thirties and quietly spoken, but they made sure she understood that if she didn't keep her mouth shut they'd shut it for her, permanently. Two weeks later a boy she'd known when she'd been at university rang her up at work and offered her a job and a chance to get even, and she'd accepted it without so much as a second thought.

She finished telling me her story while we were sitting in her car in Greek Street, giving Smithson time to get into our office building. I believed her and it explained a lot, like the pain inside her which I'd recognised at our first meeting and the way she seemed to shun company.

'OK,' I said, after a long silence. 'Let's see if we can win one for a change.'

She looked at me and smiled. I'd expected to see tears in her eyes, but I suppose she'd long since cried out her grief.

'Let's go,' I said, suddenly realising that her story had diverted me from asking questions about who she was working for and that I'd been the one who'd talked about the General being her boss. When I'd questioned people in the past my wits were the only instrument I'd had to discover the truth. I sighed. I shouldn't have put so much faith in the gun. It's too late now, I thought, you're just going to have to trust her.

Victoria put the car into gear and slowly cruised out of Greek Street and parked on the east side of the small garden in the middle of Soho Square. Unlike some of the large squares in London Soho Square is small and claustrophobic and it was easy to keep a close watch on the office from where we'd parked.

'How long have you been tailing Smithson?' I asked her.

'Tonight?'

In our fencing matches in the office I found her insouciant attitudes a challenge, but now I was too much on edge to affect an air of careless unconcern.

'We agreed we'd work together and I've put my gun away,' I snapped. 'So stop playing the fool. You know what I mean. Does he do this often?'

'You agreed we should work together,' she replied. 'As I remember it I didn't have much choice …' She sighed. 'I've never known him come back to the office, but it must be important to make him turn out on a Saturday night.'

'I know,' I said, craning my head to see if I could detect any shadows moving behind the closed curtains in his office on the fourth floor. 'But what?'

'Perhaps …'

I never found out what Victoria was going to say; perhaps she was going to say we ought to be careful we weren't spotted by any of Smithson's people. After all, she'd already had one unpleasant surprise that night and she may have been about to suggest we should take some precautions in case somebody did to us what I'd done to her. If that's what she was going to say I only wish she'd said it sooner because at that moment our conversation was rudely interrupted as both of the Renault's doors were flung open.

'Out!' said a man's voice, which belonged to a hand, which was holding a gun, which was pointing at my head.

Victoria and I exchanged the briefest of glances before I got out of the car, silently cursing myself for concentrating all my attention on Smithson's office window.

'Turn round and put your hands on the roof of the car,' said the man as he stuck the gun in the small of my back.

'Come on! Let's have you out of here, you fucking cow!' said another man on Victoria's side of the Renault. I could tell from his accent that he wasn't a Londoner.

'Give it to her, Frank,' the man who was looking after me said with approval.

The man he'd called Frank leaned inside the car and dragged her out by her hair. Most women would have screamed. Victoria didn't.

'Jesus, you're a tough little bitch,' he said, pushing her roughly against the side of her car.

Just to prove how tough she really was Victoria stamped on his foot with the stiletto heel on her shoe. The man called Frank yelled out in pain, a yell which stopped as she hit him in the face with her forearm. I sensed that the man, who would have discovered my Walther if he hadn't been enjoying the spectacle of his mate being tough with Victoria, was in two minds; should he help Frank, or should he deal with me? I stopped him worrying about what he should do when I spun round and elbowed him in his Adam's apple. He fell to the floor, choking and losing the fight to force air into his lungs and I kicked his gun out of his hand.

I turned, with the intention of getting round to the other side of the car to help Victoria, at the exact moment when the man called Frank butted her in the face with his head. She fell heavily against the side of the Renault and down on to the road; I knew she wasn't going to get up fighting – not after a blow like that. I struggled to get the Walther out of my jacket pocket but Frank already had his gun out; I knew if I stayed by the car he'd win the ensuing firefight and I turned and ran, ducking and weaving, into Sutton Street. His gun was silenced because I didn't hear him shoot, but I felt the hot searing pain of the bullet as it clipped the top of my shoulder and I heard it richochet off the side of a building as I turned into Falconberg Mews. I ran past the dustbins where I'd discovered the corpse and down Falconberg Court, and emerging through the small archway at the bottom of the Court I raced across Charing Cross Road, oblivious to the homeward bound Saturday night traffic. I didn't stop until I was in the small area of streets behind Centre Point.

Out of sight of Saturday night revellers I sank down on the pavement and sobbed; first Alice and now Victoria – everytime I'd got someone else involved in my personal fight with Smithson it had finished with them being captured. And you ran again, I wailed at myself, you ran again. Come on, said another part of me, what else could you have done? Victoria was down and out, there was no way you could have done anything to help her, if you hadn't got away you'd both be stretched out in the road in Soho Square, and in your case you'd be dead. I sat on the pavement, hugging myself in the same way Gwen had hugged herself earlier in the evening. After a few minutes I dried my eyes and blew my nose on Martin's handkerchief. You're alive, I told myself, so do something about it, go and get Victoria. If you love her, go and get her.

I took off my suit jacket. The bullet had ripped a small hole through it, at the back, just below the top of the shoulder line. My left shoulder was bleeding and my shirt was sticky with blood but I'd been incredibly lucky; an inch lower and the bullet would have gone through the top of my shoulder and it would have probably smashed my collar bone as it exited. As it was, it had cut a shallow groove across the bottom of my neck. It was what cowboys in westerns called a flesh wound. I loosened my tie, unbuttoned my shirt, folded Martin's handkerchief and put it over my wound. Knowing it would stop bleeding in a few minutes I slipped on my jacket and I was relieved to see that when it was buttoned up it hid the patch of blood on my shirt – the last thing I wanted was to draw attention to myself. Promising myself I'd get Victoria away from Smithson no matter who I had to kill I set off towards Soho Square, taking a route which would bring me to the office's rear entrance in Dean Street.

Time: 23.50 hours

When I arrived in Dean Street it was ten minutes before curfew and the surrounding roads were deserted. I pressed the buttons on the electronic lock in the correct sequence and the steel door which led on to a courtyard at the back

215

of the office clicked and opened a couple of inches. Easing open the door a few more inches I squeezed through the gap and closed it behind me. It was pitch black in the courtyard but I knew where I was going and I only turned on Victoria's pencil torch for a few seconds to make sure I wouldn't walk straight into one of the Department's cars which were normally parked there over the weekends. I skirted past the two small Fords and located the drainpipe which ran up the side of the building within a few inches of my office window. As long as the maintenance contractors hadn't come to fix my window in the time I'd been away from the office I'd be OK. I put my hand inside my jacket and touched my shoulder; the bleeding had stopped but the wound was very sore and I knew it would be pouring blood by the time I'd shinned up fifteen feet of cast iron pipe to the first floor – always assuming I could stand the pain. Come on, I thought, they've had Victoria for over half an hour, you haven't got time to stand here worrying about your shoulder, get up that bloody drainpipe.

By the time I'd climbed up to my office window I was sweating profusely in spite of the bitter weather and my shoulder was throbbing like hell. Ignoring the pain, I held on to the drainpipe with my left hand and with one foot on the window ledge I pushed the fingers of my right hand into the gap between the top sash window and window frame and pulled downwards. The window refused to budge. I pulled downwards again, harder this time. Without warning it suddenly slid open, my foot slipped off the window ledge and I almost lost my hold on the drainpipe. And if I hadn't managed to grab hold of the window ledge with my right hand I'd have fallen head first, down into the courtyard. Steadying myself with my right hand I inched up the drainpipe with my left, put my right foot back on to the window ledge, grabbed hold of the wooden frame of the wide open sash window with my right hand, moved all my weight on to my right foot, inched it along the ledge, and letting go of the drainpipe I swung myself to the right and my left hand closed round the top of the sash window.

Squatting on the window ledge I took a deep breath and

climbed through on to the top of the radiator which was secured to the wall immediately below the window. I took out the Walther from my jacket pocket, took off its safety and stood there for a few moments, listening for any sound, before crouching down and climbing off the top of the radiator on to the floor of my office.

I went across to the door and listened – it all seemed quiet enough. Outside in the dark corridor I listened again. There was still no sound of voices or anyone moving about. Making my way to the emergency stairs I crept up to the fourth floor. I'd expected to see the light from the main corridor on the fourth floor through the glass panel in the fire door as I reached the top of the stairs, but apart from the dim emergency lights on the staircase, which were left on at all times, the place was in darkness. I inched open the fire door and tiptoed along the corridor, feeling my way along the wall with the tips of my fingers, taking care not to let the Walther knock against any door frames. When I got to the door of Smithson's office I stopped and listened; I couldn't understand why everything was so quiet. They wouldn't have killed her, would they? Oh please God, I prayed, let Victoria be alive. I put my ear against Smithson's door, straining to catch the sound of voices – not a sound. And there was no chink of light escaping from under the door. Would they have taken her to Terry's office, or down to the basement? That's it I thought, the basement!

Convinced there was nobody on the fourth floor I went past Smithson's door and opened the door to his secretary's office. Turning on the pencil torch I crept across to the door which connected her office to his. If I knew Smithson his office would be locked up but there was always a chance his secretary might have been careless. I turned the handle on the connecting door, pushed gently and it opened. Smithson's office was dark and empty. I tiptoed back to the emergency staircase and went down to the second floor; Terry's office was empty too. They must have taken Victoria to the basement and that meant I'd have to go down the main staircase, across the entrance foyer and past the security desk.

Back on the first floor I crouched at the top of the main staircase. I could hear someone shuffling paper in the vicinity of the security desk but I wanted to see which of the guards was on duty before I descended the stairs to the entrance foyer. It was the young one, Bill, the BNDP supporter. Fuck, I thought, it would be, it would be that little bastard, the one who enjoys fighting. To make matters worse he was sitting behind the security desk, less than two metres from the door which led to the basement. There was no other way to get to where I wanted to go. I stood up and started to walk down the thickly carpeted staircase, one step at a time.

I'd reached the sixth step and he was in full view when I stopped and spoke to him.

'Stay exactly as you are, Bill,' I said quietly, holding the Walther with both hands and pointing it at him. 'Or I'll shoot you.'

The way his head snapped up from the newspaper he was reading told me I had the advantage of surprise.

'Drop your newspaper and stand up,' I ordered, still speaking quietly.

He did as I told him, but I caught his instinctive glance towards the panic button on his side of the security desk.

'Don't even think about it,' I cautioned.

It was wired through to the main security switchboard at the Elephant and Castle and if he pushed it the guards on duty there would alert the police and there'd be a car, filled with armed policeman, outside in Soho Square in minutes.

'Put your hands on your head.' He did as I told him. 'Now, come out from behind the desk, slowly, Bill, slowly. Stop.'

He stopped in the middle of the foyer and, still pointing my gun at him, I descended the staircase and walked across the entrance hall to within a couple of metres of him.

'Take your gun out of its holster and drop it on the floor.' He unclipped the flap on his holster. 'Just use your finger and thumb,' I cautioned. 'And then put your hands on your head.'

He took out his standard issue Smith and Wesson

revolver and dropped it at my feet.

'All right, Bill,' I said, as he put his hands on top of his head. 'Where's Victoria?'

He looked at me insolently. 'She's gone, Mister Gorman,' he said, emphasising the Mister. 'Her and Mister Smithson.'

'What do you mean? Gone?'

'I mean gone,' he said, in the same insolent voice. 'They went with Terry.'

'Keep your hands on your head,' I said, covering him with the Walther as I walked behind the security desk and opened the basement door.

There were no lights on beyond the door. Shit! I thought, they must have taken her away during the time I was jogging round to Dean Street.

I closed the door and walked over to Bill.

'Where have they taken her?'

He shrugged his shoulders. 'I dunno. Mind you,' he said and smiled at me, 'Terry always did fancy her.' He ran his tongue over his lips and winked at me. 'Stuck up cow. She doesn't fool me, I bet she can't get enough of it. That was your trouble, she doesn't go for all that chat, she just wants to be fucked. But don't you worry, Nicky boy, a nice AIDS-free girl like that, Terry'll give her one for you, and then Frank, and I bet she'll still be begging for it.'

His foul mouth etched out a scene in my mind of them holding Victoria down with her legs pulled wide apart while Terry explored her body with his grubby hands. He had no worries about Victoria, she wasn't a suspected heavy; Bill was right, he'd rape her first, then Frank, and then Terry would get down to the hideous orgy which gave him most pleasure. And the task of getting her to talk would give an added bite to his appetite as he tore, cut and ravaged her flesh.

I looked at Bill through a red mist. I could see that despite the gun I hadn't done enough to impress on him how serious I was about rescuing Victoria. I thought again about the Lee Marvin movie. I'd been playing out his role for most of the evening, but now it was different, now, courtesy of Bill's taunts, I really was in the grip of the same cold blooded ferociousness which had possessed the movie's criminal anti-hero. I stuck the end of the Walther's barrel hard into Bill's stomach and as he doubled up I whipped the gun's barrel across his face. He fell on to his knees and blood from his newly broken nose dripped on to the beige carpet.

'Where have they taken her?' I repeated, walking behind his kneeling body and pressing the gun against the nape of his neck.

'To see Emmerson.' His voice had lost its insolence.

'Where?' I jabbed the gun into his neck.

'At his house in Leicestershire.'

'Have they hurt her?'

'No.'

'You see, Bill,' I said, soothingly, 'it's easy when you try. Now, how many of them are there?' I jabbed him again with the Walther.

'Four,' he said. 'Her and Smithson and Terry and Frank.'

'Who's Frank?'

'He works for Emmerson. He's his farm manager.'

'And the other man? What happened to him.'

'You killed him, you bastard. He choked to death.' He spat some of his blood on to the carpet. 'He's in there.' He nodded his head in the direction of the basement door.

I hadn't given the man a second thought since I'd run away from Victoria's Renault. I don't know whether I'd meant to kill him; it had been him or me and I'd just hit him as hard as I could. Perhaps if there'd been more time I might have chosen to hit another part of his body, but there hadn't been time for thinking, I'd had a fraction of a second and I'd aimed for his most exposed and vulnerable feature. I looked down at Bill and the blood stains on the carpet. I'd killed someone, I should have felt sorry, or something, but God help me, I didn't.

'On your feet, Bill,' I said, taking the gun away from his neck and stepping back from him.

He levered himself off the floor and turned to look at me, holding his broken nose.

'We'll get you for this, Gorman,' he said. 'No matter what, we'll get you for this.'

'Fuck the BNDP,' I said evenly. 'What's it to you anyway?'

'What's it to me? Who do you think you're talking to?' he snarled, his pride stung by my remark. 'I'm a Group Leader.'

'Are you?' I said sarcastically, but I was genuinely impressed. I'd always assumed he was nothing more than an ordinary Party member, but in the BNDP's rank structure a Group Leader was the equivalent to a major in the army and to achieve it involved passing intellignce tests, an oral examination on Party dogma and a strenuous cross country exercise. For reasons I found it difficult to understand, those kids who'd have died rather than participate in organisations like the Boy Scouts seemed to flourish under the para-military discipline inside the BNDP. Bill had done well to get to be a Group Leader at such a young age and I took it as an indication of Smithson's power in the BNDP that they'd attached someone of his rank to work as a humble security guard in order to look out for his interests.

'OK then, Group Leader,' I said, pointing the gun towards the basement door. 'Let's go.'

I don't know whether it was delayed shock from the fight in Soho Square, or the news that I'd killed someone, or, more probably, because for a fleeting moment the picture of Terry hurting Victoria passed across my mind, but I know I relaxed my vigilance. Bill may have sensed it too, or he may have thought I was going to kill him. In any event he took me by surprise when he suddenly turned and lunged forwards. His fist struck the side of my head and sent me sprawling across the floor of the main entrance. I rolled away to my left and the stabbing pain in my shoulder was more efficacious than smelling salts in reviving my dulled senses. Incredibly, my first reaction was to get to my feet and fight him, until I realised I was

221

still holding the Walther and that he was bending down to retrieve his revolver from the floor.

'Don't!' I shouted as his fingers closed on his gun.

I'd never fired a gun before. The bang from my Walther was deafening and for a split second I was paralysed by its sound and the buzz in my ears. But I'd missed him as he rolled over to his right, and as he levelled his gun at me I squeezed the trigger in panic – Bang! Bang! Bang! Bang! Bang! Bang! Spent bullet cases flew out of the Walther's chamber as the automatic pistol in my hands lived out a life of its own, completely outside my control. Four out of the six bullets hit Bill, each one causing a small geyser of fine red spray to erupt from his head and body. I thought he moved and I squeezed the trigger again. The Walther emitted a muted click. I struggled to my feet and went over to him. If he had moved it was simply his body settling on the carpet. Trembling uncontrollably from shock induced by the sheer noise and speed of my act of violence, I pushed Bill over onto his back and looked, horrified, at what the bullets from the Walther had done to his body at short range. I didn't feel the detachment I'd felt in the past when I'd seen victims of a brutal death. This corpse was different to the one I'd found by the dustbins on the way back from the pub – I'd been the one who'd shot the bullets which had reduced his skull to a mangled bloody stump.

I sat next to the human being I'd killed, holding my head in my hands and trembling. A week ago at this time I'd been with Rob, sitting on the sofa in her living room, talking and drinking coffee, and if anyone had told me then that in seven day's time I'd have killed two people I'd have laughed out loud.

Come on! Come on! A voice inside my head spoke to me. Why don't you wake up? What did you think was going to happen? You're the last person who should be surprised. Look at the job you do, for Christ's sake! Where do you get the right to be so fucking self righteous. Stop fooling yourself; you're not an observer, someone who's simply passing through, untouched by everything that's happening around you, you're part of it, you hunt people for money. And what happens to them after you've caught them? Do you think they're tucked up in a nice warm bed in a Special Care Centre, given hot milk and a bedtime story? What happens to them when you're totting up your bounty money and dreaming of a nice quiet life in the country? You want to stop dreaming and do something, something to put right the hurt you've done to people.

Wiping my eyes on the sleeve of my jacket, I stood up and went over to the security desk. After I'd extracted seven bullets from my jacket pocket I re-loaded the Walther. OK, I replied silently to the voice which had stripped away the last of my pretensions about myself, you're right, you're fucking right. I looked at Bill, lying in the middle of the wide red stain that was slowly creeping outwards across the carpet. He was proof that I never had been a spectator. My conscience, if that's what it was, had stripped my motives down to the essential. I was hiding from myself, and I'd been hiding from myself ever since Ann had been killed. Come on admit it, I thought, it's guilt. You know why you've been hiding and you know what the psychiatrist couldn't find out because you were too bloody guilt-ridden and too bloody smart to tell him. Perhaps if you'd been honest then you wouldn't be here now. Take it out and look at it. Remember that Friday night? The day before Ann died? Remember the row you had when she came home from work and gave you what she thought was a wonderful surprise? Remember what you said when she told you she was pregnant? Remember how you shouted about how irresponsible she was to do such a thing when you'd just moved into your new flat in Finchley? Do you remember? Do you remember how you went on and on about the cost of the mortgage? And how she needed to keep working so you could pay it? And how she cried when you suggested she should have an abortion?

I leaned against the desk and wept hot, bitter tears of remorse as I remembered how we'd rowed until I'd left her sitting at the kitchen table, crying, and gone to bed in our spare bedroom. The next morning I'd woken up to find that she'd packed a suitcase and was going to spend the weekend at her sister's. Even then I hadn't found the grace to say I was sorry and that I wanted the baby and that everything would be all right financially. Instead I watched her sullenly as she'd picked up her suitcase and walked out of the kitchen and through the front door. At the very last moment I'd run to our front door but by the time I'd raced down the steps to the ground floor and outside into the road Ann had driven off in our car.

When I'd rung her sister's an hour or so later to say I was sorry and would she mind if I went down there on the next train I was surprised to find Ann hadn't arrived. Her sister, who knew nothing of Ann's reasons for visiting her, said that perhaps Ann had stopped off on the way to see her friend Jill. I rang Jill, but Ann wasn't there either. I was well past the initial feeling of worry when the doorbell rang. When I opened it and looked into the faces of the policeman and policewomen I knew Ann was dead and in that instant I knew that I was the one who'd killed her and our unborn child. It hadn't been the wet road, or the guy who was driving the lorry, or the thousand and one things that can contribute to a road accident. It had been me because I'd been the one who'd been responsible for her being out on the road in the first place. I'd buried that piece of knowledge deep inside me and played the role of the loving, innocent husband whose wife had been cruelly taken from him at their moment of shared happiness until the guilt which I'd hidden from family and friends had turned into a canker.

At every consultation with my psychiatrist, during the time I'd been a voluntary patient, I'd known he was searching for something other than straightforward grief to explain my mental turmoil, but I knew enough about psychiatry to avoid answering his questions. And when I'd finally discharged myself from hospital I'd done it out of fear that he was getting closer and closer to my secret rather than because of a feeling of renewed well-being. I'd lied to him and I'd lied to myself and my punishment had been hard labour in the SHA's Tracing Department, working alongside the other psychopaths who'd been attracted to the gruesome job of hunting sick and frightened people for money. Well, Gorman, I said to myself, looking again at the body of the man I'd shot to pieces, in the past couple of hours you've killed two members of the BNDP, your days as a tracer are over, my friend, in fact your chances of surviving at all don't look very good, so in the time that remains you better start doing something useful with your life.

I went into the men's room on the ground floor and splashed water on my face. All right, I said out loud to my reflection in the mirror after I'd dried my face, you got Victoria into this, it's up to you to get her out. And Alice too, I thought. Although I'd been wondering about Alice since I'd left Motte's gallery. I switched off the light and went out into the entrance foyer. For a moment I considered dragging Bill's body out of sight, but his blood was still leaking on to the carpet, and I couldn't see the point. Instead, I went up to Smithson's office, switched on his desk lamp, smashed the glass-fronted doors on one of his bookcases with the butt of the Walther, took a copy of *Who's Who* from it's bottom shelf and flicked through the pages until I found the entry for James Emmerson.

I copied down the address of his country home in Leicestershire before switching off the desklamp and going into Smithson's secretary's office and removing the AA book she kept on a small bookcase by the side of her desk. In the light from Victoria's pencil torch I flicked through the maps until I found the village in Leicestershire where Emmerson lived. Before I left her office I went over to the window which overlooked the Square; Victoria's car was where she'd left it. Taking the AA book with me I went down to my office and picked up an anorak I kept on a hook behind the door and a first aid box.

In the men's room on the ground floor I peeled off my shirt and cleaned and dressed my shoulder as well as I

225

could with one hand. It was sore and my recent physical exertions had caused it to bleed again, but I wasn't about to die from it, and my anorak would hide the stain where the blood had seeped through to my suit jacket. After I'd cleaned my blood off the wash basin I went back to the entrance foyer and let myself out of the main door into Soho Square. I knew it was very unlikely that anybody would have heard the shooting; all the offices in Soho Square were closed over the weekend and our steel-lined door and thick bullet-proof windows would have masked most of the sound. If the keys were still in Victoria's Renault it made more sense to take that rather than one of the office cars. Apart from the noise I'd make opening the steel doors in Dean Street her car was a bloody sight faster and more manouevrable than the Department's Fords.

The key was still in the Renault's ignition. I turned it and the turbocharged engine throbbed and gurgled with power as I touched the accelerator. I estimated it was about a hundred miles to Emmerson's house and I'd be there in a couple of hours in Victoria's little motor. Perhaps, if I get Victoria away from Smithson, I thought, the gods will set it against what I did to Ann. Please God, I said to myself as I drove down Sutton Street, please let Victoria be alive when I get there.

VI

SUNDAY,
27 FEBRUARY 1999

Sunday, 27 February 1999

Time: 02.25 hours

I turned into the M1 Motorway service station at Toddington, having successfully got through the Luton traffic checkpoint with Victoria's All Areas Pass. I drove up to the petrol pumps and filled the Renault's tank to overflowing. I'd have no trouble in going anywhere in England with the All Areas Pass and I wasn't worried about whether I'd be able to buy petrol outside the area designated by my ordinary ID card, but I was pretty sure that the next twenty-four hour service station was north of Leicester, at least thirty miles past the exit which was the quickest route to Emmerson's house. In the old days, when motorway service stations were open all round the clock, I'd have stopped further away from London but the travel restrictions and curfew had cut night-time traffic to a trickle and the reduced volume of business was insufficient to sustain more than half of the service stations. Although most of them were open during the day the majority closed by eight o'clock every night to give their staff plenty of time to get home in safety.

The temperature seemed to have dropped another couple of degrees and the wind whipped at my camouflaged patterned anorak as I replaced the Renault's locking petrol cap and ran into the brightly lit office. I gave some banknotes, my ID and the All Areas Pass to the man behind the counter. He looked at my ID before sliding it across the counter towards me, quickly, as if the merest contact with someone in my trade was enough to taint him.

'It's quiet tonight,' I said, making sure Victoria's pass was safely in the inside pocket of my anorak.

'Yes,' he agreed. 'Apart from your lot and them,' he nodded in the direction of the window, 'there's never anybody about much after midnight.'

I turned to see who he was referring to at the same moment that the office door opened and two traffic policemen came inside, they were wearing bright yellow reflective coats over their flak jackets.

'Alright, Bob?' one of them asked the man behind the counter.

He nodded. 'Yes. No problem.'

'And what are you doing out?' The other policeman asked as he came and stood by me. He was tall and thin, with worried eyes. Out of the corner of my eye I saw his companion's reflection in the glass which made up one side of the office and I caught the movement of his hand as it slid over the butt of his revolver. I pointed to my tracer's ID card on the counter. 'I'm on a job,' I said.

He picked it up off the counter and studied it. 'You're out of your area,' he said. 'This is only valid for Greater London.'

'I know,' I said, quietly. I'd come too far to have an argument with a traffic cop. I started to reach into my inside coat pocket, but stopped when I saw his body stiffen.

'It's OK,' I said. 'I'm getting out my All Areas Pass.' I spoke loudly so the copper standing behind me would hear. 'Alright?'

The traffic policeman next to me nodded and I took out Victoria's pass and handed it to him. He looked at the front and turned it over and examined the SEATAG stamp.

'What are you doing with a grade one pass?' His worried eyes were alight with interest.

It was a question which had occurred to me when I picked it off Victoria's lap and looked at it in the light from

230

her torch, and if Smithson hadn't come out of his house and driven off I would have asked her. Grade two passes had the name of the person entitled to use it written on a line above the circle where the issuing office put its official stamp. A grade one pass was unrestricted and required no name. The person carrying it could go anywhere they wanted. By definition, therefore, the person carrying it had a very high security clearance. It was one of the factors which had led me to suspect that Victoria was working for the General, because it was unlikely that anyone below that rank could have authorised its issue. I knew that the traffic cop knew that it was almost unbelievable that a tracer would have been given one.

I took the pass from him and slipped it back inside my pocket. 'I'm on secondment to SEATAG,' I said, looking straight into his eyes.

'A tracer? On secondment to SEATAG?' he asked incredulously. 'What the fuck would you be doing working for SEATAG?'

'Have you got a phone?' I said to the man behind the counter.

He looked at me in surprise. 'Yes.'

'OK then, I want you to ring SEATAG HQ and ask to speak to the Duty Adjutant. I'll give you the number,' I said, still speaking quietly as I took the All Areas Pass out of my pocket to read out their telephone number which was printed on the back of it. 'When you get through tell him I'd like to speak to him.' I nodded towards the policeman standing next to me. 'Give me your numbers would you? In case the adjutant wants to make an official complaint.'

His worried eyes assumed a look of panic.

'Now there's no need for that,' he protested quickly. 'We're just doing our jobs, that's all.' He turned and appealed to the policeman who was standing behind me. 'Aren't we, Gordon?'

'Look.' It was his companion that spoke. 'We're only checking, that's all.'

Make them sweat, I thought. I leaned on the counter

and picked up my ID, slipped it back into my wallet and put it in my pocket.

'All right, I'm sorry,' I said, picking up my change from the counter. 'It's been a long day and I'm tired.' I patted the tall, thin policeman's arm and his eyes resumed their normal worried look. 'I'm sorry. Let's forget it.'

He smiled and nodded and stood aside to let me pass. As I reached the door the other policeman opened it and saluted. 'Good night sir,' he said. 'Safe journey.'

I walked slowly back to Victoria's Renault, got in, started it, and drove away from the petrol station, glancing occasionally in the rearview mirror. I wasn't surprised there was no sign of a police car following me – even I'd been impressed by my performance. Anyone who screwed around with someone carrying a grade one All Areas Pass could land themselves in serious trouble and I guessed the two cops were anxious to stay off the motorway for the next half hour and with a bit of luck the'd radio through to their mates who were on patrol to caution them against stopping my Renault.

Time: 03.45 hours

In the moonlight the chimneys on Hunter's Lodge were clearly visible, pointing upwards over the top of the trees which surrounded it. There were half a dozen large houses in the immediate vicinity of the village and it had taken me much longer to find Emmerson's house than I'd anticipated. Nearly four hours since Victoria was captured, I thought. Four hours! By now she might by lying in a shallow grave somewhere in the Lodge's grounds. I remembered how quickly she'd adjusted to the shock when I'd wrenched open her car door and threatened her with my gun, and the way she lashed out at the man called Frank. She can't be dead, I told myself, someone as brave and tough as her doesn't just die. God help you if you've hurt her, I thought, seething with pent up rage. Smithson, Emmerson, Terry Bannister – I'll kill each and every one of you. It was different from the feeling of remorse I'd felt about Alice, it wasn't that I'd forgotten about Alice, she'd given me temporary security and the warmth of her body, but there'd been nothing genuine about our lovemaking and on her part I was certain she'd done it to keep me at her house. Victoria was different; I thought I knew her well enough to know she wouldn't go to bed with someone unless she was in love with them.

I felt through my pockets and collected the remaining spare bullets for Motte's Walther and put them all into the side pocket of my anorak; seven in the magazine and eleven spares. Would it be enough? I cursed myself for failing to strip Bill of his Smith and Wesson and ammunition pouch. Never mind, I'd have to make do with the Walther, but what worried me was the length of time it took to load the bloody thing. In the light from the moon I cocked the automatic and took out its magazine and pushed another bullet on top of the other six – that gave me eight shots before I had to reload.

Wait a minute, I thought, Victoria didn't have one in her handbag, but perhaps ... I leaned across the steering wheel and rummaged in the parcel shelf on the passenger side. The plastic folder containing the Renault's driver's manual seemed unusually heavy. I opened it and an automatic pistol slipped out on to the passenger seat. I picked it up – it was small, about half the weight of the Walther and it had been designed for concealment, or as a ladies' gun. I took out its magazine, cocked it to make sure its chamber was empty, slipped out one of the five bullets in the clip and compared its size with one of the Walther's; they were the same calibre. I checked how the pistol's safety catch worked, pushed the magazine back into the butt and repeated the procedure I'd used a few minutes earlier with the Walther. I had a total of fourteen shots before I had to reload; as long as I didn't find myself up against a submachine-gun I'd have a reasonable chance. So, I asked myself, what are you waiting for? I turned the car round and drove the couple of hundred yards back into the village and parked it in a line of cars in the main street where it would be less conspicious.

In less than ten minutes I was standing by the side of the main road in a gateway to the field which ran up to the boundary of Emmerson's country property. I looked up at the brilliant moon and remembered I was breaking another promise I'd made to myself – the one I'd made on the night I'd crossed the field to Motte's house – to shun the country and stay in the concrete and steel of London. Forget it, I thought as I mounted the gate and dropped feet first into the wet grass, you been making false promises to yourself ever since Ann died. But no more, I thought, no more.

Time: 04.10 hours

I swung my leg over the top of the wooden two bar rail fence, dropped to the ground and ran and crouched behind one of the trees which surrounded the front of Emmerson's house. I'd learned from my experience at Hemel Hempstead; and on the way over from the gate I'd kept in the shadow of the hedge that ran by the side of the road until I'd found the fence. I moved through the small stand of fir trees until I reached the asphalted turning circle at the front of the house. Hunter's Lodge was a tall, compact, ugly property. From my vantage point I could see the stable yard and stables which straggled out from the house. The doors to the stables were shut and the whole place had an air of neglect, not the sort of decaying neglect you sense in houses that have long been unoccupied, but the feeling you get about houses that are unloved and uncared for. The place seemed unkempt and I guessed that Emmerson didn't spend much time there. As far as I could tell the house didn't have a garage and there weren't any cars parked outside in the drive. Oh shit! I swore softly. Did that mean Bill had lied to me? Had I come all the way from London for nothing?

If there were no signs of life at the front of the house perhaps I'd find something around the back. I retraced my path through the trees until I reached the fence, where I turned left and followed it. After twenty or so yards I found the driveway which ran down to the house from the main road. It was constructed of crushed stones, worn smooth over the years by the passage of car tyres, and like the house it was poorly tended, with deep ruts and tufts of grass. I estimated the overall distance of the Lodge from the main road at something like a hundred metres. I climbed the fence and moved quickly across the driveway, climbed over the fence on the other side into another field and continued my leftward circle. After another twenty metres I came to the end of the trees and to the discovery that the whole area at the back of the house was devoid of any cover in which I could hide.

The light cast by the moon was sufficiently bright for me to see the surrounding countryside and I saw in a second what I hadn't appreciated when I'd first seen Hunter's Lodge from the main road at the end of the village; the house stood on the top of a hill and the land at the back fell steeply away into a wide deep valley. A wood started halfway down the hill, about two hundred metres from the house, and continued across the valley floor and up the side of the hill opposite. I'm not very good on land measurements, but I thought the wood must cover at least seventy or eighty acres. To the north, about three or four miles away I could see the lights of a town. I turned and looked at the house. Whoever had built it had capitalised on the views, and whereas the front of the house had small, almost pokey windows, those at the back were set in large bays. Of more concern to me at that moment was the fact that all the curtains on those windows seemed to be open. Did that mean the place was empty? I took the Walther out of my anorak, slid down its safety catch and ran as fast as I could across the untidy garden towards the back of the house. In spite of my feelings that there was nobody at home my muscles were tensed, anticipating the blinding pain of a bullet and the sound of a shot.

After looking through all the bay windows into the rooms on the ground floor and seeing dustsheets covering the furniture all my suspicions were confirmed – the place was deserted. I thought about breaking in, except I couldn't see the point and I was certain the burglar alarms, fixed on the front and the back of the house, would be wired into the local police station. I put the safety catch back on my gun and hugged myself, suddenly conscious, once my adrenalin had ceased flowing, that the temperature was well below freezing. What about the stables, I thought, perhaps ... Perhaps nothing, I said to myself, you've fucked up, Victoria's not here. Still, I thought, you shouldn't leave before you've checked them out.

I walked disconsolately across the steeply-sided garden until I came to a wooden door set into a brick wall, about twelve feet high, which ran out from the side of the house, to form the back wall of the northern end of the stables. The door led on to a paved area which formed a small courtyard. On the left of the courtyard, on the side of the stables, there were a couple of doors and two tiny windows. I guessed they were small outhouses in which, at sometime in the past, the house's domestic servants would have done the washing. The back door to the Lodge stood opposite them, on the other side of the courtyard. I tried the handle but it was locked.

As I walked under the low narrow archway which led from the courtyard to the stables I felt tiredness begin to creep through my bones. I hadn't slept for nearly twenty-four hours, my shoulder hurt and the determination which had driven me on for the previous four hours was ebbing away. By the time I'd walked into the last stable and shone the pencil torch into each of its loose boxes and found nothing more than lumps of old horseshit, I was exhausted. I put my gun into my anorak pocket, sank on to a pile of straw and rested my back against the wooden spar at the entrance to one of the loose boxes. Come on, I urged my sagging brain, that little bastard Bill lied to you. Think! Where else could they have taken her? I closed my eyes and tried to sort out a plan. I'd have to go back to the car and drive to London and start again ... Perhaps they'd taken her to Smithson's house in Dulwich ...? Or to Emmerson's place in London …? I'd have to find out where he lived … Wasn't it somewhere near Holland Park …? and …

Time: 11.10 hours

I emerged out of a deep sleep with a start and looked out of my sleep-filled eyes. Jesus Christ! I'd fallen asleep in the stable. I looked at my watch – ten past eleven – I'd been asleep for six hours! In spite of my anorak I was cold. I struggled to my feet. My head swam and I had to hold onto the side of a loose box until my feeling of giddiness passed. My mouth was dry and tasted of horseshit and my shoulder was sore, worst of all I felt utterly dejected because I'd failed Victoria. Come on, Gorman, I told myself, forget about how you feel, think about how she feels, if she's still able to feel. I pushed myself away from the loose box and staggered towards the stable's partially open door and as my hand touched it my ears heard the sound of an engine. Someone was coming down the long drive to the Emmerson's house, and fast. Could I make the thirty yard run across the asphalted turning circle and get under the cover of the fir trees before it emerged at the bottom of the drive? Even as I thought about it I knew it was too late. I swung the stable door shut. Damn you! Damn you, you fucking asshole! I swore silently at myself as the noise of the vehicle's engine announced its arrival in front of Emmerson's house. Now you're fucking trapped!

While I watched through a chink in the stable door a Ford Transit van, painted in the SHA's dark blue, drove up to the farthest stable, stopped, and reversed up to the narrow archway at the entrance to the small courtyard. It was one from the office's motor pool. Frank, Emmerson's farm manager, the man who'd butted Victoria in the face, got out of the driver's side and went round to the back of the van and opened its rear door. Terry got out first, followed by Smithson and then … Oh, thank Christ, I breathed … Victoria. The van's open rear door obscured my view but as far as I could tell she was unhurt. Frank

237

went into the small courtyard and opened the back door of the house and all four of them went into the Lodge. So, I thought, Bill had told me the truth and unwittingly he'd helped me gain the advantage. It wouldn't be like the fight in Soho Square; I knew the layout of the ground; the element of surprise would be working for me; and for the first time in the last couple of years I had a sense of conviction about what I was doing. Suddenly I didn't feel weary anymore.

I checked my two automatics and put Victoria's back into my anorak pocket, making sure its safety catch was on and waited for three minutes, watching the second hand sweeping round my watch and debating whether to keep the old leather gloves I'd found in my anorak's pockets on, or to take them off. As the second hand completed its third sweep of the watch's dial I decided I'd do better with warm hands. Outside, the sky was the colour of lead – it would snow soon. This is it, I thought, in the moment before I ran over and squeezed through the gap between the side of the van and the arched entrance to the small courtyard. I crossed over to the backdoor and put my ear against it before I tried the handle; as I'd expected they hadn't bothered to lock it. Satisfied there was nobody standing behind it, waiting to surprise me, I inched it open and went into the house's large, well-fitted kitchen. On the opposite side of the kitchen were two doors. I was sure, as a result of my early morning reconnaissance that the one on the left, which was closed, led into the front entrance hall. The one on the right was partially open and I guessed it led to the cellars. I walked over to it and listened; almost immediately I detected the sound of voices. Taking a deep breath I opened the door and crept down the short flight of stone steps.

At the bottom of the steps, in the dim light cast by a single electric light bulb, I found I was in the main area of the cellar. One wall supported a series of wine racks, replete with bottles, and various species of dead birds were hanging from hooks which had been driven into the massive old wooden beams which supported the ground floor's floorboards. The sound of voices I'd heard from the kitchen were much louder but I couldn't see where they were coming from. I tiptoed across the dry flagstones and took cover behind a marble cold-keeping slab which had been built into the wall on the front side of the house and listened.

'Don't worry, my old darling,' Terry was saying, 'we'll soon see how tough you are when he gets here. You won't be so fucking high and mighty then.'

I located the sound of his voice; it was coming from a small cellar room, halfway along a passage at the end of the main cellar about twenty feet from where I was crouching. I could see a glow of light from the room's open entrance but I couldn't see them and unless they came out of the small cellar and down the passage into the main area they couldn't see me. 'He' must be Emmerson, I thought, and he must have given orders for them to lay off Victoria until he could question her himself. Why was she that important to him? Christ! He was bound to have a police escort with him. They wouldn't let the Home Secretary go prancing about the countryside on his own. Surely he wouldn't want them involved? He wouldn't want a pack of witnesses who might start talking. No. He'd tell them to wait on the main road at the entrance to the driveway down to the house while he came in alone. Would he have his personal bodyguard with him? Whatever the answers, one thing was certain – I didn't have much time.

I took Victoria's small pistol out of my anorak pocket, clicked off its safety catch and pulled back the hammers on both automatics, and with one in each hand I stood up and made my way over to the narrow passageway.

'I'll go and put the van out of sight,' the man called Frank said at the moment when I appeared in the doorway to the cellar room.

'Good ...' My intended salutation remained unfinished as my brain tried to assimilate the situation which confronted me. I'd anticipated Victoria might be tied up but the thought that Smithson would be tied up as well had never occurred to me, and the sight of him standing in

239

the middle of the cellar room, a few feet in front of her, with his wrists lashed to a steel hook in a wooden beam above his head, stopped me speaking, in mid sentence.

'Jesus!' said Frank. His eyes were fixed on my two guns.

'Gorman!' exclaimed Terry, his body momentarily frozen by surprise as I stepped across the threshold and walked a few steps into the cellar, my mind bursting with questions.

'Nick!' cried Victoria.

Smithson almost laughed. 'I was wondering whether you might turn up.' He was no longer attempting to disguise his Cockney accent. 'Do you know I spent the last week looking for you?' He gave me a look of respect. 'A proper Jack the lad, aren't you?'

'You do and I'll kill you!' I yelled, pointing the Walther at Terry as his right hand started to slide towards the pocket of his heavy overcoat. 'Put your hands on your head.' I motioned my left hand which was holding Victoria's gun at the man called Frank. 'You too.'

'Go on, Gorman, kill the bastards,' said Smithson.

'Now,' I said, when they'd both put their hands on their heads. 'Back away.'

They moved away from me until their shoulders were touching the wall of the cellar. I moved past Smithson, my eyes watching Terry and Frank, and stopped near the middle of the small room. I was about six or seven feet from them. 'OK. One at a time. Take out your guns and throw them over here.' I pointed at my feet with Victoria's gun. 'You first, Terry.'

They did as I told them, one at a time, throwing their revolvers on the floor near where I was standing.

I put Victoria's small automatic in my anorak pocket so I could untie her.

'You all right?' I gave Victoria a quick smile as I went over to her, still covering Terry and Frank with the Walther. A large blue bruise had spread across her left cheek where Frank's had butted her with his head.

'I'm OK.' Her eyes sparkled with tears of relief. 'Oh God, Nick,' she whispered.

Cold rage tightened my guts. 'He hasn't?' I asked, nodding my head at Terry.

She knew what I meant; Terry's sadistic treatment of young female heavies was no secret at the office.

She shook her head. 'No … He was saving it up until after Emmerson had finished with Smithson,' she said as I fumbled with my left hand to untie the wire which secured her wrists to a large rusty hook above her head.

'What about me?' asked Smithson, as he tried to swivel his head to look at me through his upstretched arms.

'Tell me where Alice is first?'

Smithson looked at me blankly. 'Who?'

'Alice Townsend. Where is she?'

'The woman on television?'

I nodded. 'Yes.'

'How the hell should I know? I've never met the bloody woman.'

Terry and Frank had the same blank expression on their faces as Smithson.

'You sent two men to her house last Saturday morning to kill me,' I insisted.

'Believe me, Gorman,' said Smithson, 'if I'd have sent two men to kill you, you'd be dead. Is that where you were hiding? With Alice Townsend?'

'How the bloody hell does a ragged arsed prick like you get to know someone like her?' interjected Terry.

His and Smithson's looks of disbelief confirmed the doubts which had troubled me since I walked out of Motte's gallery. And if neither of them knew I was at her house there was only one explanation for the appearance of the two gunmen; Alice herself had betrayed me. Probably when I was in the shower. And she'd wrestled with the man on her lawn because she was scared he'd kill me and that my knowledge of where to find Rayleigh's body would be lost to the General.

I pulled the wire away from Victoria's wrists and pushed her gently towards the cellar door. Now I knew why Motte had attempted to drug me when I'd gone to his gallery; he and Alice were working together and he'd guessed who I was, even before we'd gone up to his apartment and I'd told him my name.

'Hurry up and get me off this bloody hook,' said Smithson. 'Emmerson is going to kill me.'

If Smithson thought I was going to take pity on him he was sadly mistaken. 'I haven't the first idea why they've strung you up,' I said to him. 'But you can fucking well stay there.'

'You little shit!' he shouted and kicked at me.

I stepped away from the backward kick Smithson had aimed at my groin and the chance which Terry and Frank were waiting for presented itself. Twelve hours earlier, before my close quarter firefight with Bill, I'd have hesititated, or shouted 'Don't', or 'Stop', or some other useless injunction which would have cut down my thinking time. But my duel with Bill had taught me that you don't try and reason with guys like Terry and Frank, not if you want to stay alive. I gave them the same chance they'd have given me – no chance – and shot them both, twice, with two volleys from the Walther, before they'd got anywhere near their guns. Frank must have died instantly as my bullets hit him in his chest, slamming him bodily back against the cellar wall. Terry had been quicker than his partner, but not quite quick enough and the two bullets from my second volley ploughed into his lower back while he was scrabbling across the cellar floor towards his gun.

Despite that he was still alive and as he stretched out his trembling hand and his fingers clawed at the butt of his revolver I knew I had a choice. I could take two paces towards him and kick the revolver out of his reach or I could finish him off. The image of what he would have done to Victoria, once Emmerson had finished questioning her and Smithson, flashed across my mind and I made my choice, and shot him, once, in the head. Looking at Terry's shattered skull I knew how I should feel about breaking the moral imperative against killing; but I suppose it's like they say in war movies – the first time you kill is the worst. I know I felt a sense of personal triumph, not because he was dead, but because I'd known when he'd jumped out of the back of the van that if I followed him and Frank into the house only one conclusion was possible, and in choosing to follow them rather than slinking back to Victoria's car I'd at last faced up to reality.

'Fucking hell,' Smithson said softly, breaking into the silence which had descended on the cellar.

Victoria slowly sank to her knees and started to sob.

'It's OK,' I said, putting my guns into the pockets of my anorak before helping her to stand up. I held her close and stroked her hair. 'You're safe now, it's over.'

'Come on, Gorman, set me loose,' said Smithson. 'Help me and I'll give you anything you want. You want to get out of the Department? Out of London? A new identity? Just name it and you've got it.'

'Victoria,' I coaxed. 'We've got to get out of here before Emmerson turns up.' I did up the buttons on her dark grey overcoat which was streaked with dirt. 'We've got to walk about half a mile. Are you up to it?'

'Give me a minute.'

There was an old empty tea chest in one corner of the room. I up-turned it and she sat down.

'Come on, Gorman,' Smithson pleaded. 'Get me down.'

'What went wrong?' I said while I looked round the cellar floor. 'I thought you were running things.'

'So did I,' he laughed quietly to himself. 'I should've known better. There's always someone you have to pay off. Do you know that? No. 'Course you don't. You might have had a university education but you know nothing. I worked my way up from the gutter. Come on, Gorman, get me out of here, I've got money, I can pay.'

'Did you offer money to Terry?' I asked, bending down and picking up two of the spent bullet cases. I put them in my anorak pocket.

'He wouldn't have crossed Emmerson.' Smithson nodded in the direction of Terry's corpse. 'Fucking bastard. I trusted him and all the time he was spying on me for Emmerson.'

'But you've crossed Emmerson, mm? What happened? Some of that blackmail money stick to your fingers?'

'How did you know about that?'

'Victoria told me last night.'

I saw another spent bullet case lying in a pool of blood which was spreading out on to the floor by the side of the ragged hole in the back of Terry's skull.

'Tell me ...' I picked it up and wiped the blood off it on Smithson's vicuna coat. 'Why did you send me after Harris?'

'I already had Terry, Chris and young Bill looking for him, but I needed more manpower. You're a fucking good tracer I knew one of you was bound to find him.'

'And you wanted Harris to get you off the hook with Emmerson?' I looked up at his wrists, secured by wire to the large hook above his head. 'No pun intended.'

'It was my only hope of getting Emmerson off my back. It was dynamite. If I'd got my hands on Harris I could've given Emmerson conclusive proof that Rayleigh was gay and he could have done what he wanted. We could have kicked out the fucking Conservatives and taken over the government.'

'We still have something called general elections.'

'We'd have won any general election with the shit we could have thrown at the Conservatives.' He shook his head, angry at his lost opportunity. 'The minister of health? A fucking gay? Emmerson would have been prime minister and I could have had anything I asked for.'

Where the hell are the other two? I thought. Victoria and I had to get out before Emmerson came.

'And if I'd found him you were going to kill me? Is that right? That's why you lost your temper and told me to go home? So you knew where to find me?'

My eyes located the fourth bullet case in a corner of the room. That left ... how many times had I fired? Five shots? Yes. One more to find. Come on, you're wasting time, I told myself, it has to be around here somewhere.

'Is that right?' I repeated as I picked up the fourth bullet case. 'And Terry fucked it up? Instead of killing me he got Harris.'

244

'Don't be stupid,' he said. 'I didn't kill Harris. Where's the sense in that. I wanted him alive; so I could serve him and Rayleigh up to Emmerson on a plate. Even Terry understood that. We'd never have killed Harris.'

'What!' I stopped searching for the last bullet case and looked at him. 'But Chris was there. He was at Hemel Hempstead when Harris was killed.'

Smithson blinked. 'Chris?' he asked hoarsely. 'At Hemel Hempstead?'

I nodded. 'Yes,' I said, with emphasis. 'He was there.'

Smithson blinked again. 'The police fished Chris out of the Thames last Saturday morning. The last time anybody saw him was last Thursday afternoon.'

I tried to shuffle this new data into my picture of what had happened when the house at Hemel Hempstead had been attacked.

'You mean you didn't go out to Hemel Hempstead after I rang you on Thursday night?'

'Oh yes,' he said bitterly. He motioned at Victoria with his head. 'But her lot had already been there ... Jesus,' he said, and I realised we'd both arrived at the same conclusion. All the time while Chris had acted as one of Smithson's trusted confidantes, he'd actually been working in company with Victoria; the General had had two of his people spying for him inside the Soho Square office. Hang on, I thought, that can't be right, last night while we sat in her car Victoria said Chris was working for Smithson. Who had he been working for? Or did he really work for the General and did Victoria work for someone else? I gave up trying to decide who Chris could have been working for and concentrated my attention on finding the fifth bullet case.

'Him and her,' said Smithson, looking with hate at Victoria. 'The fucking pair of them were working against me.'

She was staring into space, still in shock and oblivious to our conversation.

I saw the last spent bullet case, lying at the threshold of the cellar entrance.

'Victoria?' I called softly to her and she got to her feet as I went over to the doorway and picked up the small brass case and dropped it into my pocket. When I turned round she was standing next to Smithson.

'What about him? What are you going to do with Smithson?'

I knew what she wanted me to do; I could see it in her eyes. I looked at Smithson; Emmerson would leave him hanging from the beam like the dead birds in the main area of the cellar. I'd spent the last week running and hiding from him but I couldn't do it – I couldn't steel myself to shoot him, not in cold blood.

'Come on, let's go,' I said, turning my back on her and walking out of the cellar, 'leave him to Emmerson.'

I hadn't taken more than two steps along the corridor when my ears caught the sound of two metallic clicks.

'No!' But as I turned and shouted she shot Smithson in the heart with Terry's revolver.

'Oh Christ,' I said.

She raised her head and looked at me. 'He killed Peter and my father,' she said defiantly.

'Smithson?'

'People like him. We're not playing some schoolyard game, Nick. There's no rules or codes of honour. It was my duty to kill him.'

Her defiant expression changed to a look of stunned confusion and I guessed that in spite of her tough façade he was the first person she'd killed and she was struggling with the same feelings of guilt I'd experienced after my gunfight with Bill.

'I know how you feel,' I said, starting towards her.

'Stay where you are,' she snapped, pointing the revolver at my chest.

I stood still, realising I was in the same situation as Frank and Terry had been, and that she might give me the same chance as I'd given them if I was foolish enough to threaten any quick movement.

'Are you going to kill me too, Victoria?' I said.

A tremor went through her body and the gun that was

246

pointing at me started to waver.

'Is it your duty? Or do you think I put the bomb in the car which killed your fiancé and your father? I saved your life, Victoria. Remember? I told you last night, we're partners.'

Her hand holding the gun dropped to her side and she started to sway. Stay where you are, I thought, one sudden movement and she still might shoot you.

She looked at the three bodies in turn. 'Oh please, Nick, get me away from here,' she said and as her voice broke and she started to weep, I went over and comforted her briefly before hustling her out of the cellar.

I half-carried her up the cellar steps and across the stableyard. We were nearly across the field and almost in sight of the village when she slipped and fell on the wet grass and I remembered Terry's revolver.

'Do you want to give me the gun?' I said after I'd helped her to her feet.

'What gun?' she replied dully.

She was almost exhausted when I'd first walked into the cellar and our shambling flight from the Lodge had sapped more of her physical strength than I'd anticipated.

'The gun you …' I stopped clumsily in mid-sentence.

'Terry's gun. Where is it?'

She shook her head. 'I don't know, I must have dropped it.'

'Victoria,' I said, shaking her gently by her shoulders. 'Where did you drop it? Where? Think. I know you're tired, but think.'

'In the cellar,' she said, shivering with fatigue. 'Or maybe when we climbed the fence into the field.'

Shit! I thought. I'd taken three or four minutes to find the spent bullet cases from the Walther on the off chance they might have my finger prints on them, and I'd cleaned the door handle on the back door and she'd dropped the bloody revolver, which probably had a complete set of her prints on its butt. It was my fault. I should have taken the bloody thing away from her before, while we were still in the cellar room.

'Look,' I said as I took the keys to her Renault out of my pocket. 'It's not more than a couple of hundred metres to the car. Just keep going towards the far corner of the field.' I pointed my finger in the direction she had to walk. 'Climb over the fence and you'll see the start of the village. Your car's in the main street.'

I looked at her to make sure she was understanding what I was saying to her.

'Do you understand, Victoria?'

She nodded, but her face had a blank look.

'Listen to me.' I shook her by the shoulders, more roughly this time. 'I want you to go to your car and get in it and wait for me. I'll be there in ten minutes.'

'Where are you going?'

'I'm going back to get the gun. Your finger prints are on it, if the police find it they'll be after you for murder.'

'Please, Nick, leave it. Anyway they'll find my finger prints in the van.'

'Victoria.' I sighed. 'We've both been in the back of the office van dozens of times. That won't prove you were here, but the bloody gun will. And I have to go back for it.'

Victoria touched my cheek with her hand. 'It's all right, Nick, don't worry, forget about the gun. All I have to do is make a phone call. I can get us out of this in a couple of minutes. It'll just take a phone call and we'll be safe. Honestly, it will.'

I heard what she said but I wasn't prepared to listen to her. We still had some semblance of the old-time law and order and it was certain that the police would search the house and grounds, and when they found Terry's revolver they'd have a vital clue in a murder hunt Emmerson would insist upon. And I was certain he would insist. Alive, Smithson was a nuisance to the BNDP; dead, he was a potential matyr. Truth was in the eye of the beholder, and I could see it was possible to construct an entirely different version of the true events; one in which Victoria and I had murdered five innocent members of the BNDP. In that version we would have killed two men at Soho Square and three more at Emmerson's house.

The police at the Toddington service station had got out of their car and walked immediately to the office. It wasn't difficult to imagine the line the prosecuting counsel would take: 'Did the defendant Gorman act strangely?' Too bloody right I had; 'Did you examine the Renault at the time, officer?' No, they hadn't; 'So it was possible that the young woman, whose finger prints were found on the revolver that murdered Mister Smithson, could have been lying on the back seat?' Yes, she could. Victoria might think she could get us out of trouble with one phone call, but, and she'd said it, we weren't playing schoolyard games, there were no rules or codes of honour, and I could see her boss, general or not, would find it more expedient to throw us to the wolves. I didn't see how he could do anything else, because protecting us would expose him and his operations against the BNDP to the whole world.

'Do as I tell you,' I said, putting her small automatic into the pocket of her coat. 'You may need this. Now, go to the car. Go on.' I pushed her in the direction of the village. 'Give me ten minutes. If I'm not back by then go without me.'

She stopped and turned round. 'Nick,' she pleaded.

'Go on!'

I watched her departing figure for a couple of seconds, before turning and running back towards the Lodge, trying to keep to the path our feet had left in the wet grass and looking down at the ground for Terry's revolver. Please, let her have dropped it in the field, I prayed. It wasn't in the field, nor the stableyard. I found it on the floor in the main area of the cellar, near where she'd tripped up the first step, and put it in my pocket. I went back up the steps, opened the back door and found myself face to face with two men.

Time: 11.45 hours

I said the first thing which came into my head.

'Sorry,' I said, smiling at the two men who were standing shoulder to shoulder in the small courtyard. 'We got held up. I'm just going to put the van out of sight for

Frank. Excuse me,' I added, walking past them towards the van.

If they were with Emmerson, and they knew he was coming to his house to ensure Smithson's departure from the world, what I'd said to them would have made sense, whereas if they were just two men who lived in the village, the mention of Frank's name would allay their suspicions, I hoped. Why hadn't I heard their car?

'Hold it!' There was a sound of metal snicking against metal. It was identical to the sound the Walther made when it was cocked – they weren't two men who'd strolled down from the village to see if Frank Mitchell was around. I stood still and raised my hands. My only hope now lay in keeping up my pretence that I was on their side.

'What's the matter with you? I told you,' I said, turning slowly to face them, 'Frank said I had to move the van.'

'Keep your hands up,' ordered the man who was pointing his gun at me.

They were both tall and heavily built, with hard bony faces, and dressed in collars and ties, dark overcoats and town shoes. And I knew I should have realised they were city boys.

'Look? What's going on?' I asked, like I was totally bemused by their response.

'Shut up,' said the one wearing a moustache and yellow tie. He glanced at his colleague. 'Turn round and put your hands on the van.'

'But ...'

'Fucking do it! Now!'

I turned round quickly and leant against the van's rear door with my hands outstretched.

Two hands ran up my legs and back, patted my sides and armpits, before feeling my chest.

'Here we are,' said the one in the blue shirt as his hands patted my anorak pockets. 'He's a walking arsenal,' he said to his companion as he relieved me of Terry's revolver and Motte's Walther.

'OK,' he said, after he'd stepped away from me. 'Inside the house.'

The one with the yellow tie pushed the kitchen door wide open and went inside and his partner motioned towards me with Terry's revolver. 'Inside.'

'You wait here,' said blue shirt to yellow tie when the three of us were standing inside the Lodge's kitchen. He put my two guns on to one of the kitchen cabinet's working surfaces. They were well out of my reach; yellow tie had enough time to empty his gun's magazine into me and reload it again before I could get to them.

'I'll go and tell him what we've found. OK?' said blue shirt to his partner.

'Keep him covered while I put my silencer on,' said yellow tie. He took a silver coloured tube out of the inside pocket of his overcoat.

Blue shirt looked at me in the way a seasoned veteran looks at a new recruit and grinned. 'What are you worried about?' he asked yellow tie, pointing his finger at me. 'He won't give you any trouble.'

'I know,' said yellow tie, as he attached the silencer on to the end of his automatic pistol. 'But this is a new coat. I don't want to get it dirty rolling around on the floor.' He smiled at blue shirt. 'Don't worry I shan't kill him unless the boss says so.'

'I shan't be long,' said blue shirt as he went out into the courtyard. 'You're sure you're going to be all right, dearie?' he asked sarcastically over his shoulder. 'Not too big a job for you, is it.'

'Fuck off,' yellow tie called after him as he levelled his automatic at me.

'Look …' I said.

'Shut your mouth,' yellow tie snapped. 'Stand over there. And keep your hands up.'

I walked across the kitchen and stood with my back to the cellar door, facing him.

It couldn't have been more than three or four minutes later when I heard footsteps coming over the courtyard's paving stones and into the kitchen walked James Emmerson, Home Secretary and Leader of the British National Democratic Party. I'd only seen him on TV but in the flesh it was easy to see why the popular press described him as charismatic. He was tall and well put together and his slimness and radiant good health made him look in his early forties; it wasn't until you looked more closely and saw the lines under his eyes and the deep crease marks running by each side of his mouth that you realised he was the other side of fifty. The leonine head and piercing blue eyes were his best features; they gave him the air of a Greek god, confined to walk the earth in the company of mere mortals. He was the sort of man people want to follow.

'I told Patterson to radio the police escort,' he said in his upper-class accent to yellow tie while he gave me a long appraising look. 'We don't want them panicking and driving down to the house. He'll bring the car. He should be with us in a couple of minutes.'

He pulled back the cuff on his well tailored black Crombie overcoat and looked at his watch while I wondered whether his two gorillas had approached the house on foot when they'd seen the SHA van parked outside.

'Now,' he said, speaking to me for the first time. 'What have we got here? Who are you?'

I didn't have to act scared; I was scared, scared to death, because I knew that in all probability yellow tie and blue shirt were hardline BNDP and that unless God intervened with one of His thunderbolts I was going to be dead within the next ten minutes.

'I asked you a question. Who are you?' Emmerson repeated.

'I work with Terry Bannister,' I replied. I could hear the sound of fear in my voice.

'Don't lie! Bannister is personally accountable to me and I know the names of all the people he uses. Now, who are you?'

The implication of what he'd said about Terry left me momentarily speechless. Bannister? A rat like him personally accountable to Emmerson? It revealed more about the real Emmerson than all the newspaper and television analyses of his character ever had.

'Where is Bannister?' Emmerson spoke to yellow tie.

Emmerson's BNDP bodyguard shrugged his shoulders. 'I don't know. We were in the yard when this guy came out of the house.'

Emmerson compressed his lips and came further into the kitchen.

'For the last time, who are you? And where is Bannister?'

I tried to swallow but my mouth and throat were so dry they wouldn't work.

'Loosen his tongue,' Emmerson said to yellow tie. 'We're late enough as it is. I promised I'd be there in time for lunch.'

All the smart things I might have said stayed buried inside my head; I knew clever remarks wouldn't do me any good but I was desperate to keep back the moment when Emmerson's BNDP thug started hitting me. Yellow tie walked past his boss who was standing on his left and slightly in front of him.

'Please,' I whimpered, anticipating the helping of pain I was about to receive.

I'd like to say I planned it, but like most things which intervene to save us in this life it came about by accident. I suppose the genuineness of my plea for mercy was enough to convince yellow tie that I wasn't going to put up a struggle or even attempt to resist whatever he intended to do to me, and he made the same mistake I made with Bill on the previous night – he relaxed his vigilance. When you're about to be beaten into submission your senses are much sharper than normal, perhaps it's something to do with your nerve endings. But I could see from the expression in his eyes and the way he walked that he wasn't expecting I'd give him any trouble, and if he hadn't been overconfident and let the aim of his automatic slide away from my body I probably wouldn't have. But the instant I noticed his gun was pointing at the wall by my right thigh my jangling nerve ends and pumping adrenalin fused and I obeyed the primeval command which shouted from deep inside me … Fight!

I pivoted to my right and with my left foot supporting my weight I launched myself at him in a full blooded *mae-geri*, intending to execute a double kick; the first to hit under his heart and the second to strike his face. I forgot all the instructions I'd ever received about the need to check one's blows and kicked him as hard as I could. Yellow tie's reactions were quick and he was beginning to turn as I struck. Like most right-handed people avoiding a blow he was turning to his left with his right arm across his chest to shield his body and when the sole of my foot hit his right wrist, which was protecting his chest, two things happened. The force of my blow accelerated him in the leftward turn he was making and it caused his fingers to contract on the butt and trigger of his automatic pistol; I heard the vicious zipping sound as it fired. His wrist had taken some of the force of my first kick but the second part of the *mae-geri*, my follow up kick, struck him on his right cheek. I'd intended to kick him full in the face and as he reeled away from me I thought I hadn't managed to cripple him; frightened lest he recover, I threw myself on to his back and, putting my hands under his throat, I seized the lapels of his new overcoat and held him in a basic judo chokehold. If he was conscious when he'd hit the floor he was unconscious within ten seconds of me applying the chokehold and stopping the flow of blood to his brain.

Yellow tie was an incautious man and he hadn't uncocked his gun as he'd advanced towards me to mete out the pain demanded by Emmerson. If he had it wouldn't have fired when my first kick hammered against his wrist and Emmerson wouldn't have been lying on the floor next to him, the victim of a gunshot wound. From what I could see, a single bullet had entered his face, above the jawline on his right side and had blown away most of his lower jaw and teeth. He wasn't dead, but I could see that whoever had invited him for Sunday lunch was going to have to keep it in the oven for some time. His eyes looked at me, silently appealing for help. I pushed myself away from the body of his unconscious bodyguard, picked up my two guns and ran across the courtyard and through the door which led into the garden and as I closed it behind me I heard a car sweep into the asphalted turning circle at the front of the house. I guessed blue shirt had delivered Emmerson's message to his police escort before driving the car from the bottom of the drive into the broad turning circle at the front of the Lodge, and that I had about two minutes in a downhill race to reach the safety of the wood.

Time: 11.55 hours

I scrambled over the wooden fence and dived into the trees. My headlong flight from the house under a sky of snow-filled clouds had used up a lot of my strength and I was glad it had been downhill. I lay in the cover of the wood, panting, and looking back up the slope towards Hunter's Lodge before lying on my back and practising deep breathing exercises until my heart stopped trying to burst out of my ribcage. Although I was losing several minutes it was a long climb to the top of the hill, on the far side of the valley from Emmerson's house, and a good wind might make all the difference later on. When my breathing was something like normal I started up the hill under cover of the trees which were starting to sway in the rising wind. Whoever owned the wood had neglected the principles of forestry management and it was badly in need of thinning, but as I crashed and staggered through its thick undergrowth I consoled myself with the thought that I'd be almost invisible from the house in my camouflaged anorak. Near the top of the hill I stopped to look back at the house. It was clearly visible on the other side of the valley and I could see the blue lights on the top of the police cars winking through the murk of the lightly falling snow.

I climbed the last fifty metres to the top of the hill and struggled out of the wood and started across a ploughed field. Despite the previous night's frost the earth was sodden; it sucked at my thin city shoes and I nearly lost one as I stepped between the furrows. By the time I'd

255

reached the field's farther side it was snowing heavily. I made my way along its boundary hedge until I found a five bar gate and half climbed, half fell over it. Sitting in a rising carpet of snow, sucking air into my lungs, I peered through the obliterating cascade of snowflakes. I was on the side of a deserted road and I could make out the shapes of farm buildings, about a hundred metres away, I guessed a farmhouse must be behind them. The thought that it might be part of Emmerson's farm, perhaps even the farmhouse where Mitchell, his farm manager, lived, injected a new energy into my flagging body and I heaved myself upright, took off my shoes and scraped the mud off them on the edges of the gate's wooden spars; their leather was wet and mushy and my trousers were caked in mud up to the knees. I must have looked like a strolling scarecrow.

I knew, if my sense of direction was still intact, that if I walked along the road in the opposite direction from the farm buildings it would take me towards the town, whose lights I'd seen in the distance when I'd been reconnoitring Emmerson's house in the early hours of the morning. I made good progress for the first mile but after that the wind's velocity increased to a near blizzard, whipping the snow into my mouth and eyes. A car with its headlights on passed by on the opposite side of the road. It was going my way, but I decided against trying to wave it down; hitching a ride invited the prospect of questions I couldn't answer and the subsequent possibility of a phone call to the police to report a dishevelled man picked up within a couple of miles from the massacre at Emmerson's house. Instead, I moved off the road and hoped the weather conditions were bad enough to prevent the driver from seeing me. I knew they were bad enough to keep the Army's helicopter gunships on the ground.

After about another mile of hard slogging I found myself standing at the brow of a long steep hill. Halfway down I came across a sign which told me I was walking into a town called Market Harborough. I trudged on, my mind dredging up long forgotten geography lessons. I'd reached the bottom of the hill and I was walking under a railway bridge by the time my memory had located me in a small town in Leicestershire, about fourteen miles from Leicester. The trouble was I wanted to get back to London. I passed a couple of pubs and another railway bridge which had long since been demolished. Two railway lines were a good omen, even if one of them had been torn down – with any luck the town would have a station and I'd be able to catch a train to London.

I kept going until I reached a road junction with traffic lights. There were one or two cars about and a few people on foot. No one paid any attention to me while I stood at the junction deciding whether to turn left or right. Turning left would take me into the town centre and I thought it was the most likely place to find the railway station. A man walked by me.

'Terrible weather,' he said.

I knew it was a risk but I couldn't waste half the afternoon walking around the town looking for the railway station, for all I knew it had been closed years ago as part of British Rail's privatisation plan during Margaret Thatcher's fourth term of government.

'Can you tell me the way to the railway station?' I asked, hoping the hood on my anorak would hide most of my face.

'Yes. It's down there.' He pointed. 'It's not far, you can't miss it.'

I was pleased I'd taken the risk, because he'd pointed down the road to my right, and if I hadn't asked him I'd have wasted a lot of time hunting for the station in the town centre.

I walked to the station in less than five minutes. It had a pleasant façade although British Rail had done its best to deface it. I went through the main entrance and into the booking hall, located the wall panel of timetables and studied the times of the Sunday service; the next train to London was due at 15.05. It stopped six times before it reached the capital – six possibilities that the Transport Police would board the train to check passengers' ID cards. My watch and a clock on the wall above the timetables said it was 14.45. I went over to the ticket office and pushed my ID, and the All Areas Pass under its glass window and asked the clerk for a second class single to London St Pancras. He barely glanced at them before he punched a ticket, took most of my remaining cash and shoved the ticket and my ID and pass back under the screen.

'Is it on time?' I asked him as I scooped up the coins and put them in my pocket.

His head was already back behind the BNDP's Sunday newspaper with its lead article calling for the disestablishment of the Church of England if its bishops didn't stop their campaign for the more humane treatment of AIDS sufferers – SACK BISHOPS WHO SAY WE SHOULD LOVE AIDS RATS screamed the headline.

'Let's hope so,' he said without interest.

I walked along the deserted tunnel to the London platform, transferring my Walther to a pocket in my suit jacket, and finding some comfort in the fact that if I was caught the clerk in the ticket office was likely to gain first hand experience of his Party's humanity for failing to take more interest in a citizen who looked as bedraggled as I did.

Before the station had been largely demolished under the popular euphemism of 'development' there'd have probably been a waiting room, warmed by a coal stove, on the London platform, of course British Rail's huge redundancy programme of the early 1990s meant there wouldn't have been any staff to light the stove, but at least there'd have been somewhere to wait in inclement weather. Instead of a waiting room the only genuflection to passenger comfort was a brick wall which ran along the back of the platform; it was chest high and as the snow-laden wind whipped over the top of it, freezing my head and shoulders, I wondered whether the planners had deliberately built it at that height to ensure the travelling public would suffer maximum discomfort. I turned my back to the wind and hugged myself to keep warm, my feet in the snow which hadn't been cleared from the platform. Now I was no longer on the move I was beginning to feel cold.

Just after three I was joined on the platform by two young men whose civilian clothes couldn't disguise the fact they were servicemen returning to duty at the end of a weekend leave. I guessed they were the MEATAG (the Midlands and Eastern Army Tactical Group), whose HQ was at Bedford. They stayed at the other end of the platform, chatting together and stamping their feet, while I spent the time until the train arrived reading the BNDP's posters on the walls of the platform opposite, with their thinly veiled exhortations of violence towards ethnic minorities.

The train pulled into the station at 15.08. I looked into the carriage windows as they rolled past; as I'd expected, the second class compartments were packed. I crunched along the platform through the layer of rapidly freezing snow and got into the last carriage. As a rule the Transport Police commenced their ID inspections at the front of the train. The All Areas Pass didn't expire for another fourteen days but my appearance was bound to raise suspicions and I was worried that the police might find it difficult to believe that someone who looked like a tramp could be on official government business. Still, I thought, if I can find a seat with a table the constricted space of a second class carriage would help me to hide the state of my trousers. I found a seat with a table and when the train began to draw away from the station I took off my anorak, placed it on my seat and asked the middle-aged woman sitting next to me to guard it. I didn't think there was much likelihood she'd look through its pockets and find Terry's revolver.

Standing in the tiny lavatory I tore strips off a paper handtowel and jammed them into the washbasin and filled it with warm water before taking off my suit and socks. I dropped the socks into the basin and immersed the bottom half of my trouser legs and squeezed their material gently until the most of the mud had dissolved. After I'd wrung them out I attacked the blood stain on my jacket and cleaned Martin's shoes with a paper handtowel; they'd carry me home but once there their last journey would be to the dustbin. I washed my face and combed my hair and scrutinised myself in the mirror; there was a day's growth on my face. OK, I said to myself, so you're growing a beard. I climbed back into my trousers and inspected my condition. From the knees down I looked as if I'd walked through a river but that apart it wasn't too bad and as long as I remained seated I'd pass muster if the Transport Police inspected my papers. Feeling more hopeful, I went back to my seat.

'What happened to you?' The woman who'd kept my place asked after I'd sat down.

'I slipped over and fell in the station's carpark,' I said. 'Serves me right. I should have taken a taxi.'

She re-directed her attention to her book, seemingly satisfied with my explanation.

Trains always have a soporific effect on me, even when I haven't gone without sleep, killed four people, faced the prospect of imminent death and battled through a blizzard, and although I kept cautioning myself to the contrary I eventually succumbed to the train's hypnotic motion and nodded off. When I woke up the train was standing in a station. My mouth tasted like I'd been eating sheep droppings but my head was clearer.

'Where are we?' I asked the woman sitting next to me.

'Luton,' she said, putting the side of her face against the carriage window and to look down the platform. 'The police are checking the train.'

'Is that usual?' I forced myself to make my enquiry sound casual. 'I thought they checked us while the train was moving?'

'I don't think it can be,' she replied. 'Otherwise there'd be chaos. It would throw all the timetables out, wouldn't it? Perhaps they're looking for someone special.' She gave me a conspiratorial smile. 'You never know these days do you? Perhaps someone's escaped from a Care Centre.'

I felt the weight of Terry's pistol in my anorak which I'd

260

folded up and put on my lap. She'd be smiling on the other side of her face if I was the special person the police were hunting. I looked at the people in the seats across from the gangway and further down from the carriage; a couple of young lovers, a man and his wife, someone's grandmother, a young mother and her baby, if it was me they were looking for a lot of innocent people would be hurt when the shooting started. And I was going to go down fighting, no matter what. I watched the young woman cuddling her baby – there was something about her which reminded me of Ann. I made my decision and started to unwrap my anorak. I'd go to the toilet, put five new bullets into the Walther's magazine and get off the train. There were a couple of luggage trolleys on the platform outside the carriage window; they'd provide cover, and I'd put down a couple of policemen before they killed me.

Someone shouted in the next carriage. A carriage door slammed and seconds later a young man ran past the window, followed moments later by two policeman in hot pursuit. There was the sound of one gunshot. The woman and I looked at each other. After a few minutes the two policemen came past the window; they were dragging the young man's dead body behind them. The woman pressed her face to the window.

'Poor lad,' she said. 'See,' she turned back and looked at me, 'I told you they were looking for someone.'

I nodded to her and began to re-fold my anorak to enable me to get my hand inside the pocket which contained Terry's Smith and Wesson.

The train started with a jerk and then moved smoothly out of the station. From my aisle seat I saw two more officers of the Transport Police enter the carriage at the far end and begin the process of checking peoples' ID. I took out my ID and the All Areas Pass and placed them on the table in front of me. They'd found the person they were looking for, perhaps I'd make it. Just to be on the safe side I slid my hand into my anorak's pocket, gripped the cold butt of the pistol and slipped off its safety catch. I looked again at the young woman who reminded me of Ann; she was rubbing her baby's back. The last thing I wanted was a shoot out, but my travelling companions shared the same burden of guilt as I did for the harsh uncertainty of our lives; they had the vote and they'd have to take their chance in the circumstances they'd let politicians create. If it came to shooting, so be it, what came after I'd no idea and I really didn't care.

I watched as the two policeman worked their way towards me, checking people's ID cards. Neither of them looked more than twenty years old and I knew they'd do what they'd been trained to do – any sign of trouble and they'd reach for their guns. I pulled back the hammer on the revolver. Any second now, I thought, when the policeman inspecting ID cards on my side of the carriage reached my seat.

'Papers,' he said, holding out his hand. He had a large nose and acne.

I picked them off the table with my left hand and gave them to him. He examined them carefully and stared down at me. At the first sign of trouble I'll shoot him where he stands without taking the revolver out of my anorak pocket, I thought.

'I've never seen one of these before,' he said, waving the All Areas Pass at me.

'No?' There was no curiosity in my question. I wanted to sound like a bored official who wasn't surprised that a callow youth like him hadn't seen one before. I smiled at him. 'They're quite common.'

'I suppose so,' he said.

He passed my papers back to me and did as fair an imitation of touching his forelock as his peaked cap allowed.

'Have a good journey,' he said.

He checked the papers of the three passengers who were sitting next to me and as he handed back the woman's papers she asked him what had been the cause of the trouble at Luton.

'Nothing to trouble yourself about, madam,' he said as he gave me a look which implied only he and I knew what

262

was going on in the world outside the train's fuggy atmosphere.

I nodded to him almost imperceptibly and he patted his chest in a tiny display of pomposity before moving on down the aisle. When the two policemen had completed their task they passed down the carriage, their duty done it would be tea and a smoke in the guardsvan.

I eased back the hammer on the Smith and Wesson, took my hand out of my anorak pocket and settled deeper into the seat and asked myself what I was going to do once the train reached London. After a while I decided I didn't care if it was an axiom of my business that the hunted generally returned to their lair, that was where I was going. Apart from anything else I couldn't think of another option. It was the only place I could rest and in the few hours I'd be there I'd have to consider what to do with the rest of my life. For a short time at least I hoped that if anybody was looking for me it would be the last place they'd think of. It would take the police some time to find out the part I'd played at Emmerson's house – two or three days at least, probably. There was the mess I'd left at the office but with the killings in Leicestershire the police would probably be looking for a political connection; they'd want to interview everyone who worked at Soho Square of course. If they'd already been round to my flat they'd have discovered I hadn't been there since Thursday, although for someone in my line of work there wasn't anything remarkable in that. With luck they'd have left a message with my landlord, who lived on the ground floor, telling me to report to the nearest police station. It would be when I failed to appear that they'd begin to suspect I'd been involved in the killings.

The only person who could positively place me at Emmerson's house was Victoria, and as long as she'd done as I'd told her she'd have been on her way back to London by the time the police cordoned the area round the village. If she made it back to London without her All Areas Pass what would she do? It was certain she'd report in to someone in the General's organisation. And then what?

Oh God, I thought, what difference does it make whether I'm killed here on the train or at my flat, except that if I'm killed at the flat at least I'll be in my own home. I needed a hot bath, a change of clothes, food, sleep and money, and in that order, and the only place where they were all available was at home. Whether it was Victoria's people or the police who came after me, the trick was to be as far away from London as possible when they rang my doorbell. If I could get back to my flat and collect my things I'd have the means to get out of London to somewhere I could hide permanently. Going to see Wally Jacobs, the forger, and getting him to make up false papers wasn't the way I'd have chosen to vanish, but there was no other alternative. I drifted into a light doze with the feeling that as long as I was careful and lucky everything might turn out all right, and I didn't wake up until the train pulled in to St Pancras station.

I dawdled along the platform so that I could see if the police were at the ticket barrier but the only hint of officialdom was the two railway staff who were collecting passengers' tickets. I handed mine in and walked across the station concourse, skirting around two or three large gangs of BNDP skinheads who were on their way back from a Party rally in Hyde Park. I passed a group of them as I went down the stairs to the underground; they were in an ugly mood and I was glad I was white and well-built. I thought for a moment of the young Pakistani couple I'd met in Baker Street on Saturday evening and hoped they'd have had the sense to keep out of central London in favour of the relative security of their homes in Willesden. I bought myself a ticket from the automatic machines before walking along the tunnel to the Victoria Line.

A lot of people were on the platform and I stood with my back to the SHA's poster telling citizens it was their duty to report suspected AIDS carriers, by phoning the SHA's freephone number and giving the name of the suspect in the knowledge that their information would be treated in complete confidence. Further along the platform there were more SHA posters, with pictures of current pop stars warning their fans of the dangers of casual sex. I let two trains go by and jumped on the third at the very last moment before the doors closed. I was the only person to get off at Warren Street and I waited until the doors closed and the train rattled away, into the tunnel and out of sight, before crossing over to the Northern Line and catching the next train to Finchley Central; it seemed a pointless exercise but I wanted to be sure I wasn't being followed. Coming out of the station at Finchley I hailed a cab and spent the last of my money to avoid the walk to my flat through the bitter cold streets.

Time: 18.50 hours

I pressed my landlord's doorbell and waited.

'Yes? Who is it?' His voice spoke at me from the microphone by the side of the front door to the house which had been divided into three flats.

'It's Nick Gorman. I'm afraid I've lost my key. Could you let me in please?'

'Bloody hell. Some people.' He was that kind of person.

The electric lock buzzed and I went and stood outside his door on the ground floor. Bolts were slammed back and a security chain rattled and he opened it and peered out at me.

'Why can't you be more careful? It's a good job I keep spares. Where did you lose them?'

It was in my mind to say if I knew where I'd lost my keys I wouldn't be standing outside his door asking for a spare, but I did know where I'd lost them; they were in the pocket of Martin's sheepskin coat at Alice Townsend's house.

'I don't know,' I said as he passed me a key.

'There you are,' he said. 'Don't lose that one. I don't know, you'll be losing your head next.'

I'd never realised he had the gift of prophecy.

'Thanks,' I said, pocketing the key.

I was halfway down the hall when he called. 'How's

your mother?'

Considering she'd been dead for nearly five years it was an odd question to ask.

'How did you know?' I called back.

'A couple of your friends turned up on Friday morning. They said she'd been taken ill and they needed to get in touch with you urgently. I let them into your flat, I wouldn't normally but they showed me their ID and I know you work for the SHA. Is she any better?'

'Yes thanks,' I replied. 'When did they go?'

'I don't know, I was out most of the day. They pushed a note under my door saying they'd found you. You've got some good friends there,' he confided. 'The big one – whatisname? – Terry – he was very concerned about you.'

'Yes,' I said. 'Terry's a good mate.'

'Oh, yes, and the police called too.'

Act naturally I told myself. 'When did they come?'

'This morning. I'd just had my breakfast. Are you in trouble with them?'

'No,' I said casually. 'It's about something at the office. What did they say?'

'They said that if I saw you I was to tell you to report to the nearest police station.'

'It's only a routine enquiry. Don't worry,' I reassured him. 'I'll go in first thing tomorrow morning. Well, good night.'

He slammed his door shut without answering.

I climbed the stairs to the second floor and went to my flat. Before I inserted the key he'd given me in the lock I took out Terry's revolver and flattened myself against the wall. I'd seen enough movies to know the drill off by heart. I turned the key, opened my front door and prepared to launch myself into a forward roll through the front door. Instead I told myself I was being silly and walked inside and turned the lights on. The flat was exactly as I'd left it apart from a couple of dirty teacups Terry's people had left on my small dining table. I'd expected to find that they'd ripped the place apart. It would have been a senseless act of destruction because they were looking for me, not something I'd hidden, but I thought Terry might have done it out of spite. I closed the front door and secured its bolts and security chain before concentrating on my first priorty – a hot bath.

After a long, hot bath and a plateful of eggs, bacon and hot toast I felt human again. When I'd put the dirty crockery in the dishwasher I went into my living room for the address book I kept by the phone and checked Victoria's home number on the list which the office distributed to all staff in case of emergency. Against my better judgement I dialled and waited for her to reply. Listening to the ringing tone, I told myself as long as I didn't tell her where I was I'd be safe. She didn't answer, even though I let it ring for a long time, and I put the phone down wishing I followed my better judgement. Did it mean she'd been caught? Or was she somewhere safe, reporting what had happened to her during the last twenty-four hours? I went back into the kitchen and took a packet of cheroots from the drawer of the small pine dresser and lit one. What if she was dead? Going back into the living room I glanced at the front door, the one Ann had walked out of the last time I'd seen her alive. I slumped on the sofa and hot tears filled my eyes before I could stop them, as emotions I'd denied since I'd walked into the cellar room at Emmerson's house refused to be suppressed any longer.

When I felt calmer I turned on the radio; I'd missed the TV news but I knew the pop music stations had regular news flashes. I listened to the end of the current number one record in the popular music charts while I reloaded Motte's Walther and checked that I understood the Smith and Wesson's mechanism. In the news flash which followed the end of the record there was no mention of the events at Emmerson's house and the lead item concentrated on the effects of the snow storms which had swept across the Midlands and the south of England. I turned off the radio and pushed the dining table against the front door, before going to bed, taking both guns with me. The kitchen door was reinforced and I knew it would take the police, or the soldiers from SEATAG, time to break it down, certainly time enough for me to put the end of the Walther's barrel into my mouth and pull the trigger.

VII

MONDAY,
28 FEBRUARY 1999

Monday, 28 February 1999

Time: 10.00 hours

I didn't wake up until mid-morning and I got straight out of bed and pulled back the curtains. I looked out of the window into the street. The sky was a cloudless blue and the sun was fast melting the snow on the rooftops opposite. After I'd dressed and had breakfast I tried Victoria's number again. I didn't care about my better judgement; I just wanted to hear the sound of her voice and to know that she was all right. When she didn't reply I thought of ringing the office to see whether she'd reported for work, until I convinced myself that that really would be stupid. Was she all right? The question kept harrying me as I went to the bedroom and packed a couple of changes of clothes and my shaving kit into a medium sized Samsonite travel bag I'd bought for the last holiday Ann and I had been on before she was killed. Afterwards I went to my hiding place, behind the chest of drawers, next to the bedroom window, and gathered together my birth certificate, bank deposit book, passport and the small bundle of banknotes I kept for emergencies and put them into the inside pocket of my anorak along with my ID and the All Areas Pass. I put the Walther in the hip pocket of my jeans, slipped into my anorak and put Terry's revolver into one of its large patch pockets; like the Walther, the Smith and Wesson was mine now, until death did us part.

Going back to the living room I moved the dining table away from the front door, unlocked the bolts, took off the security chain and looked round the room for the last time.

I wasn't sorry to be leaving, it hadn't been decorated since Ann and I had moved in and it contained too many bad memories which I'd tried to ignore, but they'd always been there, waiting to pounce on me when my psychological defences were low. The only thing I'd miss were my books and videotapes of favourite movies which I'd recorded off the TV in the dark lonely hours when I hadn't been out on the streets hunting people for money. I thought about the bank deposit book in my anorak inside pocket, next to my heart. The money I'd amassed since I'd become a tracer had been earned by cunning and the controlled exercise of terror against other human beings – it was dirty money – but without it I'd never escape from London.

I walked out of the flat, shut the door on my past life and ran down the stairs. I needed a complete set of forged papers by the end of the day or my idea of fading away into obscurity would melt away like the snow on the pavements in the street. Once I'd got out of London the next problem would be to get on to the SHA's computer under my new name so I could have legitimate blood tests. Forged blood test certificates cost the earth, that's why people killed for them, and if I had to pay for a new one every three months I'd be broke inside two years. I knew it was possible to get on to the computer; a computer expert who I'd traced and arrested had nearly got away with it. I'd kept her secret to myself and I knew where she'd gone wrong and as long as I didn't repeat her mistake I didn't think I'd be found out. I let myself out of the service entrance at the rear of the house. Forged papers were my only hope until then and Wally Jacobs was a good forger, but once he knew the purpose of my visit his price would go up, because he'd know I couldn't reveal what went on in the basement of his little printing business without being arrested myself. Nobody did any favours for a tracer on the run and dirty money or not my first port of call would have to be my bank.

I hailed the first taxi that passed and told the driver the address of my bank and when he pulled up outside it I asked him to wait.

'How long, guv?'

'Until I come back. I shan't be long.'

He looked at the meter and swivelled round in his seat to get a better look at me through the thick safety glass which kept him safe from violent passengers. His eyes took in my camouflage anorak and I could see he thought I was a runner who'd skip without paying my fare.

'I want a tenner before you leave this cab,' he insisted.

I peeled off a twenty pound note from my small bundle of banknotes, rolled it up and pushed it through the grill.

'Here,' I said. 'Will this do?'

He reached over and took the twenty pound note out of the plastic ledge on his side of the screen.

'Sorry, guv. But you can't be too careful. I had a couple of runners last week. Bastards! It's got so you have to watch everybody. Do you know? One of them was dressed in a business suit, he had a brief case, posh voice, everything. Jumped out of the cab and ran away. I ask you, if people like that can't be trusted what the bloody hell's the world coming to? What with the curfew and all. I mean, there's not much point giving us curfew passes if there's nobody about after midnight, is there? It's got so I can hardly make a decent living.'

I tutted in sympathy and got out of the cab.

'You'll wait here?' I asked, putting my lips close to the speaking grille in the window on the front passenger door.

'Don't worry, guv.' His amplified voice sounded through the speaker below the grille. 'I'll be here, but be as quick as you can, I'm waiting on a double yellow line.'

I crossed the pavement, went into my bank and joined the end of the queue. There were eight people in front of me and only two of the six windows were open for business. It was always the same whichever bank you went to, the lack of an able-bodied workforce with the necessary educational qualifications to staff places like banks persisted in spite of the high salaries. It took ten minutes before I was at the head of the line. The two people at the windows in front of me were local shopkeepers and I watched with growing exasperation as the clerks emptied their blue linen bags and started counting the banknotes, stamping cheques and weighing bags of coins. I silently cursed the pair of them for failing to put their wretched money into the bank's nightsafe when they'd finished business on the previous Saturday. It seemed an age before one of the clerks handed back the linen bag and payment books to the shopkeeper at the nearest window. He was grossly fat and I tapped my foot on the floor in an attempt to control my fury as he laboriously put the book in his bag and folded it on the counter. Eventually he moved away from the window and the clerk touched her buzzer to indicate she was ready to grant an audience to her next customer.

I went to the counter and dropped my deposit book into the tray underneath her window.

'I want to withdraw five thousand in cash and I want a banker's draft for the rest, please,' I said. 'No, leave a hundred pounds in the account, would you please?'

She was short and dumpy with thick black glasses that accentuated her fat cheeks, and when she looked at me through the window I knew I was going to have trouble.

'Do you have any identification?' she looked at the name in my deposit book, 'Mister Gorman?'

I took out my bundle of documents from the inside pocket of my anorak.

'I can't give you any traveller's cheques without a Foreign and Commonwealth Office certificate. Besides you're at the wrong window,' she said the moment she saw my passport. 'The Overseas Department is at the end of the counter, and they're only open on a Wednesday.'

'I don't want any travellers' cheques,' I said, passing her my ID card.

'Then why are you carrying round your passport?' Mind your own fucking business, I thought.

'My brother's very ill,' I said. 'He's in India working for his company and I have to show it when I go to the Post Office to fill out my travel forms.'

She nodded – not with sympathy – but with pleasure from solving the puzzle of why I was walking around with my passport.

I signed the form she passed over to me, indicating it was my will to close my account, and pushed it into her tray.

'Who shall I make the banker's draft out to,' she asked, pen poised over a slip of paper which would record my transaction, before it was fed into the bank's computer.

'To payee or cash, it doesn't matter which.'

She looked up at me. 'I'm sorry you can't have a banker's draft unless it's made out to a person or a company. You can't fill it out to payee. It's against the rules.'

Christ! I thought, by the time I'm ready to cash the bloody thing Nick Gorman won't exist. I'd have another name and the draft would be bloody useless.

'But I want it that way,' I protested.

'It doesn't matter what you want,' she said severely. 'I've told you, I can't do it, it's against the rules. You have to make it out to somebody.'

I was becoming desperate. I'd been in the place for over twenty minutes. I glanced over my left shoulder and saw that the man at the front of the queue was staring at me with barely concealed hatred. I knew how he felt and I guessed that the cabbie was getting upset too.

'OK,' I said. 'Forget the banker's draft. I'll take the whole ninety thousand in cash.'

She looked at me as if I was a lower form of life. Nobody was strong on customer relations – with everyone battling to recruit labour, any labour, employees knew they were in the driving seat as far as the bosses were concerned.

'I'll have to check that. We might not have that sort of money in the vault. It is Monday you know.'

She left the counter and went over to confer with one of her senior colleagues. I stood by her window, seething inside and drumming my fingers on the counter. I watched as her colleague listened to her. He shook his head. Did that mean I wasn't going to get my money. When I'd left my flat I'd intended to pop in to the bank and collect my money without drawing any attention to myself. After this performance I'd have caused less fuss if I'd have burst through the bank's doors wearing a stocking mask and carrying a sawn off shotgun. She left her colleague and re-joined me at the window.

'Yes we can do that.' She sniffed. 'You can have your money.'

It was nice to know she'd finally recognised it was my money. 'I'm afraid you'll have to wait while we count it,' she added.

Christ! I thought. How long will that take?

'OK,' I said. There wasn't much else I could say.

She picked up her pen. 'How would you like the money?'

'I'll take a thousand in tens and the rest in the largest notes you have.'

She clicked her tongue. 'I can do some of it in hundreds and fifties, but most of it will be in twenties.'

I know, I thought, it's Monday. I tried to envisage ninety thousand pounds in banknotes; I'd no idea how bulky it would be. I looked down at my travelling bag and hoped it would be big enough.

'Could you put it in an envelope for me?' I asked tentatively.

'No problem,' she said, as she turned off the light over her window. 'I think we've got some big ones.'

She left the window and on her way to the bank's vault she rounded up another clerk to help her count the money. I stood at the counter and tried to ignore the angry looks from the people in the queue, which by now had reached to the door on to the street. I thought of going outside to tell the taxi driver I wouldn't be long but I decided it would be safer to stay where I was; one false move from me and the waiting crowd might turn into a lynch mob. Over five minutes ticked by before she returned with the cash.

'It's nearly all in twenties,' she said.

'There's no need to count it in front of me.' I smiled at her. 'I trust you.'

Now I could see the money I felt better. I grabbed the big brown envelope she passed under the window and dropped the bundles of banknotes inside it as she started to count up to ninety thousand in denominations of five hundred.

'Thanks,' I said, moving away from her window.

I bent down and unzipped my bag and crushed the envelope on top of my clothes. The woman who'd taken my place at the window looked down at me.

'It's all right for people like you,' she said loudly. 'Some of us have to work for a living.' She turned to look at the long queue of customers and most of them muttered in support.

I grabbed my bag and walked quickly out of the bank, ignoring the angry stares of the people who were jammed against the street door. Now I had the money I didn't care. And I'd left a hundred pounds in my account in case the rumours about the banks notifying the police of anyone who closed a deposit account in excess of five thousand pounds were true. By a miracle the taxi was still waiting for me. I opened its back door and I was inside, with the door shut behind me, when I realised the man behind the wheel wasn't the same driver I'd given my twenty pound note to. In that moment the taxi drove off so quickly the force of its forward movement threw me onto the back seat.

'Hey!' I shouted as I struggled to sit upright.

The driver hit his brakes hard and stopped and I pitched forwards out of the seat and smacked head first into the security screen behind his head, both doors were wrenched open and two men jumped in. I was still lying on the floor of the cab, struggling to get the Smith and Wesson out of my anorak pocket when the man with the beard stuck the one he was carrying against the side of my throat.

'Don't!' he said.

His partner rapped on the plastic security screen with his knuckles and the taxi accelerated away into the London traffic.

Time: 12.15 hours

The clean-shaven one took my revolver, patted the rest of my body and hitched up my anorak and pulled the Walther out of my hip pocket. Then he searched my bag. He whistled when he looked inside the bank's envelope and showed it to his hirsute comrade in arms. After that neither of them uttered a sound during the rest of the journey.

At first I thought we were driving into a tunnel and it wasn't until I saw a concrete pillar that I guessed we were in an underground carpark. The taxi stopped and reversed into a parking bay and as its engine died the clean-shaven one, with a deep cleft in his jaw, seized hold of my shoulders and pulled me off the floor. I'd always thought Terry Bannister was a big man, but the man who almost lifted me bodily off the floor of the taxi was the size of a small house, and strong, tough and very fit. He pushed my face up to the window and held it there. A car in the bay opposite to the taxi flashed its headlights twice before the driver started its engine and drove away. It was difficult to see clearly in the car park's dim fluorescent lighting but I was sure the person who was driving the car was Alice Townsend. The man with the beard got out of the taxi.

'Out!' He was another big, strong silent type. And his accent spoke of a Scot.

I scuffled backwards out of the taxi on my knees and stood up. The Scot pushed me hard in my back and if I hadn't put up my hands to protect myself my face would have hit the side of the taxi's roof.

'Spread your legs out!' he ordered.

278

He ran his hands over my body and when he was sure I wasn't carrying another weapon he grabbed the hood of my anorak and pulled me away from the taxi. I went with the movement and then turned fast to my right and drove the point of my elbow under his heart. Anyway, that's what would have happened if he hadn't known his business. He did; and as I turned he moved around with me, pushing his left hand down hard, between my shoulder blades. At the point when I'd lost my balance he brought the top of his gun's barrel up, sharply, against my exposed right side. It cracked against my ribcage and I crashed against a black Daimler which was parked next to the taxi and landed on the floor.

'Nice try, son,' he said in his soft Scottish brogue as I lay face down on the car park's concrete floor. 'You'd be good if you practised.'

I lunged at his ankles, trying to catch them in my hands in the hope that I could up end him, but he danced away and when my hands flopped back down on the concrete he stepped forwards and stood on the back of my right hand.

'Mister Gorman!' The man's voice which had admonished me had an upper-class accent with a clipped military style. 'I'm very attached to this car, I hope you haven't marked its coachwork.'

The man with the beard took his foot off my right hand and I rolled over on my back and tried to see the man who'd spoken to me from inside the Daimler; although the car's smoked glass windows hid his face, all my instincts told me I'd been spoken to by the General.

'What did you find on him?' the military voice asked the Scot.

'Two guns and a bag containing clothes and money.'

'How much?'

'About a hundred thousand, sir.'

'All right. Help him off the floor before he does anymore damage,' the military voice said to the man who'd put me there in the first place.

My sparring partner hauled me to my feet and brushed down my anorak before opening the Daimler's front passenger door and pushing me firmly inside. I'd thought about trying another move but I could see it wouldn't get me anywhere; I'd already had an advanced lesson in unarmed combat and the pain in my ribs told me he was a man who took his skills seriously. He closed the door and stood a few paces away from it; if I swung it open quickly there was no chance that I'd hit him. He was joined in his vigil by his clean-shaven partner who stood by the side of the driver's door and somehow I knew they were professional soldiers from some kind of crack unit, like the paras or the SAS. I put my hand on the other side of the steering wheel; the key wasn't in the ignition.

'That's better, Gorman, isn't it?' said the General's voice. I turned round to look at him; the screen which separated passengers from their chaffeur's inquisitive ears was down but the thick black velvet curtains on his side were drawn. 'Now, suppose you tell me who you're working for.'

'I work for the Special Health Authority. I'm a tracer,' I said, wondering what he looked like; his voice was young – perhaps around fifty.

'I know that,' he interrupted. 'I'm not interested in your cover, I want to know who you're working for. Is it the Labour Party? Or the Social Liberals, or whatever it is they call themselves these days?'

I sighed. 'I've told you. I work as a tracer.'

'Mmm,' he muttered. I heard him turn on the interior light in the back of the car. 'Well,' he said. He was flicking through some papers. 'There's nothing in your file to suggest any sort of political allegiance ... Mmm' he muttered again, while I wondered which file he was talking about. 'Why did you hazard your life to rescue one of my people?'

'Victoria? Did she get away? Is she all right?'

'Yes,' he replied. 'To all three questions.'

I sighed again. This time from relief that she was safe.

'Now, suppose you answer my question. Why did you rescue her?'

I thought about my state of shock after I'd killed Bill

and the effect it'd had on me. Unless I'd got it all wrong and there was a priest sitting in the back of the Daimler, instead of the man I thought was the General, it wouldn't make any sense to explain how, when I'd faced up to the real source of my continuing grief over Ann's death, I'd been determined to do something to set my record straight.

'I care for her,' I said.

It was a simple straightforward answer and it had the ring of truth. I don't know whether I believed it myself – so much had happened since I'd made my last attempt to invite Victoria out to dinner – but love was an emotion which was responsible for countless acts of selflessness and I thought he'd understand that more than he'd understand the nature of my life after Ann had been killed.

'You must do,' he said quietly in a way which led me to think he believed me.

'Tell me, Gorman, did you shoot Emmerson too?'

'Yes.' I said.

Again, it seemed simpler to admit it rather than bore him with a story of how I'd attacked Emmerson's bodyguard and how, as a result, he'd accidentally shot his boss. And technically I'd told the truth, if I hadn't hit Emmerson's bodyguard the gun wouldn't have gone off and Emmerson wouldn't have been shot. In a court of law I'd have argued the fine distinction between manslaughter and culpable homicide, but I wasn't in a court of law and I was pretty sure the man in the back of the car wasn't with the BNDP; if he was we wouldn't be having a cosy chat in the back of his Daimler, instead, I'd have been experiencing what it felt like to be doused with a bucket of water and exposed to electric shocks.

'Is Emmerson dead?' I asked, suddenly realising that the question had never entered my mind since I'd run out of his house.

'He's exceedingly unwell …' He paused. 'I doubt he'll be opening his mouth to make those rabble rousing speeches he's so fond of for a very long time … You're quite the dark horse, aren't you, Gorman?' I heard him flicking through the pages of my file again. 'For someone who's never been in the armed services and who's only knowledge of combat seems to have been restricted to the sport of karate, you seem to be a lethal sort of chap. According to our count you've killed four people and seriously injured a fifth in the last twenty-four hours. Is there anyone else who's lying out there, dead or injured, that we should know about?'

'No ... Anyway, it only happens when I get mad.'

'Then I must remember not to annoy you.'

He fell into silence and I thought it was my turn to ask a few questions.

'Alice Townsend works for you, doesn't she?'

'What makes you think that?'

'She was driving the car which flashed its lights when I arrived in the taxi a few minutes ago. Why did she do that? To confirm it was me?'

'There's little point asking me questions when you already know the answers,' he said.

'And Motte too?'

'Motte? Yes, he's one of mine.' There was a tone in his voice that implied he regretted Motte was on his payroll.

I looked out of the side windows at the two soldiers standing to casual attention by the sides of the Daimler. 'Where is Motte by the way? He seems to work closely with Alice Townsend.' I smiled to myself. 'Should I smarten myself up in case he joins us?'

'He's in New York with his young lady. You remember her, Gorman? She's the one you nearly frightened to death; another minor casualty of your weekend crusade.'

'I'm sorry about that.' I was; Gwen hadn't deserved the treatment I'd lavished on her. But I was also impressed by his ability to achieve the near impossible task of getting two people out of England at almost a moment's notice. And his reference to Gwen confirmed he was the General.

I hesitated before asking my next question. I thought I already knew the answer but it would be nice to have his confirmation and I knew that by asking it I wouldn't be giving myself away, or undermining my negotiating position, because I knew I didn't have a negotiating position; the two men standing alongside the Daimler could handle me without even working up a sweat and they'd do whatever their senior officer told them.

'You had Harris killed, didn't you? It was your people who stormed the house at Hemel Hempstead, wasn't it?'

'Excuse me,' he replied and I heard the glass partition behind my head glide upwards in its runners. It stopped with a soft clunk, cutting off all sound from the rear of the car.

I looked out of my window at the bearded Scotsman and wondered why the General had temporarily suspended my interrogation. Was there someone else in the back of the car? And was he holding a conference with them about my fate? I had a pretty good idea what that was. Fuck it, I thought, why don't you just get on with it, your polite manners don't fool me, when your two lads put me back into the taxi I'll be making my last trip.

The glass partition whispered its descent.

'Well?' I asked him.

'You're an intelligent man, Gorman, so I'll come straight to the point. I'm looking for a certain ...' He paused. 'Package ... Do you know where it is?'

It was the question I'd been expecting since the bearded Scotman had pushed his revolver into my throat.

'How big is this package?' I fenced, although I knew he knew I knew we were talking about Rayleigh; it would have been the first thing Alice Townsend would have reported when she'd phoned Motte on Saturday morning when I was in the shower.

'It's man-sized.'

'Do you know where he is, lad?'

I almost jumped in surprise when the other person behind the curtains joined in my conversation with the General. Leonard Harper, the Chairman of the Conservative Party has very distinctive vowels and years spent making his fortune in the City and rubbing shoulders with the rich and powerful has never quite extinguished the speech of his Manchester childhood. It was a voice which attacked the BNDP almost daily on the TV and radio and the newspapers said he was the Prime Minister's most trusted adviser. The fact that he was in the back of the Daimler was proof that they still hadn't found Rayleigh and that I was dealing with one of the Conservative Party's most senior representatives. Well, I thought, at least you know who you're talking to. So, are you going to tell them or not? I knew where I stood as far as the BNDP was concerned but how did I feel about the Conservatives?

'Please leave this to me,' the General was saying to Harper. 'We agreed not to confuse the situation.'

'Then get on with it, we're wasting time,' Harper replied curtly.

There's never much love lost between the military and their political masters and the tone of Harper's reply suggested he wasn't enjoying this novel situation where for once a politician was taking a back seat and keeping his mouth shut.

'Let's suppose I do know something about this package you're looking for,' I said. 'Then what?'

'Come on, lad,' said Harper. 'This is important. If you care at all for your country you'll tell us what you know.'

I recalled Doctor Johnson's quote about patriotism being the last refuge of the scoundrel. Come on, I told myself, do something positive, either tell them what they want to know or tell them to piss off. I decided to compromise.

'Let's suppose you answer my question first. Did your people kill Harris? Tell me and I'll answer your question. Do we have a deal?'

'Don't push your luck,' said the General.

'Look, General,' I said, 'I've been pushing my luck as you call it for the last five days and quite frankly, unless you answer my question, you and Mister Harper can go to hell.'

It was the General's turn to sigh. I scented a victory, a minor one in the circumstances, but a victory nevertheless.

'Yes and no,' he said.

'What does that mean?'

'Yes, my people stormed the house. No, they weren't

supposed to kill him. It was a botched job.'

I remembered Harris's scream as the submachine-gun's bullets tore into his body. A botched job. Was that all he meant to the two men who were sitting behind me?

I glanced at the big Scotsman; it was difficult to believe that someone like him would panic and start spraying bullets into a room without making sure he wasn't killing the person he was under orders to capture. And what was Chris doing there? He'd been tough, but he wasn't in the same division as the Scotsman and his pal.

'Why did you use Chris?'

'Who?'

'Chris Brand. He was a tracer like me; we shared the same office at Soho Square. He was killed. Don't you remember? You had his body dumped in the Thames.'

'Tell him, for God's sake,' Harper said to the General. 'He's probably guessed most of it anyway.'

'Your colleague worked for Motte,' said the General, speaking to me. 'After Motte and Alice Townsend left Hemel Hempstead Motte arranged the raid using his own people. The man always was a bloody fool. God knows what he was thinking of. He should have reported in so that the matter could have been dealt with properly.'

'But he didn't, because he thought he'd get extra Brownie points for doing it on his own,' I interrupted. 'That's about right, isn't it? He never stayed at Alice Townsend's, did he? I know that, because nobody had slept in the bed in her guestroom – the sheets were clean and fresh. He went back to his gallery and organised it all from there. And when his people arrived at Hemel Hempstead they found my car and went ape.'

'That's about the size of it,' said the General. 'Now it's your turn, Gorman.'

When it comes down to it Harper and the General aren't all that different from the BNDP, I thought. But, perhaps in the present state we're all in, the end does justify the means. What the hell, they were going to get it out of me one way or another.

'Rayleigh's dead,' I said. 'I think he had a heart attack.

285

You'll find him in a house in Paddington – 23 Falcon Row … Satisfied …? What happens now? Do I get to have a swim in the Thames, like Chris?'

'Have you told anyone else about this, Mister Gorman?' It was Harper who asked the question.

'No. You're the only two people who know.'

'Splendid,' said Harper. 'Were you there when Rayleigh died?'

'No. I arrived shortly after.'

'What about the Cabinet papers?'

For Christ sake don't give anything away, I thought. 'What Cabinet papers?'

'Rayleigh had one of his boxes with him,' said Harper. 'Did you see any papers?'

'There were some papers on his desk I think.' I said it as if I'd never given Rayleigh's papers a second glance.

'Did you read them, Gorman?' said Harper, ignoring my tone of disinterest.

'Oh sure,' I said sarcastically. 'But not until I'd made myself a cup of tea and watched the late night news … For Christ's sake, I'd found a Secretary of State in a place I knew he wouldn't have been found dead in. Trouble was he was dead. I did what anybody else in their right mind would have done, I walked out of the house and shut the door behind me.'

Both the General and Harper went quiet. Had I convinced them? I knew they must have known what was in the Cabinet papers, at least, Harper would have done. Would the scheme to turn the Special Care Centres into deathcamps come to a grinding halt now that Emmerson was *hors de combat*, I wondered, or would it proceed as planned? I hadn't had much time to think about the question since the previous day but thinking about it now I couldn't see the politicians had too many alternatives if they wanted to escape an even bigger calamity than we were presently facing. I was glad it would be Harper and not me who'd have to take the decision; I'd felt bad enough when I'd been an idealistic young hospital manager, closing wards the Thatcher government wouldn't pay to keep open.

'So what happens now?' I repeated.

'To you?' asked the General.

'Of course to me,' I said. 'I know what will happen to Rayleigh. His body will be whisked down to his home in Chichester where a doctor you trust will declare him dead from a heart attack and sign the death certificate; you'll have him screwed in his coffin and under the sod before anyone knows anything different, and then you'll issue a press release to say he passed away in the bosom of his family. Isn't that the way it works? And while he's getting a memorial service in Westminster Abbey I'll get a byline in local newspaper saying "Man found in Thames".'

The General chuckled. 'You do have a vivid imagination, Gorman. Actually I was going to offer you a job, working for me.'

'What!' I said. The expression 'You could have knocked me down with a feather' didn't even begin to capture my sense of astonishment.

'Why not? Don't tell me you're a communist. No one who does your job could possibly be that.'

'No, I'm not a communist,' I agreed. 'I'm a practising agnostic.'

'That's good, Gorman,' he said with approval. 'In my experience it's the fanatics who cause the problems, I always prefer men who are objective and detached about the things they do. You can rely on them, and that's a vital feature of this sort of work.'

'Precisely what is "this sort of work"?' I said. 'Because I can tell you now, if you want me to kill people you can stick your job.'

'Don't worry, Gorman, you won't have to kill anybody, unless they try to kill you of course. Anyway I wouldn't choose you for that kind of work, it requires a specialist and I doubt that you're the type who'd take to it easily.'

The clean-shaven soldier standing by the driver's door coughed. He was the type who'd kill without compunction; I'd known that when I'd seen the controlled violence in his cold blue eyes when he'd first jumped into the taxi.

'You see, Gorman,' said the General, 'in the secret war we're fighting against the BNDP it's very difficult to be sure who's on your side. Special Branch, MI5, MI6, the whole lot are staffed with people who've always favoured the Right in politics. That was fine when the only real threat was the Russians or left wing terrorists, but now … Well, you don't need me to tell you, half of them are on our side and half of them are in the bloody BNDP.'

'And your problem is you're never sure which half is for or against you,' I said. I could see how a war between the Right and the far Right could produce problems like that.

'Precisely,' he said. 'We've all worked together for years, most of us know one another, or we know someone who's worked with someone else. It's almost impossible to maintain tight security. That's why both we and the BNDP are always on the lookout for people who've never worked for any of the intelligence services; man or woman, it doesn't matter as long as they've got potential.'

'And you think I've got potential,' I said.

'Miss Townsend recognised it straight away. She says you have excellent qualities – and I'm not talking about what happened in her bedroom. And I'd say the way we've seen you behave since Saturday morning demonstrates that she's right.'

If my position hadn't been so serious I'd have laughed out loud. This is almost high farce, I thought. Here I am, sitting in a car which cost as much as I could earn in a year, being offered a job whose duties haven't been defined, by a man whose face I've never seen, who might or might not be a real general, in company with the Chairman of the Conservative Party. If this was sometime in 1930 and if I was an Oxford undergraduate called Burgess or Maclean or Philby it would be perfect.

'I doubt Harris would have been killed if you'd been in charge of our operation at Hemel Hempstead,' the General said emphatically. 'And you'd have taken the obvious precaution of posting a couple of men outside Alice Townsend's back door. Well? Wouldn't you?'

I shrugged. 'Yes. I would … Did Motte set that up too?'

He sighed. 'Yes ... Tell me,' he said briskly, 'do you know the official figure for deaths of suspected HIV carriers occuring at the time of their arrest?'

'Six months ago we were killing seven in a hundred,' I said. 'It's always a possibility; an HIV suspect threatens you, so you call out the police. And since they don't get the bounty money they're not too bothered if they kill the heavy or not.'

'You're wrong, the real figure, the unpublished figure, is eighteen per hundred arrests ... And,' I heard him shuffling through paper again. What was he trying to prove? 'you have the remarkable record of zero. Somehow, Gorman, you've managed to maintain an above average record of arrests without killing a single suspect. It shows you use your head. I think you'll do very nicely. Well, what do you say? Are you in or out?'

'Can I think about it?' I nearly added, 'I've got a lot on at the moment' except that I didn't think Harper and the General were the types who'd appreciate my kind of humour.

'Certainly,' said the General. 'You've got three minutes to give me an answer.'

'Thanks,' I said, but the glass screen was already separating us and I guessed he hadn't heard me.

I rejected the idea of telling him to keep his job and daring him to do his worst towards the end of the first minute after the screen had clunked against its rubber stop on the roof of the car. I wasn't some tough guy in a movie, like Lee Marvin. I could see the worst he could do; they were standing outside the car, both of them ready, willing and able to do whatever worst he ordered – a bullet in the back of my head seemed most likely, followed by a big splash when they dropped my naked corpse into the Thames. And when the police fished me out they'd record me as yet another victim of the dirty war which was being fought beneath the ordinariness of daily life. I'd no money, no friends, no job, my current blood test date would expire in thirty-six hours' time and the police wanted to talk to me about the mess at the office which a security guard would have discovered when he arrived for his Sunday shift. I was up to my neck in shit and all I'd got was the lifeline he'd thrown to me. He might be lying, but it was a chance I'd have to take.

I put my right hand over my shoulder and tapped on the glass screen with my knuckles, knowing I was making another compromise in what would probably be the start of a long chain of compromises.

'What do I have to do, what's the pay and when do I start?' I said when the screen was down.

'Excellent. Good to have you with us, Gorman.'

For a moment I half expected him to put his hand through the curtains for me to shake it.

'Right,' he said brusquely. 'Arrangements have been made for someone to show you the ropes. Don't talk about this conversation to anyone. I repeat, anyone. You understand? All our people operate on a need to know basis.'

'If that's the case aren't you breaking your own rules by talking to me,' I said.

'This was one of those occasions when we needed to know,' said Harper. 'I doubt we shall meet again, so, good afternoon young man, and thank you.'

'Yes,' said the General. 'Now that Emmerson's indisposed the game's wide open. Thank you.'

I heard him tap on his window and my door was opened by the bearded Scotsman. 'Look after yourself, Gorman,' said the General.

'Hang on a minute,' I said. 'Why is there a news blackout on Emmerson? Is there going to be a Cabinet reshuffle? There's a lot I still don't know.'

'I'm afraid that's a condition we all suffer from,' he replied. The rising screen cut off my attempt to give him an equally facetious reply. I got out of the Daimler as the man who'd been driving the taxi donned a chauffeur's peaked cap and climbed into its driving seat. When it drove out of the parking bay I tried to see its number plate, but the Scot was hustling me into the back of the taxi and his body blocked my view.

'Who was the officer in the Daimler?' I asked him after he'd settled next to me in the taxi's backseat.

'I've no idea,' he said.

'Honestly?'

'That's right,' he said. 'Now just sit there quietly and count your money.'

I picked up my bag off the taxi's floor and unzipped it. The envelope was still inside.

'Don't worry,' the Scot said before I could open it. 'We're not thieves.

Time: 13.05 hours

I sat in the back of the taxi thinking about all the questions I'd have liked to ask the General. I couldn't have asked him anything which would have revealed I'd read the two Cabinet papers; like had there been a conspiracy to get Rayleigh out of the Cabinet by taking the SHA away from him? Not a BNDP conspiracy, but a Conservative conspiracy to get rid of a man whom Alice had told me might consider a link up with elements of the Labour Party. There were other questions I could have asked him though; such as why had Motte wasted so much time once Harris turned up on his doorstep? Had Harris been working as an undercover agent for Motte, or for Rayleigh? And why hadn't Alice phoned her contact to alert them I was at her house when I'd been freshening myself up in her guest-room before our late night supper? Had she already decided to recruit me? There had to be answers but I knew I was never going to get them.

We'd been sitting inside the taxi, with me reviewing all the possible answers to my unasked questions, for less than a couple of minutes when one of those Toyota sports cars which looks a bit like a Ferrari turned into our aisle of parked vehicles, its tyres squealing in protest as it accelerated around a concrete pillar. I watched as it drove past the taxi, stopped and reversed into the parking bay vacated by the Daimler. Its driver sounded the horn and the Scot got out of the taxi and beckoned me to follow him. If I'd had somewhere to go I might have thought about attempting to run; but I hadn't and I didn't.

'Don't forget your bag,' said my clean-shaven minder. 'We're keeping your guns, you won't be needing them.'

I looked at him in alarm.

'It's OK, stop worrying,' he said, raising his voice so I could hear him over the Toyota's deep throaty roar as its driver gunned the engine.

His reassurance sounded genuine but his cold-looking eyes stayed ice cold and I didn't stop worrying.

'In you get,' said the Scot opening the Toyota's passenger door. Its low swept-back roof prevented me from seeing its driver. 'Good luck,' said the Scot as I bent low and eased myself backwards into the passenger seat. 'It's OK,' he said to the driver. 'He's got everything he needs.'

The car moved off in the moment he shut my door.

'Put your seatbelt on,' said Victoria, spinning the wheel and making the tyres squeal as she turned out of the line of parked cars into the exit gangway. 'We don't want to get stopped for something stupid like that.'

I put on my seatbelt and took out a cheroot from the packet I'd taken with me from the flat while she fed the automatic barrier with pound coins.

'Fancy meeting you here,' I said, after I'd lit it with her cigarette lighter. 'Where are we going?'

She glanced at me quickly as she stopped to wait for a gap in the traffic. 'Scotland.'

She hit the Toyota's twin air horns, drove into the stream of oncoming traffic and cut in front of a Ford in the outside lane. It's driver hooted angrily. She ignored him and turned right at the lights and accelerated fast down Park Lane. 'I hate driving in London,' she said. 'Just because you're a woman they think you'll give way.' She hit the horn again to dissuade a man from driving out of a sidestreet. 'Open your window will you it's like a saloon bar in here.'

I did as she told me and concentrated on my cheroot.

The way she was driving it might be the only pleasure I'd ever have again and I decided it was safer if I didn't divert her attention from the road; my questions would keep.

We were on the MI motorway driving north when I reopened the conversation.

'Have you ever met the General, Victoria?'

'Who's he?'

'He was in the Daimler.'

'What Daimler?' She looked in the rearview mirror. 'I can't see a Daimler.'

'Not here. Back in the underground car park.'

'I didn't see a Daimler. What are you going on about?'

I counted to ten and tried again. 'The General is the man you get your orders from. You told me that on Saturday night, if you remember.'

'You said I worked for a general, I thought it was safer not to argue with you in case you shot me.'

'I'd never have done that, Victoria.'

She looked at me.

'Anyway,' she continued. 'What does your general look like?'

'He ...' I hesitated. I hadn't the first idea what he looked like.

'Look, can we just stop it,' she said. 'I don't know any generals, but if you say I work for a general, then I work for a general. OK? Are you satisfied now? The next time I speak to my contact I'll tell her she's a general. She'll be surprised of course, but I'll tell her you said she was a general and that she'll just have to get used to the idea.'

'All right,' I said, wondering if I was seeing their need to know rule in action. 'You don't work for a general. Can we call a truce?'

Victoria took her left hand off the steering wheel and punched me gently on my arm. 'OK,' she said.

She passed me her cigarettes and I took one out and lit it for her.

'I want to know why you came to Emmerson's house,' she said, breathing smoke out of her mouth as she talked.

'You owed me for last month's tea money,' I said. 'You

293

didn't think I was going to let you get away with something like that, did you? It'd have been all round the office that I was a soft touch. Next thing I'd have known everyone would have been borrowing money off me.'

'Please, Nick, be serious. Why did you? I've been thinking about it all the time since Sunday. I ...' She stopped talking and glanced out of her side window. 'Pass me a tissue would you?' I took a tissue out of a packet which was in the driver's courtesy tray and passed it to her. She wiped her eyes. 'I promised myself I wouldn't do this.'

I leaned over and patted her leg gently. 'Come on,' I said. 'There's no need to get upset. You were in trouble. You didn't think I was going to walk out on you, did you? I told you on Saturday night, we were partners.'

'That's not an answer.'

She didn't have to tell me that – I knew it wasn't an answer. I looked out of my window at the names on the sides of the trucks we were overtaking. When I'd said we'd be partners I'd had a gun in my pocket and at the time I'd said it I wasn't sure how I felt about Victoria; and she was still half convinced I was working for Smithson. And since my trip back to London from Emmerson's house I hadn't had much time to reappraise my feelings about her. Who are you trying to fool? I thought. Why did you ring her flat when you got back to London? You know bloody well why you rang her. Grief's a peculiar thing, I thought.

'What?' asked Victoria and I realised I'd spoken my last thought out loud.

'I said grief's a funny thing ... It's difficult to explain. My wife was killed in a car accident a couple of years ago and ...'

'I reminded you of her?' she suggested.

'No, you're nothing like her ... I blamed myself for her death. That's why I became a tracer ... It's too complicated to explain ...' I paused. It *was* too complicated to explain. 'When you were captured by Terry I had to ask myself some questions ... I should have asked them a long time ago.' I shrugged my shoulders. 'I stopped hiding from myself, that's all.'

'Oh ... I see,' she said. The tone of disappointment in her voice surprised me.

'No. I don't think you do. It's true that I did it for myself but that's only half of it. I did it to save you too.' A pale flavour of the anger I'd felt in the instant before I'd killed Terry burst into my mind. 'It was the thought of what they'd do to you that drove me on.'

Victoria started to speak and then stopped and stubbed out her cigarette and then lit another one.

'I thought I couldn't feel anything ever again after my mother died. I'd lost Peter and my father, everyone I loved. But I was wrong. When Bannister captured me ... uuugh.' She shivered. 'They took us to a house somewhere in north London ... and when they took me into a different room from Smithson I thought Terry and that other man were going to rape me. If they hadn't been under direct orders from Emmerson not to do anything until he'd had a chance to question me I know they would have. And they were going to do it when he'd finished with me – Terry described it in graphic detail. Bastard! I hated him. If they hadn't put someone to guard me I'd have killed myself. And when we got to Emmerson's house and they tied me up to that hook in the cellar ...' She started to gnaw the back of her hand as she relived her fear. 'But then you suddenly appeared ... God! You should have seen your face. I knew you were going to kill them.'

'I was.'

She stubbed out her cigarette and passed me the packet for me to light her another one.

'You smoke too much,' I said after I'd lit one and given it to her.

'I know. I'm going to stop while we're in Scotland.'

I took another cigarette out of the packet and lit it to prevent myself asking the question which was forming on my lips. By the time I'd dropped the packet back into the courtesy tray behind the gear lever I thought I could make it sound like a casual enquiry. 'So we're staying up in Scotland together?'

She nodded. 'I've been given the job of training you ...

To teach you the way we work ... and you'll have to practise your karate and weapons training.'

'Plenty of running and physical jerks,' I said, imitating a hearty gym instructor. 'I see.'

'It'll take about six weeks,' she said.

'What about our blood tests? Mine runs out at midnight tomorrow.'

'Don't worry, Nick, it's all been taken care of.'

'And what happens after I've finished my training?'

'I don't know. It depends what our orders are. By then we'll have new identities. They'll have arranged for your flat to be sold by the way, and they'll invest the money for you.

'But will I be around to spend it?'

'That depends how good you are at the job ... We'll be working together, you realise that, do you?'

I thought of the idea of spending six weeks with her in Scotland and of the prospect of us working together once she'd trained me. Had the General guessed why I'd rescued her and put us together on purpose, or was it just one of those quirks of fate? Knowing my luck we'd probably be staying in some sort of army camp full of hard, fit young officers.

'Where are we staying? In an army camp?'

'That wouldn't be very clever, would it? No, we're staying well out of sight in a small cottage on the west coast. Why? Would you rather stay in an army camp?'

'No,' I said, shaking my head vigorously.

She looked at me and pouted.

'Why did you come after me?' she asked a few moments later.

'I told you.'

'No you didn't.'

I took a deep breath. In some ways nothing had changed between us; she was years younger than me and our social backgrounds were poles apart; when she'd been at boarding school, obsessed with a young girl's passion for horses, I was already married and earning a daily crust in a low status job in hospital administration. Would I break the habit of a lifetime and take the risk of exposing my feelings to a woman I hardly knew? 'I know we used to tease one another a lot,' I said. 'But I've never been pushy with women and I always knew I'd never take it farther than a laugh and a joke. But if you really want to know, I followed you to Emmerson's house because I care about you.'

'Why do you find that so difficult to say?'

'I don't know, perhaps it's the way I was brought up,' I said, remembering the way my father had bottled up all his emotions towards me and my mother.

'I always liked you, Nick. You know that, don't you? Even though I thought you were working for Smithson, like Terry and Chris.'

Should I tell her that Chris was on her side? I thought. I decided against it; I'd stick to the General's orders – if she didn't know about Chris, she didn't need to know.

'You'll have to let go of your grief over your mother and father and Peter, Victoria,' I said. 'Otherwise it'll eat you alive, believe me.'

'I know that now. After I'd killed Smithson things started to change. When you didn't come back after ten minutes I was going to go after you, but then Emmerson and his police escort came past and I just sat in the car trying to decide what to do.'

'You did the right thing, Victoria. We'd have both been killed if you hadn't stayed in the car.'

'But when I thought you'd been killed ...' She stopped talking and looked briefly out of her window. 'I've been very lonely Nick ... I'd like to start my life again ... How about you?'

'Yes, but will either of us ever have the chance? I mean, look at what we'll be doing.'

'You can always find excuses,' she replied. 'You don't get involved with someone until you've got a job, you don't get married until you've got somewhere to live, you don't have kids because of the mortgage – there's hundreds of excuses. Before my mother died she talked about all the things she hadn't done, like not telling my father she loved him often enough. I don't want to die feeling like that.'

'Yes,' I said. 'I know what you mean.'

For the next five minutes neither of us spoke.

As we approached the Toddington service station she slowed down and moved over into the slow lane.

'I must have something to drink, Nick,' she said. 'Or I'll get a headache. How about you? Do you want something?'

'I could do with a coffee and something to eat,' I said while I looked over my shoulder to see if we were being followed.

'Don't worry,' she said. 'I've been keeping an eye on the mirror ever since we got on to the motorway.'

She drove up the slipway into the service area and parked the Toyota in an empty corner of the sparsely populated car park. And after I'd put my bag in the boot we walked across to the cafeteria which had been built at the time when the traffic on the motorway was a constant roar. On our way to the self service restaurant we passed by a small group of skinheads.

'Hello, darling,' one of them said to Victoria. 'Why don't you ditch him and come with us?'

'No thanks,' said Victoria, slipping her arm through mine as we kept on walking. 'I'll stick with him.'

'What so special about him?' one of them called after us. Here we go, I thought, psyching myself up for the inevitable fight.

'Ignore them!' she whispered to me. 'I'll handle it.'

'Oh come on,' she called back, 'give him a break, we've just got married.'

'You lucky bastard,' one of them shouted to me as they descended the stairs.

'That was pretty good,' I said as I picked up a tray from the stack at the end of the self service bar.

'That's what partners are for, isn't it?' she said, inspecting a danish pastry.

After we'd eaten we went to the shop to buy her some cigarettes.

'Isn't it awful?' said the woman behind the counter as she counted out Victoria's change.

'Terrible,' Victoria agreed.

'What's terrible?' I asked Victoria when we were going through the glass swing doors into the car park.

'She was talking about the one o'clock news. Didn't you know?' she said archly. 'They broke the news about Emmerson. It seems he accidentally shot himself in the face yesterday while he was at his country home in Leicestershire. Very seriously hurt they say. There's a new Home Secretary now, he's in the BNDP of course, but they say he won't be a patch on Emmerson.'

'How will your ...' I corrected myself, 'our people use what you found out about Smithson?'

'I've no idea,' she said. 'Have you ever been to Scotland?' she asked, changing the subject.

Oh God, I thought, you're back to being a functionary Gorman.

We were walking across the car park when I asked her how she'd got back to London.

'I drove to the next village and rang my contact and they sent someone out to get me,' she said.

'From London?'

'No. Someone local.'

I was impressed. If they could move that quickly they must ... wait a minute, I suddenly thought; the motorist in the snow storm and the two soldiers at the station. Were they the General's people? Had they been detailed to keep an eye on me? Is that what the old bugger had meant about observing my potential.

'Victoria ...? Oh shit!' I said as I saw our Toyota. While we'd been inside eating danish pastries and drinking coffee two armoured personnel carriers had parked on either side of it and a group of soldiers were standing by their vehicles, talking and smoking.

Victoria squeezed my arm. 'Act naturally,' she hissed.

'Let's hope they have a soft spot for newly weds,' I hissed back.

The soldiers regarded our approach with disinterest and

for a moment I thought they were an ordinary unit until one of them stopped leaning against the back of one of the personnel carriers and I saw the SEATAG insignia, painted above its rear number plate. I could have touched the soldier nearest to me when I picked up the signs of tension in his body movements and caught the look of recognition which passed between their officer and Victoria. Before I could blink, the rear doors on the personnel carriers were swung open and Victoria had jumped inside. As strong hands grabbed my arms and lifted my feet off the floor and bundled me in after her the knowledge that she'd betrayed me in the line of duty choked my throat and crippled my will to resist. You bitch! I screamed silently as the armoured doors clanged shut behind me. How could you do this to me!

I struggled to my feet and looked at Victoria in the dim glow of the personnel carrier's interior light. 'You ...' My mouth couldn't articulate the words I wanted to scream at her smiling face with its flushed look of triumph. I saved her! And she'd killed me. They all killed me – the General, Harper, Victoria, the whole fucking lot of them! All the time they'd known, and she'd known. She'd known from the moment the General's thug had put me into her car that this was going to happen! All that crap we'd talked was to make me think I was safe. But all the time ... I fell on to my knees and buried my face in my hands. Why hadn't they just killed me? Why go to all this trouble? Why? Why?

'Nick? Are you OK?' She was kneeling by my side, with her arm round my shoulder. 'They didn't hurt you, did they? Stupid bastards! They were told you weren't to be damaged.'

'What?' I said softly and swallowed hard.

'You didn't ...? You didn't think I'd ...?'

'Yes,' I said, nodding my head. 'Yes, I did.'

'I'm sorry, I thought it would be better if I didn't tell you. We couldn't have gone all the way to Scotland in the car. This way there'll be no record. They'll drive the car back to London and ditch it. Look,' she pointed, 'your bag's in the corner over there, you don't think we'd have bothered to take it out of the boot of the car if we were going to kill you, do you?'

'I thought …'

'Nick …' she said reprovingly before she kissed me.

I pulled her to me and kissed her and held her tightly.

'I thought you said you were never pushy with women,' she said and touched the end of my nose with her lips.

'That's while things are still at the laugh and a joke stage. We're past that, aren't we?'

'I think so,' she said, kissing me again.

My question had been rhetorical, but it was good to hear her reply.

THE SNOW BEES

Peter Cunningham

Patrick Drake is ambitious. He's a high flyer who wants to get to the top of the corporate ladder – fast. And a business trip to sort out a fiasco of a French vineyard looks just like the fast track to promotion.

It isn't. He reports back to head office and then he's fired.

From muck-raking in a molehill of missing money, he steps on a minefield of murderous activity. In a tightening web of terrorism and violence he finds himself facing the naked savagery of the international cocaine trade. Fighting to clear his name – and to save his life – he unravels a threat of fear and fanaticism that runs from South Africa to Spain, from Ireland to the United States. And at any moment he may feel the fatal sting . . .

'Ripping' *Oxford Times*
'Gripping' *Standard*

0 7474 0137 3
THRILLER

CONTROLLING INTEREST

Bernard Bannerman

'The body of a woman solicitor was discovered by staff arriving yesterday morning at the Holborn offices of the prestigious London solicitors, Mathers. Katrina Pankhurst, 32, had been shot. Police are investigating.'

A murder on the premises is bad news for a law firm. It discourages clients. It also discourages recruits which is damaging to a firm like Mather's with a reputation, a lot of clients, but very few partners. But, as Dave Woolf, one-time lawyer, part-time boozer and (almost) full-time private eye realizes, a thorough professional would prefer a murder to a leak any day of the week.

Also by Bernard Bannerman in Sphere Books:
THE LAST WEDNESDAY

0 7474 0383 X
CRIME

All Sphere Books are available at your bookshop or newsagent, or can be ordered from the following address: Sphere Books, Cash Sales Department, P.O. Box 11, Falmouth, Cornwall TR10 9EN.

Please send cheque or postal order (no currency), and allow 60p for postage and packing for the first book plus 25p for the second book and 15p for each additional book ordered up to a maximum charge of £1.90 in U.K.

B.F.P.O. customers please allow 60p for the first book, 25p for the second book plus 15p per copy for the next 7 books, thereafter 9p per book.

Overseas customers, including Eire, please allow £1.25 for postage and packing for the first book, 75p for the second book and 28p for each subsequent title ordered.